Absolute MacInnes

ABSOLUTE MACINNES

THE BEST OF COLIN MACINNES

Edited by TONY GOULD

ALLISON & BUSBY
LONDON - NEW YORK

This selection first published 1985 by
Allison & Busby Limited
6a Noel Street, London W1V 3RB
and distributed in the USA by
Schocken Books Inc.,
200 Madison Avenue, New York, NY 10016

British Library Cataloguing in Publication Data

MacInnes, Colin
    Absolute MacInnes.
    I. Title   II. Gould, Tony
    828'.91409   PR6063.A239

    ISBN 0-85031-600-6

Set in 11/12pt Bembo by
Top Type Services Ltd.,
5 Franthorne Way, London SE6
Made and printed in Great Britain by
Richard Clay (The Chaucer Press) Ltd.,
Bungay, Suffolk

Contents

FOREWORD

Colin MacInnes, like George Orwell, was a better essayist than novelist; but — like Orwell again — he is chiefly remembered for works of fiction. If Orwell's popularity rests largely on *Animal Farm* and *1984*, MacInnes's main claim to fame is the trilogy of "London" novels, *City of Spades, Absolute Beginners* and *Mr Love and Justice,* which deal with the various subcultures of the metropolis: the worlds of Africans and West Indians, of teenagers, and of the ponce, the prostitute and the policeman. Because these novels were rooted in personal observation and experience and dealt with milieux not usually treated in English novels, they quickly acquired the label "documentary", a label which MacInnes himself deeply resented.

"In contemporary England, which is altering so startlingly and rapidly," he said on the radio in 1960, when reviewing Clancy Sigal's *Weekend in Dinlock*,[1] "great areas of social life exist with new types of person and activity that English novelists have hardly explored at all [...] what rich undigested material for novels our shifting society can provide! Often such novels — some of my own, for instance, if I may mention this — have been called 'documentary': which I don't think — if they *are* novels, as I hope — is all the story. 'Documentary' suggests intelligent, imaginative research in some chosen field of genuine preoccupation. Of course, if one wishes accurately to portray a social scene, such enquiry must be undertaken; but often, I think, the novelist — if such he is — proceeds by saturation in a social setting, and by intuition — presumably intelligent — about it, rather than by any documentary research in the social scientist's sense."

A social scientist worthy of the name might find this a false distinction and object that he or she too "proceeds by saturation in a social setting, and by intuition" as well as by "documentary

1. "Comment", BBC Third Progamme, 21 January 1960.

research". But leaving that aside, what really got under MacInnes's skin about the documentary label was that it implied a lack of artistic creativity.

"Speaking for myself," he wrote three years later,[2] "I think there is some matter-of-fact reality in essays I have written, but very little in my novels. Those about London have been called 'documentary' by critics who suppose that any exploration of unusual social areas has a factual intention. In reality, these books are dreams, whose intention is to try to heighten reality and explain and criticize it, but not to record it in a literal way. The figures, for instance, in *Absolute Beginners* are all emblematic: 'real', I hope, as created essences, but never to be found intact in actual life.

"I think what happens is this. You live a thing — for instance, getting to know Africans, a painfully delightful process. A vision then forms itself in your mind about this world, and critical thoughts also arise about the society that surrounds it. Out of all this — fact, vision, criticism — you try to spin a legend. The intention of trying to change the fact by making the legend is also there...."

This is a good description of MacInnes's own practice, in the London novels at least, but his need to labour the point is also perhaps a reflection of his anxiety about his own creativity. That he had great potential as a novelist in the traditional sense is illustrated in his early novel, *June in Her Spring*,[3] that this talent remained, to some extent, undeveloped, may well have something to do with the fact that he was the son of a novelist, Angela Thirkell, whose work he largely despised. As he writes of his mother, "Her example [...] reinforced an inherent dislike for writing as an end in itself — instead of as a revelation, however modest."[4]

Yet the fact that *June in Her Spring* remained MacInnes's favourite among his novels, and that when he was working on

2. "Out of the way", *New Society,* 3 January 1963.
3. The Hogarth Press are reissuing both *June in Her Spring* and MacInnes's other Australian novel, *All Day Saturday,* along with the collection of essays, *England, Half English,* which contains the best of his non-fiction at the time when he was writing his London novels.
4. "Mum's the Word", *New Statesman,* 7 June 1963. See page xxx.

City of Spades he wrote of it dismissively to a friend, "This Negro one will never be much more than picaresque,"[5] suggests that there is a certain amount of wisdom after the event about his descriptions of his creative processes and attitudes. (His later, historical novels, *Westward to Laughter* and *Three Years to Play*, though they show considerable ingenuity, particularly in the use of language, fail to do what he claims the best historical novels do — namely, serve "as allegories of their own times"[6] — and do not therefore qualify for inclusion among the best of MacInnes.)

Given his talents as an off-beat journalist and social observer, though, MacInnes was perhaps wrong to insist on the distinction between creative and other sorts of writing. Novelists, even good novelists (great novelists, or great anything, are another matter) are not uncommon; good essayists are. MacInnes's enduring claim on our attention is that he was a very good writer with uncommon insight into his own times. That should be praise enough for anyone — even for him.

5. Letter to Francis Wyndham, 26 November 1956.
6. Review of *Bomarzo*, by Manuel Mujica-Lainez, *Spectator*, 29 August 1970.

Colin MacInnes: *Curriculum Vitae*

1914   Born 20 August in London, second son of Angela and James Campbell McInnes (the "Mac" spelling of his surname was MacInnes's own later adaptation, apparently in order to make it easier for the French to comprehend).

1917   In November Angela divorced James McInnes for cruelty and adultery.

1918   Angela re-married — to George Thirkell, an Australian engineer and, for the duration of the war, army officer.

1919   George and Angela Thirkell, Graham and Colin McInnes sailed for Australia on board the requisitioned German ship *SS Friedrichsruh* (a nightmare voyage later fictionalized by Angela under the title *Trooper to the Southern Cross*). Eventually they settled in Melbourne, where the boys went to school at Scotch College under the name of Thirkell.

1928   Angela took her first trip home with her third and last son, Lance.

1929   Angela left Australia and George Thirkell for good, taking her youngest son with her but leaving the older boys to finish their studies.

1930   Colin left school and followed his mother to England.

1931   Visited France and Germany; then, rather than return to Australia to go to university, took a job with the Imperial Continental Gas Association in Belgium.

1934   First meeting — since infancy — with his father, James Campbell McInnes, whom his brother Graham had searched out in Canada and encouraged to visit Europe.

1935   Return visit to his father and brother in Canada; though he never saw his father (who died at the end of the second world war) after this, he and his brother (who chose to settle in his father's adopted country) now both reverted to their original surname.

1936   Resigned from the Gas Company.

1937   Became an art student at the Chelsea Polytechnic.

1938   Gravitated to the Euston Road School of Drawing and Painting.

1940   Joined the Wiltshire Regiment.

1941   Transferred to the Field Security Section of the Intelligence Corps; in November, posted to Gibraltar, where he remained for two years.

1944   Traversed northern Europe and Germany in the wake of the invading Allies, interrogating spies, Nazis and Nazi sympathizers.

1946   Demobilized on 25 April. Became freelance lecturer and broadcaster on art, having decided to be a writer rather than a painter.

1947   Became art critic of the *Observer* in November, but resigned the following May after a row over the coverage of the Royal Academy exhibition at Burlington House.

1950   First novel, *To the Victors the Spoils*, published by MacGibbon & Kee and nominated "Book of the Month" by the *Daily Graphic*.

1952   *June in Her Spring* published and largely ignored by the press because it touched on the taboo subject of homosexuality.

1955   Seven-week British Council lecture tour of East and Central Africa; followed by his arrest in an East End gambling club, and subsequent acquittal, on a drugs charge.

1957   *City of Spades* published and well received.

1958   In the Hospital for Tropical Diseases; also declared bankrupt, having failed to pay income tax for some years.

1959   Visited Poland in August in company with the jazz musician, Kenny Graham. *Absolute Beginners* published in September, a year after the Notting Hill race riots: "New book, for a giddy week," he wrote to a friend, "hit the Top Six."

1960   *Mr Love and Justice* published. Visited Nigeria just before Independence.

1961   Estranged mother, Angela Thirkell, died in January, having cut her second son out of her will. *England, Half English*, a selection of essays, published in September. In October he went to the Anarchist Ball at Fulham Town Hall and became an "anarchist sympathizer" and proselytizer; his other current obsession was the return of the Elgin (or Parthenon, as he preferred to call them) marbles to Greece.

1962   *London, city of any dream*, a book of photographs to which he contributed an introductory essay, published by Thames & Hudson. From October he wrote a weekly column for the newly founded *New Society* under the rubric "Out of the way" until the pressure of recurring deadlines became too much for him and he opted for a more flexible approach.

1964   Revisited Australasia, courtesy of Time-Life Books; returned via New York.

1966   *All Day Saturday*, his second novel with an Australian setting, and *Sweet Saturday Night*, a study of the Music Halls, published. As "press officer" for an organization of Blacks in Notting Hill called Defence, and the only white man involved, he became a kind of propagandist for the Black Power leader-cum-hustler Michael X.

1969   *Westward to Laughter*, the first of two historical novels, a satire on *Treasure Island*, published.

1970   Second historical novel, *Three Years to Play*, cast in the form of a fictitious background story to Shakespeare's *As You Like It*, published. Visited Peru and suffered from altitude sickness in the Andes, but was enchanted by the Amerindians.

1971   April to June: second British Council tour of Africa; his behaviour was so outrageous that officials were forced to put a stop to it. Later in the year the *Oz* trial (on youth and censorship) and the trial of the "Mangrove Nine" (Blacks versus the police) brought out the better side of MacInnes.

1973   *Loving Them Both*, an extended essay on bisexuals and bisexuality, published by Martin Brian & O'Keeffe.

1974   His last novel, *Out of the Garden*, published.

1975   Large journalistic output kept up, including the series "Captain Jockstrap's Diary" for *Gay News*. Long essay, *"No Novel Reader"*, companion piece to *Loving Them Both*, published by Martin Brian & O'Keeffe.

1976   Operation for cancer of the oesophagus. On 23 April, died of a massive haemorrhage. Buried at sea on 30 April.

1979   *Out of the Way: Later Essays* published posthumously.

PART I
The London Novels, and related writings

City of Spades has two narrators — Montgomery Pew, "newly appointed Assistant Welfare Officer of the Colonial Department", and a visiting Nigerian, Johnny Macdonald Fortune. Pew has a friend called Theodora Pace, who lives in the flat below his and works for the BBC. In the following extract, the inexperienced Pew learns a little of what he is up against in his new job.

from *City of Spades*
(1957)

I went upstairs sadly, and changed into my suit of Barcelona blue: a dazzling affair that makes me look like an Ealing Studio gangster, and which I'd ordered when drunk in that grim city, thereby, thank goodness, abbreviating my holiday in it by one week. As I drank heavily into Theodora's gin, the notion came to me that I should visit these haunts against which it was my duty to warn others: the Moorhen, the Cosmopolitan dance hall, and perhaps the Moonbeam club. But first of all, I decided, adjusting the knot of my vulgarest bow tie (for I like to mix Jermyn Street, when I can afford it, with the Mile End Road); it was a more imperative duty to inspect the Welfare hostel. So down I went by the abandoned stairs and corridors, and hailed a taxi just outside the Zoo.

It carried me across two dark green parks to that SW1 region of our city which, since its wartime occupation by soldiers' messes and dubious embassies, has never yet recovered its dull dignity. Outside an ill-lit peeling portico the taxi halted, and I alighted to the strains of a faint calypso:

"I can't wait eternally
For my just race equality.
If Mr England voter don't toe the line,
Then maybe I will seek some other new combine"

somebody was ungratefully singing to the twang of a guitar.

I gazed up, and saw dark forms, in white singlets, hanging comfortably out of windows: surely *not* what the architect had intended.

I walked in.

There I was met by three men of a type as yet new to me: bespectacled, their curly hair parted by an effort on one side, wearing tweed suits of a debased gentlemanly cut, and hideous university ties. (*Why* do so many universities favour purple?) They carried menacing-looking volumes.

"Can I be of assistance to you?" said one to me.

"I should like to speak to the warden."

"Warden? There is no such person here by nights."

"We control the hostel ourselves, sir, by committee," said another.

"I, as a matter of fact, am the present secretary."

And he looked it.

"Oh," I said, "is Mr Fortune possibly in? A Lagos gentleman."

"You could find that for yourself, sir, also his room number, by consulting the tenancy agenda on the public information board."

He pointed a large helpful finger at some baize in the recess of the dark hall. I gave him a cold official smile, ignored the baize board, and walked upstairs to examine the common-rooms and empty cubicles.

This Colonial Department hostel smelt high, I soon decided, with the odour of good intentions. The communal rooms were like those on ships — to be drifted in and out of, then abandoned. The bedrooms (cubicles!), of which I inspected one or two, though lacking no necessary piece of furniture, yet had the "furnished" look of a domestic interior exhibited in a shop window. And over the whole building there hung an aura of pared Welfare budgets, of tact restraining antipathies, and of a late attempt to right centuries of still unadmitted wrongs.

And all this time the nasal calypso permeated the lino-laden passages. As I approached the bright light from a distant open door, I heard:

"English politician he say, 'Wait and see,'
Moscow politician he say, 'Come with me.'
But whichever white employer tells those little white lies,
I stop my ears and hold my nose and close my eyes."

I peered in.

Sitting on the bed, dressed in a pair of underpants decorated with palm leaves, was a stocky youth topped by an immense gollywog fuzz of hair. He grimaced pleasantly at me, humming the air till he had completed the guitar improvisation. Whereupon he slapped the instrument (as one might a child's behind) and said, "What say, man? You like a glass of rum?"

"I'm looking," I told him, "for Mr J. M. Fortune."

"Oh, that little jungle cannibal. That bongo-banging Bushman."

"I take it," I said, accepting some rum in a discoloured tooth-glass, "that you yourself are not from Africa?"

"Please be to God, no, man. I'm a civilized respectable Trinidadian."

"The Africans, then, aren't civilized?"

"They have their own tribal customs, mister, but it was because of their primitive barbarity that our ancestors fled from that country some centuries ago."

This was accompanied by a knowing leer.

"And the song," I asked. "It is of your own composition?"

"Yes, man. In my island I'm noted for my celebrated performance. It's your pleasure to meet this evening no less a one than Mr Lord Alexander in person."

And he held out a ring-encrusted hand with an immensely long, polished, little-finger nail.

"Perhaps, though," he went on, "as I'm seeking to make my way in *this* country, you could help me into radio or television or into some well-loaded night-spot?"

"Alas!" I told him, "I have no contacts in those glowing worlds."

"Then at least please speak well of me," he said, "and make my reputation known among your friends."

"Willingly. Though I have to tell you that I don't care for calypso...."

"Man, that's not possible!" He stood up in his flowered pants aghast. "Surely all educated Englishmen like our scintillating music?"

"Many, yes, but not I."

"Now, why?"

"Your lines don't scan, you accentuate the words incorrectly, and the thoughts you express are meagre and without wit."

"But our leg-inspiring rhythm?"

"Oh, that you have, of course...."

"Mr Gentleman, you disappoint me," he said. And taking a deep draught from the rum bottle, he strolled sadly to the window, leaned out, and sang into the opulent wastes of SW1:

> "This English gentleman he say to me
> He do not appreciate calypso melody.
> But I answer that calypso has supremacy
> To the Light Programme music of the BBC."

I made my getaway.

Prying along an adjacent marble landing (affording a vertiginous perspective of a downward-winding statue-flanked white stair), I saw a door on which was written: "J. Macdonald Fortune, Lagos. Enter without knocking." I did so, turned on the light, and saw a scene of agreeable confusion. Valises up-ended disgorging the bright clothes one would so wish to wear, shirts, ties and socks predominating — none of them fit for an English afternoon. Bundles of coconuts. A thick stick of bananas. Bottles, half empty. Rather surprising — a pile of biographies and novels. And pinned on the walls photographs of black grinning faces, all teeth, the eyes screwed closed to the glare of a sudden magnesium flare. A recurring group was evidently a family one: Johnny; a substantial rotund African gentleman with the same air of frank villainy as was the junior Mr Fortune's; his immense wife, swathed in striped native dress; a tall serious youth beside a motor-bicycle; and a vivacious girl with a smile like that of an amiable lynx.

On the table, I noticed an unfinished letter in a swift clerical hand. I didn't disturb it, but....

"Dear Peach,

"How it would be great if I could show you all the strange sights of the English capital, both comical and splendid! This morning I had my interview at the Welfare Office with — well, do you remember Reverend Simpson? Our tall English minister who used to walk as if his legs did not belong to him? And spoke to us like a telephone? Well, that was the appearance of the young Mr Pew who interviewed me, preaching and pointing his hands at me as if I was to him a menacing infant...."

Ah!

"...I have made visits, too, this afternoon, both of which will interest Dad— tell him I'm writing more about them, but don't please tell our dearest Mum or Christmas that I give you this message. Just now I have returned here to my miserable hostel (hovel! — which I shall be leaving permanently) to change to fresh clothes and go out in the town when it's alight.

"And Peach! It's true about the famous escalator! It can be done, early this morning I made the two-way expedition, easily dashing up again until...."

Should I turn over the sheet? No, no, not that....

I closed the door softly and walked down the chipped ceremonial stair. At its foot, the secretary waylaid me.

"And did you then discover Mr Fortune?" he enquired.

"No."

"Will it be necessary for me to convey to him some message of your visit?"

"No."

He frowned.

"As secretary of the hostel committee, may I ask of your

business on our premises?"

I gave him a Palmerstonian glare, but he met it with such a look of dignified solemnity that I wilted and said, "I am the new Assistant Welfare Officer. My name is Montgomery Pew."

"And mine, sir, is Mr Karl Marx Bo. I am from Freetown, Sierra Leone."

We shook hands.

"I hope, sir," he said, "you have not the same miserable opinion of our qualities as he who previously held down your job?"

"Oh, you mustn't think that. Come, come."

"May I offer you a cup of canteen coffee?"

"I'd love it, but really, I'm in somewhat of a hurry...."

I moved towards the massive door. Mr Bo walked beside me, radiating unaffected self-righteousness.

"Here in London, I am studying law," he told me.

"That means, I suppose, that you'll be going into politics?"

"Inevitably. We must make the most of our learning here in London. Emancipation, sir, is our ultimate objective. I predict that in the next ten years, or less, the whole of West Africa will be a completely emancipated federation."

"Won't the Nigerians gobble you up? Or Dr Nkrumah?"

"No, sir. Such politicians clearly understand that national differences of that nature are a pure creation of colonialism. Once we have federation, such regional distinctions will all fade rapidly away."

"Well, jolly good luck to you."

"Oh, yes! You say so! But like all Englishmen, I conceive you view with reluctance the prospect of our freedom?"

"Oh, but we give you the education to get it."

"Not give, sir. I pay for my university through profits my family have made in the sale of cocoa."

"A dreadful drink, if I may say so."

He tolerantly smiled. "You must come, sir, if you wish, to take part in one of our discussions with us, or debates."

"Nothing would delight me more, but alas, as an official, I am debarred from expressing any personal opinion, even had I one. And now, for the present, you really must excuse me."

And before he could recover his potential Dominion status, I was out of the door and stepping rapidly up the moonlit road. "To the Moorhen public house," I told a taxi driver.

He was of that kind who believe in the London cabby's reputation for dry wit.

"Better keep your hands on your pockets, Guv," he said, "if I take you there."

Montgomery at the Moorhen

Though fond of bars and boozing in hotels, I'm not a lover of that gloomiest of English institutions — the public house. There is a legend of the gaiety, the heart-warming homeliness of these "friendly inns" — a legend unshakeable; but all a dispassionate eye can see in them is the grim spectacle of "regulars" at their belching back-slapping beside the counter or, as is more often, sitting morosely eyeing one another, in private silence, before their half-drained gassy pints. (There is also, of course, that game called darts.)

It wasn't, then, with high eagerness that I prepared to visit the Moorhen. Nor was I more encouraged when the driver, with a knowing grimace, decanted me on a corner near the complex of North London railway termini. The pub, from outside, was of a dispirited baroque. And lurking about its doors, in groups, or half invisible in the gloom, were Negroes of equivocal appearance. One of these detached himself from a wall as I stood hesitating, and approached.

"What say, mister?" he began. "Maybe you want somesings or others?"

"Not that I'm aware of," I replied.

"Oh, no?"

"No...."

"Not this?"

Cupped in the hollow of his hand he held a little brown-paper packet two inches long or so.

"And what might that be?"

"Come now, man," he said with a grin of understanding and positively digging me in the ribs. "Is weed, man."

"*Weed?* What on earth should I want with weed? Now if you

21

had seedlings, or even the cuttings of a rose ....,"

"I see you's a humourisk," he said.

As a matter of fact, I wasn't quite so ignorant, for I had read my Sunday papers. But this was the first time I'd seen the stuff.

"All sames," he went on, closing his fingers over the little packet, "if you need some charge later in your evenings, come to me. Mr Pay Paul is what's my name."

I thanked him remotely, and pushed open the door of the Moorhen's saloon.

Within, where dark skins outnumbered white by something like twenty to one, there was a prodigious bubble and clatter of sound, and what is rare in purely English gatherings — a constant movement of person to person, and group to group, as though some great invisible spoon were perpetually stirring a hot human soup. Struggling, then propelled, towards the bar, I won myself a large whisky, and moved, with the instinct of minorities, to the only other white face I could see who was not either serving behind the bar, or a whore, of whom there were a great many there, or a person of appearance so macabre as scarcely to be believed. The man whom I addressed was one of those vanishing London characters, the elderly music-hall comical, modelled perhaps on Wilkie Bard, all nose, blear eyes, greased clothes and tufts of hair. "Cheerio!" I said to him.

He eyed me.

"Crowded tonight."

"Yus." (He really said "Yus".) "More's the pity."

"Oh, you think so? You don't care for crowds?"

"Course I do — when they're rispectable. But not when they're darkies like what's here and all their rubbish."

"Rubbish?"

He gazed all round the room like a malevolent searchlight and said, "Jus' look for yourself. And to think a year or so ago this was the cosiest little boozer for arf a mile."

"But if," I said, "you don't like it, why do you come here?"

"Ho! They won't drive me out! They drove out me pals, but they won't drive me."

"Drove them?"

"They left. Didn't care for it as it got to be ever since the

Cosmopolitan opened opposyte."

"That's the dance hall?"

"Yus. They let those darkies overrun the dance hall, but they haven't got a licence there. So what did they do? Came trooping over the road for drinks like an invasion, and turned this place into an Indian jungle."

"And the landlord let them?"

"He can't refuse. At least he did try to for the sake of his regulars, but when he saw all the coin they dropped on to his counters, he gave up the fight, and me pals all had to move on. But not me. This is my pub and I'm staying in it till something happens and they all get thrown out again." And this outpost of empire stared at me with neurotic, baleful zeal.

A juke-box that had been blaring out strident three-pennyworths now stopped. I edged my way over to an argumentative group around it, one of whom, a hefty, vivid-looking Negro, was shouting out what sounded rather like:

"Ooso, man. See molo keneeowo p'kolosoma nyamo Ella Fitzgerald, not that other woman. See kynyomo esoloo that is my preference."

The speaker was wearing pink trousers, a tartan silk shirt bedecked with Parker pens, and a broad-brimmed hat ironed up fore and aft like a felt helmet. A watch of gold, and silver chains, dangled on his gesticulating wrists.

A smaller man beside him, an ally apparently, turned to the others and said, "Is best let Mr Cannibal have his own choice of record if someone will please give him a threepence bit."

No one offered, and I ventured to hand the giant a coin.

"Oh, this is nice," said the smaller man. "Here is this nice personality who gives Mr Cannibal his tune!" He took the coin from me with two delicate fingers, put it in the juke-box, then said smiling wide, "So I offer you a cigarette? And then maybe you offer me a light in your own turn?"

I took the Pall Mall, and held out my Ronson to his own. His fingers encircled it as if to guard the flame when, hey presto! the lighter was flicked from my hand, and this person had scurried through the throng towards a farther corner.

I looked about me and saw amiable laughing faces whose eyes

23

dropped politely when mine caught theirs. I began to make my way through them towards the robber and found that, while not exactly stopping me by standing full in my tracks, they presented hard shoulders that made progress difficult.

When at last I reached the corner, I saw an ancient hair-stuffed sofa tottering against the wall. On it were seated Mr Cannibal, the little nuisance who'd taken my lighter, and a third man who wasn't talking, only listening. He was small, tightly built into his suit, at ease, alert, alarming, and compact. He glanced up at me: our eyes locked: his glare had such depth that my own sank into his, and while for two seconds I stood riveted, this stare seemed to drain away my soul.

I blinked, hemmed in behind a wall of dark faces and drape suits. Abruptly, I shook my brain, moved a pace towards the thief, and said to him: "Can I have my lighter?"

The gabbling conversation in jungle tones went on until the third time of asking. Then the little thief looked up and said, "What is this stranger? You ask for some light from me, or what?"

It was a shock to see how with this race, even more than with our own, an expression of great amiability can be replaced, on the same face, within seconds, by one of cold indifference and menace.

"No," I said, enwrapping myself with draped togas of torn Union Jacks. "Not a *light*, but the *lighter*."

He took it out of his pocket and tossed it up and down in his hand.

"You wish to *buy* this?" he asked.

"No. Merely to have it back."

"You mean you say that this my lighter is *your* lighter?"

"Well, my dear chap, you know it is."

The giant got up, and so did the lighter-lifter, but not the third man, who sat looking at eternity through his lashes.

"Then what I ask," said the culprit, "is if your words mean that you call me now a thief?"

The giant stood looking like the Black Peril. The third man now glanced up at me again. When his eyes fixed once more on mine, I felt myself absorbed into a promiscuity of souls closer even than that which can bind, and then dissolve, two animal bodies in each other.

"No," I said, faltering, "Keep it." And as I moved off: "I hope it brings you luck."

Rage and disgust filled my heart. "That idiot at the Welfare Office was right!" I cried out to myself, as I heaved back through the crowd. "Disgusting creatures! Bring back the lash, the slave trade! Long live Dr Malan!"

Standing in the doorway was a figure different from the gaudy elegants inside — one dressed in dungarees, half-shaven, with anthropoid jaws and baby ears, more startling even than alarming. He gave me a great meaningless grin, held out a detaining hand and said (this is the rough equivalent), "You want some Mexican cigaleks?"

"No, no."

"At sree sillins for twentik, misters...."

"Oh, really? Well, yes, then."

He slipped them to me discreetly. Lighting up, awaiting for the return of my shattered poise, I asked him, "How do you get these, then?"

Conspiratorially, he replied: "From him G.I.s who sells me in cartoons wisouts no legal dutiks. So you better keep him secrix."

"They sell them to you here?"

"No, out in him streek, because of Law and his narks that put the eye insides. Anysing from G.I. stores you wants I gess you: sirts, soss, ties, jackix, nylons, overcoats, socolates or any osser foots...."

"You make a good profit?"

He looked bland.

"I must have profix for my risks. That is my bisnick."

"Do other boys here have things to sell?"

"Oh, misters! Here is him big London Spadiss markik place! Better than Ossford Streek hisself!" And he roared out laughing loud, doubling himself up and slapping himself all over. Then he looked coyly discreet. "Those bad boys," he said, "they relieves you of somesink?"

"Yes. You saw? They stole my lighter."

"A Ronsons?"

"Yes."

"Of course. Was Mr Ronson Lighter who took it. That is his professins: when he sees Ronson lighter, he muss steal him."

"And who are his friends?"

"The Billy Whispers peoples. Gambian boys, real bad. Billy hisself, and Jimmies Cannibals and Mister Ronson Lighter, this that robs you."

"What do they do for a living?"

"Prey!"

His eyes gleamed sympathetically and, I thought, with envy. Then he went on:

"That is their seats over in him corners. This is the seats of all bad Asfrican boys where they go gather makin' deals. No Asfrican boy who is not top London hustler go near their corners, and no Wess Indians dare go by never. Mister, if you have loot, or goods, or wishes they can prey on, please keep clear of him Billy Whispers and all his surrounding mens."

He told me this as one who reveals a precious, precarious State secret. Then he looked severe.

"Those boys they sink I stupit — 'Boos-a-man' [Bushman] they call me, becos I come out from my home in him interiors, not city folks like those wikit waterfronk boys...." He ruminated, flashing his eyes about. "They sink I stupit because of no educasons. But [crescendo] my blood better than their blood! My father sieftan [chieftain]!"

"Yes?"

"Yes. I seif's son."

Diffidence but enormous pride: as if making a huge joke that was no joke, as if calling on me to recognize a splendid truth even if incredible.

"Then why do you leave your people and come here to England?"

"I? Oh, to see these sights. To live. Also, to learn my instrumink."

"Your...."

"My sassofone. I work stoke in him governmik boiler-room by nights, to get loot for lessons for my instrumink. Then, when my time come, I go home to fashinate my cousins with my tunes."

"And how are your studies progressing?"

"Whass say?"

"Are you mastering your instrument?"

"Man, up till now is my instrumink who is most times mastering me. Ah! But lissen!"

And we heard:

"You leave your mother and your brother too,
You leave the pretty wife you're never faithful to,
You cross the sea to find those streets that's paved with
    gold,
And all you find is Brixton cell that's oh! so cold."

"Thass Lord Alissander! He always come playing here evening, hopin' for sillins and publicitix."

He plucked at my arm and led me out to the corner of the street. Mr Lord Alexander was leaning against the pub wall, strumming and singing in the middle of a softly humming circle.

"Give us some bad song now, man!"

"Some little evil tune, Lord Alexander!"

"Oh, no! No, no, not me in this respectable country...."

"This little Miss Commercial Road she say to me,
'I can't spend much more time in your society.
I know you keep me warmer than my white boy can do,
But my mother fears her grandson may be black as
    you.'"

There was laughter; but on the far side of the street, standing against the brick fence that lined the bombed-out site, were two figures in mackintoshes who were now joined by a tall police Inspector with the shape of an expectant mother. The Bushman took my arm:

"Lissen, man," he whispered, "I soot off now, that look to me like him Law be making his customary visicts. Come! We soot off to him Cosmikpolitan dansings, and find whass cookings there...."

Looking back, we saw the three coppers sweeping on the group, which scattered; and then Lord Alexander being led off, the uniformed Inspector carrying the guitar as if it was a truncheon.

Nicked

From *New Society*, September 1965

MacInnes's later account of his own arrest and trial, when compared with the trial of Johnny Macdonald Fortune (which forms the second of two "Interludes" in City of Spades*), will be seen to have many features in common with that fictitious event.*

This is what can happen when you get arrested.

Ten years ago, in the days when casinos were illegal, I went to a squalid gambling house in the East End. You reached it up a clanking metal stair, and there were two rooms, one serving food and with people sleeping for the night upon the floor, and another — separated by a grubby hanging blanket — where the card games were played. I was standing by the fire taking in this scene when six CID officers raided the place.

These were not local lads, but gentlemen from the Yard. They took us all into custody — and even roped in someone who was entering from the street as we were leaving. At the local nick they had us in one by one to interrogate us. I was somewhat alarmed to see the man who went in before me come out crying; the more so as Negroes do not often cry.

When my turn came, the detective-inspector called out: "You!" To which I answered something cheeky like, "I've got a name, you know." He waited till I was ahead of him, then slugged me from behind in the neck, so that I fell spreadeagled into the interrogation room.

They wanted to fingerprint me. I refused to be fingerprinted. (You can — technically — refuse this until they have a magistrate's order.) On a sign from the inspector, two of them took me into a separate room, said, "So you're not going to cooperate — huh?" and beat me around a bit. I said, "Stop behaving like in Yankee films" — and they hit me some more.

Then I was handed over to a nice elderly chap who reasoned with me and gave me a fag. Why be so awkward? — why refuse to be printed? They could do that anyway when they got me down to Brixton, he said. I accepted the fag, but still refused the printing. About two hours later I and the dozen others were hustled off to jail — after I'd also refused to sign blind for the articles they said they'd taken from me. (I got the impression, by the way, that the local lads at the police station didn't terribly care for the way the Yard CID were handling things.)

I had not, incidentally, been charged (though no doubt a charge sheet was made out), nor had I at any time been cautioned. So two more myths about Judge's Rules (the third being the non-use of violence) turned out — as I'd always expected — to be myths indeed.

On Monday we came up before the magistrate and learned we were *all* being charged with being in possession of dangerous drugs. These alleged drugs were not produced, for at this stage they only asked for a remand and did not oppose bail. In my own case they requested from the magistrate that I should be fingerprinted. He put it to me that I couldn't possibly object to this (rather, as the sergeant-major says, "You don't mind going on fatigues, son, do you?"), so I accepted. The detective-inspector did the job. "I was a bit surprised," he said to me, "by that lad who cried. He really did seem upset." "Well," I answered, "you were a bit energetic, weren't you?"

As to whether anyone *was* in possession of dangerous drugs, I simply don't know for sure. I know I hadn't any myself — and the reader can believe this or not as he pleases. I should imagine *some* were — it was that kind of a place — but I think it most unlikely that those who were dossing down on the floor for free had anything. Anyway, everyone denied it, and they stuck to this during the three times we came up (after another remand) before the magistrate.

I had meanwhile, somewhat naturally, sought advice from various sources. It was suggested to me that a bribe might help to get the charge, if not dropped, not pressed, but as I refused this contact's offer to do the necessary I cannot vouch for its possibility: all I can say is that it was proposed seriously by a knowledgeable and non-criminal person. My other advisers said I should certainly ask for trial by a judge and jury, since magistrates would always accept police evidence — so I elected (thank heaven!) to do this, even though it cost hundreds of pounds and meant waiting for months.

The reader may be wondering why I did not heroically denounce the police for their behaviour. I was advised that to do this would be to lose the case, since no one would believe me, and I would antagonize judge and jury. The thing to do, I was told, was to suggest there had been an honest error on the Law's part. So this is what I did and I am ashamed to this day I did not have the guts to say what really happened.

The packet of drugs and loaded cigarette I was supposed to have, I didn't see until the third appearance in the magistrate's court. Where these came from I do not know, but I have a fair idea, and I expect the reader — if not too credulous — has as well. I did ask my lawyer, "Look, if I'm supposed to have had those things, wouldn't my fingerprints be on them? And as they aren't can't we ask to have them examined?" Silly boy, he told me: they'll simply say that having *seen* you hold them there was no need to check them for prints, and that since my arrest they have of course been handled by dozens of official people.

In due course I appeared at the Sessions and was acquitted. The reason was simply that the police hadn't done their homework. So that when they were asked what I was supposed to have said, or where I was standing, or what I had on — simple questions of that kind to two officers (the second of whom was not allowed to hear what the first one had said in court before giving testimony himself) — they contradicted themselves. And owing to the fact that ten of the accused had already been convicted (in the magistrate's court), and the one other who could afford a lawyer had gone before a different tribunal, I had the advantage of appearing before the judge and jury alone. No doubt a collar and tie and an adequate accent were also a help.

If the reader might imagine I am still seething with indignation, or that this experience made me a copper hater, he would be quite mistaken. For what I have always (in essays and fiction) tried to establish about police work is that in certain cases, to get convictions, the police *must* use violence, perjury, and even be open to corruption. Those whom I blame are the public who will not accept this, especially when they sit on juries; or lawyers who through naivety or a mistaken sense of public policy either accept these occurrences as normal, or refuse utterly to believe them.

The police very rarely bring a charge without grounds, simply through malice. But when they *do* bring a charge they are not over-scrupulous on how they make it stick — nor can they afford to be, with public and official pressures on them to get convictions. Nor, in this case, did I detect any *personal* animosity — I had a little chat after it was all over with the two officers who testified against me, and they were quite amiable about losing; nor have they made things specially awkward for me since. And as they quite rightly pointed out, if you go to a dodgy place like an illegal gambling house on a Saturday night, you can easily involve yourself in — to say the least of it — misunderstandings.

I do have, however, four reproaches to make to this excellent detective-inspector and detective-constable. The first is, I don't think they should have swung this charge on me merely through guesswork. If a search revealed I had nothing, I think they might have let it go at that.

My next grouse is that I don't think they need have been quite so rough. And my next that they made no attempt whatever to find out who I was — or indeed ask me anything but my name and address and to be fingerprinted. I don't of course mean that because I am "educated" I was entitled to favoured treatment, but I do think if they'd asked me a question or two they might have had second thoughts.

My last reproach — not my business, really — is a professional one. When they went into court they should have dovetailed their stories better. As it was, cross-examination made their tales less and less credible.

I must confess I don't like policemen as a category much, yet they do have qualities that I admire. I think they are brave (they have to be) and dedicated, and as human persons they are often fascinating. (I suppose anyone who moves in muddy moral waters must be.) The people I don't much care for are those who still believe in the Dixon of Dock Green image: this is just so silly and, factually speaking, dishonest.

As for the gentle reader of my story, I imagine his reactions thus. If he is of the respectable classes, he will take me for either a liar or one who seeks to rock the foundations of society. If a criminal, he will say, "Why on earth is he making such a fuss about the obvious?" If a lawyer, he will probably think these things are best not written of. If the reader be simply one without direct experience, and seeking after facts, my strongest advice to him, so far as the Law is concerned, is to steer clear of it if possible and, if he falls into its clutches, be patient, brave and prudent.

from *City of Spades*

The trial of Johnny Macdonald Fortune took place in a building, damaged in the Hitler war, which had been redecorated in a "contemporary" style — light salmon wood, cubistic lanterns, leather cushions of pastel shades — that pleased none of the lawyers, officials or police officers who worked there. The courts looked too much like the board-rooms of progressive companies, staterooms on liners, even "lounges" of American-type hotels, for the severe traditional taste of these professionals; and all of them, when they appeared there, injected into their behaviour an additional awesome formality to counter-act the lack of majesty of their surroundings.

On the morning of the trail, Mr Zuss-Amor had a short conference with Mr Wesley Vial. In his wig and gown, Mr Vial was transformed from the obese, balding playboy of the queer theatrical parties he loved to give at his flat near Marble Arch, into a really impressive figure; impressive, that is, by his authority, which proceeded from his formidable knowledge of the operation of the law, his nerves of wire, his adaptable, synthetic charm, his aggressive ruthlessness, and his total contempt for weakness and "fair play". Mr Zuss-Amor, by comparison, seemed, in this decor, a shabby figure — like a nonconformist minister calling on a cardinal.

"Who have we got against us?" said Mr Zuss-Amor.

"Archie Gillespie."

"As Crown counsel in these cases go, by no means a fool."

"By *no* means, Mr Zuss-Amor."

The solicitor felt rebuked. "What was your impression of our client, Mr Vial?"

"Nice boy. Do what I can for him, of course — but what? The trouble with coloured men in the dock, you know, is that juries just can't tell a good one from a bad."

"Can they *ever* tell that, would you say?"

"Oh, sometimes! Don't be too hard on juries."

"We'll be having some ladies, I believe."

"Excellent! He must flash all his teeth at them." Mr Vial turned over the pages of the brief. "There was nothing you could do with this Muriel Macpherson woman?"

"Nothing. I even went out and saw her myself. She's very sore with our young client, Mr Vial. Frankly, I think if we *had* called her, we'd have found ourselves asking permission to treat her as a hostile witness."

"'Hell hath no fury,' and so on. On the other hand, Gillespie tells me he's not calling the sister Dorothy. Very wise of him. He's relying on police evidence — which, I'm sorry to say, will probably be quite sufficient for his purpose."

"Pity you couldn't have had a go at the woman Dorothy in the box, though, Mr Vial . . . ." The solicitor's eyes gleamed.

"Oh, best to keep the females out of it, on the whole. I'll see what can be done with the two officers. I've met the Inspector in the courts before . . . always makes an excellent impression. Looks like a family man who'd like to help the prisoner if he could: deeply regrets having to do his painful duty. I don't think I know the Detective-Constable . . . ."

"A new boy in the CID. Very promising in the Force, I'm told. Man of few words in the box, though. Difficult to shake him, I think you'll find."

Mr Vial put down the brief. "And yet, you know, it *should* be possible to shake them."

"If anyone can do it, you can."

"I didn't mean that. I mean this charge: it's bogus. Just look at it!" (He held up the brief.) "It stinks to high heaven!"

"You think this boy's telling the truth — or part of it?"

"I think he's telling the whole of it. I pressed him hard at our little interview, as you saw. And what did he do? He lost his temper! I've never seen such righteous indignation! I'm always impressed by honest fury in a defendant."

Mr Zuss-Amor nodded, frowned, and scratched his bottom. "Why do they do it, Mr Vial?" he said.

"Why do who do what?"

"Why do the police bring these trumped-up charges?"

"Oh, well...." The advocate sighed with all his bulk, and hitched his robe. "You know the familiar argument as well as I do. The accused's generally done what they say he's done, but not how they say he's done it. The charge is usually true, the evidence often false. But in this case, I think both are phoney.... Well, we'll have to see...."

The two CID officers were having a cup of tea in the police room. "It's your first case with us in the vice game," said the Inspector, "but you don't have to let that worry you. The way to win a case, in my experience, is not to mind from the beginning if you lose it."

"But we shouldn't lose this one, should we, sir?"

"I don't see how we can, Constable. But just remember what I told you. They'll keep you outside until I've given evidence, of course, but you know what I'm going to say in its essential outlines. If they ask any questions in examination that we haven't thought of, just say as little as possible: take your time, look the lawyer in the eye, and just say you don't remember."

"He's rough, isn't he, Inspector, this Wesley Vial?"

"That fat old poof? Don't be afraid of him, son. He's sharp, mind you, but if you don't let him rattle you, there's nothing he can do." The Inspector lit his Dunhill pipe. "It's obvious what he'll try," he continued. "He'll make out that he accepts our story, but he'll try to shake us on the details, so as to put a doubt into the jury's mind."

The constable sipped his beverage. "They're not likely to raise the question of that bit of rough stuff at the station, are they?"

"Vial certainly won't — he knows no jury would believe it. But the boy might allege something, even though Vial's probably told him not to. Let's hope he does do. It'd make a very bad impression on the court. Drink up now, Constable, we're on in a minute or two."

The constable swallowed. "I'm sure you know best about not calling that girl Dorothy, sir. But don't you think if we'd had her to pin it on him good and proper...."

"Mr Gillespie said no, and I think he's right. I've told her to keep out of the way and keep her trap shut till the trial's over — and she will. You never know how it will be with women in the box: she may love this boy, for all we know, and might have spoken out of turn; and if we'd called her for the prosecution, we might have found ourselves with a hostile witness on our hands."

In the public gallery, a little minority group of Africans was collecting: among them Laddy Boy, who'd brought an air cushion and a bag of cashew nuts; the Bushman, who'd got a front seat, leaned on the railing and immediately gone to sleep; and Mr Karl Marx Bo, who planned to send by air mail a tendentious report on the trail to the Mendi newspaper of which he was part-time correspondent, if, as he hoped it would be, the result was unfavourable to the defendant.

Theodora and Montgomery arrived much too early, and sat in great discomfort on the benches that sloped steeply like a dress circle overlooking the well of the court. They wondered if they could take their overcoats off and, if so, where they could put them.

"It doesn't look very impressive," said Theodora. "It's much too small."

"It looks exactly like Act III of a murder play. Which is the dock?"

"Just underneath us, I expect."

"So we won't see him."

"We will when he's giving evidence," said Theodora. "That's the witness-box there on the right."

"Box is the word for it. It looks like an up-ended coffin."

Mr Wesley Vial met Mr Archie Gillespie in the lawyers' lavatory. "I do hope, Wesley," the Crown counsel said, "your man's English will be comprehensible. I take it you'll be putting him in the box?"

"Time alone will show, Archie. But if you want any evidence taken in the vernacular, we can always put in for an interpreter and prolong matters to your heart's content."

"No, thank you," said Mr Gillespie. "Crown counsel don't draw your huge refreshers." He dried his hands. "Who's the judge?"

"Old Haemorrhoids."

"My God. It would be."

The lawyers looked at each other resignedly. There was a distant shout, and they adjusted their wigs like actors who've heard the call-boy summon them to the stage.

Johnny Fortune had been brought up from Brixton to the court in one of those police vans where the prisoners half sit in metal boxes, hardly larger than themselves. They'd arrived more than an hour before the case began, and the court jailer, after searching him yet again, said, "Well, we won't put you in the cells unless you really want to go there. If I leave you in the room here, will you behave yourself?"

"Of course."

"You want some cigarettes?"

"They not let me take any of my money."

"Oh, pay me when you're acquitted!" said the jailer with a hearty laugh, and gave Johnny Fortune a half-filled pack of Woodbines and a cup of purple tea. "I see you've got Vial," he went on. "That'll cost you a bit, won't it? Or should I say —" the jailer laughed roguishly — "cost your little lady and her customers?"

Johnny stood up. "Mister, put me in your cells. I do not wish your tea or want your Woodbine."

"No offence, lad, don't be so touchy. I know you all have to say you're innocent — I get used to it here. Come on, keep them — you've got an hour to wait." The jailer patted his prisoner on the shoulder, and went over to gossip with a lean, powdered female constable in civilian dress, who, as they talked, looked over the jailer's shoulder at the folds in Johnny Fortune's trousers.

□

Everyone stood, and the judge came in wearing a wig not of the Gilbert and Sullivan variety, but a short one, slightly askew, that made him look like Dr Johnson's younger brother. The jury was new, and the case their first, so they had to be sworn in by the usher. Two of them were women: a WVS housewifely person, and the other with a beret and a tailored suit whose nature it was impossible to guess at. A male juror turned out, when he swore, to be called "Ramsay Macdonald", on hearing which Mr Vial made a slight histrionic gesture of impressed surprise to Mr Gillespie, who ignored him.

One of the two policemen in the dock nudged Johnny, and he stood. The clerk, a quite young man with a pink, pale face, read out the charge in a voice like an Old Vic juvenile's; and when he asked Johnny how he pleaded, looked up at him, across the court, with a pleading expression on his own wan face.

"I plead not guilty."

Mr Zuss-Amor, flanking his advocate, twitched his shoulders slightly. You never could tell with defendants: he'd even known them get the plea wrong at the outset.

Mr Archie Gillespie's opening statement of the case for the Queen against the prisoner was as methodical as one would expect from a Scottish lawyer of vast experience and entire integrity. He had the great psychological advantages of believing the facts in the brief that he'd been given, or most of them, and of being quite dispassionate in his advocacy. He had no feeling of animosity towards the prisoner whatever, and this made him all the more deadly.

He began by explaining to the jury what living on the immoral earnings of a common prostitute consisted of. It was a distasteful subject, and a painful duty for the members of the jury to have to hear about it. But they were, he did not doubt, men and women of ripe experience, to whom he could speak quite frankly. Very well, then. As everyone knew, there were, unfortunately, such women as common prostitutes — selling their bodies for gain (Mr Gillespie paused, and gazed at a female juror, who licked her lips) — in our society; women whose odious commerce was — subject to certain important restrictions — not actually illegal, however reprehensible on moral grounds. But what *was* illegal — and highly so, and he would say, more revolting and abhorrent — was the practice of certain men — if one could call them men — of battening on these wretched creatures, and living on the wages of their sin; and even, in a great many cases — though he would not necessarily say it was so in the present instance — even of forcing them out on to the streets against their wills. It was not for nothing, said Mr Gillespie, removing his spectacles a moment, that such men, in the speech of a more robust age, had been known as "bullies".

The judge manifested a slight impatience, and Mr Gillespie took the hint. He explained to the jury that two police officers would tell them how observation had been kept on one Dorothea Violet Macpherson, a known and convicted common prostitute, who had been seen, on several nights in succession, to accost men in Hyde Park, receive sums of money from them, entice them into the undergrowth, and there have carnal knowledge of them. These officers would further tell the members of the jury how the said Dorothea Violet Macpherson was subsequently followed to an address in Immigration Road, Whitechapel, where she lived in two rooms with the accused. (Here Mr Gillespie paused, and spoke more slowly.) These officers would then tell how, on a number of occasions when observation was kept on the accused and on the said Dorothea Violet Macpherson, she was seen to hand over to him large sums of money that had come into her possession through her immoral commerce in the purlieus of Hyde Park.

The Crown counsel now glanced at Mr Vial, who sat looking into the infinite like a Buddha. "No doubt my learned friend here will suggest to you," he declared, "that the accused was not present on these occasions or, alternatively, that the sums of money in question were not passed over to him or, alternatively again, that if they were, they were not those proceeding from the act of common prostitution." Mr Gillespie waited a second, as if inviting Mr Vial to say just that: then continued, "It will be for you, members of the jury, to decide on whose evidence you should rely: on that of the witness, or witnesses, that may be brought forward by the defence, or on that of the two experienced police officers whom I am now going to call before you."

The Detective-Inspector walked in with a modest, capable and self-sufficient mien. He took the oath, removed a notebook from his pocket, and turned to face his counsel.

"Members of the jury," said Mr Gillespie. "You will observe that the Detective-Inspector is holding a small book. Inspector, will you please tell the court what this book is?"

"It's my police notebook, sir."

"Exactly. Officers of the Crown, when giving evidence, are permitted to refer, for matters of fact — and matters of fact only — to the notes they made of a case immediately after they have performed their duties. Very well. Now, Detective-Inspector, will you please tell my Lord and members of the jury what happened, in your own words?"

In his own words, and prompted only slightly by Mr Gillespie, the officer related the detailed minutiae of the events the counsel had already outlined. By the time of the third, fourth and fifth seeing of Dorothy taking money in the park, and seeing her giving it to Johnny in the Immigration Road, the tale began to lose some its human fascination, even though its cumulative substance added greatly to the "weight of evidence".

Mr Gillespie sat down, and Mr Wesley Vial arose.

"Detective-Inspector," he said. "Do you know who the defendant is?"

"Who he is, sir? He's an African."

"Yes. Quite so. An African. But can you tell us anything about him?"

"I have, sir."

"Yes, Inspector, we know you have. But I mean who he is? His family? His background? What sort of man the court has got before it?"

"No, sir. He said he was a student."

"He said he was a student. Did you enquire of what?"

"No, sir."

"You didn't. Did you know this young man's father, Mr David Macdonald Fortune, wears the King's Medal for valour which was awarded to him when he was formerly a sergeant in the Nigerian police force?"

"No, sir."

"You didn't bother to find out what sort of man you had to deal with? It didn't interest you. Is that it?"

The judge stirred himself slightly, as if from a distant dream. "I can't quite see the relevance of that, Mr Vial," he said, in a melancholy, croaking voice. "It's not the accused's father who's before me."

Mr Vial bowed. "True, my Lord. But your Lordship will appreciate, I'm sure, how vital it is for me, in a case of this description — that is, a case where the defendant is a citizen of one of the colonies of our Commonwealth — to establish clearly his social standing and reputation. The members of the jury" (Mr Vial inclined himself courteously towards them) "may not be as familiar as we have grown to be, my Lord, with what very different sorts of African citizen are now to be found here in England among us: some, no doubt, with a background of a kind that might render an accusation of this nature unfortunately all too credible, but others — as I hope to show you is the case at present — in whom such conduct would be as totally improbable as it would were I, my Lord, or Mr Gillespie here, to be said to indulge in it."

There was a hush, while everyone digested this. "Yes. Well, do proceed, please, Mr Vial," said the judge.

The defending counsel turned once more to the Crown witness.

"You have, in fact, Inspector — apart, of course, from the present case — nothing to say against the defendant?"

"No, sir. He's got no police record."

"Exactly. He's got no police record. And has he, at any time, made any statement in writing, or any verbal statement concerning the charge, by which he admits his guilt in any particular whatever?"

"No, sir."

"So we're left with what you and your officers have seen, Inspector."

The Inspector didn't answer. Mr Vial looked up, and barked at him, "I say, we're left with what you tell us that you've seen.

Will you please answer me, Inspector?"

"I didn't know you were asking me a question, sir."

"You didn't know I was asking you a question. Very well. Now, I want you to tell us about these happenings in Hyde Park. You saw this woman accost various men at various times on various evenings, take money from them, and disappear with them into the..." (Mr Vial looked at his notes) "...yes, into the undergrowth, I think it was. Now let us take the first evening: the evening you tell us that the defendant later received twenty-eight pounds from this woman. How many men accosted her?"

"Five or six, sir."

"Five — or six? Which was it? You may consult your notebook if you wish."

"Six, sir."

"So each man would have paid an average of four pounds thirteen shillings and fourpence for this woman's services?"

"Not necessarily, sir. She could have had some money in her bag before she went inside the park."

"In her what, Inspector?"

"She could have had some money in her bag before she went there."

"What bag?"

"The bag she put the money in, sir."

"Oh." Mr Vial picked up a document. "But in the magistrates' court, I see you told his Worship that this woman put the money in her raincoat pocket."

"Yes, sir."

"Sometimes she put it in her raincoat pocket, and sometimes she put it in her bag, is that it?"

"Yes, sir."

"I see. And then she went with these people into the undergrowth. How dark was this undergrowth?"

"Quite light enough to keep her under observation, sir."

"Come now, Inspector. Are you telling the court a woman of this description would take a man, in a public locality like Hyde Park, into a place that was dark enough for her purposes, but light enough to be observed by two police officers —

standing at a certain distance from her, I suppose?"

"We were quite near enough, sir, to see whatever happened."

"You were quite near enough. And she never saw you?"

"No, sir."

"On no occasion? Not once on all these evenings when you and your colleague stood peering at her while she went into the undergrowth with all these dozens of men?"

"She gave no sign of being seen, sir."

"Not even when you followed her home?"

"No, sir."

"What did she travel home on? A bus? A tube?"

"She usually took a bus to Victoria station, and then a tube, sir."

"She usually did. Aren't prostitutes in the habit of taking taxis? Isn't that notorious?"

"Not all of them, sir. Not always." The officer consulted his notebook. "She took a taxi one night, but it's not been referred to in my evidence."

"So you followed her by bus, or tube, or taxi to the Immigration Road — and then what?"

"We saw her go into the house, sir."

"Saw her how? Did you follow her inside?"

"No, sir. We kept observation from the street."

"So you must have seen her through the window. Is that it?"

"Yes, sir."

"This window had no curtains, I suppose. Is that what you have to tell us?"

"Yes, sir, it had. But they weren't always drawn over it."

"Not always drawn across the window in the depths of winter?"

"Not always, sir."

Mr Vial paused for quite ten seconds. "Officer," he said, "if you, or I, or anyone else in his right mind were going to hand a large sum of money over to somebody else, even for a perfectly legitimate reason, would we really do it in front of an open, uncurtained window on the ground floor of a house in a busy street of a not particularly salubrious neighbourhood?"

"That's what they did, sir."

"And if the transaction was a highly illegal one, as it would be in the present instance, wouldn't there be all the more reason to hand the money over behind closed doors and out of sight?"

"These people are very careless, sir. They're often under the influence of alcohol, and other things."

"They'd need to be! They'd certainly need to be, to behave so rashly!" Mr Vial gazed in amazement at the judge, at the jury, at Mr Gillespie, and back again at the Detective-Inspector. "Now, Inspector," he said gently. "Please understand I'm not questioning your good faith in any respect. You're an experienced officer, as my learned friend has said, and there can therefore be no question of that at all.... But don't you think, from what you tell us, it's possible you were mistaken?"

"No, sir. She gave him the money like I said."

"On half a dozen occasions, a prostitute takes money out of her handbag, or raincoat, or whatever it was, and hands it over to a man in a lighted room without the curtains drawn across in full view of the general public, and does it all so slowly that anyone standing outside could count the exact number of pound notes? Is that what you're telling us?"

"Yes, sir."

"Thank you, Inspector." Mr Vial sat down.

The Detective-Constable was called. Examined by Mr Gillespie, he confirmed his colleague's account in all essential particulars. Mr Wesley Vial rose again.

"How long have you been with the CID, Detective-Constable?"

"Two months, sir."

"This is your first case as a CID officer?"

"Yes, sir."

"Before you joined the CID, did your duties bring you in contact with this sort of case at all?"

"No, sir. I was in Records."

"You were in Records. Now, Constable. Since this case was first brought in the magistrates' court, you have discussed it, naturally, with the Inspector?"

"I've talked about the case in general, sir. I haven't discussed the details of the evidence."

"Of course not. The evidence you gave is entirely your own, isn't it? But you've relied on the guidance of your superior officers to a certain extent as to how you should put it to the court?"

The judge made a slight noise. "I don't think you should ask the witness that, Mr Vial," he said. "You needn't answer, Constable."

"As you say, my Lord. I have no further questions."

The Detective-Constable left the box and went and sat by the Inspector, who gave him a slight, official smile. "Call the defendant," said the usher.

Johnny Fortune left the dock, walked firmly through the court and took the oath. The assembly regarded him with a slightly increased respect; for whatever the outcome of the case, a person in the witness-box seems a very different person from one sitting between two policemen in the dock.

Mr Vial faced his client with a look stern as Gabriel's, and said: "John Macdonald Fortune: do you know what living off the immoral earnings of a woman means?"

"Yes. I do know."

"Have you lived off the immoral earnings of this woman?"

"No. Never."

"Have you ever lived off the immoral earnings of any woman?"

"Never! Never would I give my blood to such a person. Never!"

Mr Vial sat down. Mr Gillespie arose.

"You say you're a student," he began. "A student of what?"

"Of meteorology."

The judge leaned forward. "What was that word?"

"Meteorology, my Lord. I'm not quite sure what it is, but no doubt we'll discover. And how long is it since you attended your last lecture?"

"Is some months now."

"Why? Is your college on holiday?"

"No. I give up these studies."

"So now you're not studying anything?"

"No."

"You've not been a student for some months, in fact?"

"No."

"And what have you lived on?"

"I work in a labouring job."

"How long did you work in this labouring job?"

"Some few week before I get arrested."

"Some few weeks. And at the time you were living with this woman, were you working?"

"Listen to me, sir. I live some few week when I have no money with this woman."

"So you *did* live with her? You admit that?"

The judge croaked again. "There's just a point here, Mr Gillespie, I think. It's possibly the language difficulty, you know." He looked at Johnny. "You say you lived *with* this woman. Do you mean simply that you lived in the same house, or flat, or room, or do you mean that you lived there as man and wife?"

"She not my wife."

"We know that," said Mr Gillespie. "What his Lordship means is, did you have any carnal knowledge of this woman?"

"Have what?"

"Did you have intercourse with her?"

"One time I have sex with that woman, yes. One time. But I take no money from her. Never."

"I see. You took no money from her. Who paid the rent?"

"She pay it."

"Who bought the food?"

"She buy some small food some time."

"So you're telling us you lived in the same room as a common prostitute, alone with her, that you had intercourse with her, that you accepted board and lodging from her, and that you took no money from her? Is that it? Answer me, will you?"

"Listen, man. I answer you. Never I take no money from that woman. Not even pennies for my bus fare."

"You really expect the court to believe that?"

"I swear on this book here what I say will be true. And what I say is true."

There was suddenly a yell from the public gallery. It was the

Bushman. He shouted, "God is black!" and was hustled out by a constable. The judge closed his eyes during this episode; then opened them, and said, "Please continue, Mr Gillespie."

"I have no more questions, my Lord."

"Mr Vial?"

The defending counsel bowed and shook his head. Johnny went back to the dock.

The judge blinked around the court. "Mr Gillespie, Mr Vial. Is there anything further before you address the jury?"

The counsel shook their heads.

"Then I shall adjourn for luncheon before your final address."

Everyone rose, the judge did so rather more slowly, and disappeared beneath the rampant lion and unicorn.

Mr Zuss-Amor stood with Montgomery outside the court, waiting for Theodora. "Well, there it is," said the solicitor. "I need hardly tell you that I think he's had it."

"What does Mr Vial say?"

"He won't commit himself. But our boy made some horrible admissions. And that interruption from the gallery didn't help at all."

"That wasn't Johnny's fault."

"I know it wasn't, Mr Pew: but it made a very bad impression. Was that boy drunk, or what?"

"No. Just voicing his feelings, I expect."

"I wish he'd voiced them elsewhere."

"I didn't think the police officers were all that brilliant, anyway."

"Oh, they're not so clever in court as they are outside it, I admit. But they do know when to keep their mouths shut."

"The Inspector was the more convincing...."

"He should be, he's been lying longer."

"I don't like that place. Everyone acts as if the wretched prisoner's the only person there who doesn't matter."

The solicitor didn't answer that, but said, "I wish your friend Miss Pace would hurry powdering her nose. I could do with a gin and orange."

Crossing the corridor, Theodora was detained by a pale youth in a drape suit whose face was vaguely familiar. "Hello," he said. "I let you in at Mr Vial's party, don't you remember? They call me Alfy Bongo."

"Oh, yes. Excuse me, please."

"I follow all Mr Vial's cases whenever I can."

"Please excuse me."

"Just a minute, miss. You know your boy's going down this afternoon?"

"What do you mean — my boy?"

"He is, isn't he? I remember you two that evening. I know how you feel about him."

"Excuse me!" She hurried on.

He sidled after her. "There's only one thing could help him, isn't there."

She stopped. "What?"

"If there was some other woman to speak for him."

"What do you mean?"

"Someone like you who might have been his girl at the time they say he was poncing on that chick."

Theodora looked at him intently.

The Inspector and the Constable were drinking Worthingtons in the saloon bar round the corner. "I was all right, then, sir? You're not dissatisfied?"

"All right for a beginner, Constable. Cheers!"

"We'd never have had all this fuss if we could have kept it in the magistrates' court."

"That's out of our hands, lad, when the prisoner's got the money. I wouldn't worry about the result, though, and the sentence will be stiffer here."

"Why didn't you just take him in for hemp, Inspector? That would have been more certain, wouldn't it?"

"Of course, but he might have got away with only a fine. Even with magistrates, you can't be sure."

"I didn't like the defending counsel. He's murder."

"I'll get that degenerate one day, if it's the last thing I do."

47

The court jailer, who'd heard how the case was going, was not quite so nice to Johnny. "Here's your dinner," he said, handing him a paper bag.

"I want no dinner."

"You'd better get into the habit of doing what you're told, you know. It might come in handy after this evening."

"He's being awkward," said the Brixton warder.

Theodora dragged Mr Zuss-Amor away from Montgomery into the private bar. "At this stage," she said, "can we call any further witnesses?"

"We could if we had one who's of any use .... Why?"

"I've been Johnny Fortune's mistress."

"Go on!"

"I saw him during the time they say he was with that woman, and gave him money, and looked after him."

"Yes...? Now look, Miss Pace, it's nice of you to think of trying to help him. But can you expect me to believe that — let alone a jury?"

"I'm pregnant by him."

"Oh. You are? No kidding?"

"Oh, don't be so stupid and familiar. I tell you I've seen the doctor!"

"Have you!"

"I love Johnny — can't you understand? I want to marry him."

"You do?" The solicitor shook his head dubiously. "And you're prepared to swear all this in court — is that it?"

"Yes."

"Well...I'll have to see Mr Vial and hear what he thinks."

"Hurry up, then."

"You'd better come with me. He'll want to question you a bit."

When the trial resumed, Mr Vial asked the judge's permission to call another witness. "I apologize, my Lord, to you, and to my learned friends, for any apparent discourtesy to the court. The fact is that my witness, who is, as you will see, a person of irreproachable character and reputation, has felt hitherto a quite understandable reluctance to appear in a case of this description; but since the evidence she will give — "

"Is this a woman, then?" said the judge.

"Indeed, my Lord."

"I see. Go on."

"Thank you, my Lord. Since, as I say, the evidence she will give, with your permission, will be of capital importance in establishing the innocence of the defendant beyond all possible doubt, she has felt it her duty — greatly, I may say, to her credit — to overcome any natural scruples and appear before the court."

"Have you anything to say, Mr Gillespie?" asked the judge.

"Not at this juncture, my Lord. I think any observations I may wish to make would best be kept until I have an opportunity of hearing this witness, and of cross-examination."

"Very well, Mr Vial."

Theodora entered the box and took the oath. She looked firm, tranquil, dignified and womanly, though with a slight hint of the repentant sinner.

Mr Vial quickly established that her name was Theodora Huntington Pace, her age twenty-eight, her state a spinster, and her occupation that of Assistant Supervisor of Draft Planning at the BBC. She had known the defendant since the previous summer, when she first met him at an interview in connection with his participation in a series of radio programmes. "Please continue, Miss Pace," said Mr Vial.

"I got to know Mr Fortune very well," she said, in steady, almost semi-official tones. "I grew to admire his qualities of character and intelligence, and soon became very fond of him."

"And this feeling of yours, Mis Pace. It was reciprocated?"

"Yes," said Theodora. "I think it was."

"Please tell the court what happened then."

Theodora slightly lowered her voice, and looked up steadily. "I became his mistress."

"I see. And then?"

"I asked Mr Fortune to come and live with me, but he is very independent by nature, and preferred we should have separate establishments."

"And during the period that we have heard about in court this morning. You saw the defendant?"

"Frequently."

"And is it not a fact that you were able to help him financially when this was necessary?"

"I know Mr Fortune comes from a substantial business family in Nigeria, and that he would have no difficulty in calling on them for money if he needed it. He is, however, I'm sorry to say, something of a spendthrift..." (she paused slightly)..."and on occasions when he was hard up I had no reluctance whatever in lending him whatever money he might want to tide him over."

"So that during the period in question, he was in no need of money?"

"Why should he be? No. He had only to come to me."

"Thank you, Miss Pace."

Mr Gillespie got up.

"Miss Pace," he said. "In view of what you have told the court this afternoon, why did you not come forward this morning to speak for the accused on this very serious charge?"

Theodora glanced towards the dock, then said quietly: "Mr Fortune forbade me to."

"He forbade you? Why?"

"He wished to face this charge alone. Knowing his innocence, and being sure of an acquittal, he did not wish my name to be mentioned in any way."

"I see, I see. And now he's *not* so sure of an acquittal — *is* that it?"

"I heard Mr Fortune giving evidence this morning. English is not his mother tongue, and an African has greater difficulty in expressing himself clearly than many of us realize. With this language handicap I didn't feel he was doing his case justice, and I therefore felt I ought to appear myself, even if against his wishes, to tell the court what I knew."

"Did you, Miss Pace! Then please tell my Lord how you

account for the fact that if the accused, as you say, had only to come to you for money, he chose to live with a prostitute in an East End slum?"

"Mr Fortune, as I have said, is a very independent man, and preferred to live his Bohemian student life in a quarter inhabited largely by his fellow countrymen. He told me, of course, of his staying for a while in the same house as this woman — which he regarded as an interesting way of catching a glimpse of the seamier side of London life."

"So this man, who has admitted he was a penniless labourer, prefers living in squalor with a prostitute when he has a rich mistress willing, and no doubt anxious, to accommodate him at any time?"

"I need hardly say that I would have preferred him to live in more conventional surroundings."

"With you, in other words."

"Yes."

"But he didn't. Miss Pace: you have heard the accused admit that he had intercourse with this woman. Did you know of this?"

"No. I expect he was ashamed to tell me of this momentary lapse."

"I expect so, indeed. How old did you say you were, Miss Pace."

"Twenty-eight."

"And the accused is eighteen?"

"Nineteen, now."

"Is there not a considerable discrepancy between your ages?"

"Yes, unfortunately."

"And you ask us seriously to believe — "

The judge leaned forward. "I don't wish to hinder you, Mr Gillespie. But as the witness has admitted her relationship with the defendant, I really don't think you need press this point any further."

Theodora turned towards the judge, and said softly, "I am pregnant by him, my Lord. I hope to marry the defendant."

The judge nodded slightly and said nothing. He turned to Mr

Gillespie. "I have no more questions, my Lord," said the Crown counsel.

Theodora left the box, and the two lawyers addressed the jury.

"You must not attribute," said Mr Gillespie, "any undue weight to the testimony of Miss Theodora Pace. Remember that this woman who admits — indeed, I should say, glories in — an illicit relationship with the accused, is no doubt under the domination of her obsession. Keep firmly in your minds, rather, the contrast between the evidence you have heard from the two police officers, and that of the accused himself. If there may be, in the evidence of these officers, some slight discrepancies — of which my learned friend has naturally tried to make the most — you must surely conclude that the evidence of the accused is totally, utterly incredible. It simply cannot be believed! No, members of the jury: your duty in this matter is quite clear. Banish from your minds any thought that a verdict against the defendant might be imputed to anything in the nature of racial prejudice. In a British court, all men are equal before the law: and if you believe the defendant to be guilty, as you are bound to do, you should return a verdict in that sense with the same impartiality as you would show were he a fellow citizen of your own."

To which Mr Vial, raising himself like Moses bringing down the tablets from the Mount, rejoined:

"My learned friend has asked you to discount the evidence of Miss Theodora Pace. But is her testimony not supremely to be believed? Here is a woman — a courageous woman, I would say, whatever you may think of her moral conduct (which is not what is on trial today) — who is prepared to risk — possibly even to sacrifice irrevocably — an honoured and established position in society, to bear witness to the truth, whatever the cost! Is this mere infatuation? Is this what my learned friend has called the consequences of an *obsession*?

"But even more to be believed — yes, even more — is the evidence of the defendant. My learned friend has told you that this evidence is 'incredible'. But is it? Is it incredible? I have no small experience of hearing witnesses in court, and from this I have learned one important lesson." Mr Vial, who contrived to speak not like an advocate, but like the impartial spirit of justice itself, now looked very grave. "Only a too fluent witness, members of the jury, is to be mistrusted! Only a story that has no flaw — one which the witness, or witnesses, have carefully manufactured, polished and rehearsed — is likely to be untrue. Did you not notice — and were you not impressed by it? — that the defendant at no time sought to deny facts that might have seemed prejudicial to his case? Did you not hear how he freely admitted to some few, small, discreditable facts because he knew, in his heart of hearts, that on the major issue — the essential issue you are called upon to decide — he was without guilt of any kind?" Mr Vial stood a second, hand raised aloft. "The defendant was an angry witness, members of the jury! He was angry because he is honest: he is honest because he is innocent!

"Have a care how you deal with John Macdonald Fortune! This young man is a guest among us, who possibly has behaved foolishly, as young men will, but who has not behaved dishonourably. In this country he is a stranger: but a stranger who, coming from a country that is British, believes he is entitled to receive, and knows that he certainly will receive, that fair treatment and equal justice from his fellow men and women which has always been the glory of the British jury."

Mr Vial sat down. The judge, his moment come at last, began his summing-up.

When he recapitulated the case of the prosecution, which he did in meticulous and admirably balanced detail, the case for the prosecution sounded quite unanswerable; but when he came to recapitulate the case for the defence, this case sounded quite unanswerable too. It was, in fact, impossible to tell what the judge thought, or even what he recommended; though he did, at one point in his dry, interminable, penetrating survey of the evidence, look up a minute at the jury and say this:

"I need hardly remind you, I suppose, that you should attach great importance, not only to the substance of the evidence that has been put before you, but equally to the demeanour of the witnesses, and to the force, the weight, I might say, of the actual words they used. Now the defending counsel, you will remember, asked the accused at one point" (the judge consulted his notes) "if he had ever lived off the immoral earnings of any woman. To which the defendant answered in these words: 'Never. Never would I give my blood to such a person. Never.'" The judge blinked at the jury. "You will have to decide whether these words which the defendant used convey to you the impression of veracity... of authenticity...."

When the judge finished — rather abruptly and unexpectedly — the clerk put the fatal question to the jury. After some slight muttering, they asked if they might retire.

"Will you be very long, do you think?" the judge asked the foreman.

"There seems to be some considerable disagreement, my Lord," the foreman answered, glancing round at the eleven.

"I see. Very well, you may retire."

In the emptying court, Mr Vial strolled across to the dock, leant on its edge and, ignoring the two policemen, said casually to Johnny, "I thought the judge's summing-up was very fair, didn't you?"

"I thought you was wonderful," said Johnny Fortune.

In the corridor outside, Theodora stood with Mr Zuss-Amor. "Splendid, my dear," said the solicitor. "I'm sorry to say the Press were scribbling busily, though. I hope you don't lose your job."

Smoking an agitated cigarette, Montgomery was accosted by the Detective-Inspector. "Well," said the policeman, "whichever way it goes, there's no hard feelings on my part for your young friend. It's only another case to us."

As the court reassembled, the usher in charge of the jury

(who had sworn publicly, before they retired, upon the sacred book, that he would not divulge a word of their deliberations) whispered, as he passed by, to the two officers guarding Johnny in the dock, what their still secret verdict was. Johnny heard it too, and one of the officers patted him gently on the back of the knee.

The judge returned, and so did the jury. They did not, despite the nature of their impending verdict, gaze benevolently at the accused as juries are traditionally supposed to do, but sat like ancient monuments on their hard seats.

The clerk asked the foreman how they found. He said, "Not guilty."

Mr Vial then rose and said, with infinite deference, to the judge: "May the prisoner please be discharged, my Lord?"

"He may."

A week later, Johnny was re-arrested on the charge of being in possession of Indian hemp. Montgomery could borrow no more money quickly anywhere, and Theodora was in hospital with a breakdown and a miscarriage. "I'll come over to the court for free, if you really want me to," Mr Zuss-Amor told Montgomery, "but why don't you tell him to plead guilty and settle before the magistrate? Believe me, if they don't get him for *something*, they'll never let him alone. And it'll only be a fine."

It was, but no one had any money, and Johnny went to prison for a month.

from a letter to Mrs Longmore
March 1959

I was most flattered to think of you speculating on the
hypothetical futures of the people of C[ity] of S[pades]. I
have, as a matter of fact, often speculated on this myself,
and would suggest to you the following — or something
like it — bearing in mind that the whole thing happened
about ten years ago (there is internal evidence of the date
dotted about here and there — e.g., "Please, Mr Attlee,
don't steal my majority").

J.M. Fortune Esq. has almost certainly by now made
quite a bit of loot, in transactions of at any rate technical
legality, and has gone into politics, and is awaiting his hour
in 1960, when he will become a city politico of some
consequence, I imagine, but not on the national level, as the
paper work would be too heavy. He has certainly married,
advantageously, and while not exactly faithful to his
consort, is secretly a bit scared of her, and treats, her,
publicly, with immense respect. Four children, possibly five,
all spoiled. News has reached him of William [his son by
Muriel Macpherson], via the Afro-English bush telegraph,
and he has even sent some expensive and unsuitable gifts via
friends travelling northwards, but has not corresponded
with Muriel and has, indeed, almost forgotten her. As for
Theodora, he has even forgotten her name. He is a little
stout, but extremely handsome, and in spite of everything,
is known among his friends for sticking up for the English
when they are (generally quite rightly) maligned, and has a
number of English businessmen among his drinking cronies.

M. Pew is in Granada television, where he is renowned
for unreliability, but somehow gets his programmes on the
air, and has projected a number of rather sensational series
on Commonwealth Minorities (the one on the Maltese won
him a Television Critics' Award). He drinks less, still
spends well ahead of his income, and has taken up with a
Norwegian girl at London University, and they are

thinking, rather vaguely, of getting married. He has a
formal luncheon with Theodora every so often, but finds it
increasingly difficult, with the passing years, to remember
to arrange it. He has written about eighteen times to
Johnny, who once came up with a picture postcard of Lake
Street, Lagos, but has otherwise remained silent, except
that strangers arrive every so often with messages and, after
drinking half a bottle of scotch, depart.

Theodora, after working successfully for some years in a
Mayfair advertising agency, has married an estate property
dealer, lives in SW3, and gives elegant and slightly boring
parties. No children. She told her husband all about Johnny
before they married, and he regarded this as an amusingly
unconventional episode, which secretly offended her, and
made her slightly despise him. She doesn't entertain
Africans any longer, but when she's out in the streets, and
sees one passing by, she always stares at him intently.

William M. Fortune-Macpherson is now, as you correctly
divined, a hefty, vivacious lad who is the apple of his
mother's eye, but a terrible trial. He leads a ferocious gang
of juveniles in the Kilburn area, shows a marked talent on
the double bass, and will very possibly become a musician
(though Muriel would prefer him to be a professional man
of some kind, and is very concerned about getting him into
a grammar school).

Muriel herself has had three offers of marriage (one
African, one Cypriot, one Scottish), but has settled for
tranquillity. There is a photograph of Johnny on her
bedroom chest-of-drawers, a coloured enlargement in a
silver frame. By day, she works as supervisor in an Oxford
Street store that sells separates to teenagers, and is known
to be rather severe with her employees.

Dorothy has moved north, to Moss Side, Manchester, and
is not doing very well....

It would be nice to record that Detective-Inspector
Purity has come unstuck, but truth compels us to record
that he has been promoted to Superintendent, and is in the
running for Chief Constable of a small north western

county. He has completely forgotten J. M. Fortune's name and very existence.

Mr Wesley Vial is going strong, exactly as before, except that he has at last taken silk, and is now Wesley Vial, Esq., QC. He thought of going into industry when he had a prodigious offer from a director he'd defended in a fraud case, but has decided he loves the courts too much, and anyway, he's rather lazy. The parties at Marble Arch continue as before.

Alfy Bongo, and two like-minded pals, have opened a Chinese restaurant in the W2 area, and are doing very nicely. The place is known to aficionados as *Chop Alfie*.

Mr Lord Alexander is now horribly successful, his dreadful calypsos have lost all their original Trinidadian authenticity, and he appears on his own television spot and sometimes with the Edmundo Ros band. He owns a Jaguar and forty-three shirts.

Karl Marx Bo is Assistant to the Minister of the Interior of the northern province of his native land, and is plotting to supplant him.

Billy Whispers was drowned in the Bay of Biscay. The very predictable fight with Johnny took place, and Johnny's messmates pushed Billy over the side and told the captain it was an accident. The inquest at Lagos returned an open verdict.

Jimmy Cannibal is in Dartmoor.

Ronson Lighter has gone "back home," and conducts a haulage business smuggling cattle over the frontier into Dahomey [....]

Last but by no means least, Mr Zuss-Amor. He chanced his arm once too often, and got struck off, but not before making a deal with a defendant of consequence whereby he acquired a large capital sum that, together with his earlier considerable savings, he has invested in a bookmaking business, and has trebled his income, and lives at Hove. But he still hankers after the courts, and drops in at the Brighton Sessions from time to time to criticize the performance of his former colleagues.

Oh, and the Bushman! He's a chief now, back home, and is mobilizing a resistance movement among his fellow chieftains to the expected inroads of the city politicians, come independence.

Well, if you don't care for these solutions, make your own! Almost anything could have happened to them all!

...Seerioh! as the Bushman might say.

Yours

Colin MacI.

The dedication of City of Spades *is "For Ricky". Richard Hawton Samuel Erizia was, as MacInnes wrote to a friend, "the onlie begetter of J. M. Fortune". His actual story, though, sadly differed from that mapped out for J. M. Fortune Esq. in MacInnes's letter to Mrs Longmore.*

from "Welcome, Beauty Walk"
Encounter, October 1960 (*England, Half English,* 1961)

THE BOOMA BOYS
The Nigerian warriors came home from the Burma war filled
by the same impatience with the past that flung their English
comrades into Clement Attlee's grim embrace. Among them
was a residue of restless souls whose misconduct in Lagos won
them the name of "Burma boys". When the late 1940s raced
into Nigeria (as they never did to war-sodden, static,
"welfare" England), this name became "Booma", and the
"boys" really boys: for a new generation of good-bad lads
sprang out of the Lagos pavements who were too young to have
fought overseas, but old enough to demand that the future
happen quickly now. Many of these vivid scamps, innocent as
rogues under twenty-three can be, were suddenly gripped by a
deep urge to know the world; and as swallows do, they took off
from Africa for England with nothing but a compelling instinct
as their baggage, stowing away, signing on and deserting,
sometimes cajoling minimal fares from rightly reluctant
families. Their landfall was in the big English dock cities, and
they loped ashore blithely confident that the world loved them
and owed them a treasure.

This was the first mass exploration in reverse; the encounter
with Englishmen and women not as they appeared in Africa,
but as they are. It lasted until the early 1950s by which time the
Anglo-Booma boys had prospered, floundered, died, or drifted
home, and Nigerian emigration had become regulated, with
motiveless journeys hindered by both governments. Properly
so; for these English Nigerians were good citizens of neither
country — only of a precarious realm of their own creation
which had nevertheless the beauty that in spite of squalors, it
was the only honestly integrated Afro-English society. It was
because they had "no reason" for coming to England that these
wild ones had the best. Never again will young Nigerians know
this shock of a first confrontation; nor will young Englishmen.

Into the London chapter of this community I happened a

decade ago without conscious intention, and I cannot remember how: only that one summer day I knew no Nigerians, and a few months later, scores. From these exiles I heard constantly of Africa long before I went there, so that names of tribes, regions, cities, and even streets grew familiar though unknown. One day in this novitiate, a Yoruba friend brought with him an Ijaw countryman who said (not exactly "asked") he was looking for a place to stay, and how about if he stopped with me a while? This was Hawton, who was brave, intelligent, generous, selfish, and slothful save in emergencies... the ideal temperament for a soldier and a leader, which he would have been if his manhood had come in other times than tired peace. With him as guide and guarantor, I learned the bush paths of Afro-London, and how to address its denizens appropriately on strange occasions. After a year of staying for a while, Hawton "cut out" from London and settled in Manchester, Moss Side: the most homogeneous and least unwelcoming African reservation in the Black Man's Grave. Two years ago now, pneumonia (which is for Africans what malaria was for us) drowned one of his lungs, and the other the next day; and life that he enjoyed so much, and scattered so much on his friends, abandoned him in thirty-six hours, surviving only in his infant Afro-Mancunian daughter.

LAGOS INTERIORS

Lake Street, Lagos, was as Hawton had evoked it in his tales of waterfront scallywaggery — a comfortable slum behind the Marina, blocked from sight of the lagoon by modern offices. I passed several times before the house wondering how, or whether, to announce myself. I knew Hawton's mother lived there with his elder and younger brothers Easter-day and Eugene, but not if they knew of my existence or would welcome memories. Faltering along Broad Street, my doubts were resolved when with a great shout of "Collins!" Jimoh erupted, a cherished old-timer of the London scene, the first of many I re-met in Lagos who belonged to the old boys' club of Tottenham Court Road before the deadline when the

Paramount was closed down. Jimoh, who knew Hawton, made off to Lake Street to explain matters, and next day I found myself facing Hawton's mother: she uncomprehending and remote. It seemed I and my story had scant reality, did not connect up with the reluctantly believed and unproved fact of her son's death in that place "England". I told her what I could, which Jimoh "translated" — that is, re-phrased in Afro-English, for he being a Yoruba and she an Ijaw, no intimate translation of my words was possible.

Later I met the brothers and a seaman cousin, and everything fell into focus — thanks greatly to this seaman relative. All I had told the family about my friend convinced them I knew Hawton well...and yet some token of physical reality was missing. Eyeing this mariner, I suddenly recalled that Hawton once brought home to Camden Town a relation from a ship who saw I was limping with a dislocated toe, asked leave to look at it, and had immediately (and without permission) seized it and set it straight; an incident I could scarcely have invented and he fail to remember. It was indeed the same man: incredulity vanished, and this cousin became the essential witness who had seen Hawton and me in London when he was still alive. Afterwards, by their unspoken wish, I had separate sessions with each brother. Easter-day is a good man carrying a sorrow: which and why? He had gone into the police force where Hawton's father had been a prominent and successful figure, had come unstuck, and the love affair with a career — perilous for a young man — had turned sour on him. My guess is that Easter was born a trusting man, and that this instinct had been shocked and wounded...so that though he exudes confidence and strength, it is Samson's when his locks are shorn. He was deeply and patiently concerned about all the circumstances of Hawton's death — and obsessively so about his daughter. I was soon manoeuvred into the role of emissary to the Lancastrian mother, to ask her if the child could be surrendered and adopted by its African relations. I asked Easter-day had he thought if the girl herself would like to be in Africa? An infant Mancunian suckled on telly, cold rain, and rock salmon with soggy chips? And I warned him not to expect

her to be grateful, or to be astonished if she hankered for
England later on...Easter-day bowed his head to all this
European sagacity, and asked me to write him when the child
could come.

Eugene, the junior brother, is a Nigerian angry young man
(non-literary): startlingly like Hawton physically, but with
more practical energy and less glamour. Independence delights
him, as it does everyone in the Federation; but the emerging
political-social set-up makes no appeal. Again and again I heard
this from the young: good work is scarce, all wages are too low;
the drop in status from the few rich to the poor millions is
catastrophic; and they are looking beyond the national
revolution to the economic, and despise the new Nigerian
bourgeoisie. It is sad so late in the day — and after it has ful-
filled its historic task so valiantly and done so much for one and
all — to have to write yet again with disparagement about this
persecuted class; but I must record that the Lagos bourgeoisie is
quite sensationally unattractive. To begin with, because
aggressively vulgar ostentation coupled with complacent
ignorance of everything except export and import prices is so
uncharacteristically African: for though Africa has known
brilliant traders always, commercial suburbanites are a horrid
novelty. Worse still is that though technically a "bourgeoisie"
in the Marxist sense, this Lagos lot is culturally petty-bourgeois
in the extreme: their social tone corresponding conveniently
and disastrously to that of the outgoing managerial
"expatriates" (polite local term of hostility) whom they
imitate in many ways while striving to eject these helpful aliens
more rapidly ("Nigerianization"). Of new-rich clubs in the
federal capital, I append this last malicious vignette: of the sight
of dozens of stout young men robed in shapeless curtain
material, thickly bespectacled, in little bonnets set at jaunty
angles on fat heads, shouting at servants and laughing loud and
heartlessly before rolling off too fast and noisily in tank-like
cars: the international hall-mark of the philistine parvenu in
every rich society, irrespective of its political belief. (Car
owners of the world, unite: you have nothing to lose but your
manners and someone else's life.) In spare, tense contrast was

Eugene, his voice kind and furious, plagued visibly by a frustrated idealism and a dangerous generosity. What independent Nigeria offers to the youth it has excited is bureaucratic posts which many will delight in; but Eugene and his sort peer over the heads massed in celebration, scanning Africa for a vision.

The night I left Lagos, he took me late over to the mainland to see Rose, Hawton's beloved sister he spoke of so often as if of a guardian angel. We reached the house after midnight and Rose and her husband and two children were already sleeping. After a minute or two of knocking and of parleying with Eugene, the door was thrown open and there they all were: children tucked tidily away, wife and husband dressed and ready for conversation, all in one room: a deft illustration of three African graces — the faculty for instant, unconditional hospitality; the effortless cohesion of the family unit, the children always in evidence but never in the way; and the sublime ability to receive you wherever they are, simply, without any "explanation" or apology. Rose as a young matron is superb; as a girl she must have been a startling beauty. She is also, as not so many African women are, engaging in her manner; for most of her sisters lean heavily on the stark fact of being female to amaze the male. (It is not surprising to find policewomen rampant in the largely non-Moslem south; bossiness from a static position of strength coming naturally.) Rose, once initial courtesies were cleared away, was concerned only, as her brothers were, with Hawton's child: she brushed aside politely any hint of legal obstacles, and told me to get things moving, please. I am struck by the paradox of this family's instinct to retrieve part of their flesh, and of their neglecting, for two years until my arrival, any practical measures to ensure this.

from "Britain's Mixed Half-Million",

Africa South in Exile, vol. 5, No. 2, Jan-Mar 1961

We come now to the massive immigration of the late 1940s and 1950s: which — so far as West Indians are concerned — shows no sign of abating in the decade we have now entered. To consider, however, the smaller African (in fact, chiefly — for various causes — West African) immigration first, and the reasons for it: since the motives of these immigrants were in most cases very different from those which impelled the Caribbeans to come here. It is only exceptionally that one may find Africans in England who decided to emigrate because of extreme economic hardship in their homeland: not that poverty does not exist there — indeed, it does — but West Africa, however thickly populated and as yet undeveloped economically, is manifestly richer potentially, and very clearly going to be richer. Thus, the male visitors were either seamen, or students, or traders or, in a very great many cases, a category that has no Caribbean counterpart — young men who were propelled here by a *wanderlust* that possessed so many Africans when, as a consequence chiefly of the war, the world burst suddenly into Africa, and Africans wanted to burst out in the world. A subsidiary reason was the desire to escape from the tender emotional and material blackmail with which African family and tribal life enfolds males: offering them security and status, but at the price of strictly individual freedom. There is, indeed, scarcely a West African in England who would not, materially, be better off "back home" (some, indeed, come from homes whose wealth would amaze the citizens of the English slums they live in). If any reader doubts all this, let him question an African who has come here for no apparent "reason"; and also recall how an identical instinct has impelled young Englishmen to emigrate in the past.

The case of the West Indians is much simpler: they have always been an emigrating people. Their islands cannot hold nor sustain their bursting populations, and a young West Indian (like an Irishman half a century or more ago) must seek his fortune elsewhere to prosper, even to survive. Unquestionably, if immigration into the US had not been drastically restricted in the late 1940s, or if West Indians could freely have entered other desirable Latin American countries, they would never have wished to come in such numbers to the British Isles. They came here because it was the only door left, if not open, at any rate ajar.

[...] The Africans, it is true, though at first surprised and wounded when they discovered everyone was not delighted to see and greet them, soon shrugged their massive shoulders with resigned indifference: for I have yet to meet an African who does not think that to be one is an enviable thing, and that anyone who does not realize this is an imbecile greatly to be pitied. In addition, independence was already in the air, and colonial occupation had been relatively brief: so that there was no real conflict of loyalties, and the oblong blue passport was regarded merely as a matter of provisional convenience. But with the West Indians, it was very different. For generations, they had been nurtured on the idea of England, the distant mother, whose destinies they had shared for more than 300 years: whose history they knew far more intimately than most of us have ever learned theirs: and whose language they spoke (with embellishments and, to my own ears, in many ways, enrichments) with the intimacy (unknown to Africans) of a cherished mother tongue. England had sent their ancestors to the Caribbean, and had kept them there, in circumstances about which they were ready to be indulgent. In spite of everything, they felt themselves to be British: for centuries, they had helped make their mother rich and strong. Now, nationality laws which this motherland — not they, who had no power to — had just enacted, threw open welcoming doors. Well ... times were hard, the Americas uninviting, so they would sell up or save, and cross the air or ocean to nestle at this broad maternal bosom. When they arrived, in tropical suits in winter, and with hard savings spent on fares, they found no one to greet them (except whores, rent-sharks and hostile journalists), and the first doors they knocked on, slammed. Even worse: having herself issued the tacit invitation by the nationality acts, when she found she was taken at her word, mother England (or her press and public) clamoured that the laws were wrong....

from "A Short Guide for Jumbles"

Twentieth Century, March 1956

(England, Half English)

But is it really possible for a white man and a coloured to be friends?

One hastens to say "Yes"; but then, remembering the *distant* look that sometimes comes into the opaque brown eyes — that moment when they suddenly depart irrevocably within themselves far off towards a hidden, alien, secretive, quite untouchable horizon — one must ultimately, however reluctantly, answer, "No."

[Later:]

The first thing I want to say about this piece is that the years which have passed proved to me what I didn't then believe — that an African or a West Indian, and an Englishman can be friends. A great deal, of course, is against this happening. Superficially — but horribly effectively — the colonial relationship of their countries stands guard against a developing intimacy. (Older readers will recall the same malevolent, inhibiting spectre that haunted their relationship with Indian friends.) Next, is another dreadful, attendant ghoul — the continuing presence of the whole world-wide "colour" situation. Lastly — and ultimately the only real obstacle — there are the truly formidable differences of social and psychical background. Even in, say, Anglo-American friendships, this factor may present a real difficulty: in Anglo-African or Caribbean, it is obviously greater; but given goodwill and fortune, it is surmountable...

"Today, youth has money, and teenagers have become a power," MacInnes *wrote in December 1957 in the essay "Young England, Half English", which is sub-titled "The Pied Piper from Bermondsey" in*

honour of Tommy Steele. No sentence MacInnes ever wrote has been quoted so extensively as his description of this pied piper: "He is Pan, he is Puck, he is every nice young girl's boy, every kid's favourite elder brother, every mother's cherished adolescent son." Not only was MacInnes the first "outsider" to spot Tommy Steele's potential, he was also among the first to understand the significance of the teenage revolution. His view of teenagers, as he recognized, was an optimistic one. "But it would be equally possible to see," he wrote in "Pop Songs and Teenagers", "in the teenage neutralism and indifference to politics, and self-sufficiency, and instinct for enjoyment — in short, in their kind of happy mindlessness — the raw material for crypto-fascisms of the worst kind." And his second London novel, Absolute Beginners, *shows how the teenage idyll of, among others, a young photographer (who remains nameless) and his girl Suze (short for Suzette, as in* Crepe Suzette*) is rudely shattered by the Notting Hill race riots....*

from *Absolute Beginners*
(1959)

IN JUNE

It was with the advent of the Laurie London era that I realized the whole teenage epic was tottering to doom.

"Fourteen years old, that absolute beginner," I said to the Wizard as we paused casually in the gramophone section to hear Little Laurie in that golden disc performance of his.

"From now on," said Wizard, "he's certainly Got The Whole World In His Hands."

We listened to the wonder boy's nostrils spinning on.

"They buy us younger every year," I cried. "Why, Little Mr L.'s voice hasn't even dropped yet, so who will those taxpayers try to kidnap next?"

"Sucklings," said Wizard.

We climbed the white stair to the glass garden under the top roof of the department store, and came out on the glorious panorama, our favourite rendezvous.

I must explain the Wiz and I never come to this store to buy anything except, as today, a smoke-salmon sandwich and ice coffee. But in the first place, we have the opportunity to see the latest furnishings and fabrics, just like some married couple, and also to have the splendid outlook over London, the most miraculous I know in the whole city, and quite unknown to other nuisance-values of our age, in fact to everyone, it seems, except these elderly female Chelsea peasants who come up there for their elevenses.

Looking north you don't see much, it's true, and westward the view's entirely blocked up by the building you're inside. But twisting slowly on your bar stool from the east to south, like Cinerama, you can see clean new concrete cloud-kissers, rising up like felixes from the Olde Englishe squares, and then those gorgeous parks, with trees like classical French salads, and then again the port life down along the Thames, that glorious river, reminding you we're on an estuary, a salt inlet really, with crazy seagulls circling up from it and almost bashing their beaks against the circular plate glass, and then, before you know it, you're back again round a full circle in front of your iced coffee cup.

"Laurie L.," I said, "'s a sign of decadence. This teenage thing is getting out of hand."

The Wiz looked wise, like the middle feller of the three old monkeys.

"It's not the taxpayers," he said, "who are responsible. It's the kids themselves, for buying the EPs these elderly sordids bribe the teenage nightingales to wax."

"No doubt," I said, for I know better than ever to argue with the Wizard, or with anyone else who gets his kicks from an idea.

Mr Wiz continued, masticating his salmon sandwich for anyone to see, "It's been a two-way twist, this teenage party. Exploitation of the kiddos by the conscripts, and exploitation of themselves by the crafty little absolute beginners. The net result? 'Teenager' 's become a dirty word or, at any rate, a square one."

I smiled at Mr W. "Well, take it easy, son," I said, "because a sixteen-year-old sperm like you has got a lot of teenage living still to do. As for me, eighteen summers, rising nineteen, I'll very soon be out there among the oldies."

The Wizard eyed me with his Somerset Maugham appearance. "Me, boy," he said, "I tell you. As things are, I won't regret it when the teenage label's torn off the arse pockets of my drip-dry sky-blue jeans."

What the Wiz said was at any rate partially true. This teenage ball had had a real splendour in the days when the kids discovered that, for the first time since centuries of kingdom-come, they'd money, which hitherto had always been denied to us at the best time in life to use it, namely when you're young and strong, and also before the newspapers and telly got hold of this teenage fable and prostituted it as conscripts seem to do to everything they touch. Yes, I tell you, it had a real savage splendour in the days when we found that no one couldn't sit on our faces any more because we'd loot to spend at last, and our world was to be our world, the one we wanted and not standing on the doorstep of somebody else's waiting for honey, perhaps.

I got off my stool and went and stood by the glass of that tottering old department store, pressed up so close it was like I was out there in the air, suspended over space above the city, and I swore by Elvis and all the saints that this last teenage year of mine was going to be a real rave. Yes, man, come whatever, this last year of the teenage dream I was out for kicks and fantasy.

from *Absolute Beginners*

I'd like to explain this district where I live [the area of W10 and 11], because it's quite a curiosity, being one of the few that's got left behind by the Welfare era *and* the Property-owning whatsit, both of them, and is, in fact, nothing more than a stagnating slum. It's dying, this bit of London, and that's the most important thing to remember about what goes on there. To the north of it, there run, in parallel, the Harrow road I've mentioned, which you'd hurry through even if you were in a car, and a canal, called the Grand Union, that nothing floats on except cats and contraceptives, and the main railway track that takes you from London to the swede counties of the West of England. These three escape routes, which are all at different heights and levels, cut across one another at different points, making crazy little islands of slum habitation shut off from the world by concrete precipices, and linked by metal bridges. I need hardly mention that on this north side there's a hospital, a gas-works with enough juice for the whole population of the kingdom to commit suicide, and a very ancient cemetery with the pretty country name of Kensal Green.

On the west side, still in the W10 bit, there's another railway, and a park with a name only Satan in all his splendour could have thought up, namely Wormwood Scrubs, which has a prison near it, and another hospital and a sports arena, and the new telly barracks of the BBC, and with a long, lean road called Latimer road which I particularly want you to remember, because out of this road, like horrible tits dangling from a lean old sow, there hang a whole festoon of what I think must really be the sinisterest highways in our city, well, just listen to their names: Blechynden, Silchester, Walmer, Testerton and Bramley — can't you just smell them, as you hurry to get through the cats-cradle of these blocks? In this part, the houses are old Victorian lower-middle tumble-down, built I dare say for grocers and bank clerks and horse-omnibus inspectors who've died and gone and their descendants evacuated to the outer suburbs, but these houses live on like shells, and there's only one thing to do with them, absolutely one, which is to pull them down till not a one's left standing up.

On the south side of this area, down by the W11, things are a little different, but in a way that somehow makes them worse, and that is, owing to a freak of fortune, and some smart work by the estate agents too, I shouldn't be surprised, there are one or two sections that are positively posh; not *fashionable*, mind you, but quite graded, with their big back gardens and that absolute silence which in London is the top sign of a respectable location. You walk about in these bits, adjusting your tie and looking down to see if your shoes are shining, when — wham! suddenly you're back in the slum area again — honest, it's really startling, like where the river joins on to the shore, two quite different creations of dame nature, cheek by thing.

Over towards the east, the frontiers aren't quite as definite, and the whole area merges into a drab and shady and semi-respectable part called Bayswater, which I would rather lie in my coffin, please believe me, than spend a night in, were it not for Suze, who's shacked up there. No! Give me our London Napoli I've been describing, with its railway scenery, and crescents that were meant to twist elegantly but now look as if they're lurching high, and huge houses too tall for their width cut up into twenty flatlets, and front façades that it never pays anyone to paint, and broken milk bottles *everywhere* scattering the cracked asphalt roads like snow, and cars parked in the streets looking as if they're stolen or abandoned, and a strange number of male urinals tucked away such as you find nowhere else in London, and red curtains, somehow, in all the windows, and diarrhoea-coloured street lighting — man, I tell you, you've only got to be there for a minute to know there's something radically *wrong*.

Across this whole mess there cuts, diagonally, yet another railway, that rides high above this slum property like a scenic railway at a fair. Boy, if you want to admire our wonderful old capital city, you should take a ride on this track some time! And just where this railway is slung over the big central road that cuts across the area north to south, there's a hole, a dip, a pocket, a really unhappy valley which, according to my learned Dad, was formerly at one time a great non-agricultural marsh. A place of evil, mister. I bet witches lived around it, and a lot still do.

And what about the human population? The answer is, this is the residential doss-house of our city. In plain words, you'd not live in our Napoli if you could live anywhere else. And that is why there are, to the square yard, more boys fresh from the nick, and national refugee minorities, and out-of-business whores, that anywhere else, I should expect, in London town. The kids live in the streets — I mean they have *charge* of them, you have to ask permission to get along them even in a car —

the teenage lot are mostly of the Ted variety, the chicks mature so quick there's scarcely such a thing there as a *little* girl, the men don't talk, glance at you hard, keep moving, and don't stand with their backs to anyone, their women are mostly out of sight, with dishcloths I expect for yashmaks, and there are piles and piles of these dreadful, wasted, negative, shop-soiled kind of *old people* that make you feel it really is a tragedy to grow grey.

You're probably saying well, if you're so cute, kiddo, why do you live in such an area? So now, as a certain evening paper writes it, "I will tell you."

One reason is that it's so cheap. I mean, I have a rooted objection to paying rent at all, it should be free like air, and parks, and water. I don't think I'm mean, in fact I know I'm not, but I just can't bear paying more than a bob or two to landlords. But the real reason, as I expect you'll have already guessed, is that, however horrible the area is, you're *free* there! No one, I repeat it, no one, has ever asked me there what I am, or what I do, or where I came from, or what my social group is, or whether I'm educated or not, and if there's one thing I cannot tolerate in this world, it's nosey questions. And what is more, once the local bandits see you're making out, can earn your living and so forth, they don't swing it on you in the slightest you're a teenage creation — if you have loot, and can look after yourself, they treat you as a man, which is what you are .... If you go in anywhere, they take it for granted that you know the scene. If you don't, it's true they throw you out in pieces, but if you do, they treat you just as one of them.

The room I inhabit in sunny Napoli, which overlooks *both* railways (*and* the foulest row of backyards to be found outside the municipal compost heaps), belongs to an Asian character called Omar, Pakistani, I believe, who's regular as clockwork — in fact, even more so, because clocks are known to stop — and turns up on Saturday mornings, accompanied by two countrymen who act as bodyguards, to collect the rents, and you'd better have yours ready. Because if you haven't, he simply grinds his teeth and tells his *fellahin* to pile everything you possess neatly on the outside pavement, be it rain, or snow, or mulligatawny fog. And if you've locked the door, it means absolutely nothing to him to smash it down, and even if you're in bed, all injured innocence and indignation, he still comes in with his sickly don't-mean-a-thing kind of smile. So if you're going to be away, it's best to leave the money with a friend, or better still, pay him, as I do, monthly in advance. And when you do, he takes out a plastic bag on a long chain from a very inner pocket, and tucks the notes away, and says you must have a drink with him some time, but even when I've once or twice met him in a pub, he's never offered it, of course. Also, if you make any complaint *whatever* — I mean, even that the roof's falling in, and the water cut off — he smiles that same smile and does positively sweet bugger-all about it. On the other hand, you could invite every whore and cut-throat in the city in for a pail of gin, or give a corpse accommodation for the night on the spare bed, or even set the bloody place on fire, and he wouldn't turn a hair — or turn one if anybody complained to him about you. Not if you paid your rent, that is. In fact, the perfect landlord.

The tenants come and go, as you might expect, but among the regular squatters I have a few particular buddies, of whom I'd specially name the following three.

The first of them, on the floor below me (I'm on the top), is a boy called The Fabulous Hoplite. I'm hoping you'll not scoff at his name, because Hoplite would certainly not care for it if you did, as he's a most sensitive and dignified character, who was formerly a male whore's male maid, if the truth be told, but has now retired from that particular scene. According to report, the Hoplite has been in business with some of the city's top poof raves, and was even more in demand by the gentry than the mostly glamorosos he'd shacked up with. How I know him, is on account of his being a friend of Wiz's who he admires (but nothing doing), and it was through them that I actually got my room. What the Hoplite does for a living now, apart from a bit of free-lancing on the side when conditions get too rough, is act as contact man for various gossip columnists, because though you might not think this credible, considering his background, Hoplite gets around on the Knightsbridge-Chelsea circuit in quite an important way, no doubt owing to his being very handsome in an elfin, adolescent sort of style, and certainly very witty, or should I say sharp-tongued, but most of all, because he's really very *friendly*; I mean, he really *does like* people, which a lot of people think they do, but which it seems, as a matter of fact, is really very rare.

Next, on the first floor, in in fact the best room, but I somehow don't think he'll last there, on account of really critical moments with Mr Omar, is a young coloured kid called Mr Cool (which I need hardly say is not his baptismal name, I don't suppose). Cool is a local product, I mean born and bred on this island of both races, and he wears a beardlet, and listens to the MJQ, and speaks very low, and blinks his big eyes and occasionally lets a sad, fleeting smile cross his kissable lips. He's certainly younger than I am, but he makes me feel about nine or so, he's so very poised and paternal, though what the hell he does to keep himself in MJQ LPs I haven't an idea — I really haven't. I don't think it's anything illegal, which is what you might expect, because the kid is always so skint, he's only one suit (a striped Italian black), and no furniture to speak of except for his radiogram, so that either business, whatever it may be, is bad, or else, for reasons best known, he's covering up.

I miss out various rooms and floors, and come now to my particular pal, who lives in the basement and really is a horror, called Big Jill. Now Jill is a Les. and, what is more, you may not believe this, but a Les. ponce, that is to say, she keeps a string of idotic chicklets on the game, and just sits back in her over-heated, over-decorated, over cooking-smelling basement and collects. She's in all day, and goes out as sun sets to an overnight club where she's behind the counter, and holds her court among her little Les.-ette fans. And then, in the wee small hours, she has a way, when she comes home, of stopping in the area before she goes in and yelling at the upper windows at the Hoplite or myself, to ask if we want to come down and have anything to eat. Which, as a matter of fact, we quite often do, not really for the food, but because old Jill is very wise, in spite of being not far in her twenties, and is my chief and only confidant about Suzette who I ask her advice about but, as I need hardly tell you, haven't produced for her inspection, for all my contacts with Suze are at her place over there in W2.

from *Absolute Beginners*

But this particular evening, I had to call at a teenage hut inside
Soho, in order to contact two of my models, by names Dean
Swift and the Misery Kid. Now, about Soho, there's this, that
although so much crap's written about the area, of all London
quarters, I think it's still one of the most authentic. I mean,
Mayfair is just top spivs stepping into the slippers of the former
gentry, and Belgravia, like I've said, is all flats in houses built as
palaces and Chelsea — well! Just take a look yourself, next time
you're there. But in Soho, all the things they say happen, do: I
mean, the vice of every kink, and speakeasies and spielers and
friends who carve each other up, and, on the other hand, dear
old Italians and sweet old Viennese who've run their honest,
unbent little businesses there since the days of George six, and
five, and backward far beyond. And what's more, although the
pavement's thick with tearaways, provided you don't meddle
it's really a much safer area than the respectable suburban
fringe. It's not in Soho a sex maniac leaps out of a hedge on to
your back and violates you. It's in the dormitory sections.

The coffee spot where I hoped I'd find my two duets was of
the kind that's now the chic-est thing to date among the juniors
— namely, the pig-sty variety, and adolescent bum's delight. I
don't exaggerate, as you'll see. What you do is, rent premises
that are just as dear as any other, rip up the linos and tear out the
nice fittings if there happen to be any, put in thick wood floors
and tables, and take special care not to wipe the cups properly,
or sweep the butts and crusts and spittle off the floor. Candles
are a help or, at a pinch, non-pearl 40-watt blue bulbs. And a
juke-box just for decoration, as it's considered rather naive to
use one in these places.

This example was called Chez Nobody, and sure enough,
sitting far apart from each other at distant tables, were the
Dean and the Misery Kid. Though both are friends of mine,
and, in a way, even friends of each other, these two don't mix in
public, on account of the Dean being a sharp modern jazz
creation, and the Kid just a skiffle survival, with horrible

leanings to the trad. thing. That is to say, the Kid admires the groups that play what is supposed to be the authentic music of old New Orleans, i.e., combos of booking-office clerks and quantity-surveyors' assistants who've handed in their cards, and dedicated themselves to blowing what they believe to be the same note as the wonderful Creoles who invented the whole thing, when it all long ago began.

If you know the contemporary scene, you could tell them apart at once, just like you could a soldier or sailor, with their separate uniforms. Take first the Misery Kid and his trad. drag. Long, brushless hair, white stiff-starched collar (rather grubby), striped shirt, tie of all one colour (red today, but it could have been royal-blue or navy), short jacket but an old one (somebody's riding tweed, most likely), very, very, tight, tight, trousers with wide stripe, no sox, short *boots*. Now observe the Dean in the modernist number's version. College-boy smooth crop hair with burned-in parting, neat white Italian rounded-collared shirt, short Roman jacket *very* tailored (two little vents, three buttons), no-turn-up narrow trousers with 17-inch bottoms absolute maximum, pointed-toe shoes, and a white mac lying folded by his side, compared with Misery's sausage-rolled umbrella.

Compare them, and take your pick! I would add that their chicks, if present, would match them up with: trad. boy's girl — long hair, untidy with long fringes, maybe jeans and a big floppy sweater, maybe bright-coloured never-floralled, never-pretty dress... smudged-looking's the objective. Modern jazz boy's girl — short hemlines, seamless stockings, pointed-toed high-heeled stiletto shoes, crêpe nylon rattling petticoat, short blazer jacket, hair done up into the elfin style. Face pale — corpse colour with a dash of mauve, plenty of mascara.[...]

If you have a friend who's a junkie, like I have the Dean, you soon discover there's no point whatever discussing his addiction. It's as senseless as discussing love, or religion, or things you only feel if you feel them, because the Dean, and I suppose all his fellow junkies, is convinced that this is "a mystic way of life" (the Dean's own words), and you and I, who don't jab hot needles in our arms, are just going through life missing absolutely everything worthwhile in it. The Dean always says, life's just kicks. Well, I agree with him, so it is, but personally, it seems to me the big kick you should try to get by how you live it sober. But tell that to the Dean!

Why I'd not recently seen him, is that he'd until then been away inside. This has fairly often happened to the Dean, owing to his breaking into chemists' shops, and as he suffers a lot when he's cut off from the world and all it gives in there, he doesn't like you to refer to it when he emerges. At the same time, he *does* like you to say you're glad to see him once again, so it's all a trifle dicey.

"Hail, squire," I said. "Long time no see. How is you are we? Won't you say tell?"

The Dean smiled in his world-weary way. "Doesn't this place stink?" he said to me.

"Well, certainly, Dean Swift, it does, but do you mean its air, or just its atmosphere?"

"The both. The only civilized thing about it," the Dean continued, "is that they let you *sit* here, when you're skint."

The Dean gazed round at the teenage products like a concentration camp exterminator. I should explain the Dean, though only just himself an ex-teenager, has sad valleys down his cheeks, and wears a pair of steel-rimmed glasses (which he takes off for our posing sessions), so that his Dean-look is habitually sour and solemn. (The Swift part of the thing comes from his rapid disappearance at the approach of any cowboys. You're talking to him and then, tick-tock! he's vanished.) I could see that now the Dean, as usual when skinned and vicious, was going to engage in his favourite theme, i.e. the horror of teenagers. "Look at the beardless microbes!" he exclaimed, loud enough for everyone to hear. "Look at the pram products at their plotting and their planning!"

And, as a matter of fact, you could see what he meant, because to see the kids hunched over the tables it *did* look as if some conspiracy was afoot to slay the elder brethren and majorities. And when I'd paid, and we went out in the roads, even here in this Soho, the headquarters of the adult mafia, you could everywhere see the signs of the un-silent teenage revolution. The disc shops with those lovely sleeves set in their windows, the most original thing to come out in our lifetime, and the kids inside them purchasing guitars, or spending fortunes on the songs of the Top Twenty. The shirt-stores and bra-stores with cine-star photos in the window, selling all the exclusive teenage drag I've been describing. The hair-style saloons where they inflict the blow-wave torture on the kids for hours on end. The cosmetic shops — to make girls of seventeen, fifteen, even thirteen, look like pale rinsed-out sophisticates. Scooters and bubble-cars driven madly down the roads by kids who, a few years ago, were pushing toy ones on the pavement. And everywhere you go the narrow coffee bars and darkened cellars with the kids packed tight, just whispering, like bees inside the hive waiting for a glorious queen bee to appear.

"See what I mean," the Dean said.

And the chicks, round the alleys, on that summer afternoon! Heavens, each year the teenage dream-girl has grown younger, and now, there they were, like children that've dressed up in their fashionable aunties' sharpest clothes — and suddenly you realize that it's not a game, and that these chicks mean business, and that it's not so much you, one of the boys, they aim their persons at, as their sheer, sweet, energetic legs walk down the pavement three by three, but no, at quite adult numbers, quite mature things, at whose eyes they shoot confident, proud looks there's no mistaking.

"Little madams," said the Dean.

"There you go!" I answered.

Here Dean Swift stopped us in his tracks.

"I tell you," he said, pulling his US-striped and rear-buckled cap down over his eyes, "I tell you something. These teenagers are ceasing to be rational, thinking, human beings, and turning into mindless butterflies. And they're turning into butterflies all of the same size and colour, that have to flutter round exactly the same flowers, on exactly the same gardens. Yes!" he exclaimed at a group of kiddos coming clicking, cracking prattling by. "You're nothing but a bunch of butterflies!"

But the kidettes took no notice of the Dean whatever,

because just at that moment... there! in his hand-styled car with his initials in its number, there sped by the newest of the teenage singing raves, with beside him his brother, and his composer, and his chicklet, and his Personal Manager, so that all that was missing was his Mum. And the kids waved, and the young Pied Piper waved his free hand back, and everyone for a few seconds was latched on to the glory.

"Singer!" cried the Dean out after him. "Har, Har!"

from *Absolute Beginners*

The Wiz was wearing a gladiator Lonsdale belt with studs on it, and this he unbuckled as he came into the Dubious,* like a soldier that's been relieved from guard. But still he looked wary, as he always did, and no doubt in his sleep as well, as if the world was in the other corner of the ring where he did battle, and himself a lonesome hunter on the London jungle trail. "Come over behind the music," I said to him, and we got on the other side of the performers, so that their sound made a barrier that hedged us from the lush-swilling visitors around the counter.

"What's new?" I asked the Wiz.

A nice thing about Wizard is that he forgets a quarrel absolutely. A battle, with the Wiz, is always for a purpose, like a meal, and once it's over, he just doesn't seem to think of it any more at all. He eyed me with approval, and I could see that once again I was his old reliable, perhaps the only one he had outside eternity.

"I've news for you," he said.

I must admit at feeling anxious, because the Wiz's bits of news are apt to sweep you out to sea until you can get adjusted to them.

"I'm thinking," he said, "of going into business with a chick."

"Oh, are you. Clever boy. I'll visit you at Brixton," I said, disgusted.

* *Editor's note:* a Soho drinking club.

80

"You don't approve?"

"How can I? You're not that kind of hustler."

"Try anything once...."

"Oh, sure. Oh sure, oh sure. Next thing is breaking and entering."

I got up to fetch some drinks, and also to have time to think of this. Because I'd always imagined one day Wiz might go that way, but always decided he had brains enough to do better than that, and not get himself into some bower-bird's clutches. Because say what you like, in that set-up it's the female party who controls the situation, even if she gives the male one all her earnings, and he crunches her on Sunday evenings after the weekly visit to the Odeon. The simple reason being that her own activity, whatever you may think of it, is legal, and the boy's is not, and all she has to do if there's an argument is dial Detective-Sergeant Someone round the corner.

"Health, wealth and happiness," he said sarcastically.

"Happiness! You should talk!"

There was a silence. Then,

"Go on," said Wiz. "Let's have it."

"What use, if you've decided?"

"Let's have it all the same."

I groaned, I really did.

"It's just, Wiz, that it's not your kind of thing. Tell me one ponce you know who's got real brains."

"I know of several."

"I don't mean craft or cunning, I mean *brains*. Constructive brains."

The Wiz said, "I could introduce you to several bookies, club owners, car-hire proprietors, who've built up their business by loot they made when on the game before retirement."

I said, "I could introduce you to several Saturday-midnight-at-the-chemist's, and several in-and-out boys, and several corpses, who've had just the same idea."

"Ah. Well, we disagree."

I said to the lunatic, "It may be all right for creatures who are young in *mind*, as well as age, but, let's face it, Wiz, you're too mature already. You *know* too much what you'd be doing."

The Wizard smiled, if you can call it that. "And this," he said gently, "comes from a kiddo known around the town for flogging pornographic photos."

Oh well, hell!

"In the first place," I said....

"And don't forget the second — and the third...."

"In the first place," I continued, "you know very well only *some* of my snaps are pornographic, and I'm on that kick for giggles as much as loot. In the second, as you say, you know I'm pulling out of that activity as soon as ever — as I've often told you. And in the third, yes, as you also say, are you really comparing poncing with what I do?"

"Not really," the Wizard said, "because it's more straightforward, and it's better paid."

"Oh, if you say so, Sporting Life."

There was another pause for refreshments between rounds.

"And who's the lucky chick?" I asked him.

"Oh, girl I know. Of course," he said, "you'll understand it's not wise to say *who*, specially to anyone who disapproves."

"How right you are, young Wizard. Anyway, whoever it is, I pity her. You'll have a dozen on the game before you're nicked."

"I'd not be surprised," the Wizard said.

I drained my non-alcoholic beverage.

"Well, let me tell you, genius," I said, "two things, and do just listen. The first is, cute little number though you may be, you're really not the fixer type, the hustler type, because you're too damn delighted by the sport of it to take it seriously enough. The other, which you know full well, and should be ashamed of yourself for, is that you really have got brains, and if you'd had even a fragment of education, you'd have done big things, boy, and it's not too late. It's really not too late: why don't you study?"

"The school of life," Wiz answered.

"Brixton class."

"So what? Each occupation has its risks."

"Fool."

"Yeah? Oh, well...."

The Wizard looked up at the ceiling, because the combo had stopped its operations for a moment. And me, I really felt I must say *something* to stop this thing; not because I disapproved of it (although I did), but because I knew that, if the Wizard did it, then I'd lose him.

But he got in first, now. "I'll tell you something," the Wizard said to me. "I've thought it over carefully — and I'm safe as houses. Look!" And I looked at him. "Imagine me in the dock! What mug — even a magistrate, let alone a jury — is going to believe a baby-face like me could be a ponce?"

I waited, then said, "If you could see yourself in a mirror now, this very moment, you'd realize you don't look young at all. Not at all, Wiz, you don't — you look damn old."

"Oh, I do?" said Wiz. "Well, then, let me tell you something else. This is an old, old thing, this whore, and ponce, and client business. Since A. and Eve, there's always been the woman, and the visitor, and the local male."

"Be the visitor, then."

"Nobody likes the easy-money boy, there I agree. But the reasons he's disliked for, kiddo, are all very hypocritical. The client shifts his shame on to the ponce, see, and the ponce is willing to carry it for him — give him a clear, social, respectable alibi. Then, no man likes paying for what the ponce is paid for. And most of all, boy, the world is jealous of the ponce! Well, kid, and rightly!" And he smiled a great big aren't-I-clever smile.

"Fine, fine," I cried. "We'll have to get you testifying before those Wolfenden creations."*

"Oh, *them*," said the Wizard. "The last person they'd ever want to ask about the game is anyone who *knows* about it... a whore, a ponce, even a client. You know what the Wolfenden is for?" he went on, leaning across and grinning at me. "It's so as to play down the queer thing in our country, and hide it behind the kosher game. It's so as to confuse the two, and get all the mugs muddled, so that if they call down fire and brimstone,

* *Editor's note:* Sir John Wolfenden was the chairman of the Committee set up in 1954 to consider the law and practice of prostitution and homosexuality (conveniently lumped together).

they don't know on what."

"Not so loud, Wiz," I cried, because the combo had broken up, and someone hadn't yet put on the pick-up once again.

So there it was. Already, I was speaking *secretly* to the Wiz, like I had never done before, becoming a part of his squalid little plot, and, believe me, I was revolted.

"Christ!" I exclaimed. "What's happening to me? My girl, I've lost her to the Spades and queers, and now my friend, I'm losing him to the girls."

"Don't compare me with Spades," said Wiz.

"Now, be intelligent, I wasn't. I was comparing Suze with you."

"Nice! Perhaps it's you who's worrying most about all this, little latchkey-kid."

"Oh, perhaps!"

"Well," said the Wizard, making as if to rise, "when the cowboys start to fill me in, I'll have you buzzed immediately for bail."

"Don't talk to me like that, Wiz, *please!*"

"Oh, I know you'll come running...you adore me!"

This was evidently it, and I reached up and slapped the Wiz real hard. Real hard, I did. He didn't look all that surprised, and he didn't retaliate at all. He just rubbed his cheek and walked off over to the bar, so that I realized this was how he wanted it to be. Oh, fuck, I thought.

So I went out of the Dubious to catch the summer evening breeze. The night was glorious, out there. The air was sweet as a cool bath, the stars were peeping nosily beyond the neons, and the citizens of the Queendom, in their jeans and separates, were floating down the Shaftesbury avenue canals, like gondolas. Everyone had loot to spend, everyone a bath with verbena salts behind them, and nobody had broken hearts, because they all were all ripe for the easy summer evening. The rubberplants in the espressos had been dusted, and the smooth white lights of the new-style Chinese restaurants — not the old Mah Jongg categories, but the latest things with broad glass fronts, and dacron curtainings, and a beige carpet over the interiors — were shining a dazzle, like some monster telly screens. Even those horrible old anglo-saxon public-houses — all potato crisps and flat, stale ale, and puddles on the counter bar, and spittle — looked quite alluring, provided you didn't push those two-ton doors that pinch your arse, and wander in. In fact, the capital was a night-horse dream. And I thought, "My lord, one thing is certain, and that's that they'll make musicals one day about the glamour-studded 1950s." And I thought, my heaven, one thing is certain too, I'm miserable.

from *Absolute Beginners*

IN SEPTEMBER

I was up very early on that morning, as if with a private alarm clock in my brain, and it was one of the most beautiful young days I've ever seen. The dome of the heavens, when I looked out up at it over my geraniums, was pale pink glowing blue, with nothing in it but a few stray leaves of cloud, lit up gold and green by sun you couldn't see behind the houses. The air was fresh, blown right in from the sea, and there wasn't a sound except from hundreds of thousands of pairs of lungs, still slumbering there in Napoli. Peace, perfect peace, I thought, as I sucked in the warm air of my native city. And it was also, as it happened, my nineteenth birthday.

I put on some music and abluted, then made two Nescafés and carried one down for Hoplite. The cat was absent. Waste not want not, I decided, so carried them further down to Cool. Another cat out on the tiles last night. No use disturbing Big Jill that early, so I drank both cups on the front doorstep, and stood there taking in the scene.

And I saw this. Coming down the street, from the N. Hill Gate direction, were a group of yobbos, who most probably had been out at some all-night jungle-juice performance too, and who straggled across the street and pavement in that *messy* way they have, and whose bodies were all *wrong* somehow — I mean with lumps and bumps in the wrong places — and whose summer drag looked hastily pulled on. And coming up the street, from the Metropolitan Railway direction, were two coloured characters — not Spades, as it happened, but two Sikh warrior products, with a mauve and a lemon turban, and with stacks of hair. Well, when the two groups met, the Sikh characters stepped to one side, as you or I would do, but the yob lot halted, so as it was difficult to pass by, and there was a short pause: all this just outside my door.

Then one of the scruffos turned and looked at his choice companions, and grinned a sloppy grin, and suddenly approached the two Sikh characters and hit one of them right in the face: with his fist pointed so that the top knuckles got inside the skull. So long as I live, I swear, I shall never forget the look on that Asian number's face: it wasn't at all fear, it wasn't at all rage, it was just complete and utter unbelief and surprise.

Then the other Sikh one shouldered up beside his buddy, and the yobbos drew away a bit, then both the two groups separated, and the oafo lot went off laughing down the hill again, and the Sikhs started chattering and waving their arms about. They walked on a little bit, then turned and looked back, then went off chattering and waving again up hill out of sight and sound.

Now, you will be asking, what about me? Did I run out and take a poke at the chief yobbo, and bawl the bunch of little monsters out? The answer is — I did not. First of all, because I simply couldn't believe my eyes. And next, because the whole thing was just so *meaningless*, I suddenly felt weak and sick; I mean I've no objection, really, to men fighting if they want to, if they've got a *reason*. But this thing! Also — I don't like to say this much, but here it is — I myself was scared. It doesn't seem possible such sordids as this lot could frighten you, and certainly one wouldn't, or even two or three of them.... But this little group; it seemed to have a horrid little mind, if you can call it that, all of its own, and a whole lot of unexpected force behind it.

I ran down in the area and called Big Jill. She took a while coming to the door, and shouted had I no discretion, there were chicks sleeping on the premises, but I shoved past her into her kitchen and told her what I'd just seen. She listened, asked me several questions, and said, "The bastards!"

"But what should I have done, Big Jill?" I cried.

"Who — you? Oh, I dunno. I'll make you a cup of tea."

As she started banging crockery about, and pulling her red slacks on over her huge hips without any by your leave, I found that I was shivering. When she handed me the cup, she said, "You might like to take a look at this."

It was a leading article in the Mrs Dale daily which the Amberley Drove character,* who you may remember, wrote for, and it was about the happenings a week ago up there in Nottingham. It said the chief thing was that we must be realistic, and keep a proper sense of due proportion. It said that many influential journals — including, of course, this Mrs Dale production — had long been warning the government that unrestricted immigration, particularly of coloured persons, was most undesirable, even if such persons came here, as by far the bulk of them undoubtedly did, from countries under direct colonial rule, and countries benefiting by the Commonwealth connection. But Commonwealth solidarity was one thing, and unrestricted immigration was quite another.

Then it had a word to say about the coloured races. England, it said, was an old and highly civilized nation, but the countries of Africa and the Caribbean were very far from being so indeed. It was true that the West Indian islands had enjoyed the advantages of British government for many centuries, but even in these the cultural level was low, to say the least of it, and as for Africa, it should be remembered that, a mere hundred years ago, some parts of that vast continent had never even heard of Christianity. In their own setting, coloured folk were no doubt admirable citizens, according to the standards that prevailed there. But transported unexpectedly to a culture of a higher order, serious difficulties and frustrations must inevitably arise.

"Must I go on reading all this balls?" I shouted at Big Jill.

"It's up to you," she said.

*Editor's note: a journalist ("Mrs Dale's Diary" was a very middle-class serial that ran on BBC radio for what seemed like decades).

Then it went on to give you the facts about the coloured communities who'd come to settle here in the UK. Many were toilers, it did not deny, as could be seen by those courteous and efficient public transport servants, but many were layabouts who thrived on the three-pounds-ten they got from the National Assistance. This led to labour troubles, and we must remember that the nation had been passing through a slight, though of course temporary, recession. Pressure on housing was another problem. It was true that many coloured folk — for reasons that were more than understandable, and need not be detailed here — found difficulty in securing accommodation in the better sections of most towns. It was also true that many West Indians, in particular, had saved up enough from their wage-packets, over the years, to purchase houses, but unfortunately these were generally speaking little other than slum property, which further deteriorated when they moved into them, to the disadvantage of the rate-paying citizens as a whole. Moreover, it was not unknown for coloured landlords to evict white tenants — often old-age pensioners — by making their lives impossible.

Then there was the matter of different customs. By and large, said the article, English people were renowned for their decent and orderly behaviour. But not so the immigrants, it seemed, or very many of them. They liked haggling in the shops, prodding fruit before they bought it, leaving the hi-fi on all night, dressing in flashy clothes and, worse still, because this made them more conspicuous, driving about in even flashier vehicles, which they had somehow managed to acquire.

Then there was the question of the women. (Old Amberley certainly went to town on this woman question!) To begin with, he said, mixed marriages — as responsible coloured persons would be the very first to agree themselves — were most undesirable. They led to a mongrel race, inferior physically and mentally, and rejected by both of the unadulterated communities. But frequently, of course — and this made the matter even graver — these tainted offspring were, in addition, the consequence of unions that were blessed neither by church nor state. More, said the piece. The well-known propensity and predilection of coloured males for securing intimate relations with white women — unfortunately, by now, a generally observed phenomenon in countries where the opportunities existed — led to serious friction between the immigrants and the men of the stock so coveted, whose natural — and, he would add — sound and proper instinct, was to protect their womenfolk from this contamination, even if this led to violence which, in normal circumstances, all would find most regrettable.

But this was not all: it was time for plain speaking, and this had to be said. The record of the courts had shown — let alone the personal observations of any anxious and attentive observer — that living off the immoral earnings of white prostitutes had now become all too prevalent among the immigrant community. No one would suggest — least of all this journal — that in each and every such immoral union, the guilty male was a coloured person since, of course — as figures published recently in its columns had unfortunately made it all too clear — the total estimated figure of active prostitutes in this country did not itself fall far short of the total numbers of male coloured immigrants of the appropriate age. Nevertheless, the disproportionate number of coloured "bullies" could not be denied.

"Christ!" I said, putting the damn thing down. "I just can't go on with this!"

"Stick it out," Big Jill said. "I'll make you another cuppa."

Several conclusions, this Drove one continued, flowed inevitably — and urgently — from these grave matters and, more particularly, from the recent disturbances at Nottingham, which everyone — and especially his Mrs Dale daily — so greatly and so vehemently deplored. The first was, that immigration by coloured persons, whether having an identical citizenship status as ourselves or not, should be halted instantly. Indeed, the whole process should be reversed, and compulsory repatriation should be given urgent and serious consideration by the government. Meanwhile, it went without saying, law and order should be enforced most rigorously and impartially, however great the provocation may have been —

and there may well, it must be admitted, have been provocation on both sides. But it was only a minority — chiefly persons known by the name of "Teddy boys" — who had actually been guilty of a physical breach of the Queen's peace, and these youths should undoubtedly be restrained; though many might feel that such young people — who were far from being characteristic of the youth of the country as a whole — were psychopathic cases, in greater need of medical attention than of drastic punishment by the courts of law.

The occurrences at Nottingham, A. Drove wound up, could in no way be described as a "race riot". No comparison with large-scale disturbances in the southern states of America, or in the Union of South Africa, was therefore tenable. By the swift and determined action of the Nottingham authorities, we could rest assured that no more would be heard of such lamentable incidents — which were entirely alien to our way of life — provided, of course, immediate action along the lines suggested by the Mrs Dale daily was taken without fear or favour.

I put this thing down again. "The man isn't even funny," I said to Jill. "And I don't believe he's even stupid — he's just wicked!"

"Take it easy, breezy," said Big Jill.

"And there's quite a lot of things that he's left out!"

"I don't doubt you're right," she said to me.

"And the whole point is — he's not denounced this thing! Not denounced this riot! All he's doing is looking round for alibis."

Jill sat down and started on her nails. "He's just ignorant," she said, "not wicked."

I cried out: "To be ignorant, and *tell* people, *is* wicked!"

She looked up from her nail polish. "All it comes to," she said, "is if you've got a black face in a white or off-white neighbourhood, *everything* you do's conspicuous. You just stick out like a sore thumb."

"Everything you do!" I said, picking up the Dale daily and rolling it into a tight sausage. "But what *do* they do, different from all the hustlers living in this slum?"

"You tell me," said Jill.

"Look! There's more coloured unemployment than white.

Everyone knows that. And not only layabouts; you see them queueing at the Labour every day for hours."

"Yeah," said Big Jill.

"And you know what it's like when they try to get a room: 'no children, no coloureds'."

"I suppose," said Jill, "if you hate the one, you also hate the other."

"As for white illegitimates, are there none around here, would you really say?"

"I don't know many myself who aren't," Big Jill said.

"And what about white chicks?" I cried. "Don't they *like* it? I mean, hasn't everybody seen them hanging around the Spades?"

"I've seen more than a few," Jill said.

"And those ponces. Are none of the bastards Maltese, Cypriots, even home-grown products, just occasionally?"

"Plenty," Big Jill said, looking up.

"Oh, sorry, Big Jill."

"It's okay, baby."

"What's the matter with our men?" I said to her. "Can't they hold their own women? Do they have to get this pronk (and I bashed the Dale daily onto the chair back) to help them and protect them?"

"I should have thought," said Jill, beginning on her right hand, "there should be more than enough girls to go round for everybody."

I stuffed the rolled paper among the tea-leaves. "The whole thing, anyway," I cried, "is that what really matters is being missed. And here it is. If every Spade in England was a hustler, that's still no excuse for setting on them ten to one."

Big Jill didn't answer me this time, and I got up.

"I don't understand my own country any more," I said to her. "In the history books, they tell us the English race has spread itself all over the damn world; gone and settled everywhere, and that's one of the great, splendid English things. No one invited us, and we didn't ask anyone's permission, I suppose. Yet when a few hundred thousand come and settle among our fifty millions, we just can't take it."

"Yep," Big Jill said.

"Upstairs," I continued, "I've got a brand new passport. It says I'm a citizen of the UK and the Colonies. Nobody asked me to be, but there I am. Well. Most of these boys have got exactly the same passport as I have — and it was *we* who thought up the laws that gave it to them. But when they turn up in the dear old mother country, and show us the damn thing, we throw it back again in their faces!"

Big Jill got up too. "You're getting worked up," she said.

"You bet I am!"

She looked at me. "People in glass houses..." she said.

"What does that mean?"

"Listen, darling. Personally, I live off mysteries, and that doesn't give me the right to be particular. As for you, you peddle pornographic pictures round the villages, and very nice ones they are, I don't deny. But that makes it rather hard for you, it seems to me, to preach at anybody."

"I don't dig that," I said, "at all. You can hustle, and still be a man, not a beast."

"If you say so, honey," Big Jill answered. "And now I must turf you out, the chicks will be screaming for their breakfast."

"Oh, fine then, Big Jill." I went to the door, and said to her, "You are on my side, though, aren't you?"

"Oh, sure," she said. "I'm all for equality.... If a coloured girl comes in here she's every bit as welcome as the others...."

"I see," I said to her.

She came over and put her hammer-thrower's arm across my shoulder. " Don't worry, son," she said, "and don't take things too much to heart that aren't your business. The Spades can look after themselves... they're big strong boys. A lot of them are boxers...."

"Oh, yes," I said. "But remember what I saw just now. Put Flikker and twenty Teds inside the ring tooled up with dusters in their gloves, and there's a sort of handicap."

"Flikker's been sent away," she said.

"Oh, yes? He has?"

"He's on remand in custody."

"This is the first time I've liked a magistrate."

Big Jill came out into the area. "It's not the Teds you have to worry about," she said, "but if the men join in it, too. The men round here are rather a tough lot."

"I've noticed that," I said to her, going out to take the padlocks off my Vespa.

"Where are you off to, baby?"

"I'm going to take a look around my manor."

As soon as you passed into the area, you could sense that there was something on. The sun was well up now, and the streets were normal, with the cats and traffic — until suddenly you realized that they *weren't*. Because there in Napoli, you could feel a *hole*; as if some kind of life was draining out of it, leaving a sort of vacuum in the streets and terraces. And what made it somehow worse was that, as you looked around, you could see the people hadn't yet noticed the alteration, even though it was so startling to you.

Standing about on corners, and outside their houses, there were Teds; groups of them, not *doing* anything, but standing in circles, with their heads just a bit bent down. There were motor-bikes about, as well, and the kids had often got them out there at angles on the roadway, instead of parked against the kerb as usual, for a natter. Also, I noticed, as I cruised the streets, that quite a few of those battered little delivery vans that I've referred to — usually dark blue, and with the back doors tied on with wire, or one door off — had groups around them, also, who didn't seem to be mending them, or anything. There were occasional lots of chicks, giggling and letting out little yells, a bit too loud for that time of the morning. There were also more than the usual number of small kids about. As for the Spades, they seemed to creep a bit, and keep in bunches. And although they often did this anyway, a great number of them were hanging out of windows and speaking to each other loud across the streets. As I continued on, I came to patches once again where all was absolutely as before; quiet and ordinary. Then — turn a corner, and you were back once more in a part where the whole of Napoli seemed like it was *muttering*.

Then I saw my first "incident" (as A. Drove wrote it) — or, as you know, my second. Here it was. Coming along, pushing a pram and wearing those really horrible clothes that Spade women do (not men) — I mean all colours of the spectrum and the wrong ones put together, and with shoes like Minnie Mouse — was a coloured mum with that self-satisfied expression that all mums have. Beside her was her husband, I imagine it was — anyway, he was talking at her all the time, and she wasn't listening. Then, coming from the opposite direction (and there always seems to *be* an opposite direction), was a white mum, also with kiddie-car and hubby, and whose clothes were just as dreadful as the Spade mum's were — except that the Spade's girl's looked worse, somehow, because you could see, at any rate, that she was *trying*, and hadn't given up all hope of glamour.

Well, these two met and, as there's no law of the road on pavements, both angled their prams in the same direction, and collided. And that started it. Because neither would give way, and the two men both joined in, and before you knew where you were, about a hundred people, white and coloured, had appeared from absolutely nowhere. Quite honestly! I was watching the thing quite closely from near to, straddling my Vespa on the roadway, and one minute there were two (or three) people on each side, and next minute there were fifty.

Now, even then, if in normal times, the thing would have passed off, with the usual argument, and even then, if someone had stepped in and said, "break it up," or "don't be so fucking idiotic," all would have gone well — but no one said this, and as for coppers, well, of course there wasn't one. Then somebody threw a bottle, and that was it.

That milk that arrives mysteriously every morning, I suppose it brings us life, but if trouble comes, it's been put there — or the bottles it comes in have done — by the devil. And dustbins that get emptied just as regularly, and take everything away — they and their lids, especially, have become much the same thing: I mean, the other natural city weapon of war. They were soon both flying, and I had to crouch behind my Vespa, then pull it over, when I got a chance, behind a vehicle.

Even then, it was still, in a way, if you'll believe me, rather *fun*; I mean, the bottles flying, and the odd window smashing, little boys and girls running round in circles shouting, and people weaving and dodging, like they were playing a sort of enjoyable, dirty game. Then there was a scream, and a white kid collapsed, and somebody shouted a Spade had pulled a knife. It's always those attacked who give the pretext — don't we know! Anyway, there was some blood for all to see.

Then, just as suddenly, the Spades all ran, as if someone had told them to on a walkie-talkie from headquarters somewhere — and they dived round corners and inside their houses, slamming doors. Honest! One minute there were white and coloured faces battling, and the next there were only white. There was a lot of shouting and discussion after that, and a few more bottles through the windows where a Spade or two was peeping out, and the white kid was carried on the pavement where I couldn't see him, and the law arrived in a radio-car and told everybody to disperse. And that was that. All over.

Then, a bit later, came incident number two — or three. Along another road I was prospecting, I saw driving along quite slow, because anyway it was pulling up, one of those "flashy cars" A. Drove was on about, and four Spades in it — and the driver handling the thing in that way Spades often do, i.e., very expertly, but as if he didn't realize it was a *machine*, not a wonderful animal of some kind. Well, two of those delivery vans I spoke of sandwiched it like the law cars do in US films, and out from the back and front of them came about sixteen fellers — those from the back spilling out as if they were some peculiar kind of cargo the van had on board that day. And these were not Teds, but *men* — anyway, up in the twenties, somewhere, I should judge — and this time there was no previous argument whatever, they just rushed at that vehicle, and wrenched the doors open, and dragged out the Spades, and crunched them. Of course, they fought back — though once again, there was that same brief hesitation as I'd noticed with the Sikhs, that same amount of complete *surprise*. Two were left lying, and got kicked (those boys certainly knew all about vulnerable parts), and two made way, one weeping; and about a hundred of my own people gathered round about to watch.

And about those who watched, I saw something new to me,

and which you may find quite incredible — but I swear it's the truth I'm telling you — they didn't even seem to *enjoy* themselves particularly — I mean, seeing all this — they didn't shout, or bawl, or cheer; they just stood by, out of harm's way, these English people did, and *watched*. Just like at home at evening, with their Ovaltine and slippers, at the telly. Quite decent, respectable people they seemed, too; white-collar workers and their wives, I expect, who'd probably been out to do their shopping. Well, they saw the lads get in the Spades' car, and drive it against a concrete lamp-standard, and climb back in their handy little delivery vans, and drive away. And once again, that was that. Except that a few coloured women came out and tended the men lying there, who the bystanders I spoke of had come up a bit nearer to, to examine.

Then came another incident — and soon, as you'll understand, I began to lose count a little, and, as time went on, lose count a bit of what time was, as well. This one was down by the Latimer road railway station, among those crisscross of streets I mentioned earlier, like Lancaster, and Silchester, and Walmer, and Blechynden. In this part, by now, there was quite a muster; I mean, by now people realized what was happening — that there were kicks to be had if you came out in the thoroughfare, and besides, the pubs were emptying for the afternoon. And they all moved about like up in Middlesex street at the market there on Sunday, groups shifting and re-forming, searching. People were telling about what had happened here, or there, or in some other places, and they all seemed disappointed nothing was happening for them then and there.

Well, they weren't disappointed long. Because out of the Metropolitan Railway station — the dear old London Transport, we all think so safe and so reliable — came a bunch of passengers, and among them was a Spade. Just one. A boy of my own age, I'd say, carrying a hold-all and a brown paper parcel — a serious-looking kiddy with a pair of glasses, and one of those rather sad, drab suits that some Spades wear, particularly students, in order to show the English people that we mustn't think they're savages in grass skirts and bones stuck in their hair, but twentieth-century numbers just like we are. I think he was an African; anyway, there's no doubt that's where his ancestors all came from — millions of them, for centuries way back in time.

Now, this kiddy must have been rather dumb. Because he evidently didn't rumble anything was at all unusual — perhaps he'd come down from Manchester or somewhere, to visit pals. Anyway, down the road he walked, stepping aside politely if people were in his way, and they all watching. All those eyes watching him, and the noise dropping. Then someone cried out, "Get him!" and the Spade dug it quick enough then — and he started running down the Bramley road like lightning, though still clutching his hold-all and his parcel, and at least a hundred young men chasing after him, and hundreds of girls and kids and adults running after *them*, and even motor-bikes and cars. Some heathen god from home must have shouted sense into his ear just then, because he dived into a greengrocer's and slammed the door. And the old girl inside locked it from within, and she glared out at the crowd, and the crowd gathered round there, and they shouted — and I'm quoting their words exactly — "Let's get him!" and "Bring him out!" and "Lynch him!"

They cried that.

But they didn't get him. What they got, was the old greengrocer woman instead, who came out of another door, and went for them. Picture this! This one old girl, with her grey hair all in a mess, and her old face flushed with fury, she stood there surrounded by this crowd of hundreds, and she bawled them out. She said they were a stack of cowards and gutter bastards, the whole lot of them, but they started shouting back at her, and I couldn't hear. But she didn't budge, the old girl, and her husband had got the shutters up inside, and by and by the law made it's appearance with some vans as well this time, and they got through the crowd, and started milling round, and collected the young African, and moved among the mob in groups of six and told it to disperse — with truncheons out this time, just for a change.

I went off after this to be a bit alone. I rode out of the area to the big open space on Wormwood Scrubs, and I sat down on the grass to have a think. Because what I'd just seen in there made me feel weak and hopeless; most of all because, except for that old vegetable woman (who I bet will go straight up to heaven like a supersonic rocket when she dies — nothing can stop that one), no one, absolutely no one, had reacted against this thing. You looked round to find the members of the other team — even just a few of them — and there weren't any. I mean, any of us. The Spades were fighting back all right, of course, because they had to. But there were none of us.

When this thing happens to you, please believe me, it's just like as if the stones rise up from the pavement there and hit you, and the houses tumble, and the sky falls in. I mean, everything that you relied on, and all the natural things, do what you don't expect them to. Your sense of security, and of there being some plan, some idea behind it all somewhere, just disappears.

from *Absolute Beginners*

There's no doubt night favours wickedness: I mean, I don't think the night's wicked, and I love it, but it opens the trap for all the monsters to come out. I went down by Westbourne Park station, and took a ride along the scenic railway to the Bush. The train was packed with sightseers from the West, who hopped out at different stations for the free display. From the height between the stops, you could see the odd fire and firemen and, at sudden glimpses as the train rocked by a street at right angles, the crowds, and law cars prowling, or standing parked with cowboys packed in them, waiting for action, like bullets in a clip. And when the train halted, at Ladbroke and by Latimer, you could hear loud-speakers blaring something harsh and meaningless, like at Battersea pleasure gardens, in the funfair there. And all along the ride there were patches of blue-black darkness, then sudden glares and flares of dazzling light.

But at the Bush, I was amazed. Because when I crossed over, beyond the Green, to that middle-class section outside our area — all was peace and quiet and calm and as-you-were-before.

Believe me! Inside the two square miles of Napoli, there was blood and thunder, but just outside it — only across one single road, like some national frontier — you were back in the world of Mrs Dale, and What's My Line? and England's green and pleasant land. Napoli was like a prison, or a concentration camp: inside, blue murder, outside, buses and evening papers and hurrying home to sausages and mash and tea.

I bought a late-night edition by the telly theatre there. They were playing it up — big headlines, no paper can resist that — but also trying to play it down. Reactions from Africa and the Caribbean, it said, had been unfavourable, but much exaggerated. There was a bit of gloating in South Africa and the US South, which, in this difficult situation, was greatly to be deplored. The cardinal fact to remember was that neither at Nottingham — nor even at Notting Hill, so far — had there been any loss of actual life. Meanwhile a cat at Scotland Yard had issued a message to discourage sightseers. I threw the thing away. The law never wants you to see what it can't handle. Then I went back inside the area again.

I walked down an empty street that was lit, as a lot of them are round there, by lamps put up in Queen Boadicea's day, when I saw, coming along, three coloured cats, keeping together. I looked around to see if they were being chased or anything, but they weren't, so I went up and said, "Hi, boys, what's cooking?" — when I saw that one of them had a spanner, it looked to be (anyway, something metal), and they made a rush. Boy, did I gallop! With those three sons of Africa racing after me and hissing! I made for a pool of light, and dodged round some vehicles, and batted across a road straight into Mr Wiz. "Hold it!" he cried, and the coloured cats saw I had an ally, and melted like a falling gleam. "Boy!" I cried, slapping the old Wiz like a carpet-beater. "Am I glad to see your wicked face! Where the hell have you been, man, I've been seeking for you!" The Wizard took my arm, and said, "Cool it, kiddo," and just round two corners we found ourselves in the middle of a large assembly.

This lot were being addressed by a thing from the White Protection League, whose numbers were also distributing leaflets round the throng. The speaker on the portable platform was a man of quite ordinary appearance — i.e., the kind you'd find difficult to describe if someone asked you after — except that now he was lit up and jet-propelled by a sort of crazy, electric frenzy. He wasn't talking to *anybody* —to any human cat you could imagine, even the very worst — but out into space, out into the night to some spirit there, some witch-doctor he was screaming to for help and blessing. And looking up at him, in the yellow-coloured glare, were the white faces he was protecting, all turned, by the municipal lamps above, into a kind of un-washed violet grey.

I nudged Wiz. "He's round the bend," I said.

Wiz didn't answer.

"I said he's flipped, boy!" I shouted, above the noise of the loudspeaker.

Then I looked at Wizard. And on my friend's face, as he stared up at this orator, I saw an expression that made me shiver. Because the little Wiz, so tight and sharp and trim and dangerous, had on a little smile, that showed his teeth a bit, and his wiry little body was all clenched, and something was staring through his eyes that came from God knows where, and he raised on his toes, and shot up his arms all rigid, and he cried out, shrill like a final cry, "Keep England white!"

I stood there for a moment, while the mob roared too. Then I grabbed Wizard's neck clothes with all the strength I have in my body, and I yanked him round about off balance, and I hit him with all my life behind it, and he stumbled. Then I looked round quick, and saw how it was, and ran.

from "The Criminal Society",

Spectator December 1961 (*Out of the Way,* 1979)

The intense interest in crime among all sections of society is suspect. The don deep in his murder book, the millions rapt in sex stories of their Sabbath papers, the key place criminals hold in literature, films and television, whether vulgarized or intellectual, all attest that in some sense the criminal is hero of our times. Concurrently with this vicarious preoccupation, we are alarmed by the rise in actual crime. In our lives, not fantasies, the criminal has become the villain whose elimination can purify society. He has grown from the squalid, pitiful wretch he really is to be the fearful antagonist of an imaginary civil war. He is our black African to the Afrikaner: the man doubly feared because half-admired and felt subconsciously to be a part of us.

Why is anyone surprised crime flourishes in England? The spiritual forces of our country are traditional and not renewed: vestigial Christian and liberal, patriotic and humane — we have no dynamic faith. Our living, vital creed, expressed by politics, mass media and our own behaviour, is candidly material. The criminal is the arch-materialist, and we respect his logic as much as we reject his methods.

A crime-rate is the thermometer of a society's fevers. A rising prison population proves the danger is growing outside prisons as much as in them; and in the long run, crowded prisons assure the opposite of security and social health. In countries where there are more prisons there is more crime; and the "improvement" of prisons and prison conditions, unless society improves as well, does not affect the ratio.

It is just as rash to suppose that the more the police, the less the crime will be; and we must notice again that nations with police forces proportionally larger have greater crime problems than our own. Those who propose as sovereign remedy "more police" must recognize other dangerous possibilities. Policemen are bound to have some vested interest in the existence of crime, just as soldiers have in war, though each will deny this and perhaps not even know it. The stronger police forces become, the more their administrative acts will be directly judicial: the more they will feel "we are the law". The extreme instance of this is in authoritarian countries of all kinds, where the police force grows to be the nation's fourth estate — sometimes even its first.

Our chief fault is to treat our police as figures of myth. National vanity demands that they both get their man and remain knights in shining armour (or behave like that dishonestly silly stereotype of the television serial*). Our personal attitudes to them vary between sycophancy and fear, excessive adulation and resentment. This is not even to give police officers credit for being the serious professional men they are. Small wonder that in face of these fickle and foolish attitudes the police are uneasy about their "public image"; and if they present a contemptuous poker-face to the public one cannot blame them.

Nor should we blandly assume our justice is so superior to others' without direct experience of its operation, especially on the socially weak, nor without comparison with courts in other lands. The laws of a society at any moment are a rough approximation to whatever may be its inherited moral concepts. But because laws are passed more often than repealed, so that socially obsolete statutes may survive for centuries, and because these laws are enforced and interpreted by venerable judges whose social codes may be a half-century out of date, much of our criminal law is archaic and thus savage. So unless our purpose be to fill prisons for the sake of filling them, we should try to make sure that no one, in any decade, is made criminal by acts no longer deemed so in society as a whole. A lot of our thought about "suppressing crime" should be directed to eliminating laws wilfully creating it. I know men once convicted for gaming "crimes" now tardily made innocent by recent legislation; others among the thousands who, in 1961, are still gaoled for failure to pay debts they are least able to refund from prison; others again convicted for "loitering with intent", which charge, notoriously, can mean anything whatever.

* Editor's note: i.e. Dixon of Dock Green

My own belief is that a criminal tendency is never necessarily hereditary, though degeneracy can be, and although "criminal families" do exist in certain social contexts. Nor do I believe any man of any age, if not insane (and often even if he is), to be irredeemable. On the contrary, I believe criminal activity is an extension, in violent and precise form, of the criminal tendency in all society; and to have been chiefly created by conditions of life that society imposes on potential and actual criminals. So long as one thinks of criminals as being different in essence, as well as in fact, from anyone else, it will not be possible to understand their motivation or reduce their numbers.

These beliefs are derived from some knowledge of criminals and of social contexts in which they are most prone to exist; also from study of many "non-criminal" temperaments including, of course, my own. I have in my support the spiritual concepts of the Anarchists and of the Christians, as I understand them. Ranged against me — and firm in the belief that judgement and hell are for the world and not eternity — I have, I think, the majority of my countrymen, who see evil, always, as something in others, never in themselves; and who have not the informed imagination to perceive how hard it can be for those underprivileged, socially and intellectually, never to become involved in criminal deeds.

An interest in crime, such as we all manifestly possess, does not lead necessarily to thought about its origins, nature or the means of reducing it; and, as I have hinted, an obsessive interest may well indicate a hidden love. So I think the initial imperatives are to become conscious of our inner attitudes to crime and to learn more about it in a committed, yet objective spirit, much as we are gradually doing with mental illness.

At present the whole theme is wrapped in passion and obscurity. Judges make formidable pronouncements, as if they spoke as some kind of doctor, called a Diagnostician, who could assess sickness by indirect report, without ever having himself entered a hospital or even lanced a boil. The police and prison officers enfold their activities in mystery, and we encourage them to do so by default. Criminals see themselves praised in public fantasies and their real deeds more publicized than a statesman's. Moralists thunder about "juvenile delinquency" in terms that reveal they know as much of "juveniles", and of their social customs, as they do of delinquent Esquimaux. We listen to these violent voices, taking sides; but we attend less to the probation officers who could tell us how they try to stop men from being criminals or from returning to crime again. These officers are concerned with remedy, not punishment. But so hard and slow is their work — as growth itself is — that though they may act and speak in wise and practical terms, their conclusions are so tentative and conditional that they make no sensational appeal.

Like the earlier City of Spades, Mr Love and Justice *—the third and last of MacInnes's London novels — has a double focus. Frankie Love is a seaman who becomes a ponce; Edward Justice is a policeman. The novel switches from one viewpoint to the other as each pursues his opposite but complementary career until they finally come together.*

From *Mr Love and Justice*, 1960
MR LOVE

Frankie Love and the girl sat in a café (known to the local girls as "judge's chambers") waiting the arrival of the solicitor's clerk. "Now, I don't know," Frankie said, "why you want to mix *me* up in all your bits of trouble."

"Trouble? It's not trouble! Anyway, you're my friend, aren't you?"

"I'm your friend, yes, but until I get a ship or even a job I want to keep clear of law, and courts, and solicitors — the lot."

She laughed. "Oh, don't be so silly, Frankie! This isn't *trouble*! A soliciting charge? I've had dozens of them."

"Then what you want me here for?"

She looked at him seriously. "Well, Frank," she said, "this *is* a bit different as a matter of fact: it is a bit dodgy, and I felt the need of a pal around to give me courage."

"Courage to do what?"

"Well, I'm not pleading guilty this time for once."

"You usually do?"

"Always. In the first place I almost always *am*, in the second, what can you do with magistrates against copper's evidence? and in the third — well, if you plead not guilty it's a fiver instead of forty bob; or if the charge was hotted up to something worse, he might even send you to the Sessions."

"Who might? What Sessions?"

"The magistrate. And if he did the law would have a barrister, and juries just don't like whores — however often some of them have had a go with one of us."

"Why you taking a chance, then?"

"Well — just because I'm sick of it!"

"Of what?"

"I'll tell you. There's a young fellow — vice-squad copper — who's always asking me to take him home for free. Well, some of the girls do that — but I just won't: not if I don't *like* the feller, anyway. Last time he said, 'Do what I say, or else.' And this is the 'or else': he's bringing a charge."

"The bastard!" Frankie cried, genuinely revolted. "That's not right!"

"I don't think so either."

Frankie pondered. "But he'll get you all the same, from what you say."

The girl looked round the café and said gently, "Perhaps not, you know — it all depends on the date of the alleged offence the charge is for."

"How come?"

"Well, I've been having my whatsits this last week. With some of the girls that makes no difference — they just ram in some cotton wool and soldier on. But me, no, I'm particular: I stay at home those days — of which fact I've got witnesses."

"But, baby — he's not a mug. He won't bring a charge unless he saw you at it, will he?"

She stared at him, amused. "Boy, are you crazy? He wouldn't even bother to leave his desk! He'd make the charge blind. Against a known and convicted common prostitute? It's a pushover!"

"Unless you can prove...."

"That's it: an alibi."

"I see."

"You do? Smart boy! Here comes the shark from the solicitor's."

With a cheery wave and a cry of "How do, girl!" there now approached a tall, mackintoshed, somewhat lumbering young man with dark greased hair and a sharp but uncritical regard. He sat at their table, said, "How do?" to Frankie without asking who he was, and called out for a cup of tea and a cheese roll.

"Money, money," he said cheerfully, holding out his hand. "The old firm doesn't even move without a sub."

From the black bag the girl handed him some notes which he counted, folded each one of them singly, and stuffed them in a hip pocket, saying, "Ta very much, dear."

"It's we who keep your wife and kids for you," the girl told him.

"Don't I know it! And the magistrates! Have you ever thought of that? What wouldn't the courts cost the poor old taxpayers if it wasn't for all you girls and the thousands of forty bobs your little cases attract?"

"Let's talk business, son," the girl said. "We'll be on very soon."

He shifted his glasses on his nose and said, "Well, I know you girls *never* want to hear advice, which is all we're really useful for, however, mine is — let's get it over — please, dear, plead guilty."

"You know why I'm not."

"Oh, I do! And I understand your feelings! But do you *really* want to take the law on single-handed? Do just think a bit of the consequences!"

The girl frowned. "Not the law, stupid — only this one feller."

The clerk looked at her. "I'm surprised at you," he said. "Look! The law may have their internal wrangles and suspicions, and all be ready to shop one another if it means promotions. But to the outside world — and particularly, excuse me being frank, a girl like you — it's one for all and all for one, they live or hang together."

"I think he's right," said Frankie.

"You do? What do *you* know about it?" she cried.

Frankie got up. "I'll be seeing you," he said. "It's none of my business anyway."

She grabbed him by the seat of his slacks and yanked him down. "Don't go," she said. "I'm sorry — I'm wrought up. I always am a bit just after my monthlies."

There was a pause. Then the lawyer said, "Look, dear, there's another aspect. He might have brought this not to get his vengeance or anything like that, but just because he wanted a little birthday present."

"You think so?"

"Well, it's possible, isn't it? Vice-squad boy? Now, if that's so...I shouldn't tell you this, my gov'nor wouldn't like it...why don't you settle with him? After all; even if you plead guilty it's forty bob, and if you don't there's us to pay as well in addition to all that might happen up at the Sessions if he brought in a brothel-keeping charge or something."

"They take bribes?" said Frankie.

"Oh, don't be silly!" the girl answered.

The lawyer gave Frankie a rather puzzled look. "Well, naturally," he said. "Imagine yourself please, for a moment, in their position. Girls sitting on a gold-mine, you've got complete powers of arrest, and the courts believe your word, not theirs. Your wages are maybe twelve or so a week. What would *you* do?"

"I wouldn't bring false charges," Frankie said. "I don't say I'd be all that particular about everything, but I couldn't bring false charges."

The lawyer smiled slightly, and the girl was still silent. Then the lawyer said, "Would you like me to see this feller for you?"

"Isn't it too late?" she asked.

"Oh, to withdraw the charge, it is. But not how it's pressed... there's evidence and evidence, you know."

The girl, suddenly, slammed her bag on the Formica table. "You're all a bunch of sharks!" she cried. "I'll plead guilty — give me back my money!"

"Now, don't be silly," said the lawyer, his glasses almost falling off his nose in his surprise. "You've got me down here, and you've asked me my advice...."

"You'd better give it back," said Frankie.

The lawyer turned on Frankie Love, completely unimpressed. "Now *please*," he said. "Don't *you* join in."

The girl put her hand on Frankie's arm. "He's right, dear," she said. "I was a bit vexed, that's all" — and she got up.

"So you won't be needing me in there," the lawyer said, preparing to rise too. "If you're going to plead guilty it's best for you there's no defence forces whatever to be seen."

"I know," she said. "But stick around, will you, in case there are complications."

The lawyer nodded, and called for another tea and roll. Frankie said to her, "You want me to come with you?"

"Oh, no, dear. But mind this for me, will you? They don't like to see that we're not destitute in there." And she walked out leaving her bag beside Frankie on the table.

Gingerly, he put it on the seat beside him, the lawyer watching casually. Then Frankie said, "Apologies for speaking out of turn just now."

"Oh, quite okay! I know how you feel about all this."

"How *I* feel?"

"Well — yes," said the clerk, retreating slightly behind his spectacles and munching the second cheese roll. "I hope she'll not be long," he added. "It all depends where her name is on the list."

"You handle a lot of these cases?"

"Hundreds. And I mean hundreds. My guv'nor deals in vice business almost exclusively, and we're greatly in demand. And though everyone believes we're scoundrels (which of course we are — har-har), we do have our uses because, believe me, without a lawyer you're just a dead duck in advance. With us to help you, you only lose a leg or maybe, if you're fortunate, a few tail feathers."

"What: you work chiefly for these girls?"

"By no means! Very rarely, in fact — their cases are usually so simple. No. For the vice barons: the gaff landlords and the escort-businesses that handle call-girls and, of course ... " the lawyer dropped his eyes " ... the easy-money boys, the ponces."

"Those bastards."

The clerk looked up sharply. "Yes, those ones," he said.

Frankie Love had his hand resting on the girl's bag. Suddenly, the penny dropped.

"Here!" he cried. "You think *I'm* one? *Me?*"

"Well, son — aren't you?"

Frankie raised his fist and cried, "You dirty little lump of shit!"

The lawyer shot back his chair two feet without rising, looked quickly round the cafe and said, "Well, excuse me, *aren't* you?"

Frankie was impressed by the total sincerity of the lawyer's complete surprise. He lowered his fist and said, "Well, I'll be buggered! Do I look like one?"

The clerk carefully adjusted his seat and picked up his tea again. "Boy!" he said, "Who *does?* Just do me a favour, will you? Just attend the courts for a week and *look* at them. Except for the odd exception, they all look exactly ... well, like you and me or anyone at all."

Frankie laughed. "Well, I'll be fucked!" he said. "Just fancy that!"

"You use a lot of bad language, son," the lawyer said.

"Excuse me again: I didn't mean it."

The lawyer said, "Forgotten — excuse *me*, too." He paused. "What is your profession, then, if I might ask?"

"Seaman."

"Seaman. Got a ship?"

"No."

"Got some other job?"

"No. Not yet."

"Pardon this question: please don't take it amiss: you ever taken money from that girl?"

There was quite a wait, and for the first time in many years, Frankie blushed. "I *have* borrowed a few quid from her," he said.

"*Borrowed.*"

"That's what I told you."

"All right — all right. Don't hang me, sailor." The clerk stirred his cup thoughtfully, then said, "I'm going to tell you something if you want to hear it, but on two conditions. The first is you don't hit me, please. The second is you don't tell the girl because, after all, she's supposed to be my client. Do you agree?"

"Go on...."

"You seem a nice boy, and I think I ought to tell you. So here it is. If a vice copper saw you near the courts with a woman coming up on a soliciting charge, and waiting in a caff holding her bag while she went in, and he knew you'd had money from her, and he knew you'd got no job, he wouldn't *ask* you if you are a ponce, believe you me! He'd know you *were* one, and a bloody foolish one at that!"

Frankie Love looked at him steadily, then rose and said, "Thanks. Would you do something for me, please? Give her this bag. And tell her if she comes near me again I'll crunch her."

[...]

Like children (and most men), Frankie was attracted by what, for reasons of pride more than real inclination, he had rejected. The episode near the courts had left him speculating — naturally — on what, if he *had* been her ponce, the life would have been like: and as with so many of us, what we have speculated on at length becomes with time the thing we mean to do. A few weeks' reflection, too, had taught him that essentially the girl, by her oblique and crafty offer, hadn't really meant him any harm: her manoeuvre had in its way been flattering; and also — for Frankie was unusually free from self-delusion — had been one that, things being as they were, might as well be rationally considered.

The chief — in fact, the only real — reason against it all was that Frankie thought ponces were bums, and seamen princes. But suppose you were a prince without a throne? That it was criminal didn't worry him particularly, since Frankie's code of honour (which most certainly existed) at times coincided with, but at times departed completely from, those enshrined by any established sets of laws. For example: he wouldn't hesitate a second to wound a man — or even, if it came to that, to kill him — if it was to help a friend — a rare and real one. And as for the sexual aspect, this didn't worry him at all: because for Frankie, sex *was* love: and sexual attachment the only profound relationship with a woman that he considered possible. The money, of course, would be — well, obviously — useful. Like many seamen, Frankie wasn't greedy about money and only felt the urgent need of it for explosive blow-outs when ashore in port. On board — with food and a berth and working clothes — he felt no need of it at all and even forgot at times, completely, how much back pay the company might owe him. But to be *destitute*: and on land! That was a real horror, a most shameful and miserable misfortune.

So — all things considered — hadn't he been a fool to turn her down so finally and abruptly? Quite clearly, poncing would be dangerous...you'd need to find out a lot more about the tackle and ropes of *that*. As obviously, a great deal would depend on how far you could trust the woman; and — more to the point —dominate her. Because in Frankie's sharp and hard experience a woman, like a ship, was reliable only if you had her under strict and complete control.

Nevertheless: the sea, certainly, came first — and far away so — if it would have him back. No woman and no fortune would hold him from that great and utterly dependable she. So, filled with the determination of a wise and right decision, he spent an energetic day among the nautical layabouts of Wapping. But though he drank a very great deal — and they — no one, apparently, could fix anything or even make a practical suggestion. And as night fell he grew not just dejected and intoxicated, but — worst of all for a man whose mind and spirit waxed and waned in power with the strength of his animal energy — he grew spiteful, tired and angry. "Oh, well," he said, "anything rather than the Labour" — and he set off on foot to her address.

Repeated ringing brought no answer: till he became aware from the movement of a curtain that there was someone up there. He withdrew ostentatiously; returned and waited a whole hour in a nearby doorway (fortifying himself from a hip flask) and then, when another lodger entered, ran up and got his foot inside the door. This man (in fact, the landlord) vigorously protested, but Frankie simply lifted him up and placed him on one side, walked up the stairs, banged on the door, heard angry shouts, heaved against it several times and broke inside. The girl was standing by the table holding a breadknife, and her companion, a short, dark man, remained sitting watchfully beside his loaded plate.

"Get out!" the girl cried.

"Not me," said Frankie, " — him."

"You're drunk!" she shouted.

"Of course. Is he a customer? Tell him to go!"

"He's not. He's what *you* were too bloody high-and-mighty to want to be."

And now the man made a rush. Frankie was used to the Maltese, and didn't underestimate them at all. They're fast, fearless, and mean business, he knew. He raised a whole leg quickly and braced himself against the wall; the Malt ran into it and lost his knife. Unfortunately for him his shoes were off his feet, and Frankie (recalling an episode in Williamstown, Victoria) had gone for both of them with all his eleven stone while keeping a fraction of a weather eye on the girl and, more particularly, her breadknife. But she didn't use it or move, and the Maltese was in agony. Frankie kicked him again, ripped his slacks down by a swift tear at his belt (another Victorian expedient), then closed in, heaved him to the open door and literally "threw him down the stairs".

The girl ran out and cried, "Give him his coat here or he'll call the law!"

Frankie threw it down after him. "You want me call the law?" the Bengali landlord echoed.

"No, no — I'll see you straight: a fiver!" cried the girl.

The front door slammed on the Maltese. They went back in the room. "Well!" said the girl. "You *are* a lively boy!" He grabbed her and got to work ferociously.

An hour or so later they sorted themselves out and resumed the meal abandoned by the Malt. She was gazing at him with frank admiration and also (but perhaps he missed this) with a triumphant, proprietary glint. Downing his VP wine, he said to her, "Hand me that thing."

"My bag?"

"You heard."

She passed it over with a smile and he upended it. "Not much," he said.

"Others have been at it."

"Not any more."

"No? Hi! You're not going to be one of *those*, are you?" she cried as she saw him stuffing all the notes into his slacks pocket.

"One of what?"

"One who takes *every*thing."

"Why — is this all you've got?"

"Sure."

"Don't kid me!"

"Darling, why should I? You'll soon find out."

"Nothing hidden?"

"*Hidden*? Are you crazy? In this dump? My bag's the only safe place — it never leaves me."

He put it down. "Haven't you got any savings?" he asked her.

"*Savings*? Darling! What you take me for!"

"Well — we're going to change all that; we're going to save."

"Are we? Well, dear, I'm all for it — but it's going to be up to you."

"Okay. I'll see to it."

"Nice of you. Meantime, could I have a couple of quid for pin money? Only two...."

"Of course."

"*Thank* you. You *are* good to me!"

He kissed her and upset some crockery. She disentangled. "And will you tell me," she said, "just *how* you're going to save this money?"

"*How*? Put it in the bank."

"Oh, yes? The GPO? The Midland?"

"Well — why not?"

She looked at him. "Darling," she said, "I love you, but honest, you worry me, you've got a *lot* to learn."

"Well — teach me."

"Suppose you're nicked — just on suspicion. And they find you've got a bank account. What then?"

"I see."

"You do? Well, then. What next?"

"We'll put it in your name."

"Oh! So you trust me! Suppose I walk out on you?"

"You won't."

"Won't I? Dear, in this business you just *never* can tell."

She got up, picked up her chair and came round and sat beside him. "Listen," she said. "Let's get a few things straight. I love you, Frankie, but there'll be rows enough if I know you — and I know me — and there's some we can skip by right from the start avoiding misunderstandings."

He lit a fag. "Okay," he said. "I'm new on board. Please clue me up."

from *Mr Love and Justice*

MR JUSTICE

The Detective-sergeant had told Edward that "if anything at all big comes up" he was to inform him and not try to tackle it alone. "If you prove to be any good," his senior had added, "something certainly *will* turn up, because a good copper always attracts crime to himself. But don't forget — it's only with arrest that the real problem of our job begins. There's the prisoner to be dealt with for his statement and so on, and beyond that the whole machinery of the courts we've got to persuade." But Edward had vivid recollections of his disappointments when in uniformed days any discovery of his own produced, if reported, a host of seniors who did all the fancy work and took the credit. And knowing success is never blamed, he decided to chance his arm and handle the suspected brothel case alone.

Accordingly, and by appointment, he met the nark at the public-house in question: or rather the nark, as agreed, merely handed an empty glass at 10.15 p.m. (publican's time) to the individual he accused of being a pimp in order that Edward might be sure of his identity. That, so far as the nark was concerned, ended the proceedings; after this Edward was on his own.

The pimp, surprisingly, was little more than a teenager — twenty-one or two, Edward thought, and looking younger than his age. He was so surprised by the boy's appearance that against all professional etiquette he ventured a glance, in search of confirmation, at the nark — who very properly ignored it. The pimp, also, was a songster: for between his errands and still holding wallop-stained glasses in casual festoons, he'd pause at a microphone to nasally intone appalling Irish melodies much appreciated by the Celtic boozers who the farther they got from Erin's isle, adored it all the more.

At closing time, Edward lingered in the street carrying (a subtle touch, he thought) a quarter-filled can of paraffin whose purpose was that wherever he might be observed to loiter, the assumption would be he was visiting or coming from a neighbour to collect or supply this useful household fluid. At the back of his mind there was also the notion it might come in useful to hurl at somebody, if need be. For Edward was now learning what all young coppers do: that their job, at night, and even sometimes in the day, can be very dangerous. The only security he felt was that he was alone: always the safest situation for any probing, nocturnal prowler. This wisdom confirmed the Detective-sergeant's diagnosis that he was born to the purple of the CID: who've soon understood that the real reason why plain-clothes men are told to work, if possible, in pairs, is not for their own protection but that one can be the witness of an assault upon the other, and bring any vital messages home to base.

By now he was following a carolling party piloted by the pimp, the paraffin in his can playing lapping harmonies to their graceless melodies. The Cypriot café was not far off, and from its exterior Ted had no difficulty in observing they descended immediately to an invisible basement room. After a while of strolling and hesitation he entered, parked his paraffin tin, and ordered kebab and ladies' fingers. He ate these slowly and drank two Turkish coffees till he was the only surviving customer. Hints began to be dropped, even by the courteous Cypriots, that the time had come for him to be on his way. He therefore retreated to the road again, where he spent a tiresome, embarrassing hour of vigil.

But this delay served a purpose: his mounting irritation was now firmly concentrated on the drunks and gamblers in the cellar. Of course, he knew well — even recruit training had taught him that — you should always try to remain quite *impersonal* in your feelings about suspects, and not ever become too interested in them as individual human beings. On the other hand, a little spite and resentment would spice the eagerness to effect a capture. Edward was soon rewarded by the exaggeratedly cautious appearance of three Irishmen and the pimp. Observing (with recollections of the text-books) Alternative B, he "followed" them from in front assisted, like a blind man's guide-dog (who, after all, doesn't know either *where* he's going), by the sound of their lurching feet behind. Soon the feet stopped, and he looked cautiously back to identify the brothel.

This word (brothel) conjured up scandalous, alluring visions. What it in London in most cases consists of is a dilapidated house with several girls in rooms with minimal accessories. But even in this basic, utilitarian form it still has, on account of the ancient mystique of the word and its frankly anti-social purpose (and the curiosity and venom these variously attract), a certain faded glamour. But not to Edward Justice. Edward did not condemn prostitutes because they were "immoral"; he did so because they sought to destroy in the most flagrant possible way his own deep belief in love. He therefore approached the establishment with intense interest and disapproval.

Lights shone from curtained windows, but the place was otherwise discreet. He knocked and nothing happened. Then he went away, returned and gave — a happy bow at a venture — three short knocks and one long. A light came on in the hall, the door opened hiding the person behind it, then closed on Edward who found himself confronting a forty-ish man in jeans. "I don't think we've met," this person said.

"No. I'd like to see one of the girls."

"Busy, mister. What you got in that can?"

"Oh, that? It's for the wife."

"She know you're here?"

"Not likely."

"No. Well, there it is. You can call back, or if you like you can have a Maxwell House with me downstairs while you're waiting for a vacancy."

Edward accepted. The basement room was scented in a savagely "oriental" manner, and its furnishings were the Harrow road emporium's version of Ali Baba's cave. The stranger put on a kettle, then surprised Edward considerably by trying to give him an affectionate kiss. He preserved his calm, however. "You're one of those," he said, disengaging politely.

"One of the many," his host cried gaily. "We horrid creatures crop up *every*where!"

"So you don't cause jealousies among the girls."

"Oh, I wouldn't say *that*. After all, in a certain way they're very fond of me, and I'm very necessary to them, too."

"You own this place, then?"

"*Me?* Living in the basement? Silly! No — I'm their maid."

"A male maid, like."

"Check!" cried the male maid, pouring water on the Maxwell House. "And now," he continued, bringing the coffee over, "a question or two to *you*, please. Who sent you here?"

"The Cypriot boys."

"Which one?"

"Dark feller."

"Darling! *All* Cypriots are dark! Nicky, was it? Constantine?"

"Nicky, I think."

The male maid shook his head at Edward. "Naughty!" he said. "There *is* no Nicky."

"Well, mate, I don't know his bloody name but he just sent me."

Hand on a jeaned hip, the male maid eyed him. "Do you know what?" he said. "I think I've been a very, very stupid boy. I think you're quite probably a c-o-p."

"Who — me?"

"You, darling."

The male maid, darting like a gold-fish, had raced through the door, slamming it behind him, and as Edward jumped up he heard the sound from the backyard behind of an outside lavatory chain being vigorously pulled up and down like a ship's siren. By the time he got to the first floor there were signs of considerable movement. Edward banged on the nearest door whence a loud female voice bellowed at him to fuck off. The second door on the landing opened, and he was face to face with a squat woman of thoroughly unwelcoming demeanour who, blocking the whole doorway, said to him, "Let's see your warrant."

"Open that door there," said Edward.

"Listen, young man. Show me your warrant or else hop it. If you don't, I'm on the blower to Detective-constable you-know-who."

"*Who?*"

"Who will *not* be pleased you've come here pissing in his garden."

"What you mean?"

"Son, I'm beginning to think you're stupid. What you suppose I pay twenty a week for to you people? Get going, now. And sort it all out with your own mates: they'll tell you."

By now doors had opened, figures appeared, and several very truculent males had gathered at strategic points on stairways. Silence fell a moment, and everybody watched. Edward had never felt so solitary in his life.

"You 'll hear more of this," he said, and walked downstairs. There were shouts of laughter and crude cries of abuse.

By the door, the male maid handed him his paraffin tin. Bursting with rage, Edward knocked it out of his hand, grabbed him and manhandled him out into the street. "I'm being *arrested*!" cried the male maid. "First time in *years*. A thrill!"

As he marched his capture up the dark and empty roads, Edward recalled as best he could in his emotion all the golden rules of an arrest: for this, though far from being his first, was his first one in the expert CID. He longed to get at his black note-book, for facts noted down in this, he knew, had a magical effect on juries and even magistrates. An officer, by law, can produce his note-book when in court and consult it (for matters of *fact* alone, of course) when in the witness-box. The conception that these factual jottings may be fantasies or added long after their supposedly immediate inscription — or that the defendant, too, might be permitted to produce a similar jury-impressing book — does not seem to have occurred to legislators. Edward knew all this: but to him the black book was the reassuring symbol of his office: and he liked to enhance the tenuous reality of the confusing happenings of fact by giving them, as soon as possible, this inscribed, oracular dimension.

But how do you get at your note-book if you're frog-marching a delightfully wriggling suspect in the dark? The more Edward thought of the whole episode the less he liked it. On a sudden decision he stopped at a corner, let the male maid go and said, "All right — I'm turning you loose. Now skip!"

"Oh, *are* you!" said the maid, rubbing his skinny arms.

"Hop it now," said Edward.

The male maid stood his ground and cried, "Copper, I *refuse* to be released."

Edward had not quite expected this. "Oh?" he said, as nastily as possible.

"Look, big boy," the atrocious male maid answered. "You've messed things up for us tonight, and I'm going to mess up a thing or two for you."

As to his next move, Edward didn't hesitate. He hit the male maid very hard in the face, and turned and walked away. When he paused after several hundred yards to make some notes of the occurrence (and of others) in his book, he was dismayed to see the maid still following at a distance. He hurried on; and reaching the highway, by the expedient of showing his card to a uniformed man and of declaring the male maid had urinated in a public place, he shook him off and returned (determined to say nothing of all this) to the station.

Immediately on arrival, he was sent for by the Detective-sergeant. This officer, more in exasperation than in anger, blew him up. "You'd like to know," he said to Edward, "what you've done wrong. Well, I'll tell you: everything."

"Sir?"

"First and foremost — and even *you* should know this, constable — you don't tackle *any* case — any case at all — without prior notification and permission unless, of course, it comes upon you suddenly like a smash-and-grab or something."

"Yes, sir."

"This is a *Force*," the officer said. "Not a collection of Robin Hoods."

"No, sir."

"Next. If you want to enter a house without a warrant, I've no objection: these little matters can usually be ironed out and brothels, of course, don't expect you to have one anyway. But *please* don't enter any house at all without first checking if your colleagues happen to know much more about it already than you ever will. Particularly, constable, any suspect premises we've decided to let stay open for our own particular purposes."

"I'm sorry, sir, I don't...."

"I expect not. Look! That gaff, as gaffs up this way go, is perfectly well conducted and a very useful place indeed to pick up *real* suspects in: the sort of criminal you *should* be interested in."

"I see, sir."

"You see!"

"I suppose, sir," Edward said cautiously, "the woman phoned you...or someone."

"Oh — brilliant! Let me tell you something, son. That good woman you upset is much more useful to the Force at present by her information than *you* look like shaping up to be."

"Yes, sir."

"And now you've crashed in there like a cow in a china-shop, what use is she going to be to us? Eh? Answer me that! Or *ask* me before you do these things. That's what I'm here for: come and ask me!"

"But, sir," said Edward full of contrition, "brothels *are* often raided, aren't they? Brothel-keeping cases *do* come up...."

"Naturally, boy! But do use your loaf! You only raid the place when any advantages it may have to the Force are *less* than the prestige of a cast-iron brothel-keeping case. If vice has got to flourish, it had better flourish underneath our eyes until we're ready to clamp down on it."

"Yes, sir."

The Detective-sergeant lit his pipe. "You'll soon see how it is," he said. "Sometimes, of course, the order comes to us from on high, and then we close the place up anyway. Or maybe the Madam forgets her place and fails to be co-operative. Or maybe there's a change of personnel here at the station and somebody new in charge just doesn't like her face. Those vice hustlers know all that, and so do we: the whole thing's perfectly well understood. Except, of course, by idiots like you."

"Yes, sir."

A constable entered, saluted and said, "There's a poof

downstairs, sir, wants to bring an assault charge."

"Against who?"

The constable looked at Edward.

"Oh, no!" the Detective-sergeant cried. Then, to the constable, "Throw him out."

"He's very persistent, sir. He says if we won't wear it here he'll take it to another station."

"*Does* he?" the Detective-sergeant said, an ominous glint appearing in his clouded eyes. "Just wheel him in, constable, will you?" He then turned to Edward. "You've broken," he said, "the first rule of the business: which is to make an arrest, and fail to bring a charge and make it stick."

Edward said meekly, "Can't we just charge him, sir, with being a queer?"

The Detective-sergeant didn't even bother to answer. The male maid appeared and the uniformed constable withdrew. The Detective-sergeant got up, punched the male maid five or six times very hard in an extremely dispassionate manner in the stomach, then threw him across a chair and said, "I know you're a masochist and enjoy it, but don't provoke me or there might be an accident. Now, listen. What happened down at your place tonight just didn't happen. Do you understand? If I hear a squeak out of you, or anybody, I'm taking *you* in *not* on a vice charge which I know you wouldn't mind, but on a charge of robbing a client there and, believe me, everything will be present and correct: witnesses and stolen goods, your own sworn statement — the whole lot. You poofs have a high time in the nick, three in a cell, as we all well know. But this wouldn't be months I'd get you, sonny, it'd be years. And think of it, you might grow old and grey and unattractive, specially if I dropped a hint about you to the screws. So. Just apologize to my officer for all the trouble you've caused everyone, withdraw your charge as you pass the desk on your way out, and get back to bed again with your current husband."

The male maid left in silence: though not without a yearning, reproachful glance at Edward.

Then the Detective-sergeant said: "Now you, son. Please understand: I can't have anything more like this from you, either. You've got to improve your performance quite a bit or I'll lose my patience with you."

"Yes, sir."

"All right. Fuck off home."

Edward stood at attention in salute, but hesitated before moving off. "Well?" said the Detective-sergeant.

"Sir: it's just a question, sir, of procedure. This hitting them. I know the rule is you never do. But could you tell me please, sir, when you *can* do?"

A cracked smile appeared on the Detective-sergeant's life-battered countenance.

"Well, son," he said, "number one, in public, never. The citizens don't like it. Also, they don't believe we *do* it. Of course, if you're quite obviously attacked it's another matter."

"Yes, sir. And in here?"

The Detective-sergeant rose and said, "Well, constable, that depends. Personally, I don't happen to be a sadist and never do it unless it's clearly necessary to get certain results. Others do, I know, just for the heck of it: but not me."

"No, sir."

"If you *do* do it," the officer continued, "the first thing to remember is not to mark them: not to hit them where it shows next day in daylight. Never forget: they've got to be produced in court in twenty-four hours — or forty-eight, of course, if the day of arrest happens to be a Saturday."

"And if you *do* happen to mark them, sir?"

"You say they went berserk and had to be restrained. Of course, you know — sometimes they do: I could show you a scar or two to prove it."

"But, sir. If you bash them — don't they tell the magistrate?"

"Sometimes....It has been known....I've not met with one magistrate yet, though, who's believed it.... Or even if they do, well, so long as they think the charge you've made against the prisoner's quite authentic it doesn't seem to worry them unduly.... As for juries, if a prisoner pleads violence or a forced confession, in my experience all it does is tell against him in the verdict."

"I see, sir."

"Don't *rely* on that, though, constable. There's no point at all in using force just for the sake of it, unless it serves a purpose. Because — and you might as well remember this if you possibly can — your real battle isn't with the criminal but with the courts. It's only *there* that you can get him his conviction. You've got counsel up against you, and solicitors, and the witnesses for the defence, and juries and magistrates and judges — and the press, please don't forget *those* little parasites. They've all got to be defeated or convinced before your man gets his complimentary ticket for a seat in Brixton."

"I'll remember, sir."

"I do hope so. In the Force, constable, the greatest asset that a man can have, in my opinion, isn't all the ones you read so much about but purely and simply a sense of *order*; of thoroughly methodical procedure. If you train yourself to be methodical and avoid confusion like the plague, then you may end up Chief Constable — just think of that! Not, on your present showing, that it's very likely," he added, turning out the light and opening the office door.

from *Mr Love and Justice*

Examining the area, Edward liked it. There is about Kilburn a sort of faded respectability, of self-righteous drabness, that appealed to him. For the true copper's dominant characteristic, if the truth be known, is neither those daring nor vicious qualities that are sometimes attributed to him by friend or enemy, but an ingrained conservatism, an almost desperate love of the conventional. It is untidiness, disorder, the unusual, that a copper disapproves of most of all: far more, even, than of crime, which is merely a professional matter. Hence his profound dislike of people loitering in streets, dressing extravagantly, speaking with exotic accents, being strange, weak, eccentric or simply any rare minority — of their doing, in short, anything that cannot be safely predicted.

So Kilburn was reassuring: but on the other hand it had something else that equally appealed to Edward which was that, although proper, it was also in an indefinable way equivocal. As you walked through its same and peeling (though un-slummy) streets, the façades of the houses hinted, somehow, that all was not as it seemed behind those faded doors and walls. This strait-laced seediness, this primped-up exterior behind which lurks something dubious and occasionally horrifying, is the chief feature of whole chunks of mid-twentieth-century London — as, indeed, of many of its inhabitants: the particular English mixture of lunacy and violence flourishing inside persons, and a decor, of impeccable lower-middle-class sedateness. This atmosphere appealed to Edward who, like all coppers, shunned clear pools (and even turbulent torrents) and preferred those whose surface, though quite still, could easily be stirred up into muddy little whirlpools. For if the copper is a worshipper of the conventional (so far as the world at large outside him is concerned), he is also in his inner person (being the arch empiricist) something of an anarchist: a lover of stress and strain and conflict, wherein he himself may operate behind that outward, visible order he admires.

from *Mr Love and Justice*

Stepney, in early morning, has a macabre, poetic beauty. It is one of those areas of London that is thoroughly confused about itself, being in transition from various ancient states of being to new ones it is still busy searching for. The City, which still preserves its Roman quality of ending very abruptly at its ancient gates, towers beyond Aldgate pump, then stops: so that gruesome Venetian financial palaces abut on to semi-slums. From the dowdy baroque of Liverpool Street station, smoke and thunder fall on Spitalfields market with its vigorous dawn life and odour of veg, fruit and flowers — like blended essences of the citizens' duties, delights and fantasies. Below the windowless brick warehouses of the Port of London Authority, the road life of Wentworth Street — almost unknown elsewhere in London where roads are considered means by which you move from place to place, not places in themselves

— bubbles, overspills and sways in argument and shrill persuasion, to the off-stage squawks of thousands of slaughtered chickens. Old Montague Street with its doorless shops that open outward into the narrow thoroughfare, and its discreet, secretive synagogues, has still the flavour of a semi-voluntary ghetto. Further south, in Commercial Road, are the nocturnal vice caffs that members of parliament and of Royal commissions are wont to visit, invariably accompanied by a detective-inspector to ensure that their expedition will reveal nothing characteristic of the area; and which, when suppressed, pop up again immediately elsewhere or under different names with different men of straw at the identical old address. In Cable Street, below, the castaways from Africa and the Caribbean perform a perpetual, melancholy, wryly humorous ballet of which they are themselves the only audience. Amid incredible slums — which, one may imagine, with the huge new blocks replacing them, are preserved there by authority to demonstrate the contrast of before-and-after — are pieces of railway architecture of grimly sombre grandeur. Then come the docks with masts and funnels strangely emerging above chimney-tops, and house-locked basins, the entry to which by narrow canals and swinging bridges seems, to the landsman, an impossibility, were it not for the cargo boats nestling snugly between the derelict tenements. Suddenly, beyond this, you come upon the river: which this far down, lined with wharves and cranes and bearing great ocean-loving steamers, is no longer the pretty, grubby playground of the higher reaches but already, by now, the sea.

A great charm of the area is that only here, in one sense, is London really a capital city at all. For what, elsewhere in the world, distinguishes capitals from their bleak provincial brethren is that they're open for business all night, and for seven days in the week. Thanks to the markets, seamen, and Commonwealth minorities, in Stepney you can eat and drink, as well as other things, at any hour you choose to; and thanks to the alternation of the Jewish sabbath with the Gentile, the shops and markets never close. All that remains astonishing, since this is England, about this delightful state of affairs is that no one has yet managed to suppress it....

...As he walked through Stepney, [Frankie] passed by the all-night caffs that cater for the exhibitionist dregs of the vice trade and where, in the morning, a few survivors from the last night's market-place remained: either disappointed hustlers of both sexes who'd returned from various squalid set-ups whither their earlier imaginings had lured them not to complain (for this was useless: and who to complain to?), but as the beast returns from the smaller, empty water-hole to the larger. Among them was a sprinkling of the different, morning clientele: lorry-drivers, local workers and a few from the West of the city who'd visited the gamble-houses and called in for breakfast to count (mentally) their losses or more unlikely gains. It is at this hour, when someone sleepy is sweeping out among this driftwood, and not in the hopeful afternoon or the intoxicated evening, that moralists should paint their portraits of Gin Lane.

from *Mr Love and Justice*

The attraction of wrestling is not so much the sport itself (if it be one), as in the survivals it enshrines of ancient customs. If anyone wants to know what an old Music Hall audience was like (when gallery boys hurled pease puddings and pigs' trotters over the cowering heads of the grilled-in musicians on to the performers), or going back a bit, what a bear-baiting public may have resembled, or further still, the spectators of a gladiatorial show — he may probably capture some of their atmospheres at a wrestling match. The audience, indeed, are much more arresting than the fighters: the faces of mild respectable men in business suits are twisted into vicious snarls; those of women, shrieking violent obscenities, wear masks of gloating ferocious glee. The bouts themselves seem to fall into two categories: comparatively straight matches of incomparable boredom in which huge hunks of living meat lie locked in painful and contorted postures; and then the "villain-and-hero" bouts, sorts of popular moralities, wherein one wrestler becomes, presumably by pre-arrangement, St George, and the other (usually the more polished performer) the odious dragon. It is a tribute to the artistry of these thespian practitioners of grunt-and-groan that though all but the dimmest-witted of the audience know the performance is a fake — or, one might say, an allegory — they accept the convention of this Jack-the-Giant-killer world entirely. So that when Jack, attacked basely from the rear by the treacherous giant who just a second ago was pleading on his quavering knees for mercy, outwits the monster and hurls him four feet high and six feet wide with a resounding crash on to the groaning mat, the audience yells the applause that may have greeted David as he returned from his encounter with Goliath.

Among the spectators of the bout between Boris the Bulgar and the Tasmanian Devil were Frank and his girl, now reconciled and firmly reunited and comfortably ensconced in ringside seats; and also among those present in ringsides likewise (complimentaries, in this case) were the newly installed tenants of their Kilburn flat, Edward and his beloved woman. Surrounding them was a cross-section of that part of the London populace which is rarely to be seen elsewhere (except at race meetings, certain East and South London pubs, and courts and jails), and whose chief characteristics are their uninhibited violence, their heartless bonhomie, and their total rejection alike of the left-ish Welfare State and the right-ish Property-owning democracy: a sort of Jacobean underground movement in the age of planned respectability from cradle to grave.

Up in the ring it was Boris the Bulgar (need one say?) who was cast for the role of villain. He was short, squat, bald and lithe, and probably hailed from Canning Town or Newington Butts. His face, if such one could call it, wore a built-in scowl when all was in his favour, a contortion of dreadful agony when his opponent secured a grip, and a look of abject ignominy when fortune momentarily failed to smile upon him. With the referee (a huge, sandy, mild-eyed man of tough but exquisite manners) he was on the worst of terms, perpetually disputing his decisions; and with the crowd even more so for he hurled back, in reply to their hoots and screams, base insults by voice and scandalous gesture. What a contrast was the Tasmanian Devil! A large, sad, slow-moving man whose whole bent, bruised body suggested a life of unjust suffering dedicated, much more in sorrow than in anger, to a resigned forgiveness of the world's worst treacheries and wrongs. How often did the Devil not break away, voluntarily, and release his victim from an impossible posture, chivalrously to show that even an animal so base must be given yet another chance! How obedient he was to the least remonstrance of the wise and patient referee! And how earnestly he looked up at the audience, apologizing with a wry smile for any faulty manoeuvre that had caused him untold agonies at the Bulgar's hands, shrugging sadly his red and massive shoulders at some outrageous piece of wickedness of his adversary, and occasionally, the fierce light of battle appearing in his brow-locked eyes, appealing to the masses as he held the atrocious Bulgar at his mercy for *their* impartial judgment (free from the prejudices that momentarily marred his own) to decide the exact nature of Boris's so richly merited fate.

This sealed, between contests and amid the patrons' recapitulative buzz, Edward's girl squeezed his hand and moved her hips even closer to his off-duty gaberdine. But Edward was staring into space. "It ought to be suppressed," he said.

"What ought, dear?" she said, surprised.

"All this," said Edward, frowning. "It's a disgrace."

"But I thought you liked it."

He looked round at her. "Oh, yes, well, I do: I mean the fight. But it's the audience I'm speaking of. I've seen more wanted men in here this evening than any day in the line-up. *And* flashing their money about — somebody's money, anyway."

"They've got to go somewhere..." she suggested.

"I know where they all ought to go...."

She squeezed him again. "Well, don't complain too much," she said. "You're doing a bit better yourself since you got your danger money."

"Mustn't talk shop here, dear," he said softly.

"Oh, I'm sorry. I liked the Tasmanian one, Edward. I think he was sexy."

"That hunk of meat? Well, that's what the whole thing's meant for, I suppose. I notice there's nearly as many women here as men...."

"Oh, yes, we love it! Those big men tied in knots!"

"Lovers' knots."

"Oh, Ted! You can be so crude!"

A stir in the audience, and the incomprehensible barking from the man in a hired tuxedo at the mike, both heralded the next pair of warriors. Frankie looked round expectantly, but his girl chewed her cashew nuts in silence. "Stay for this one, babe," he said.

"Okay, Frankie, if you say so, but never again. It's such a drag."

"This will be better: younger fellers, more your type."

"No wrestler's my type. They all look like blown-up balloons. Me, I like lean men."

"Skinny like me?"

"You're not skinny — not since you've been with me, anyway."

"Not in here, darling. Watch what you say...."

"'Been with me'. What's wrong with that? And, Frankie, just look at the audience! All those old bitches: I bet they've not had a man in years — apart from hubby."

"What's wrong with hubby? Look! Here they both come — young kiddies, like I said."

"Yeah?" The girl scanned them casually. "I'll wait till they get their gowns off," she said, "before I pronounce judgment."

"It'll be a real fight," said Frankie. "There's nothing to beat a fight between two young men, provided they're reasonably matched."

"You think they will be — in a place like this? Listen, Frankie. There's only one kind of fight I like, and that's with you on a six-foot divan."

"This'll give you an appetite," said Frankie.

By the unexacting standards of the grunt-and-groan game, the fight seemed to be a fair one. At any rate, plenty of things happened that surely no one could possibly have predetermined or predicted. When the two men bounced individually off the ropes to gain momentum, they collided and knocked each other out (apparently). At one moment a wrestler was sitting *on* the other's head, though this man was standing, and contrived to remain there for at least forty seconds. And at another, when one man staggered in dazed pain this may have been simulated, but hardly the sudden gesture of concern with which the man who'd hurt him ran up and stroked his arm. As the fight developed, two distinct personalities emerged. One fighter would attack sharply, and even when his hold seemed powerful and secure he'd break away abruptly, of his own accord, to mount a different, unexpected hostile manoeuvre. The other, in sharp comparison with the two earlier wrestlers whose expressions in combat had been perpetually bestial, wore a certain grace and freedom in the savagery of his face. When they were locked tight it was often quite impossible to tell, at moments, who was who and which limbs belonged to which: though the different-coloured shorts they wore were something of an indication. The nicest thing about them both — and professionally the most convincing — was their apparent indifference to the audience around them to whom they paid little or no court, entirely intent on battle. The bout, which lasted (most unusual in wrestling) all its rounds, seemed inconclusive, although the referee did raise one tired arm: by the audience this was of course disputed, but rather languidly, as the fight had been too good for them to enjoy it.

At the interval most patrons went out in the long bars for some solid boozing. Criminal aristocrats, all wearing hats (they looked as if they wore them in their baths, beds and tombs), stood in little squares to talk so that there was no direction from which a stranger might approach the party unobserved. Women of hideous splendour — looking like actresses in a banned play who'd strayed outside the pass-door a moment — stood absolutely motionless with a gin glass, ignoring their escorts and ignored by them. The wrestlers of the earlier bout appeared in mufti, but betrayed by squashed ears and colossal shoulders, to have a quick one and talk contracts with alarming men who never blinked and spoke with a fraction of their mouths in voices inaudible from more than eighteen inches.

Frankie and Edward glanced at each other, their eyes locked, held for a second then fell away. Then each, as men do to assess a man, looked at the other's woman, and across both their faces there passed a flicker of slight disdain.

from "A Kind of Religion"

Spectator, February 1963

I published some years ago a novel called *Mr Love & Justice*. Superficially, this is a realistic portrait of the worlds of the police and prostitution, and as such it was kindly acclaimed by not very acute reviewers for its factual actuality. But my true intention was to write a morality, or religious allegory. Frankie Love, the professional ponce "lover", has no understanding of love, which he mistakes for mere sexuality; but he does have a profound sense of justice, and this very virtue brings about his material, if not spiritual, ruin. Edward Justice, the copper and professional upholder of the law, has no sense of justice, which he equates with power; but he does possess a deep instinct for spiritual (as well as sexual) love, and this, too, encompasses his material destruction. Each man, in his acts, betrays his supposed conventional virtue, and is in turn betrayed into a fall that brings truth and understanding by the real virtue of which he is unaware.

The final scene of this novel takes place in a hospital, where both men lie wounded, and where each man finally becomes, as the result of his material fall and inner illumination, identical with the other. (Hence the title *Mr Love & Justice*, and not "Mr Love & Mr Justice", which several benevolent critics said it should have been.) I had hoped this hospital scene would be read in two ways, on two levels: both as what it is, realistically, and also as an allegory of purgatory. If read in the latter sense, the "nurses", "doctors" and invisible "specialists" take on another meaning and dimension. I planted clues all over the place, and particularly in the final paragraph, when the word "God" is used for the first and only time in the whole book.

That everyone (so far as I know) entirely missed the point of my endeavour may prove artistic incompetence, or perhaps that the religious instinct I thought I possessed was unconvincing; yet it may also be that the kind of person who happens to like what I write (or what he thinks I do) cannot imagine that a "serious" writer, yet one not overtly adhering to any denominational faith, would ever be compelled by a religious theme at all.

To try to situate the religious element which I conceive exists in myself and in others of my countrymen (but which the orthodox would doubtless consider not religious at all or, at best, heretical), may I beg indulgence for a further autobiographical fragment.

I was reared by an unbaptized mother, and have myself never been baptized. The only tangential religious instruction I received was at a Presbyterian school, where my admiration for the goodness of many of my teachers was matched by the horror I felt at their theology, once I grew to understand it. I passed through the usual phase of adolescent religiosity and then, after much reading — Marx, Freud and about older rival faiths, for instance — and considerable inquiry among believers of various sects, arrived at a total doubt about historical religions which still remains with me; yet something which I take to be religious also remains.

Before trying to define this, may I please make it clear I do not wish to give offence, do not presume to be "right", nor do I, of course, wish to suggest I am a "good" person at all. So: a personal God, an identifiable devil, miracles (including an immaculate conception) and any kind of physical after-life are to me not only incredible but paltry concepts. What remains?

On a radio interview not long ago with Norman Mailer (who, in contrast to the popular and partly self-created notion of him as a roaring boy and intellectual hipster, I take in fact to be an almost rabbinical moralist), the conversation turned chiefly on the concept of God. According to Mailer, God is not omnipotent, but dependent on us as we on Him. Satan was not thrown down from heaven — he tore himself out of it by the force of his own evil, and God could not prevent this. The whole universe — as each human life — consists of a creative and a destructive force. The meaning of our lives is to add to the positive, and repel the negative. In so far as we do so, we survive eternally in essence. If sufficient of us fail, we help drag the whole cosmos into destruction, and all life, physical and spiritual, comes to its end.

This concept (which is no doubt an ancient heresy, refuted by many a skilled theologian — not to mention by atrocious "religious" wars) has reality for me. It explains a lot of things which, in conventional theology (and despite every twist of sophisticated logic, or the armature of an unquestioning faith), remain otherwise inexplicable. It explains why God is both omnipotent and powerless, why evil and cruelty must exist as well as good and kindness, and it explains, most pertinently of all, the imperative necessity for a constant personal choice. To act well or ill is no longer a mere matter of individual salvation, nor of pleasing God: to act well or ill involves the very existence of God, mankind, the whole firmament.

I think anyone with a feeling of this kind may have a great awareness, and acceptance, of the laws of life that come directly and observably from nature, and yet will constantly be conscious of an *otherness*, of a reality both in and outside all our lives, in function of which he also lives even if, by his deeds, he may deny it. This "otherness" I can best define as a perpetual sensation that life exists in ways the brain and even imagination cannot apprehend — but of which a powerfully intuitive instinct (which I expect is what the orthodox mean by "soul") is constantly aware despite itself, and by no act of conscious volition. Accompanying this, will be a compelling sensation that the forces of good and of creation, and evil and destruction — impersonal, eternal, locked in perpetual battle — exist in everyone and thing, and even as potent essences in themselves that cannot entirely be identified nor defined by the evidence of their effects on mankind or nature.

Persons who feel all this will not be religious, like the churchman, by any hope of a reward, but simply by necessity: for the invisible life seems as inescapably real to them as does the life their five senses know in nature — and no one expects rewards for recognizing natural fact. Nor, for such persons, is this any matter of "belief" at all. To me, this very word is suspect, since it implies blind effort of a desperate will. I would rather say, not that I "believe" these things, but that after forty-eight years of thinking, reading and then questioning, then to such as I am, the concept is so real as to impose itself, and thus be beyond belief...

PART II

Life and Times

from "Born and Bred: Cultural Clans"

The Times Educational Supplement January 1975 (*Out of the Way*)

The reader may care to hear a personal account of one of these [cultural] clans, since it happens that, on my maternal side, I am a distant descendant of one of them. I would preface these notes by saying that this "dynasty", though peculiar, is not one of the most eminent; also that such is, by now, the genetic mix, I can lay no claim to any personal distinction on account of this connexion. I would add that my paternal ancestors who, with one exception, achieved no artistic fame, are far more sympathetic to me personally.

The Rev. George Browne Macdonald (1805-68), a Wesleyan minister of Highland descent, married a Welshwoman, four of whose daughters took as husbands, or became mothers of, men of unusual distinction. Thus, Georgiana (my own great-grandmother) married the painter Edward Burne-Jones; Agnes married Edward Poynter, later President of the Royal Academy and director of the National Gallery; while Alice, marrying the scholar John Lockwood Kipling, became the mother of Rudyard; and Louisa, marrying the politician-ironmaster Alfred Baldwin, became the mother of Stanley.

While the names just mentioned are those whose entries in the *DNB* are the most extensive, many others of note occurred in subsequent generations; either as direct descendants, or as relations by marriage. A cousin and I once tried to write down all the names we knew of relatives who had published books (of whatever merit), and gave up when we reached double numbers. Even in my own small family of father, mother and two sons, all have published volumes, the total number of titles (the reader will be horrified to hear) running into scores.

With the exception of infant memories of my great-grandmother, I did not, of course, know any of the "founding daughters", but as a lad I did encounter some members of the second generation and, of course, those of the third (my mother's) and of my own. These varied considerably in character and personality, and yet seemed to share certain traits which I shall try to define, as being possibly indicative of the kind of persons a "cultural dynasty" creates.

To start with their defects (the characteristic in relatives it is more pleasing to dwell on): I would say that they had, to a man and woman, an excellent opinion of themselves. I do not mean that they were haughty, nor that they felt this right to self-congratulation was not one that everyone must earn. Yet though affable enough, and tolerant of individual foibles, one felt very much on one's mettle when in their company.

They were not particularly loving people. Since, almost without exception, their marriages were devoted, and they made a great fuss over little children, this may seem a mean and unkind stricture. Yet I must adhere to it, for their love seemed, however intense, to be rather chill and demanding. And, indeed, anyone who recalls Rudyard Kipling's boyhood martyrdom, when he was boarded out with strangers at Southsea, must have wondered how his so-loving mother and aunts could have permitted this.

Though tolerant when their sympathies were engaged, they were not at all of whatever was not dear to them. Now really to be tolerant, surely, is to accept that a great many persons and peoples exist whose ways of life are quite different from one's own, and yet who are as entitled to these life-styles as is anyone. Yet in this sense, despite the real depth of their chosen culture, I think there was something almost provincial about them.

As to their virtues, perhaps their chief one was a real, total and quite unquestioning respect for art and learning. For them, art and scholarship were never a sort of icing on the cultural cake, but the very substance of it; and quite instinctively they regarded being an artist, or a scholar, as an activity quite as normal as most people would those of being a trader or industrialist.

They were too sagacious (and of too recently humble origin) to regard money as dross, and yet they did have a genuine lack of respect for it. Of course, they would despise a wastrel or a spendthrift; yet while they had no snobbish contempt for commerce, they did not regard making money as in any way meritorious. Thus, they were not in the least impressed by the rich (unless they had other personal qualities), and had no contempt whatever for anyone who, provided he had a genuine activity, was a "failure" in purely wordly terms.

In this connexion, it is clear that the Rev. George Browne Macdonald set the tone from the very start. For when Edward Burne-Jones, then a young painter quite unknown, and of no resources but his talent, asked for their Georgiana's hand, her father's three questions to her were if his health was good, if he was a worker, and whether she was sure he loved her (asked in that order). When she said yes to all three, her lover was instantly trusted, and no questions were asked of her or him as to his "prospects" or "position".

A third virtue I think they all possessed — though it is one less regarded now than then — is that they were immensely patriotic; and by this I mean simply their being utterly devoted to England, and solicitous about its honour. As to "patriotism" of the ignoble kind, their attitude can best be illustrated by the action of my great-grandmother on the occasion of our final victory in the Boer War; when, a widow living alone in a Sussex village, she hung out a banner embroidered "We have killed and also taken possession". (She was rescued from the villagers' ire by her much embarrassed nephew and neighbour, Rudyard.)

I do not know if descendants of other cultural clans who belong to my own generation would share this view, but my own feeling about the particular one I know is one of great respect and admiration, equally mingled with alarm and a mild revulsion. For if they were inspiring people, they were also appallingly demanding. They were, in fact the sort of family that one would perhaps rather read about than belong to, and since, as I have said, my father's family (though odd enough, too, in its way) was not one of that kind of distinction, I can at least console myself with not being, as are some heirs presumptive that I know of, descended on both their mother's and father's sides from *two* such alarming cultural dynasties....

"A Pre-Raphaelite Memory"

Spectator, October 1963 (*Out of the Way*)

The Kensington house in which my grandparents lived until their deaths after the last war was one of those bleak, inconvenient neo-Roman piles that still encumber the Royal Borough. It is true it had a double frontage, so that there were large rooms on either side of the central corridor, and a grubby square of back garden that somewhat relieved its gloom. But its rooms were all too high for their width, its staircase too narrow for two persons to pass by, and its plumbing recalled that of a provincial railway hotel.

Inside, however, it was thoroughly remarkable, and not least because of the unusual temperaments of my grandparents themselves. J. W. Mackail, my grandfather, had been born a son of the manse in Ayrshire, had found his way via Gottingen to Balliol, and eventually became a classical scholar of repute, a Professor of Poetry at Oxford, and a holder of the Order of Merit. In his younger days he was a disciple of William Morris — whose earliest biographer he also was — and thus came to frequent The Grange, North End Road, Fulham, the home of Morris's closest and life-long friend, the painter Edward Burne-Jones. There he encountered, and fell in love with, the painter's beloved only daughter, Margaret. "I had thought," said the Pre-Raphaelite artist wistfully, when the young pair announced their attachment, "that he was just a nice young man who had come to visit *me*."

I am not competent to assess the quality of my grandfather's scholarship, but am told he was a thinker of synthesis, rather than of inspired originality. His literary production was at all events prodigious, and one of its most remarkable features was that, until his retirement from the Board of Education (as it then was), all his private work was done at dawn, or on his holidays. In appearance he was immensely distinguished in a rather raw-boned Scottish way, in manner kindly and withdrawn but, if provoked, he could be trenchant in the extreme: all Ayrshire, Balliol, and his own scholastic erudition speaking out with forthright disdain if he disagreed with you. I recall, in the middle

Thirties, trying to persuade him of the beauty of a poem by W. H. Auden. He listened magisterially while I read the lyric, then roundly declared — of the work of an artist who was to be a successor in the Oxford Chair — "That is *not* poetry."

But he did not tell me why, and what I found unhelpful, as a young man, about his colossal learning, is that he would but rarely unless almost forced to express any literary opinion and, when he so infrequently did, would fail to advance any reason for his holding it. He gave, perhaps unconsciously, the impression that everything worth writing had been written long before 1919, and that the last modern author worthy of note was Maurice Maeterlinck, whose English translator he had been. But although my grandfather was intellectually arrogant, in personal converse he was most benign; and my chief recollection is of a good and gentle, even timorous man, despite the rigid exclusiveness of his professional opinions.

His wife, my grandmother, was a far more complex and dominating character. In her youth she was a startling beauty in the Pre-Raphaelite manner, and her father had often depicted her both in portraits and in his huge allegorical canvases. (I use, of Burne-Jones, the term "Pre-Raphaelite" since this is habitual, if inaccurate; for strictly speaking, he was not one of the Brotherhood itself, but a disciple of Rossetti and thus a neo-Pre-Raphaelite only.) Her father's home had been, in the last decades of the nineteenth century, a considerable centre of artistic, literary and political intercourse, and she had been brought up to a familiarity with the great by whom, I imagine — as by her father and his wife Georgiana — she had been much spoiled. At her mother's death, and that later of her brother, Philip Burne-Jones, she had inherited a considerable fortune, and was thus an heiress both to wealth and fame, which factor, coupled with her own compelling temperament, made her a rather demanding woman.

Yet I could not but reflect, when I found her unusually *exigeante*, that whereas her father and husband had done great things — as had even her mother, Lady Burne-Jones, whose *Memorials* of her husband are a minor, and reticent, masterpiece — the only work of art she herself had created was her own

139

considerable personality. (Apart from voluminous, and brilliant, letters, her only writing, so far as I know, is the description of Mrs Beeton printed on the back of the postcard on sale at the National Portrait Gallery.) When we were children she was, to my elder brother Graham and myself, the perfect grandmother: fantastic, forgiving, leaping, as grandparents can, across the barrier of generations, to establish an immediate and heart-stealing relationship. But as we grew older, she set standards for us that I, at any rate, could never hope to rise to nor, to tell the truth, did I particularly wish to do so. She wanted me, I think, to be good, obedient and pure, and as I am none of these, she disapproved. What seemed to interest her less was what sort of personalities her grandchildren really *were*, or even with improvement conceivably could be.

There was, in her nature — as indeed in that of her illustrious father — a deep strain of melancholy, possibly due in part to her Celtic origins, for her father, before his elevation to a baronetcy, had been Edward Jones from Birmingham, and her mother one of the Macdonald sisters whose marriages led to the Kipling, Baldwin, Poynter and Mackail families all being related. And this melancholy induced in her a kind of resolute pessimism, though this was not unmixed with fun and fantasy. As for the innumerable gifted men and women she had frequented as a girl — who ranged from Little Tich and Yvette Guilbert to Gladstone, Tennyson and William Morris himself — she was disappointingly reticent about them. All I could persuade her to tell me of Oscar Wilde, for instance, was that when he came to her parents' house he was "a tease". On Ruskin, she was slightly more revealing. Recalling a visit to Brantwood she declared, "Whenever Mr Ruskin came into the room and found me doing something, he would tell me to do something else."

Their Kensington house was like a museum of these memories; and it was more, one felt, her house than my grandfather's, for despite his own high achievement, he had been somewhat absorbed into the Pre-Raphaelite heritage of his wife. You climbed up a steep stair from the street towards the pillared portico and, as soon as the front door opened, found yourself in a small hall with another door, of frosted glass, beyond. (In our childhood days, one of our grandmother's inventions that delighted us was to pretend this small hall was a lift, and press imaginary buttons before opening the further door of glass.) Inside was a much larger hall with massive bookcases containing huge volumes about art and, somewhat surprisingly, a collection of toys from all parts of the world that had entertained at least three generations. In a huge oak chest there was an enormous assemblage of brown-paper sheets and colossal balls of string, for these my grandmother always saved from any parcel — never tearing the first, nor impatiently cutting the second.

The dining-room beyond had a large oblong cottage table that had been her father's, and to one side a locked bookcase with volumes of their works inscribed to him by Rossetti, Morris, Swinburne and other mid-Victorian colleagues. In one corner was my grandmother's writing bureau (it seems to me somehow typical of her that she chose this unusual room for her correspondence) and, on a table by the inadequate gas fire, a back-gammon board and pieces, for my grandparents played this game together unfailingly after every meal. Among unexpected objects on the wall there was a "folk art" clock whose face represented Big Ben by moonlight, executed in a mosaic of mother-of-pearl; for my grandmother had a lively appreciation of English, and indeed Continental, *kitsch*. Near by — and somewhat incongruously — there was an unfinished portrait, by Burne-Jones, of his wife in their young days: the "Burne-Jones woman" who appeared in his earlier paintings — small, large-eyed, and of immense if rather remote inner dignity; and contrasting with the taller, more willowy heroine of his later pictures, who more strongly resembled his own daughter.

Running the whole length of the house on the further side of the central hall was perhaps the most purely Pre-Raphaelite feature of the house, the drawing-room. Its papers and chintzes were all by Morris, and except for a large and quite conventional sofa, the more decorative pieces of furniture had a splendid Pre-Raphaelite austerity (cushions half an inch thick, I recall, and elegant woodwork backs to thoroughly unwelcoming chairs). There were more paintings by her father on the walls, including a colossal water-colour (can any other artist have painted in this medium on such a scale?) of a sleeping beauty entwined in thorns, and two portraits of herself — the "blue", full face before a convex mirror, and the "grey" in profile, more restrained. There were a piano, a harpsichord and a clavichord which Burne-Jones had decorated as a gift for his child's wedding. Books lined the walls in collected, but by no means luxurious, editions, and the carpets were fine Persian that had been trodden by many feet.

A Chinese chest in one corner had a particular fascination for me. On top of it, there was a rounded brass-bound box containing the letters which her cousin Rudyard Kipling had written to my grandmother from India, when he returned there from Westward Ho to write for the *Civil and Military Gazette*, Lahore. These letters were written on the paper both horizontally and then vertically across the horizontal lines — the reasons for this being the expense of postage in those days; but the script was so clear that one had no difficulty in deciphering them. My grandmother never allowed these letters to be published during her lifetime; and indeed, she had become sadly estranged in later years from her adored cousin, both because of family altercations and, I believe, because of the support to the Boer cause her branch of the family had given at the turn of the century.

Inside this chest there was a drawer, known as the "Funny Drawer", which contained all the curious oddments that had come my grandparents' way during their long years of married life. There was, for example, a collection of all the envelopes on which their names had been grotesquely misspelt by correspondents — as "Mocktail" and "Crocktail" for versions of my grandfather's surname. Some of the items, in so austere a household, were astonishingly bawdy: for instance, a massive list of all the English family names they could discover which are indecent. An impressive object was the slate the Burne-Joneses used to keep at The Grange on which visitors, if they were out, were invited to leave any message; and one day when

Tennyson had called, my grandmother, then a girl, had filched the slate so that another had to be provided. (The Laureate's message, by the way, was simply — and quite adequately — "Tennyson" in a firm but spidery hand.)

Up the narrow staircase — the previous tenants, former Anglo-Indian officials, had abandoned the house, so my grandmother told me, because they could not sweep up and down it in sufficient style — was to be found my grandfather's study: the only room in the house that was decidedly his own, and marked by his private personality. Books, proofs and first editions rose from floor to ceiling, and upon the chimneypiece was a photograph much cherished by its owner. This portrayed an African chieftain surrounded by naked wives and warriors, with the simple words underneath this image of "Macmillan & Co.". The unfortunate ambiguity of this picture — due no doubt to an inattentive proof-reader in the advertising department of this distinguished firm of publishers — delighted my grandfather; and so much so that when Kipling begged him to surrender what he declared to be a group portrait of the directors of the company, my grandfather refused to part with it.

Passing by the most uncomfortable bathroom in the metropolis — among whose peculiarities was that in order to open the window, you had to climb into the bath — one might reach the top, or nursery, floor. In later days this housed the domestic staff, who never enjoyed even the modest luxury of piped water. This staff consisted of Annie, a kindly cook resembling any one of the three witches in *Macbeth*, a woman much addicted to Gilbert and Sullivan — of whose productions she had a vast collection of gramophone records which she sometimes played to my grandparents in the drawing-room — and who, somewhat disconcertingly, considering her profession, to all appearances ate nothing whatever, and subsisted on tea; also a succession of disgruntled house-parlour-maids, for I do not think my grandmother was the most benevolent of employers. But in earlier days, two generations had been brought up there — my grandparents' three children, and then my mother's after she took refuge in her parents' house when her first marriage ended in disaster.

It is thus that I have infant memories of the house, as well as maturer ones. I can remember, during the First World War, being carried down to the basement for fear of zeppelins, and being given a whistle to blow out of the window at the German surrender in the war to end all wars. I recall my grandmother teaching me to read (*Pauline's First Reading Book* — does this still exist?) and reading aloud to us regularly — a family tradition, for even my grandparents often read to each other in the evening, and my mother continued this splendid practice, in later years when we left for Australia, to my own and my brother's immense benefit. I even remember my great-grandmother, Georgiana Burne-Jones, when she visited us in the nursery, and I frightened her out of her considerable wits by greeting her, in bed, disguised by an animal mask from the copious chest that my grandmother kept for dressing-up.

When my grandparents had both died, and the house was gutted, I must confess that I did not feel great pangs. There had been too much of my life there, and the kind of life, despite its intense joys in childhood, was not really my own. I called, one day, when my mother was sorting out the accumulation of papers, and asked her how she was getting on. She had been burning some letters, she said. What letters? Letters to Mamma from Mr Ruskin, she rejoined. My heart missed a beat. My first vulgar reaction was that these letters were surely valuable. My second was that, whatever might be their content, they were of undeniable historic interest. But when my mother explained to me that they were the kind of letter that Mr Ruskin ought not to have written to a young girl, my third reaction was one of grudging admiration. These letters were a private, family matter, my mother considered, and thus not the concern of anybody else. And in this drastic action I seemed to recognize a gesture faithful to the austere spirit of the house.

from "Mum's the Word"

New Statesman, June 1963

During her lifetime my late mother, Angela Thirkell, caused me intense embarrassment: for there she was, an immensely successful and bad writer, and there was I, scorned for so long by the cruel world yet believing I had something real to say.

My mother was in her forties before she became an author. While in Australia she had contributed to such fashionable periodicals as the continent then boasted (I recall a somewhat camp piece that sought to demonstrate the Romans really spoke *English*), and conducted a truly ghastly "literate" radio programme for kids in which she introduced herself to the amazed Australian young as Mother Elder.

Then, in about 1930, she decided to leave her second husband, George Thirkell, and return — bearing of her possessions only clothing and her portrait in charcoals by John Singer Sargent — to her native land. As she was penniless, this involved living with her parents, which no woman with forty years, two marriages and four children behind her, cares much to do.* So to win financial independence, she purposefully took up her pen.

Encouraged by E.V. Lucas she first wrote an account of her Pre-Raphaelite childhood called *Three Houses.* This, published by the OUP, won a considerable *succès de nostalgie,* but not a fortune. About this time James Hamilton had started his firm, and began by printing the reminiscences of W. Graham Robertson, an old family friend who introduced the young publisher to the older authoress, both at this stage being novices.

It was James Hamilton who persuaded her to try her hand at novels, and if ever a publisher deserved to do well with a writer, he most certainly did; and I believe my mother realized this, for she remained faithful to his imprint without question. The novels at first did modestly, then won a book society award in the US and rocketed over there and here. From then onwards there was no stopping her, and she died leaving a modest fortune.

Since I did not like my mother nor she — for the best of reasons — me, it is perhaps hard for me to write of her

* Editor's note: Mary McInnes, born in March 1917, Angela's only daughter, died in infancy.

productions objectively. So abandoning the attempt, I will simply say I find them able in execution (if in a rather decayed "traditional" style), and in content totally revolting. I shudder to think that millions of copies of her sterile, life-denying vision of our land should have persuaded and delighted so many hundreds of thousands in our country and the US.

A curious aspect of her portrait of the English gentry is that she was never of them, and didn't really know them. By her first marriage to my dear father, James Campbell McInnes, a diabolically angelic baritone singer, she knew the London musical world of the late Edwardian and early Georgian eras. By her second to an extroverted Australian engineer she was plunged into a, to her, exotic antipodean existence. With one exception, neither world of experience appears at any point in her creations.

This exception is a straightforward account of our family odyssey to Australia, after her second marriage at the end of World War 1, written under a pseudonym and called *Trooper to the Southern Cross* (or *What Happened on the Boat* in other editions). It is funny, quite realistic, and agreeably malicious. It is also — predictably — the only book of hers I like at all.

Of course it is true that, as a girl, she did visit stately and semi-stately homes, since her father J.W. Mackail, a professor of poetry, and her mother, who was once Margaret Burne-Jones, moved peripherally in these worlds. She also descended on the country often enough when she later became a writer. But her vision of English rural life is really a fantasy seen by one yearning, from the outside, for its supposed stabilities; and this may well account for the appeal of her novels to those countless thousands who have similar hankerings for gracious country living.

A key to her performance, indeed, is to realize she was three-quarters Scot and one-quarter Welsh and hence, by birth as well as nurture, an alien to the world she evoked in over thirty books. The Lowland Scot in her may perhaps also explain her really formidable application — which her dissolute son admires and respects however much he finds the end-product repugnant.

On my own productions she preserved a stony silence, and

I'm not even sure if she read them, though I expect she did. Her tactic, if any "literary" conversation ever arose, was to avoid referring to her creations or my own — thereby hinting, I felt, she was being tactful about my incompetent obscurity and her own illustrious achievement, which was of course doubly maddening. I am sure that the thought I really didn't like what she did simply failed to occur to her at all.

Without question, the worst kind of parent a writer can have is a successful bad one. Had she not been a writer, though I don't believe I'd ever have liked her much, I don't think I'd have been so much tempted towards a kind of literary matricide. As it was, I became so obsessed by not being described as "Angela Thirkell's son" that I took neurotic precautions to try to prevent publishers or magazines mentioning this fell fact at all. Luckily, of course, I had a different surname.

What was additionally exasperating about all this is that my father was an artist, though now forgotten. He sang Vaughan Williams's earliest songs, and Graham Peel wrote most of his for him. At festivals and lieder concerts up till World War I (he was nearly twenty years older than my mother) he was a much heralded figure. How I longed, earlier on, to be "Campbell McInnes's son", and not "Angela Thirkell's". But no: hers was the reputation that till then survived, and I belonged to a name that was not even my own as if I were created by immaculate conception.

I am sorry to record that, as a writer, I found her death a liberation. This is monstrous, though I believe I can really say it was not at all due to envy. Had she been an author I admired, I think I am generous enough to have been proud of what she might have achieved, and not denied it.

As it is, I have perhaps been influenced by her indirectly — as we all are by parents of strong character who repel us. Some of the themes I have chosen — or which have chosen me — may have recommended themselves precisely because they were ones that would disgust her. Her example also reinforced an inherent dislike for writing as an end in itself — instead of as a revelation, however modest [....]

from "Through the looking glass to adolescence"

(*The World of Children*, edited by Edward Blishen — Paul Hamlyn, 1966)

Since no attempt to recall the farewell to childhood can be other than subjective, may I first offer the reader the bare facts of my own pre-adolescent condition. My mother, after divorcing my father (for the best of reasons), had re-married an Australian — or, more properly, a Tasmanian, since the latter do not like to be called the former, even though they are. I was thus, as the age of five, transported to Australia, where I was reared, till the age of nearly seventeen, in Hobart, Melbourne and, during long school holidays, on the sheep stations and fruit farms of the all-embracing bush. My mother, whom I never loved (I have always, for this reason, found the Oedipus complex difficult to credit), though I certainly feared her, conducted herself, in this colonial decor, like a suave settler in darkest Africa. Beneath a torrid sun, and often in circumstances of great material distress, she resolutely maintained the values — and the accent — of her Kensingtonian culture in London, much to the astonishment of the natives. Yet curiously, she got away with it: she was so resolute in her rejection of everything Australian (except for the beaches, for she loved swimming) that she acquired the reputation of a "character", or "card", and made countless Australian friends who almost wept when she finally departed.

My step-father, the Tasmanian, was an extroverted engineer, brilliant at technology, hopeless in business, tough, generous, kindly and totally devoid of the faculties of speculative thought or of imagination. It cannot be easy for any man — and especially one not reflective — to see every day, in his step-child, the living proof that some other man has earlier occupied his wife's bed; and though he acted justly to me, there was no point of human contact whatsoever. I do not think he hated me, but simply wished that I was not there at all.

The reader may imagine that this is the prelude to the artist's habitual tale of an unhappy childhood. But quite on the contrary. I loved Australia, I loved (dreadful admission!) my

148

school, I loved my mates, the sea, the bush, the sun, and that ingrained Australian habit of granting independence early to their children, giving them responsibilities beyond their years, and letting them fight, roam, dream, make idiots of themselves without too severe a retribution. If my mother irked me, as she constantly did, I took her swimming and swam further out than she could. If my step-father shanghaied me to mow the lawn or clean his car, I vanished with my pals till we all returned at night for the ritual flogging. Youth has such energy, and in Australia such licence, that its elders fight a perpetually losing battle.

I first became aware of adolescence when my elder brother entered that estate. Hitherto, though he was a year and a half my senior, we had played and fought together in games and battles ferocious and intense. He had once tried to kill me with an axe while I defended myself with a hastily snatched dustbin lid. On the other hand, we had ridden miles together in the eucalyptus-sodden country, on bicycles or horses, and swum in creeks, dams and gorgeous bays, singing in parts to each other and enacting fantasies of bushrangers or explorers. But suddenly all that stopped. My brother's friends became attentive to their dress, bought razors, and, instead of hitting or teasing me as before, treated me with an aloof, tolerant condescension. They stole whisky from my step-father's demijohn in the tool-shed, smoked pipes and cigarettes behind the woodpile, and chased me away when I tried to partake in any of these mysteries — the more so after, in all innocence, I had entered my brother's room to find them engaged in competitive masturbation, a sight which — in the brief glimpse I was vouchsafed of it — filled me with mingled terror, envy and fascination.

Then my brother began chasing *girls*. They phoned: he phoned. He stole my step-father's car on several occasions and then drove off, before my puzzled spying eyes, in the direction of the beach. Letters arrived which he seized from my hand, when I fetched the mail, and hid. He wrote poems, and when I found and laughed at them, he scarcely deigned to beat me. Soon it became apparent some great change had happened to

149

him which removed him, for the moment, from my society. He shared jokes with my step-father that I did not understand — and was chased from the room if I tried to. Exchanges became minimal, except when he wanted me to lend him a tie, a tennis racquet, or mysteriously vacate my room for an afternoon and not come back till tea time.

Worse befell when my own favourite mate Jack was also thus suddenly transformed. When young males reach puberty, there are savage re-groupings of old friendships, and those to whom the miracle has not yet occurred are cast out by their dearest comrades who ruthlessly seek new friends among older boys. The rejected feel like neophytes who have — all unjustly — been refused access to the temple. They experience deep pain and indignation — and yet are haunted by the feeling that they in truth do not merit the privilege of belonging to the inner circle which these erstwhile comrades have abruptly entered in confidence and glory.

I cannot speak of England or the United States, but in Australia most boys and girls know what physical changes are involved in adolescence — or, at any rate, know about these in theory. Among animals — for even city dwellers make off in summer to the bush — it is all there to be observed, conversation about humans is extremely frank, and when youth sleeps out on the beaches in the hot seasons, it is all there clearly to be seen (and heard). Yet to know what "happens" is not at all to know what the sensation is. And thus, as the child enters the brief pre-adolescent stage, there come moments of decisive revelation in which, if physical adulthood is not actually achieved, it can at any rate be more realistically imagined.

Up on the river Murray, there is a garden area of the state of Victoria where fruit is grown in endless acres with row upon row of plums, apricots and peaches extending over hill and dale for miles. On an orchard where I used to go for holidays I met, in the fruit-gathering season, a half-caste aboriginal of indeed repellent aspect, who was much taunted by the white pickers both because of the innocence of his race, his bizarre English, and his air of dumb docility — which hid in fact, however, a considerable fund of guile. Fruit-picking is exhausting work, as you climb on the ladders in the broiling sun, a huge canvas bag suspended tugging on your neck and banging awkwardly upon your belly, stretching amid spiky foliage to pluck the hot ripe fruit — of whose taste your gluttony is soon disgusted, so that these delicious globes and ovals soon seem nauseous. Since the pay is by quantity, not time, you must struggle on — and here the aboriginal had come into his own, for while the white pickers often subsided for brew-ups of billy tea during their numerous "smoke-ohs", the aboriginal toiled on, his centuries of habit enabling him to do without rest or water.

Since I was not paid for picking, being a guest of the orchard-owner and a boy, and since the men pickers had no use for me but to light fires for their tea, I used to wander off and help the aboriginal. At first I was scared of him, for his bent, millennial features seemed forbidding, and his age-old melancholy eyes were so remote as to seem utterly indifferent. Besides, he looked grubby and unkempt, and seemed to confirm all the tales I had been told of the aboriginal delight in a diet of worms and lizards, of their fecklessness, dishonesty, and sudden treacherous malice. Yet I was attracted to him as much by the fact that he accepted my company without surprise, as by the affection I felt suddenly for the first adolescent I had known who, while having manifestly crossed the perilous threshold into early manhood, did not seem to reject, as my brother and his friends had done, any lad like myself who had not yet achieved this transformation. He also shared his cigarettes without condescension and a leer, and as I, hitherto, had only smoked surreptitiously cooking herbs wrapped in lavatory paper, the extension of this privilege delighted me.

When the evening came, and the fruit was weighed, and the pickers made off to their tents beside the farm to drink and gamble, the aboriginal lingered after them and beckoned me. Lowering his eyes, then gazing at me with a crafty smile, he asked if I'd like to come down to the river for a swim. As I hesitated, both because I knew my hosts would certainly object ("You can't trust the abo, son"), and because truth to tell I was still frightened of him, he reached out one hand and, with a gentle plucking gesture, tugged reassuringly at my shirt. I looked round at the house, nodded quickly, then whispered I'd

151

meet him down by the cow tracks to the river. He set off ahead whistling, with that jaunty barefoot aboriginal prowl, while I, making a prudent detour round the milking sheds, caught up with him among the ferns and reeds that bordered the clayey windings of the Murray.

Here he immediately undressed, and plopped into the river like a porpoise. I followed timidly and, when I swam out, could no longer find him. Searching somewhat anxiously in the gathering gloom, I suddenly felt myself heaved up out of the water on his shoulders, tossed upwards like a pancake, and dropped with a whack on my back: whereupon he leaped on top of me so that I sank some feet and surfaced breathless in a rage. Seeing I was alarmed, he smiled, trod water in front of me, wiped the hair out of my eyes and patted me gently on the cheeks. Then he laughed, beckoned with a dark lanky arm, and swam slowly to the shore, turning sometimes to make sure I was following.

There, while we had a cigarette, he gazed at me craftily, then rose and, to my great surprise, stood knee-deep in the stream and bedaubed his whole body with its ochred mud. As soon as it had partly hardened, he began to trace patterns on his body which I recognized from photographs I had seen, as being those appropriate to an initiation. He stood proudly before me in the rising moonlight, flashed his teeth grinning, then advanced, pulled me to my feet, and led me to the water. There he anointed me fondly with the slime, told me to lie down, and traced similar patterns on both sides of my body. While he did this, he examined me minutely, his hands wandering promiscuously, familiarly, but without violation. As I lay next to this boy-man by the river, I felt an exaltation — he was promising me that the strength he possessed would soon be mine as well. I reached up and kissed his muddy face, but he laughed, rose briskly to his feet, dived in the stream and disappeared towards the further shore.

At home, my first pre-adolescent encounter with a girl was with Oenone — incredibly so called, but she once told me her mother was fond of poetry. Hitherto girls, who once had been companions, had become, as adolescence approached, a scourge and enemy. The former tomboys had been transformed, as they reached their early teens, into dreadful little ladies, moving in defensive, disdainful groups, and darting quelling sarcasms at any boys of their own age who approached them. For this seems to be the only period when the warfare between the sexes becomes so acute that the rival armies will not even engage in battle.

Oenone was about seventeen, and she used to work two hours in the evening tidying up, for such limited help was all my mother could afford. Because she considered me a boy, I had become her intimate in the kitchen, though to my elder brother her attitude was much more aloof and cautious. She regaled me with tales of the "boys" who took her dancing at the Bambalina Cabaret — a local dance-hall, as I imagine it now, as innocuous as could be, but seeming by her account the height of wickedness and glamour.

About this time, though as yet no untoward hair had appeared upon my body, I had joined the school cadet corps, which had a dazzling uniform like that worn by Latin American officers. When first I wore this, the sight of my youthful body in the mirror convinced me I was now a *man* and, trembling with daring, I invited Oenone, after I'd helped her with the washing-up, to come and gather fruit with me in the back garden. She smiled to herself, then laughed and agreed, and we made for the hammock that was strung, beneath the Southern Cross, between a peach tree and a nectarine. Reaching up for fruit, and being flung together by the extreme discomfort of the hammock, I began to fondle her, at which she giggled, slapped me, but didn't stop me. ("Hands off the model, son," she said. And, "Don't try anything I might forgive, but couldn't forget.") Even if I had known what to do, and even if I had been capable of doing it, I believe Oenone's prudence, if not virtue, would have halted my endeavours; but as it was, I had a melancholy gnawing sense of inadequacy. Clearly, I no longer felt towards her as a boy — the uniform no doubt encouraging this sensation — but equally, I was as yet unable to act towards her as a man. Sensing this, she was indulgent, and yet slightly mocking: I realized with a pang she did not feel I was dangerous, yet also with excitement that she felt I might become so before long.

For now I had reached the condition I am trying to evoke: that of being suspended between two states of being, not quite belonging to either, and fluctuating almost hourly between excessive reversion to childhood, and impossible demands that a manly status should already be conceded to me. The chief characteristic I remember of this brief period is its sudden swings between extremes of morbid gloom and inexplicable ecstasy. At one moment I would set off for long walks besotted with rapture, singing Schubert to the stars. At the next, I would sit on the woodpile in solitude convinced that I was cut off from all my past, and that all futures were barred to me irrevocably. My comrades having passed this state, or not yet having reached it, I found that the supports of old friendships were suddenly withdrawn. Out of a deep instinct to protect my state of isolation, I became a prodigious liar and thief, and failed in critical school examinations. My parents (who, like so many parents, must have forgotten that they, too, had once passed through this miserable condition) adopted a censorious attitude which made matters, if that were possible, worse. I tried to take refuge in consoling arts appropriate to my condition, and read ecstatic Keats and looked at glowing reproductions of Botticelli: but art, alas, though it certainly explains life and enhances it, is of no help to those whose own grip on life is insecure, and the dreams of the poets and painters only reinforced my gloom.

At this time I also became entangled with religion. I had never been baptized into any faith, and attended a school where religious instruction was minimal and formal, yet now I began to contemplate infinite things. I did not of course then understand what part of this impulse was genuine, and what larger part of it emotive and unreal, as I sat out services in church and read holy works seeking for impossible consolations. What I sought, but did not know it, were love and reassurance: but on a lad in this condition these are almost impossible to bestow except, perhaps, by some older person of infinite comprehension and wisdom, and such I was not then lucky enough to find.

I was also afflicted by curious snobberies. I began telling all my friends (who were not in the least bit interested) that I was not *Australian*, but *English* — hoping thereby to create, in the emotional void that enfolded me, the impression that I belonged to a suaver, surer world. I took to visiting, in my one good suit, older friends of my mother's and sought to impress them by the brilliant maturity of my uncouth observations. I affected, to mask the inner doubt and emptiness, an attitude of nonchalant indifference to all whom I encountered — a tactic which failed completely to impress the matter-of-fact Australians, though it no doubt irritated and surprised them.

But then the pendulum would swing upward to the skies, and life would become more beautiful than it had ever been before — and, I believe, than it would ever again be in the future. I have said how attached I was to my Presbyterian school, and at this time it took on an unexpected glamour. The masters seemed benevolent and full of consideration for my pretensions, the sportsmen young heroes out of legends, my comrades worthy companions before whom my undoubted gifts might shine. Even the buildings and the grounds seemed beautiful. The latter in fact *were*, for the astute Scottish worthies who had founded the academy had purchased a vast tract of land on the confluence of the river Yarra and a stream called Gardiner's creek. And though the sham red-brick Gothic of the school was in reality hideous, it seemed glorious to me, and I wandered among the gums along the river in the evening, long after I should have returned home, watching the oarsmen and the swimmers, and feeling part of a splendid and devoted confraternity of like-minded young.

The reader must please not laugh if I recall that, at this critical time, I was also protected by the mantle of Lord Baden-Powell. The scout troop to which I belonged was a tough and enterprising one. We often set out for the bush at night, pulling a trek-cart laden with scouty gear far out into the country. How beautiful the wild, untutored, hot, untidy Australian bush can be, so unlike the laundered countrysides of Europe, so welcoming, by its very indifference, to a fervent youthful spirit! We camped and swam and sang and built trestle bridges and cooked truly revolting food around fires whose smoke chased the myriads of mosquitoes. Most fortunately, this troop was not over-burdened with Powellesque ideology and, forgetting the ten scout laws (or most of them), we indulged to the full in a brash outdoor hedonism which was the perfect antidote to urban gloom.

Thanks to the more pretentious of my mother's friends, I was also, at long last, able to meet girls on a footing that released me both from their venom and, if they were older than I was, from my painful feeling of animal inadequacy. For one of these older ladies was mad about theatricals and since I was a cute kid and a show-off (Australian, "skite"), I shone on these occasions — or at any rate, thought I did sufficiently to give me the courage, or effrontery, to talk to these girls without fear of their claws or, worse, indifference. I began to conceive passions for some of the older of them and wrote them facetious-romantic letters to which they were often kind or indulgent enough to reply. Masking my tremors, I even became the confidant of some of my brother's sirens, who sometimes kissed me surreptitiously, filling me with shock, ardour, and frustration.

My sister died when she was still a baby, and I have always regretted I had only brothers. For however much a man may later grow to understand women — if that is ever fully possible — I believe the daily company of the other sex must be a chief key to knowing them. I have tried, in a novel (*June in Her Spring* of 1952), to describe the feelings of a girl poised on puberty, and women have been good enough to say June is convincing (and not just a young boy transposed into a girl). Yet since I had no sister to observe, and since, at this time, I had not yet loved a woman who could tell me, I must try to describe young girls as I saw them in the same stage of pre-puberty as my own.

I think they were *wiser* than we were. It is not only that boys mature later, generally, than girls do, but that the girls seemed closer to reality than we: to understanding what is possible, and what not, in human life at any juncture. With adults, among the many things which differentiate the sexes, it seems to me that women do not *boast* or *fuss* as much as men. (As to the latter, try nursing a sick man or woman, and see the difference! As to the former, it may be the physical transformation that men must achieve in sex which accounts for their anxious vainglory.) Yet even with young girls, this greater female poise is evident. This is not at all to deny passion, wildness, fervour to such girls: but these seem to come when there is a pretext for them, not just when self-induced for the mere sake of sensation without reason. Even before puberty, a girl seems to guess what being a woman will mean for her in the near future, while boys more often carry their boyhood into early manhood.

They are *kinder* than we are. Boys are barbarians, moving in irrational killer groups, fickle in feeling, vain and resentful. Girls have their mean, spiky nastiness, it is true, yet they seem more humane. Dangerous in flocks, they seemed gentler and sweeter than boys of that age were when you could catch them alone a moment.

The physical changes that come to boys as they approach puberty are, heaven knows, disturbing, but the far greater shock to girls must be horribly disturbing. The erotic reverie of the boy may be alarming, yet on the whole agreeable; the comparable change in a girl's body cannot but be unpleasant, despite the promise that it holds out — once this is kindly and truthfully explained to her — of later glory and fecundity. I remember a moment when this sharp change overtook a girl while we were gathering shrimps on an Australian beach. Far out on the rocks, beneath the huge sky of Western Port, we were chasing them in warm limpid pools, the picture of juvenile amity, when suddenly she stared at me in white alarm and fled off ashore to her mother without a word. An aunt, to explain her conduct, later told me she had had a distressing and mysterious experience. Boys joke about this, and they are little horrors to do so. For on girls it must lie heavily, though perhaps (like pregnancies and the menopause later) these are cardinal events that give to women their greater sense of reality, even if these hard reminders of our animal nature may deprive them of the man's greater faculty to brood and dream.

June in Her Spring is not an autobiographical novel, though the awkward, sensitive Benny, caught between two lifestyles — the outdoor hedonism of the Australian sheep stations, and the piano-playing aestheticism of his guardian, Henry Bond — bears more than a passing resemblance to his creator during his adolescence. It is a powerfully atmospheric story of young love thwarted. Here Benny and the eponymous June, on their first outing together, find themselves "bushed":

from *June in Her Spring*
(MacGibbon & Kee, 1952)

Disturbing words lurk at the back of consciousness in every country, and up in the district there is "bushed": often a subject for laughter in safe places, but never a word said openly and seriously...as words never are that hint of death, even "death" itself. Of course, the danger's not as great as it used to be a generation back when if you got bushed you were a man left to swim in the Pacific.... Still, every summer, there are nasty stories...children out all night and terrified when the search-party reaches them...strangers found by accident after three days of thirst....disappearances, and then the corpse that someone stumbles over — so often near a habitation if he had but known it, so often just a beside a spot where the search-party has passed, crying out, "Coo-ee!" but in vain.

To be bushed is to experience, in a concentrated hour, the slower demoralization of a nervous breakdown over days: the bottomless dejection; the hollow elation in an ensuing moment of strength; the deeper drop into a total loneliness; and then into worse —into a solitude that is not I without them, but I without I: a disintegration of the personality that bears a foretaste of the end of life.

"This is going to get us nowhere," said June. "We'll ride back the way we came and take the other track."

"Oh, if you like," said Benny, nonchalant because perturbed.

The blazes, of course, were invisible on this side of the trees, and they halted every few minutes to look over their shoulders for them. They saw one or two, but then no more.

"The best thing we can do," said Benny, "is to ride straight uphill and come to the track that way. Or better still, let's turn round again and keep on downhill, and we're bound to come out on the plain."

June said, "Where was the sun, Benny, when we left the track up there?"

"Overhead. Right overhead."

They looked up, but it was cut off by a deep net of fronds.

"There's light up there through the trees on that side," Benny said. "I'll go and see if I can get a view."

"You'll never get through to there."

"Oh, but I will. Hang on to my horse."

"No, Benny. Keep on it."

"It'll be all right. Just hold the bridle."

"I'd rather you didn't leave me here."

"I'm not going to leave you, June. I'm going to find the way."

He disappeared into the bush, sending back an occasional "Coo-ee" which she answered. Then, after a while, he shouted an inaudible message. She shouted back. Then there was a moment of silence, and his voice seemed to come from a greater distance. She dismounted, tied the horses' bridles together and clambered into the bush.

Like sightless bats, they tried to meet by sound.

"Benny!"

"Coo-ee!"

"Where are you?"

"Where are you?"

"Come back here!"

"...over here!"

"Coo-ee!"

"...what you say!"

Suddenly their voices were so near that they were ashamed of the growing shrillness, and with a cracking of branches they came face to face, grabbed each other's hands and burst into rapid laughter.

"Couldn't see much up there," said Benny. "Let's ride straight downhill like you said."

"I thought you'd gone and lost yourself."

"Me? I've got a sense of direction."

"Well, we'll need it."

"Where are the horses?"

"This way."

But not that way, not any way, despite calls for them, retracing steps, hurrying to landmarks that were not landmarks, pushing forward, crawling back, holding sweaty hands, till of one accord they started running down the hill, their limbs possessed with a tremendous physical power: leaping over logs, crashing through the bushes, until they fell against a pyramid of fallen trunks, tried to climb over it, slipped back and clutched each other. "We're bushed, Juney," he said, and she said nothing.

Then they heard an extraordinary sound: as if some giant hand were pounding on the ground and coming closer. And like an apparition, out of the bush there soared two huge grey kangaroos, elegantly, surely leaping their way among all that mess of undergrowth, unhurriedly disappearing as quickly as they had come; and leaving in two human hearts an impression of strength and wisdom, and of shame for their own ignorance and fear.

"Well, they know their way about," said June.

"They should do. This is their country."

Hand in hand they went on down the hill, no longer panicking, but hastening afraid; splashing knee-deep into a swampy creek that filled a gully, and only realizing when they clambered slowly up the other side that they were bruised, scratched, muddy, white, and panting.

They sat down on a log to consider. "We're bushed, Juney," Benny said again.

"We can't be. Not so near the stations, we can't be."

"But we may go round and round in circles. They always do...."

"Oh, shut up, Benny. Let's think; let's think. First of all, what have you got on you? In your pockets, I mean. What have you got? Is there any of the tucker? Have you any matches?"

He felt in the wrong places, remembered they were Syd's clothes and found that there was nothing but a handkerchief.

That was all June had too. They looked at the handkerchiefs, both smeared with dust and lemon butter, and put them back again.

"Well," June said, "I say what we do is follow this creek and never leave it. At any rate, we'll have water."

"And what about the horses?"

"We can't find them till we've found ourselves, can we? Anyway, they'll be all right, they've got more instinct then us...."

So they started on a long journey down beside the creek bed, sometimes losing track of it when it was hemmed in by rocks or trees, but guided by the sound of water and the greater coolness round about it. They'd known each other now a very great many years, for they were still close enough to childhood to admit a sudden intimacy that had not the support and proof of time. Rather like children, holding hands, they walked on accepting their adventure with a growing confidence, and too engrossed in the communion of flesh and spirit it gave them to think of spoiling this innocent happiness by making it that of adults. And yet, when he stepped ahead, she thought, "He's nervy now, but I can see he's one who'll grow to be strong and make them respect him and protect me." And when Benny looked at her, he thought, "If I don't live all my life close to her body I might as well die, but I can see she wants me to." Deeper in the valley, the trees grew thicker and the light grew dimmer as much by the leaves as by the fading of the afternoon. But a ray of picturesque sunlight fell upon a narrow wooden bridge they suddenly saw crossing the stream in front of them. They broke into a run, and found it carried a track they both knew well, that ran among the foothills behind Boundary.

from "Sidney Nolan: The Search for an Australian Myth", June 1957

Introduction to catalogue of the Sidney Nolan retrospective at the Whitechapel Art Gallery, 1957

(England, Half English)

The people — the "Aussies". They have terrible defects: they are cruel, censorious, incurious, flinty-hearted, and vain as Lucifer at being all these things. But their virtues! Phenomenally brave, open-handed, shrewd, humorous, adventurous, fanatically independent and, most blessed of all, contemptuous of fuss. There is indubitably a greatness about the Australian people: a bigness, a wideness, an inborn capacity for the large, the heroic gesture. If peoples are born serfs or princes — as they are — the Aussies are a kingly race.

Let us consider three key characteristics — their courage, their individuality, and their profound national instinct. Except for the incidents of the Eureka Stockade (1854), the "Kelly War" (1878-80), and the odd bomb dropped on Darwin by the Japanese, there have never been battles in Australia; but it suffices to read Alan Moorehead's *Gallipoli*, or Russell Braddon's *The Naked Island*, to catch the spirit of that Spartan contempt for death and danger which is peculiarly Australian. In the Dardanelles, they fought like the Greeks there in the Trojan wars before them, with a total disdain of the impossible. In Malaya, like the Spartans at Thermopylae, they tried to hold the swarming Japanese, though their native realism told them, long before anyone else, that they could not conceivably do so. The Australian is not just a fighter: he is a warrior, dedicated to battle.

Yet how reluctantly he dons his uniform, and how casually he wears it! Can there ever have been such appalling soldiers behind the combat areas? The defiance of all authority is the basic dogma, the very claim to his individuality, of the Australian. Small wonder that this is the country of labour power, of equality legislation, and of a fiercely democratic instinct quite unknown in England, for example, where equality is thought of as economic, not personal and social. In Australia, no one would think of saying, "Jack's as good as his master": it is "Jack's as good as Jack." Nationally, these qualities express themselves in a xenophobia that exceeds even that of the South Africans. These two peoples have one great point of resemblance — each is a minute European minority trying to survive amid the resurgent African, and Asian, millions that surround them. But between the Afrikaners and Australians, there is one essential difference. The Australians are the only people of European stock in the entire world who, living in a torrid climate, have resolutely refused to batten on coolie labour. To realize this is to see the "White Australia" policy, so shocking to liberal inclination, in an entirely different light. To bar the way to Asians was to reject the pleasures of a parasite existence, and to decide that all the manual labour in Australia would be performed by Australian hands.

It is when the positive, aggressive instinct of the Australians serves some end that is instinctively, deeply desired, that their achievement is richest and most remarkable. To take a seemingly small instance which may symbolize others that could be greater, I would name the life-savers. As everyone knows, the Australians love bathing and surfing: what is perhaps less well known is that every year some bathers and surfers get eaten, because most Australian seas are infested with sharks: tigers, grey nurses, and hammerheads, who cruise eagerly off-shore at sixty miles an hour. To indulge their favourite passions, the Australians gamble recklessly with their lives (I have seen men with shot-guns firing into the sea at sharks where half an hour ago everyone was bathing).

The public guardians against sharks — and against the more normal dangers of being engulfed in the huge "dumpers" — are the life-savers. These are picked bodies of men, all volunteers of quite incredible physical prowess, valour, and self-discipline who, on the least provocation, will lash out to sea among the grey nurses and hammerheads, carrying rescuing lines to succour those in danger (they will even succour you when in no danger at all, if they feel like it, and drag you through the waves to unwanted safety, and a restorative pummelling on the beach). To see these men at work is an impressive sight: apart from their prodigious efficiency, there seems something so un-Australian about their more-than-military bearing, though something very Australian about the initiative and ferocity of their behaviour. Here, it dawns on you, are the Australian warriors at play: the Spartans practising, of their own free will, a perilous military manoeuvre in time of peace.

from *"No Novel Reader"*
(Martin Brian & O'Keeffe, 1975)

I was fortunate to be reared in houses where books abounded, and were taken quite for granted; and although my maternal ancestors (my mother had divorced my father when I was a child) were in some ways austere, no censorship was imposed on reading anything, however apparently "advanced" or "unsuitable" for children. (Indeed, my mother carried this detachment towards the written word to the astonishing point of keeping the intimate diaries of her first marriage on shelves open to one and all; which fascinated my brothers and myself, though what my step-father thought of her insouciance, I can't imagine.) Reading aloud was a family custom, and I can recall being read to by my maternal great-grandmother and grandmother, as well as — much more extensively — by my mother. The ritual was that, after supper, the kids had to drop everything else, and appear in the drawing-room, more or less spick and span, for the evening reading — rarely reluctantly, I may add. We thus, over the years, worked through much of Dickens, Thackeray and Scott, with odds and ends of Mark Twain and Dumas. (I am sorry the custom of family reading seems to be vanishing; and I know that my grandparents, after reading to two younger generations, continued to do so for each other, well into their old age.)

This traditional fare was supplemented by a colossal intake

of popular rubbish, both English and Australian, intended for boys (and also, I suspect, for delayed adolescent adults). Retrospectively, I can see the gung-ho!, xenophobic, class-ridden tone of much of this was deplorable, but on the other hand, the hearty amorality of these tales was a pleasant corrective to the moralizings of Victorian classics, as was their much more colloquial tone.

The third influence I have to record is, rather surprisingly, that of schoolmasters — for writers are supposed to loathe their school days, whereas I found this Australian-Presbyterian academy delightful: one where the "games ethic" was kept in bounds, and scholarship not despised. Anyway, Domine One, unbelievably, turned Aussie kids on to regarding the plays of Shakespeare as a riot; chiefly by making them act (athletic hearties being assigned the female roles), and playing up the horrific aspects of these masterworks. He also lured us to visit the annual performances of Alan Wilkie and his company, a splendid thespian of the twenties who, taking on single-handed philistine and puritanical Australia (as it then was), contrived to shame and bully the nation's schools into sending their kids to his "seasons". These matinee performances were amazing: imagine a theatre packed with a thousand larrikins, treating the event as if seeing Tom Mix confronting Redskins at the local "flicks". Audience-participation was on a massive scale, and villains and heroes booed or cheered according to these characters' conduct in the plot, rather than to the renown of the actors playing them, let alone the underlying moral intentions of the dramatist. (A vivid recollection of Alan Wilkie is of his being hooted for five full minutes when he took, as Wolsey, a solo curtain-call at the end of *Henry VIII*: the kids had spotted he was the rogue, all right, and let him know it in a superb accolade of execration.)

Domine Two was a short, brisk, bald enthusiast who, besides organizing the school's football teams, had a passion for the English nature poets, whose works, by an extraordinary gift of empathy, he contrived, from 10,000 miles of physical and cultural distance, to understand intimately; and to impart this strange sympathy to totally recalcitrant kids. With the temperature at 100⁰ in the shade, and the lads gazing yearningly out at Gardiner's Creek, he would recite, in an ear-cracking Aussie accent, these poets' invocations of the English seasons (all the wrong way round from the Australian viewpoint, not to mention the flowers, and even stars, being unfamiliar). "Give a man a fair go!" he would cry, when their attention wandered, and then relate, in Browning's name, to the incredulous kids, the delights of being in England at April ("who wants a Pommie autumn, anyway?"). He stood up, too, for the Australian poets ("we've got *poets,* sir?"), at a time when these were far less considered — and indeed, far less able — than they are now.

Domine Three was an unusual blend of Lake Poet and Augustan man (and also the only Englishman of the three); and perhaps nostalgia for his native place made his praises of Pope's and Wordsworth's so English visions all the more compelling. He had, at any rate, the splendid gift of making us see that poetry is not a thing apart from the reasonable world but, on the contrary, at the very heart of it. And perhaps because of his, and these other influences, poetry, rather than prose, has always seemed to me the normal verbal art, although, apart from lampoons, I have written none myself.

A final, and perhaps strongest boyhood influence, was speech; for I cannot remember a time when I was not fascinated by how men and women express what they want to say, in whatever form, and with whatever accent. In a hybrid tongue like English, there is no such thing as an "accent", really: this is just a word for any which one does not happen to have oneself. As for turns of phrase, our grammar is so elastic, that anything can be said in almost any way, provided it is said effectively (or "with force, lucidity and ease", as Edmund Wilson dauntingly defines a good prose style).

The next influence I should record is that of foreign languages. Evelyn Waugh, asked by a schoolboy how to write English well, replied that he should learn Latin. Well — he would; yet there is this much truth in the idea, that if the great beauty of English is its infinite flexibility, it does lack, by comparison with Latin tongues, a certain rigour and precision.

No Novel Reader

Though I know only schoolboy Latin, I learned two Latin languages, and two Germanic. Of these I know French best, as a consequence of several accidents (which do not exist, according to Sigmund Freud). One of my school-mates was a French-speaking Alsatian, who insisted on talking in his mother-tongue. Then, when I returned to England at age sixteen, and after a stint with an appalling family at Sceaux-Robinson, near Paris, I got a job in a British company based in Belgium. There, for five years, I worked in offices where there were no Englishmen; and after hours, frequented Belgians of whom more were French speakers, than Flemish. In consequence, from ages seventeen to twenty-one, I read, wrote, spoke and telephoned almost exclusively in French.

I thus began a second education in French poetry and prose; and without wishing to appear at all exotic, would say this has been a major influence on my own writing. Of the qualities I have most admired in French prose (if one can generalize about a creation so gloriously diverse), are its realism: French writers are far more rarely bull-shitters than are English, and cover up far less their ignorance, especially sexual; next, its measured clarity — for instance, from the day, at Sceaux-Robinson, when the dreadful mother said, at the dinner-table, to her terrible daughter, *"Jacqueline! Tais-toi, et mange!"*, I was never thereafter surprised by the declamatory tone of Jean Racine; and then, what is rare in English writing — the quality the French call *esprit*: which is not exactly wit, but more mental daring and agility, and a love of the terse poetic paradox: a quality found abundantly in so many French writers and notably, to name one of our own century I much admire, in the works of Valery Larbaud, an artist little known in England, save perhaps as the first translator of James Joyce.

"Going into Business"

Spectator, December 1965

In 1931, I set sail for England from Australia, seventeen years old covered with pimples, and equipped with three scholarships to the University of Melbourne. The notion was that I should spend a year in Europe scanning the scene and learning languages before going back to study law.

I wandered round London and was fascinated. I lived three months in Sceaux-Robinson, near Paris, with a French family who starved me and tried to convert me to the doctrines of M. Charles Maurras. (The sons of the house, one of them epileptic, were both *camelots du roi,* and had painted "La République" on the family dustbin.) Then I went off to Germany, in the pre-Hitler era, and attended lectures on Flemish painting at Freiberg University, the idea being that the slides the professor showed me would help me to understand the language. In midsummer I returned to London and announced to my startled family that I was not going back to the antipodes.

When they asked me why, I said I wanted to go into business. I knew absolutely nothing about business, and had no real ambitions in that direction, but on two things I was totally determined. I was never again going to sit for an examination (getting those scholarships had reduced me to a nervous wreck), and I wanted to stay in Europe. And if I stayed in Europe, I knew I couldn't attend an English university because they wouldn't accept my Australian matriculation (I had checked on this), and there wasn't any money anyway.

Shaking their heads at my manifest intent to become an illiterate, yet somewhat impressed by this passion for business that had never yet appeared in any of our family, my relatives bestirred themselves. They tried to get me into Thomas Cook and Sons, but my mother patronized the contact there so much that he was unhelpful. A rich relative by marriage tried to push me into Bryant and May's, but this also came to nothing. Finally, by the good offices of Mr Reginald McKenna, a former Chancellor of the Exchequer, I was infiltrated into a gas company.

In eighteen hundred and something, Sir Moses Montefiore, that splendid Jewish capitalist and champion of his race, had hired a stage-coach and journeyed all over Europe. In the capitals he visited, he offered to supply, by contracts of ninety-nine years' duration, the English novelty of gas to their oil-lit populations. Thus the Imperial Continental Gas Association came into being, and up till the First World War it supplied most of northern Europe. And since the crafty Sir Moses had stipulated that his contracts were not only for gas but for any other form of illumination yet to be invented, the firm, in due time, supplied electricity as well.

My first interview with this illustrious firm was inauspicious. I was set papers in French, German and arithmetic. In French I did brilliantly, in German poorly, and all the sums I got wrong. (This was due both to natural incompetence and to the intimidating atmosphere of the boardroom, where I did my papers beneath a portrait of Sir Moses.) "I don't think much of your arithmetic," said the managing-director dryly. Nevertheless, thanks to sheer nepotism, I got a job at £52 per annum.

It must be remembered that Europe was then in the depths of depression, and jobs of any kind extremely difficult to get and to hold on to. Also, that for a boy of seventeen, to be independent, as so many are today, was rare in the extreme. I was thus doubly fortunate, for not only did I land a job with a first-rate firm, but within a week found my basic salary more than tripled.

It happened this way. When the Association posted anyone abroad it was, in their minds, as if they were sending him to darkest Africa, so that, in addition to his basic salary, they gave him what was called "a living allowance". And since I was almost immediately bundled off to Antwerp, I found myself earning £180 a year from the start, on which it was then quite possible to live. I lodged with a spinster and her two aged aunts in a cobbled road near the Antwerp zoo. And every day I presented myself at the offices of the *Antwerpsche Gasmaatschappij.*

This subsidiary of the Association had three English staff,

and the rest were Belgians. The manager, in his late twenties (who subsequently rose to direct the whole concern), was kind and ruthless to me. "I don't like favourites," was his greeting to me when we met at Antwerp docks — the reference being to my employment by influence rather than merit. The other two Britons were a taciturn engineer who thawed only when, desperate for partners, he invited me to his flat to play bridge; and the manager's confidential secretary who hoped, in vain, to marry him.

I was put in the office of the manager's personal assistant, an amiable sandy Fleming whose task it was to explain to me, when he could find the time, how a public utility works. We spoke in French, but, like all good Flemings, he preferred his mother tongue, and I set about learning this. In three months I mastered this peculiar language after a fashion. The only time that this was subsequently of any use to me was when I helped liberate Belgium in the 1940s, and slightly astonished the locals in north Belgian cities by my volubility.

For the first month, the only job I did was to keep a graph of the £ sterling — then, as now, fluctuating somewhat. Then I was let loose in the departments, of which I most enjoyed the saleroom, and actually one day succeeded in selling a replacement to a gas cooker to someone. The head of the sales department was a fat, florid Belgian who was constantly at odds with my boss, the personal assistant. After one of their weekly quarrels the assistant told the salesman, "*Coosemans, vous n'êtes pas un gentleman* — " which was, as a matter of fact, quite true.

My recollection of this period is all of depression and of bliss. I was lonely, wanted to be back in England, was extremely mystified by "business", but, on the other hand, there was I, seventeen and independent, free from my family and examinations. I soon moved from the spinster's household to a flat in a fashionable avenue whose rent I could not afford. I sampled Belgian food, which I think is excellent if rather greedy; I visited museums, I got to know Belgians and liked them extremely. Their chief virtue, I believe, is their indomitable instinct for life. It is a great mistake to think the

Flemings are a gross, material people. Their poetry consists in finding beauty in the commonplace, as the arts of Brueghel, Rubens and Permeke bear lively witness.

After three months, the manager summoned me and asked if I thought I now understood the business. Wisely, I said I did not — especially the *comptabilité*, which was, and has since always remained to me, totally mysterious. (I am convinced that double entry, for example, is really a philosophical, not a commercial, concept.) He advised me to study bookkeeping, which I did, by both reading appallingly dull books and taking lessons from a fellow expatriate. Then word came from London that I was to be transferred from Antwerp to Brussels. There, in the capital, was not one subsidiary, but about a dozen. The one I was sent to was the company that actually made the gas, and I was put in the department that marketed its resultant coke.

The manager here was an Irishman who believed in throwing me straight into the deep end of the pool to see if I could swim. After I was there a few weeks he told me to write his monthly report to London. Although he re-wrote my draft from top to bottom, it wasn't a bad effort and a few of my paragraphs survived in the final version. I visited gas-works, and became quite knowledgeable about prices c.i.f. and f.o.b. to various parts of Europe. Then I moved on to other companies, worked in the contracts department, sold land, and even, after a fashion (and helped out by kindly colleagues), juggled with accounts. I was beginning to think I was rather clever, and grew exceedingly conceited.

I stayed in Belgium five years altogether, with occasional missions to London. My salary rose, till in the end I was getting about £300, which was a fortune in those days for a boy of twenty-two, though I always overspent it. I travelled a lot in Belgium at the weekends, and wandered over Europe on my month's paid holiday. I am really very grateful to this firm, which gave me so much and to which I gave so little, for I only started to be at all useful to it by the time I left.

For as the years passed, it became apparent to me I could never be a businessman. This was not because I had any hostility to business (I think this, on the part of some artists, to be idiotic), but because to do this well, you have to be totally engrossed in it; and I increasingly was not. I made many friends in Belgium, and they were all painters, writers and musicians. Most fortunately, I came under the influence of several who made me read a lot and who, I can say, educated me in so far as I am educated at all. Increasingly, as I sat in my office dealing supposedly with kilowatt-hours and cubic metres, my mind wandered off elsewhere. So I journeyed to London, saw the managing director, and threw in my hand. He accepted this news with, I think, relief, and generously gave me a golden handshake of £100.

In one sense I was an idiot not to go to university when I could have, since I shall lack for ever the knowledge and disciplines this training could have given. On the other hand, I did gain some notion of affairs, got to know one foreign country really well, and learned perforce how to teach myself as best I could. I sigh for the scholar I might have been, yet do not really regret my encounter with those gasometers. And, after all: how many of my gentle readers know how to dismantle and reassemble a gas-meter...or, for that matter, how to detect when it has been fraudulently used?

"No Quiet Time"
Queen, July 1961

In a hotel lift at Eastbourne, my maternal grandmother met an angel. This occurred thirty years ago, when the "Oxford Group" — not yet cosmopolitan MRA, and still chiefly based within our modest shores — was winning unexpected converts to its revelation. My grandmother, by I know not what initial introduction and persuasion, had attended a "house party" at this maritime resort. And from Eastbourne she returned, illumined, to announce that she'd "sat on the floor with some delightful people", had encountered the celestial visitant, and had found the faith which, for more than three score years, she'd sought hitherto in vain.

The surprise of her friends and family was considerable. It was known my grandmother had sampled many sects (I recall earlier restless Quaker and Faith Healing episodes), and that she was prompted by profound religious yearnings. But she was also a woman whom, one might suppose, the tone and techniques of this Anglo-American gospel would have totally repelled. She belonged, by birth as well as marriage, to a late Victorian cultural clan whose self-chosen standards were exacting and austere: to a dynasty of painters, poets, ecclesiastics, scholars, statesmen who, though denominationally Nonconformist, were traditionalists in temper; and whose attitude to all things transatlantic was, to say the least, reserved. In temperament — indeed, in conversation and appearance — my grandmother set high standards for herself, as she did for all whom she encountered. "Quiet times" — yes, possibly; in those one could imagine her participating. But in the key Buchmanite device of "sharing"? Or in those "house parties" of effusive, miscellaneous strangers? Or in anything at all like sitting on the floor (even if among " delightful people")? No — surely not! Yet so it had turned out to be. The first explanation of her startling transformation — and one which I am sure must not be frivolously scorned — is that for anyone who, believing in Him, seeks God, then wherever they may feel they find Him is the true place where He is. I think another cause was that, being in some ways a solitary person — albeit one admired, even adored, by many of her family and countless often demanding friends — the informality of the Group's gatherings, and the — to her — exotic quality of their personalities and style of intercourse, allowed my grandmother, once in their company, to satisfy a private, long-felt wish to "let her hair down" (if such a term may be applied appropriately to her at all). In addition, I expect the Groupers — who had a well-known, frankly admitted skill at courting those deemed "influential" — contrived to blend with their seductively casual conduct an element of deference (or the appearance of it) which she felt to be her due.

So gripped thus by the Group, my grandmother — as converts invariably feel impelled, if not encouraged, so to do — set swiftly about making her own conversions. Her vigorously scattered seed fell mostly on unwelcoming ground — though she scored certain partial successes. My grandfather, her husband, an eminent professor and, as a Scots "son of the Manse", a man of obstinate opinions, assumed, in face of this assault by one he most esteemed and loved, a cautiously ambiguous posture. He didn't, I think, positively discourage her; and he agreed (or was talked into) signing some of those joint top person letters to *The Times* that were one of the means by which the Group sought to spread its influence. But he certainly didn't become (to use a political term appropriate to this Movement) a "militant". One of my grandmother's oldest and dearest friends — a formidable Surrey *châtelaine* and JP — heard patiently the eager convert out, then answered roundly, "Margaret, I can't get my religion at Woolworth's." A prime minister she tackled listened carefully (as he did always to anyone), and took scant ensuing action (as was equally his custom). An ambassador of a Power friendly (for whatever reason one may suppose) to the fortunes of the Group, was overtly — if diplomatically — enthusiastic. Following ancient precept — and indeed, contemporary practice of the Group — my grandmother tried also to spread the good word among byways, as well as highways. Her grocer, appealed to through the post, replied that he much respected her endeavours, and trusted to be favoured (as for so long, and greatly to his honour) with her continuing custom. The neatest — and I think kindest — answer came from a beloved junior male cousin, who said to her simply, and with much affection, that he felt himself unworthy of her message.

With her elder daughter, my own mother, my grandmother got nowhere. What my mother's real views on religion were, I do not to this day know. Certainly, during my childhood, she preserved on this dangerous theme a stony, enigmatic silence. Certainly also, she did not arrange for the baptism of any of her children — but then, despite my grandmother's (let alone my grandfather's) powerful religious instinct, neither had *they* ever had their children blessed in this formal way. Without being utterly unfilial, I think I can guess my mother's religious notions went somewhat thus. She approved of Henry VIII, of bishops (but not so much archbishops), and of Anglican services in rural churches. She thought that in Protestant countries one should, more or less, be Protestant, in Roman Catholic nations be a Roman Catholic, and in neither case, *vice versa*. As to any other of the world's ancient faiths and doctrines, I think she felt none of them merited a second's consideration. She once wrote a (I believe never-published) study of Christ's Mother; in which her essential supposition was that the Mother found the Son selfish, and ungrateful in all His activities, a sorry trial. (A thought possibly suggested to her, by distant and somewhat blasphemous analogy, by the behaviour, as she saw it, of her own sons to herself.) As for the Son, I think I can say that she despised Him — and for a reason I believe held more commonly than is admitted, however vulgar and point-missing it may be. And this is that Christ — unlike, for example, Henry VIII — did not, in His own lifetime, *win*: very much the contrary, in fact; He was arrested, tried, convicted by acclamation, miserably done to death — all discreditable things.

Accordingly, on the theme of my grandmother's conversion, there arose, between mother and daughter, a tension that expressed itself in "tactful", highly-charged evasions. Face to face with the older woman, the younger said not a word other than "correct" (for my mother had a due and fit respect for *any* mother). But in her parent's absence, she let all her mind — or emotion — on the subject of the Buchmanites, speak categorically out. Indeed, when one reflects on my mother's nature, and on the "Oxford Group's", one can see the Group had about it every possible element most likely to irritate and disgust her (a point I may make more vivid by explaining she was Angela Thirkell). Thus, one fatal day, when my mother was visiting her own at Kensington W8, the bell rang, and my mother answered it. Upon the neo-Grecian doorstep she discovered — all eager for cordial indulgence in some collective Buchmanite activity — a throng of youthful and expectant Groupers. The following crisp dialogue ensued:

175

Groupers: Is Margaret in?
My Mum: I think you want the servants' entrance.

A bold gambit — however brusque — for had the Buchmanites descended the precarious area steps to the inferior portal thus recommended, and tugged there at its period ball-and-wire clarion bell, no "servant" would have emerged to answer them, because there weren't any.

Disappointed by the bleak reaction of one younger generation, my grandmother next turned to that lower in seniority — my own. I was at that time about eighteen; and working in Brussels for an English company rather surprisingly engaged in marketing, to the Belgian population, gas, electricity and their derivative products. Between my infancy and my seventeenth year, when I returned to Europe from Australia, I had not seen my grandmother at all. But from my London childhood I had memories of her that were totally delightful; and from my Australian boyhood, those of letters (not to mention money orders and astonishing parcels) which revealed all the art she so outstandingly possessed of capturing the warm hearts of the young and of speaking to me through these messages (as relations separated by more than one generation often can) in a note of fantasy and understanding wisdom that were overwhelmingly enchanting to a boy. On my brief visit to London (before leaving once more for the Continent), the personal confrontation had, on the whole, confirmed all I hoped. For a wonderful short moment — and as one so rarely is by anyone at any age — I was enraptured by my grandmother. True, there were brief, occasional, sharp hints of a total later estrangement, then hidden suspended in futurity; but so few, it didn't seem to matter.

So when, at my address in Brussels, there came a letter from my grandmother, written in a hand so cherished that even the sight of its envelope excited me, I read its message with initial favour. Perhaps I felt doubtful about the Group (influenced possibly by scalding, contradictory accounts from other sources) and, despite my fondness for my grandmother, there was the built-in suspicion with which any youth reacts to any suggestion as to what he should, or should not, do. But I must try to be faithful to my young distant self, and remember the lad I was then had also religious questionings and hopes. So that the ground on which the seed this time descended was, if not rich not arid, at any rate capable of being fertilized.

My grandmother's proposal was as follows. At St Germain-en-Laye, near Paris, there was shortly to be held a "house party" of an international flavour. To this she suggested I might wish to go, and added the — to her mind — powerful inducement that Frank himself would be among those present. (My excuse for describing Dr Buchman in this familiar manner is that I am following what I believe to be Group protocol.) Meanwhile, as a sort of initiation or, as it were, *hors d'oeuvre* to the main meal at St Germain, there was to take place in Brussels — in fact that very week — a gathering of local Belgo-Buchmanites to be addressed by a prominent visiting French Grouper, the Comte de Something, at which she hinted I might also wish to be. Indeed, she added hopefully, this initial encounter would enable me — and also do so more conveniently — to judge if the later journey to France might turn out fruitful. She concluded — touchingly, disarmingly, and I believe with entire sincerity — that as she felt I was, after my grandfather, the most sympathetic member of her family, she trusted I would consider these matters kindly.

The preliminary Brussels meeting was not, to my young eyes at any rate, successful. I arrived at a *salon* somewhere near the rue de La Loi to find assembled, in a décor of Belgian bourgeois opulence, an uneasy assembly of persons sitting —metaphorically speaking — on the extreme edges of plush chairs. An additional — if accidental — cause of everyone's malaise was that the much-heralded Comte, having had to attend a *Conseil d'Administration* earlier on, was delayed there for well over an hour. And when he at last appeared — or made an entrance — I didn't take to him. To begin with, he was French; and I was just then passing through a pro-Flemish, anti-Latin phase of total absurdity and boredom. He was also too voluble, well dressed, and master of the situation; things in an older man a young one properly resents. "*Jamais, jamais, au grand jamais,*" he exclaimed (with a considerable smile) would he *ever* attend a

Conseil of *that* company (one sensed he directed many others) if he had *any* subsequent engagement. Then, after a necessarily truncated "quiet time" (my first experience of this — like sitting in a doctor's waiting-room), the Comte began a copious and elegantly phrased discourse on the virtues of the Group — about which he said both too little and too much — and on its beneficent ramifications in his native land — about which, for my taste, he said very much too much.

Appraised of my disapproval of this assembly — and of the Comte — my grandmother nevertheless persisted. She was consoling on the topic of the manifest failings of the French — or some of them, perhaps. But I would find, she declared, many amiable Britons at St Germain; also other Continentals (for instance, Swiss) more acceptable to, and appreciative of, myself; and also — not to be forgotten, she repeated — Frank in person would be there. So what about it?

To this I replied with a counter-proposal whose guile and parsimony (and thoroughly unreligious spirit) fill me, when I recall it now, with shame not, I must admit, unmixed with a part of admiration. I suggested that if I went to St Germain, my grandmother should pay for everything. If I was there converted to the faith, I'd pay her back; if not, not. I don't think she admired the proposition much; and when, after a silence longer than was usual, she answered accepting this peculiar spiritual-financial transaction, she did so in terms somewhat terse, and of notably diminished cordiality. I sensed this, of course; yet could not but feel that as I didn't really want to go (or wasn't sure whether I did), and as nothing had been said about the cost of the expedition, and as she had more money than I had, and it was *her* idea anyway... so on these terms, the deal was closed.

The venue at St Germain turned out to be a school or institution of some sort, with a large separate chalet in a mouldering garden. On arrival I was "documented" (as when visiting the Labour Exchange, then directed to an adjacent house in which an overspill of Groupers were to be accommodated. I there met my host and hostess (so to speak), who at once made it very clear (though affably) that their own sole connection with the Movement was that of being temporary — and, they said, reluctant — landlords. In my room upstairs I found there were two beds, one littered with luggage belonging to a Grouper concerning whom my only clue so far was that on his bed-table lay a large black book, embossed in gold with the title BIJBEL.

Returning to the school, I wandered forlorn until I noticed a tweedy, shaggy, pipe-sucking personage resembling a retired English colonel (and so he turned out to be) who was examining me with what, in other contexts, might have been thought an equivocal manner. I waited for him to accost me, which he did by telling me his name, and asking mine. On learning this, an expression of crafty triumph suffused his amiably blotched countenance. "Now isn't that extraordinary!" he cried. I asked him what was. "That we've come together as we have!" he answered. I said I didn't understand. A note of vexation entering his voice, he explained that my grandmother had asked him to look out for me . . . and there — lo and behold! — I was! I still couldn't see anything remarkable in this, since presumably she'd told him what I looked like, and being about nine feet tall I'm not difficult to spot. But I didn't say so to him; instead, he told me, "You mustn't be surprised by our being brought together as we have. This sort of thing's always happening in the Group."

The colonel now introduced me to Vernon Meadow and Vincent Pasture — not their real names, but accurate in spirit, and in their peculiarity of looking so very much alike: young, washed, neat, brisk, smiling, positive, assured. Not "hearty" at all, nor "evangelistic", but resembling, of our own day, a rising producer of a thoughtful telly programme, or an athletic Bow Group-inclined MP. They were specimens from those "teams" of Group-inspired (and trained) operators (I should say "disciples", and would like to say "salesmen") of which I had heard much — especially, and vituperatively, from my mother. They got me up against a wall (I don't quite mean literally), the colonel standing smiling by (as if a trusty veteran admiring subalterns of some New Model Army), and they fired friendly, remorseless questions at me, like two vice-squad coppers with a suspect. Example:

Meadow (or Pasture): And tell us: what made you want to come and join us?

Myself (suppressing the wish to admit "A free trip to Paris"): Curiosity, I suppose.

Pasture (or Meadow): Aha! Just what brought me to my first Group meeting!

Then we had supper. I hadn't noticed Frank come in — apparently a chief point about Dr Buchman is that one is not supposed to notice him; for when, later on, I told the colonel I thought the Founder "unimpressive", he positively beamed and cried, "Exactly so! It's by his being unimpressive people are impressed." Frank chose our table (I had vanity enough to be flattered), and enquired who I might be. When told, he looked at me once (and not again thereafter) then said, as if to no-one in particular, "Oh, yes. I know all about you." This riled me, because I didn't believe he could, nor did I like the idea of being "known all about" by anyone (nor did I even know much about myself). So we supped in silence, I sulky, he aloof, while the colonel rattled cordially on. I examined the Founder surreptitiously. His appearance, often described and photographed, I would myself liken to that of an inwardly — if faintly — illumined pumpkin, as if of a mask for Hallowe'en.

The Groupers, save for myself and those left washing up, now departed through the garden night towards the chalet: for there some initial mysteries were to take place from which as a prospective postulant, I was forbidden. Much later, a rather cross girl, hitherto unknown to me, appeared, collected me peremptorily, and urged me across the darkened lawn. In the chalet, "sharing" was now in progress; and I listened for an hour to those blendings of public confession, and do-it-yourself spiritual striptease. Some of them were silly, some simple, modest and affecting — and at these I did not sneer, and do not now. Others were decidedly bizarre. The colonel, for instance (and I quote exactly), prefaced a rambling account of his unregenerate pre-Grouping days by telling the perplexed assembly, "Autrefois, j'avais des squelettes dans mon armoire...." I escaped before closing time, and joined with the landlord and

lady at the house where I was staying in a treacherously
reactionary conversation about "new" religions. Upstairs,
where my Dutch room-mate soon arrived, there was a tense
little scene when he tried to carry on the good work by
proselytizing after hours, and I became very British and said
sleep mattered more than truth.

Next morning, I walked alone around the forest,
contemplated the shimmering snaked Seine, chain-smoked blue
Gauloises, and pondered on faith, my grandmother...and
Paris. The only illumination I received was to get out of St
Germain immediately. I felt I should say goodbye to someone,
so hunted round the school and found the Comte, who appeared
not to understand that I was leaving, or if he did to wonder or
care why, or in fact even remember me at all. Half-way down
the road, Vernon Meadow (or his partner) overtook me at the
gallop, stood panting, stern, and yet forgiving, barring my
escape route, and cried out, "*Go?* You can't do that!" I said
something rude, hastened to the station, and spent the rest of
the day up by the Place Pigalle.

My excursion, quest, and failure had several small sequels,
and one longer-term. Some weeks after my return, Vincent
Pasture (or the other one) arrived in Brussels, called at the
office where I worked while I was out, and left a reproachful
yet encouraging invitation for a rendezvous, which I did not
answer. About the same time there came, from the Dutch boy
of the Bijbel, a long and neatly handwritten letter, expressed in
English needless to say impeccable. He told me, in substance,
that after I'd left the room we'd shared, he found his fountain
pen was missing; had thereupon permitted himself to suppose
I'd stolen it; had then realized the sinfulness of this thought (the
more so as, apparently, the pen turned up again), and wished
now to confess his evil to me, and ask my forgiveness by return
of post. It needed no deep reading of enlightening Penguin
books (then just beginning to appear) for me to recognize that
was a "sin" cooked up to supply him with the luxury of
"confession"...and also, no doubt, present me with the
voluptuous possibility of graciously bestowing pardon. Had I
learned then what I much later did — that the only way to

answer foolish letters is not to answer them — I would have preserved a dignified (if, by implication, offended) silence. As it was, I couldn't resist a snooty answer, the gist of which was...well, one can imagine (and I can't say, on reflection, I regret it).

A graver matter was the showdown with my grandmother. I wrote a full account, probably unjust in many respects, and certainly, in all that mattered, wounding to her. I also claimed my pound of flesh (the promised expenses), and I got them. As is often the case when, between two human persons, there exist large areas of difference and dispute which are hidden from them by happier shared memories, by the illusion all is still well, and by the reluctance to "speak out" and break a spell — one disagreement on a particular event can release a whole chain-reaction of disillusionment and sorrow. This was what happened. My grandmother withdrew further within her faith — and further away from others besides myself; and I do not believe she found fulfilment there. I naturally supposed, then and for a long while after, that I'd at last "seen through" her...but how sure can one ever be, when a person one loves seems suddenly less lovable, that it is not really oneself who has deteriorated? That whatever she had been fond of in her grandson was, when she came to love him less, a quality he himself had lost?

Of the Movement itself, I subsequently learned little. Except to wonder how anyone with any moral instinct whatsoever can be other than revolted by the notion of combining, as in those much-publicized initials, the utterly contrasting concepts of morality, and of re-armament. Also to feel that any doctrine whose chief essence lies in being *anti* something else (as, in this instance, "anti-Communist"), rather than in being positively for whatever it deems better, is doomed, however plausibly presented, to confusion and sterility.

from an unpublished journal of a trip to Germany & Italy, September 1933

(Original in the Library of the University of Rochester, New York)

Friday 1 Sept:
Arrived at the Gare du Nord almost an hour too early, but found the train almost full. Cannot account for this, as trains have all run empty this year — probably the last of the holiday-makers returning from the littoral. Anyway, the train was packed when it started, people sitting uncomfortably on valises in the corridors.

I began Boswell & Johnson in Scotland. The fellow-passengers were a German husband and wife returning from La Paune, a German friend they met by accident in the compartment, two fusty mouldering Belgians, and a German lady of bad reputation, with whom the German friend had been most *galant* (helping her with luggage, buying her fruit, etc.) before the husband and wife got in, but of whom he became at once ashamed directly they did.

The Germans had two children (Anna & Pischi), who came and asked for food from time to time, with endearing baby-German. I compared them, much to their advantage, with a brace of Belgian children in the corridor, with wan and sticky faces, and dressed in horrible sailor suits. The mother of the Germans (though she had black hair, and was perhaps not pure Aryan) was most sympathetic.

I forgot to add there was also in the carriage an elderly belle, whose very elderly swain had to stand up in the corridor all the way to Verriers, and who cast vainly appealing glances on me from time to time!

The journey was quite uneventful, and the weather dull. We arrived at Aachen at 6.30, where lots more Germans got on. One began a conversation with me in the corridor, but I could not understand a word he said, mostly because of the noise. But he seemed quite content with a *ja* or *nein* or a grunt. There was a Nazi S.A. man, who swaggered up and down the corridor, followed by many a pair of feminine eyes.

At half-past seven we were in Köln, and arrived in pouring rain. I went to the Central, and after a walk to the Rhine, returned to bed. Changed a couple of £s, too, at 12.50 and 12.80!

I'm sorry to say I was woken at 2 a.m. by violent itches on the arm. A sleepy search revealed the bug, and I cut him in two with my nail scissors. But that's really Saturday.

Saturday, 2 Sept:
Breakfasted very well, and crossed the Rhine in a tram to Denz. The train was 40 minutes late (but caught itself up subsequently). I had decided to make a detour via Nürnberg in order to witness the *Reichsparteitag*. The train was packed, and the people in my carriage talked the usual talk, i.e. if America hadn't entered the war — why did the Allies steal all our colonies — Germany must expand, and so on. They asked me, didn't I agree, whereupon I disclosed my nationality. They were, however, most polite. I told them the Germans were poor diplomats, but they didn't see it. I told them that Englishwomen would laugh at a notice saying *"Die deutsche Frau naucht nicht"** (supposing it to be in English; but they didn't see that either.

We mounted the Rhine via Koblenz, Wiesbaden and Mainz, and continued via Frankfurt, Offenbach, and Wurzberg to Nürnberg.

As we neared Nürnberg, the towns we passed were literally bedecked and bedaubed with swastikas and the national flag. At Nürnberg itself, the station was a seething mass (no exaggeration) of S.A. men. I had been warned there was no hope of getting a room — but saw a hotel tout at the station. He said he had double rooms only, at R.M.8 (12/6d), so I closed with him at that.

We set off to the hotel, literally threading our way through brownshirts. On the way I saw a mob of them surrounding a car (a big, powerful grey car), yelling, "*Heil.*" I ran forward to see. It was Goering, sitting on the hood, flushed and almost smirking, as he acknowledged their salutes.

*"German women don't smoke."

An Unpublished Journal

At the hotel I was shown to my *doppelzimmer* and was eyed suspiciously by a brace of hefty Nazis in the hall. I found out that the *Reichskanzler* will make no more speeches, but is to appear tomorrow (to ticket-holders) in the Adolf Hitlerplatz. The hopes of my becoming a ticket-holder are slight, I fear. Anyway, I've seen Goering!

I dined, among brownshirts (and four Mosley fascists, who needed a wash and brush-up), and afterwards walked to the Zeppelinfeld to see the fireworks. They were not very well organized, and I returned, dog-tired, in a tram packed with S.A. men. I don't think they thought much of me — a shirker in civilian clothes, who hasn't joined the party!

Sunday, 3 Sept:
...I was called at 6 — the hall-porter had not succeeded in obtaining a ticket for me. I don't think he bothered; he probably thought I looked too poor to tip him.

I was very vague, and so, I must say, was everybody else, as to what was to be seen, and where. I made my way, feeling conspicuous among hordes of brownshirts, to the Adolf Hitlerplatz, where a tremendous arena, covered with bunting, had been erected. A small crowd had collected. But soon S.S. men (who wear black hats and trousers, and appear to act as police to the public and the lesser Nazis) formed a line, and shoved us away. No one seemed to know where one should go to see the procession. People hurried to and fro, but in opposite directions. All roads seemed to lead back to the Adolf Hitlerplatz, and to chains of black-breeched S.S. men, who steadily drove the public further and further back.

I don't think I've yet described clearly enough what the town looked like. All the houses were almost hidden under Nazi and national flags, greenery, photographs and paintings of Hitler and his followers, and various devices: *"Deutschland Erwache"*; *"N.S.D.A.P. Reichsparteitag"*; *"Heil Hitler"*, and so on. The streets were thronged with civilians and Nazis in different species of uniforms, in the proportion of about 1 to 8. Most of the Nazis were most ebullient, but those on duty took their work with tremendous seriousness and self-importance.

Transport was held up; and only large and powerful official cars, and black-painted Nazis and motor-bicycles (I had the pleasure of seeing one fall off, and spill most of his oil) sped along, ringing bells and horns.

After quite a bit of wandering I eventually found a street which was thronged with an expectant crowd, mostly brownshirts, which I joined. It was now about 8 and I had had no breakfast. If I had known that I would have been wedged in that crowd till 11.45, before the procession started, I....

The crowd waited patiently in fairly good order. Mock salutes were given to a band of nurses who walked to and fro. Eventually, at about 11, minor celebrities rolled by in swift cars. Foreign diplomats and members of the Press, and the shoddy-looking English fascists, who were lustily *heiled*.

By this time I was longing for a seat to such a degree that I think I should have accepted a dentist's chair. My back was on fire. But still no procession came by....

Then, *Dieu merci*, the celebrities appeared. Several whom I did not recognize were whisked by in official cars, loudly applauded by the crowd, who saluted, men and women alike. Finally a great shout went up as Goebbels, dressed as an S.A. officer in khaki, drove by. He sat beside the chauffeur, and raised his arm on high *à l'Italienne*. He looks very like photographs, but a little sturdier. He was grinning broadly.

A greater shout went up as my old friend Goering was driven by. He was dressed as an S.S. officer, all in black, and saluted in the manner peculiar to him, and not at all in the manner he recently prescribed for all Germans. He bends his arm right back so that the palm of his hand almost faces the sky. He is fatter than I had thought, but looks very active.

At last the Führer arrived. People high up in attic windows espied him before the crowd, and called, *"Er kommt!"* He drove by slowly, amidst thunderclaps of *"Heils"*. He stood alone in the back seat of his car, with his arm merely bent so that the tips of his fingers reached no higher than his shoulder. He was dressed in the uniform of an ordinary S.A. man, which suits him well. His face was expressionless, set in that moody and sullen cast by which he has come to be known and caricatured.

Whether it is merely the strength of association or not I know not, but he is certainly an impressive figure. He has a strangely detached air, as if this dream that he has realized is still but a dream. And yet his speeches are those of a man of action.

I have never made the popular mistake of thinking Hitler was an *"homme de paille"*. There is something unusual about him, a mixture of simplicity and mysticism. I have yet to see the picture or caricature that can catch his peculiar expression, as I have seen it, and as everyone has seen it in newspapers and in the cinema.

A peculiar impression. He seemed strangely impressive from behind! One understands his attraction to his followers. I do not believe he is a charlatan; or if he is, I don't believe that he thinks so.

Sometime after he had gone by, the procession began but I did not stay long, for I longed to sit down after standing still on an empty stomach for four hours. With difficulty I made my escape, and had lunch at the hotel.

There was a train for Munich at 1.45, which I tried to catch. But I was cut off by the procession, which continued till 4.30, so that I had to catch the 6.46, which brought me very tired to Munich at 10....

Isolated impressions.

On the train from Nürnberg, a very obvious Jew got in, and I felt sorry for him, so exaggeratedly humble and polite was he, and so meanly was he treated by the public, after they had seen his nose.

At the waiting-room in Nürnberg, I fell foul of a brace of Nazis. One of them took my seat (by accident) while I was fetching a plate of sausage. He gave it up when I told him; when he left, he and his friend saluted and said, *"Heil Hitler."* I did not realize I was being saluted, and did not respond. They said *"Heil Hitler"* again, icily and pointedly, and I saw that something was amiss. They asked why I didn't reply. I said, foolishly, I was not German. Then can't you say *"Guten Tag"*, they said. They were very dignified and officious.

The Nazis at Nürnberg were of all shapes and ages, and of all degrees of tidiness. There were several old gentlemen with tremendous beards, and young and old with huge bellies, that ill-befitted their martial clothing.

Monday, 4 Sept:
This morning I sight-saw with great energy.... I love the neo-Russian churches in S. Germany, topped with a dome, and not a spire.

The streets [of Munich] look newly brushed, and so do, and probably are, the inhabitants. Many wore Bavarian embroidered shorts, and short jackets. I bought some Hitler p.cards, and some vulgar ones too, and crossed the Isar. It is swift and beautifully green — greener than the Seine. I came back over some waterfalls.... Further on I came across the Braun Haus — it is smaller than I had expected, but pleasing to look at. The swastika floats on high, and it is well guarded. I noticed that people were not nearly so dutiful about saluting the flag as in Nürnberg — I dare say this will die out with time. The Hitler-party is, I'm afraid, not nearly so interesting and romantic as ruler as it was when it was struggling upwards....

from "Thelma Hulbert and the School in the Euston Road"

Introduction to catalogue of Thelma Hulbert retrospective at The Whitechapel Art Gallery, 1962

The term "Euston Road School" now generally refers to a style of painting, current in the late 1930s, which may loosely be described as "social realism"; "social", meaning that the themes were vaguely proletarian (railway stations, public baths, factories and so on), and "realism" in that their portrayal was — in contrast to the rival styles of surrealism and abstraction — more or less naturalistic. But originally this school was not so much a pictorial tendency as a physical place:

the School of Drawing and Painting over a pin-table saloon in the Euston Road — on the north side of it between Warren and Great Portland Street tube stations.

I first heard of the school in late 1938 when I frequented Michel St Denis's London Theatre Studio by the Angel, and got to know some of the young actor students there. I was at that time myself an art student, studying at Chelsea, and thoroughly dissatisfied both with the tuition I had at the Polytechnic and, more justly and profoundly, with my own incapacity as a painter. The teaching at Chelsea seemed to me to combine the disadvantages of being spuriously "artistic" in its ideology, while remaining academic, in the most uninspired sense, by its essential nature. I longed for something more exciting: for some artistic key that would unlock the floodgates of my own basic incompetence.

So when the young actors at the Theatre Studio told me of a party, in Fitzroy Street, where work by students of a new academy would be exhibited, I accompanied them eagerly. The studio where the work was shown had earlier been Whistler's and then Sickert's, was then Mr Duncan Grant's and was later to be Mr Victor Pasmore's. I had seen Victor Pasmore's paintings in Bond Street, and admired them; but the students' work I didn't find very endearing — it seemed highly competent, far more so than anything I had been able to do, but drab and worthy: lacking in poetry and imagination, the qualities I prized above all others, and certainly lacking in gaiety and colour.

In this mood of discouragement I clutched my Beaujolais morosely and gazed, with the angry eyes of twenty-five frustrated years, at the bohemian assembly; when by good fortune I was introduced to a man who influenced me profoundly, and one of the few of my own generation whom I loved and admired entirely.

This was Graham Bell — a name now, alas, largely forgotten, though a book of his paintings was published after the last war, and an eloquent tribute paid to his character and talents in a broadcast by Sir Kenneth Clark. He was a South African, tall, broad, tough, proud, violent, kind, gentle, sensitive, cruel, generous, dangerous and patient, affectionate and demoniacal. He had a mop of hair like a broom, tiger's or hawk's eyes, a jutting dilated nose, a bitter and sensual mouth, and chin like a knobkerry. His voice rang every change from cooing solicitude to vituperation. He could be blindly ruthless and exquisitely tender, act decisively or languidly, love you or hate you for no apparent reason. He was formidably intelligent, deeply imaginative, and had great areas of blank prejudice and stupidity. In appearance and temperament he belonged to the pages of Dostoevsky. Before the evening was over I was completely under his spell, agreed to join the school, and moved immediately from a slum in Fulham to a slum in Camden Town. The School of Drawing and Painting (please notice the modest arrogance of this austere and factual title) was founded by William Coldstream, Claude Rogers and Victor Pasmore. All three, though well known in artistic circles, had been forced by the penury of those days to do work other than painting — Coldstream in documentary films, Pasmore in the service of the LCC, and Rogers, I believe, in teaching. I don't suppose they expected that their school would provide them with much of an income — and indeed, such was their generosity to the students, I very much doubt if it did. I think that their motives were the better ones of teaching directly, in their own way and freed from art school pressures, and perhaps of trying to build up a following, among younger painters, for their own pictorial doctrines. They secured the patronage of older and more illustrious artists (among them John, Paul Nash and Duncan Grant), and rented the aforementioned premises in the Euston Road.

These consisted of two large rooms, linked by a clanging corridor, the larger back one equipped with a top light. The furnishings were minimal, but nothing essential was missing: model's "throne" (i.e. dilapidated sofa), a forest of stand-up easels, and that instrument convenient for drawing known as a "donkey". For reasons that remained mysterious to me, Graham Bell, although he was closest to William Coldstream, was not one of the three founder-instructors; though he frequently was there, as was Rodrigo Moynihan and other artists older than the students.

The methods of tuition of the three chief professors were contrasted and eccentric. William Coldstream would stand behind you, gaze long and intently at whatever you were doing, and say or do absolutely nothing whatever; it was two months, indeed, before he addressed even a word to me. This may have been due to his tactful horror at my performance, but as much, I believe, to an extreme reserve which is one of his most notable characteristics. To favoured students — as, for instance, the then young Laurence Gowing — he would unbend a little; but confided his observations to them so discreetly that they were, to those outside the intimate circle, quite inaudible. (I sat to Bill Coldstream later on but when, after twenty or so sessions of silence and total rigidity, he said he'd like to begin again, I contracted out.)

Victor Pasmore would sit beside you on an adjacent donkey and make gnomic pronouncements of an abstract nature — often most illuminating, but sometimes rather opaque; he was much addicted, I recall, to the magic properties of the Golden Section. He would then retire to a distant easel and paint a miniature canvas of the model seen over a sea of the backs of the pupils' head. The most practical teacher was Claude Rogers, whose brisk, brusque method was to paint the canvas on top of your own version. This was humiliating, but of all these tutorial devices the one that helped me most in practical terms.

Among the students, there was something of a schism between those who admired the Pasmore-Rogers style (I was in this faction), and others who adhered to the Bell-Coldstream axis. The method in the second case was to pin-point the object with an infinity of dots and lines (by much use of the plumb-line), then carve away, so to speak, the object from its background by an elaboration of vertical and hatched strokes in dim liquid colour. Most of the preliminary dots and pencilled lines remained in the final painting, and I'm not sure whether these contributed a sort of proof of probity (that is, not to disguise one's method), or perhaps an aesthetic embellishment in itself (like Walter Sickert's squaring-up left on the finished canvas), or possibly revealed an incompetence to make a final definite statement without still clinging to this initial scaffolding. The Pasmore-Rogers tendency, if also tentative, resulted in a more positive statement and certainly had more colour: though the hues in all Euston Road paintings remained tonal, rather than explorations of true colour.

As an aesthetic, the Euston Road style, or styles, had obvious limitations. It was a defensive method, based more on a determination not to err than containing any real pictorial discovery. To say it was a latter-day derivation from Whistler, Sickert and the Camden Town painters is, however, I believe mistaken. These artists (except perhaps for Sickert) were never heroes of our teachers, nor held up as examples. The admired artists were the Impressionists and, even more, the Fauves and Cubists, however little Euston Road paintings may seem to betray their inspiration.

In assessing the quality of the school — whatever it may be — one must remember the period in which it briefly flourished. The favourite styles were then neo-abstraction and Anglo-surrealism, and the Euston Road artists were in reaction against the lack of discipline and naturalism of the one, and the artificial image-confection of the other. Their aim, I think, was to adapt Fauve and Cubist innovations to make a new kind of English naturalism. I don't believe they succeeded in this, because the productions of the school remained essentially mannerist — paintings about art, rather than about nature. As for the "social content" of the pictures, I think this was really irrelevant. To choose as a theme a railway station or a factory does not ensure the consequent painting will itself be "realistic". The emphasis on "social realism" derived more from the *zeitgeist* than from any authentic pictorial preoccupation. Poets, novelists, documentary film makers and Unity Theatre dramatists were all obsessed, at that time, by "the people" and their habitat, and the Euston Road painters conformed to the almost universal trend. (It is curious, incidentally, to see this tendency repeating itself thirty years later in the doctrines of Mr John Berger and the social theories of Centre 42.)

It is the fashion, now, to sneer at the leftward inclinations of artists and intellectuals in the Thirties. I can only reply that for anyone of human feeling, it was impossible, in the Chamberlain era, to be an artist without being also some sort of a radical (even if a reactionary radical, like Roy Campbell). The political constipation of the Tory government, the poverty and massive unemployment, the mounting fascist threat and the emblematic battle in Spain, all drove anyone who loved life into opposition. In addition, it is often forgotten that, in the 1930s, England still had — perhaps for the last time — a key political role to play (or, as it happened, not to play) in Europe and the world. Our power is so shrunken today that the effect of any English political agitation has also shrunk. But in 1938, our nation could still make big choices; and as it was apparent we were mostly making the wrong ones, any active intelligence could not escape political involvement.

Thus, at Euston Road, the constant pictorial disputation was blended with political debate. Polemicists and politicians visited us and argued, we painted banners to be carried in processions and on hoardings demanding food and arms for republican Spain. We attended an infinity of meetings and marched down Whitehall telling Chamberlain he must go (which he did, but two years later) and calling for an improbable popular front of Churchill, Cripps and the Communist party. This may seem futile now, since all failed political endeavours must seem futile; but to us it seemed a desperate necessity. And as today, when I hear chairborne publicists mock and rebuke the CND, I feel it is better to be wrong, or partly wrong, and even fail, than to sit wisely on one's bottom waiting for Armageddon. If youth is not radical, it is no longer young.

I have left out, hitherto, what was most attractive about the school. This is that it was, perhaps, the last authentic master-and-pupil academy which has existed in our country. That is the best and oldest way of teaching the unteachable — art — and I cannot believe the cultural factories called Colleges of Art are in any way a substitute for this intimate older-to-younger artist relationship. We saw our teachers paint, we visited them at their studios, we ate and drank and disputed with them. They got our paintings into shows with theirs, introduced us to their patrons, and brought to the school older artists — Walter Sickert among them — and critics — as Adrian Stokes — in such a way that, although students, we could feel we were already fully involved in the artistic adventure. In personal terms, they couldn't have been kinder or more practically effective. All this, I believe, was of far greater value than any actual aesthetic they may have taught us; for an "influence" can always be overcome, or used as a basis for later, different development. Nor should it even be thought, by anyone who may find the Euston Road style uninspiring, that it lacked enterprise and variety. The "abstract expressionist" paintings which these artists and their friends showed at Zwemmer's in the Thirties were a curious precursor of today's action painting, and by their non-naturalistic inventions were far removed from what is generally thought to be the Euston Road convention.

They also introduced us into what was still an authentic bohemia. I know well the arguments against the bohemian existence, but I think the faults mostly arise from its later commercialization and romanticizing corruption. Today, young artists are mostly subsidized, and galleries are eager to consider their productions. In the 1930s, there were no grants, Arts or British Councils (or at any rate, no active art department of the latter), and the painters were familiar with the two chief conditions of a genuine bohemia which are poverty and obscurity. It is not nice, and it is in many ways inhibiting, to be, if gifted, poor and totally unknown. But at least these conditions encourage solidarity and serious (if over-earnest) artistic joint endeavour. (To be, as today, a beatnik is not the same thing at all: for beatnikry is parasitical on wealth that can be plundered, and dependent for survival on sustained publicity.)

Where office blocks arise now between Euston Road and Oxford Street, there were then dozens of studios to be had. You walked into Perkins & Bellord's, offered 30 shillings a week, and they put out their (tattered) red carpet to receive you. Cafés, since mostly bombed, and restaurants now catering for expense-account customers, were inhabited by artists, writers and musicians who met daily and exchanged ideas. People dropped in and out within an area of a few hundred yards, and the front doors were always left open. I lived at the top of the Fitzroy Street house where Victor Pasmore had the Whistler-Sickert studio, and he was most kind to me (Sunday breakfast was a favourite occasion). So, in his more reserved way, was William Coldstream, who I remember nursing me when I had a fever. So, even, was the Euston Road Venus (as she was called), Miss Sonia Brownell, with whom I went dancing at the Astoria ballroom in the Tottenham Court Road.

Then came the war, and the favourite number from the juke-boxes downstairs in the pin-table saloon was "I'm Sorry I Said I Loved You". We painted through the news of Dunkirk and felt, rightly, this was a doomed activity. Some of us tried to volunteer and were told to wait; some turned their thoughts to camouflage or to conscientious objection. The RAF was the least difficult service to get into and Graham Bell joined it, took to the air in bombers, and was killed crash-landing in, of all places, his native Africa;[*]   carrying with him to oblivion a fine talent as a painter, an even greater as a writer, and a force of nature that, had he survived, might have been turned to anything he wanted — politics, perhaps. The school soon disintegrated, and entered its niche in English artistic history.

"Gunther and Horst"
New Society, July 1966

In the pre-war Hitler era, word went round that if you, in England, were willing to offer hospitality to a German refugee, he would be allowed to leave Germany and enter England with you as guarantor.

Inspired by noble thoughts of aiding the downtrodden, I signed the form. I at that time lived in two Sickertian rooms in Camden Town, and had scant means to support myself, let

[*] *Editor's note:* In fact the fatal crash was at Newark, in Nottinghamshire, not in Africa.

alone any refugee. But the authorities made no means test, my guarantee was accepted, and I awaited the visitor to whom I was thus bringing succour.

What I romantically expected was some splendid Jewish violinist, or an ardent Marxist poet, or perhaps some sage from Heidelberg or Göttingen who would impart to me, in exchange for my generosity, perennial wisdoms. What I in fact got was an extremely ordinary German boy.

When St Paul said "the greatest of these is charity," he had a practical, as well as theological, point. By *caritas*, of course, the saint meant not just anonymous subscriptions, but a personal act involving sacrifice. And despite my high intent, it became painfully apparent to me, after the boy had been there as little as a week, that I was stronger on faith and hope than on this highest virtue.

The episode was a terrible lesson to me on the dangers of high-mindedness. Of course, it *is* right to be high-minded — but only provided that you *are*. I evidently was not; for though the lad's behaviour was impeccable, within a month I could have strangled him. (If he reads these lines, I hope he will excuse me.)

For the fact is, it is horribly difficult to share your life with anyone, unless there is some emotional — or, more probably, sexual — tie. In a barrack-room it's supportable because you don't have to be polite, and no one expects it. But for two strangers living on top of each other in an exiguous space, there must be a saintliness that neither usually possesses.

I was reminded of this incident by the arrival of Gunther and Horst. They were German students who came over to London recently. A friend asked, could I possibly put them up and, forgetting experience, I rashly said I could.

Gunther was the solemn one, aged 23, third-year student in art history. Horst was the slightly more sprightly one, aged 20, just beginning studies of world literature. They had hitch-hiked from Holstein, carrying sleeping-bags and toothbrushes. After London, they were off to Liverpool (the Marrakesh of England), Dublin and either Oxford or Cambridge.

In London they wanted to see:

Mods and Rockers
Sit-down disturbances in Trafalgar Square
Speakers' Corner
Street markets
An Indian hemp party
The colour problem
Sexual clubs
The National Gallery.

Some of the items on this programme seemed easy enough, but others fraught with difficulties and dangers. One obstacle was that they were apparently penniless and lived, so far as I could make out, on bread and salt — these were, at all events, the only items they produced from their sleeping rolls. Equipped with a few fivers, the scenes they wished to penetrate might be accessible enough. But by charm alone?

They asked me where I thought the Mods and Rockers might appear. Not having the faintest idea, I suggested Box Hill. Accordingly, one Saturday, they hitched southwards in pouring rain; returning bedraggled and reproachful to announce that nary a Mod nor Rocker had they seen. I blushed to read in the evening paper that the battalions had all been massed at a coastal resort.

The next three items, and the last, they managed successfully, though they were disappointed no one actually sat down beneath Nelson's column. (If I'd known this before-hand, I think I could have arranged for some anarchist friends to oblige.) As for the more dubious aspects of our folk-lore, I made a few phone calls and did the best I could. They seemed quite satisfied, and departed again for Liverpool in the rain, carrying large placards to show potential givers of lifts the cities they wanted to visit on the way.

Why they reminded me of my earlier experience was because of their inexorable earnestness. I have known young Germans since 1931, and this resolute solemnity is one of the things that has always struck me about them. For instance, Gunther and Horst insisted on bedding down in their revolting sleeping-bags, even though I could offer adequate divans. And all their dissertations about England seemed to me

197

preconceived and rather flat. For surely the chief point about England is its oddity, and of London, its squalid romance and, if so, both of these they seem to have missed.

How different did they seem from lads of the Weimar generation? The chief difference seems to me that they are less enthusiastic, hopeful. The Weimar republic has had a terribly bad press, and of course, those regimes that fail are always condemned by history. The fact is, I think, that historians, though they pretend not to, really admire the Hitler era, because it was violent and cruel; and historians, being mostly unbelligerent men with little direct knowledge of the world of power, are greatly impressed by this. But the poor old Weimar republic, though it had nasty nationalist undertones, was pacific and creative, and this bores historians.

It is hard, today, to recapture the atmosphere of the Weimar years. The Germans had been through every economic disaster and, by the time I first met them, were in the midst of an acute economic depression. Yet their youth seemed resilient and optimistic, rather like our modern teenagers though, being Germans, not so abysmally ignorant. On the least pretext the students I knew went walking up into the hills (much too far and high for me), swimming (nudity for both sexes was the fashion then), and would organize concerts (they could all sing perfectly) or interminable, and very knowledgeable, political discussions.

At the same time, they did suffer from the scourge of earnestness, and jokes, if any, had to be rather basic. They seemed also to have an undue respect for any authority. I remember one day we saw two cyclists nearly killed by a Mercedes-Benz at a traffic crossing. It seemed to me nobody's fault, but the driver of the car stopped, got out, walked back, slapped both cyclists smartly on the cheeks, and strode back to the car again. The cyclists were indignant, but did not protest, and my comrades justified the incident by pointing out that since the cyclists had come from the left (or was it right?) they should have given way, and therefore were in the wrong. No doubt they were, but I can't see two English teenagers taking a slapping from a stranger without hitting back or at any rate arguing.

Horst explained this to me. He, Gunther and some friends had visited a rally of SS veterans in North Schleswig and deliberately got into arguments with them — a bold thing to do, which I'm not sure I would. They told the SS: "We don't reproach you with what you did *then* — we're too young to, anyway, and can't judge what the pressures were. But we do reproach you with what you're doing *now*." They were all thrown out of the meeting, but were ready to try again.

Such evidence as I've heard and seen suggests to me that most German youth really does reject the National Socialist past. But what it lacks, compared with the Weimar generation, is any manifest *joie de vivre*. The ethos of the *wirtschaftwunder* makes little appeal, though they accept the economic benefits it offers. What I expect is happening is that Germans of all generations are passing through a period of national convalescence, and from people in this condition one should not expect wonders of temperament and creation.

So though I found Horst and Gunther bores, and was delighted when they left to stand on the Old Kent Road in the rain with their placard marked DOVER, I couldn't help feeling sympathy for them. Our own kids, delightful though they are, really have it too easy: I mean psychologically, not just financially. If the sins of the fathers are visited on the children, our own are unaware of any such sins (not that there weren't any), and because of internal prosperity that masks our external indebtedness, can live it up in relatively mindless bliss. But Gunther and Horst have to deal every day with ghosts and, in the shape of a divided country, ominous presences.

from "Pacific warrior"
New Society, June 1966

(...) Foreseeing conscription in 1940, and determined no drill sergeant would lay his horny hand on my lily-white person, I joined the auxiliary fire brigade. I had thought of pleading conscientious objection — quite dishonestly, since I am not a pacifist; I had also contemplated turning up at the barracks — as some of my enterprising acquaintances did — with hennaed hair and a revealing wiggle of the hips. But both these devices seemed too humiliating, and so I chose the fire brigade which, while involving discipline and a uniform, did maintain civilian status.

But by an accident of fortune, I had to enter hospital when the fire people signed me on, and by the time I came out their lists were full and they no longer wanted me; so the Wiltshire Regiment claimed me for its own.

Yet as soon as I reached Devizes, and began that appalling, fascinating life as a military rookie, I realized that this was what I'd really wanted all the time. And throughout six undistinguished years of military service, I grew to love the army emotionally, while totally rejecting its ethos both intellectually and spiritually. And if this seems an absurd attitude, I would only suggest that it is fairly typical, and typical also of the general public attitude today which I have described.

Let me begin with what I hated about army life. Armies are concerned with death, and I don't want to kill anyone — even when my country is in danger — and still less do I want to be killed, even for so noble a cause. Three-quarters of military discipline is mindless, obsolete and wastefully self-frustrating — apart, of course, from being highly irritating. No one can serve in any army for years without becoming to some extent an inbred malingerer and scrounger, irredeemably slothful. (In all those six years I do not recall one hard day's work by civilian standards — though I certainly remember dozens of most unpleasant ones.)

But what of the virtues of military life? First, in an unexpected way, it is egalitarian: the bullet or shell knows no favourites, and private you and the galloping major are both targets. It is also egalitarian in the sense that while authority reigns supreme, all are subject to it, whatever their rank. And further, because I believe genuine talent — of a military kind, of course — is more quickly recognized in the army than in any civilian body, promotions — with the rare exception — are by merit and results.

Next, there is what one might call the imperative of friendship. You can live a civilian life and get to know anybody or nobody, just as you please. In the army, you are absolutely forced to close human acquaintance with hundreds, literally, of men of whose lives you would otherwise have known absolutely nothing. It is a great lesson in the reality of our common clay: that men you might otherwise despise, or be indifferent to, are vital to your very survival, just as you are to theirs.

Then, despite the rigidity of hierarchies, and the imperative of orders, the life is in many ways calm, assured, blissfully irresponsible. If you do what you're told you don't have to do anything else, and your whole inner life becomes free, contemplative and protected. No one can relax as soldiers can: no one — except, perhaps, in a monastery or prison — can dream as richly.

To these I would add that the life is an open sesame to your country's present social structure, and its past social history. Today, I have no difficulty in talking to men of any class, whereas before I was in the army I just couldn't do this. In addition, since any army is, by nature, a kind of fossilization of ancient social traditions, to have lived in one is to understand these intimately.

Thus it is, that though I rejoice with the young today that they do not have to know this servitude, I am forced to think that they are missing something; and when I talk to anyone who has *not* been in the services, I am conscious of a certain emotional barrier. For the army does in some senses break you down and build you up again — and despite the tares and barnacles which mar your new personality, there is also the sense of having undergone an experience common to all mankind....

MacInnes's first novel, To the Victors the Spoils, *closely follows his own wartime experience as a Sergeant in the Intelligence Corps after the Normandy Landings. His unit operated in the wake of the invading troops in northern Europe before entering Germany. This episode, which highlights MacInnes's ambivalent attitude towards violence, takes place in Holland; and the script of the BBC talk that follows deals factually with the events which forms the climax of* To the Victors the Spoils.

from *To the Victors the Spoils*
(1950)

One day Lieutenant Vroons sent word he wanted to show us two suspects. A call for help from Vroons was unusual unless there was a hidden motive, and I drove round to the Gendarmerie with a double curiosity.

Standing on the bare boards of the guardroom were two men with the devalued, shop-soiled look that settles even on the honest — even the respectable — after spending a few hours in a police office. According to Vroons, these two had been arrested at the canal bridge "on suspicion". When I asked of what, he made a face that allowed for a variety of crimes and said, "Smuggling, at any rate, for certain."

"That's a matter for you to deal with, isn't it?"

"I thought perhaps there might be more: things of interest to yourselves. They have no papers — are illegally in the forbidden zone — refuse to give a logical explanation of their movements."

I looked at them. They stared back in an exaggeratedly injured way, and shot sharp glances at each other to decide whether their attitude should be meek or else aggressive. "I'll take them round to our place and talk to them," I said.

"No, Sergeant, what I would suggest is you question them further here with me. Let us get to the bottom of this together."

It seemed he wanted a military stooge in the room to help scare them into talking about the smuggling. "I'll take them with me," I told him.

"Well, as you wish. I will give you an escort."

"That's not necessary, just tell them to get in the car."

Back at the billet, I brought them one by one into the mess, and asked them what they'd been doing.

Most of the remarks men make, and the expressions on their faces that go with them, suggest different, underlying meanings to a wary observer; and you often feel that two or three forbidden questions would quickly bring you to the edge of secrets whose outward traces you detect in dubious statements, and see imprinted on guarded eyes. Because of our position, and even when mere curiosity was really the motive, the habit of asking these questions was growing on us. And we had learned that even when a man came into the office on some innocuous errand, a few deft, irrelevant feelers would often start a hare that could be pursued to the visitor's discomfort. But the perfect opportunity was the set interrogation of a suspect.

In simple cases, provided the interrogator is patient and asks sufficient questions over a period of time, it is always possible for him to discover whether the suspected person is telling the truth or not. Truth is so powerful a force, it needs such effort and ingenuity to try to suppress it, that it is impossible to tell a long story of supposed events without contradictions, particularly if the interrogator asks you to repeat your tale a day or so after you have first told it, and if he has made notes of what you said at earlier hearings. For if it is hard enough to lie convincingly, it is harder still to remember the lies you told.

Of course, most persons, on being subjected to an interrogation, will be sensible enough to offer a story that is largely made up of truth. But as he listens to your tale the interrogator, paying attention to how you tell it as much as to what you say, will become aware of certain passages in which the story no longer flows naturally; and he will conclude that here are the parts of it in which the facts have been altered or suppressed.

Yet when the participants in the duel have reached the point at which the one has detected these areas of untruth and the other knows they have been detected, that is only the beginning. To discover a lie is not the same thing as discovering what really happened. And at first the interrogator may pursue the suspect up a blind alley, since a reluctance to reveal the fact may not mean that a person has performed the actual deeds of which he is suspected. For instance, if these men didn't want to say what they were doing between 9 and 9.30 on the evening before last, that might not mean they were German agents, which was what interested us, but perhaps that they were looters, or were working a black-market deal. So that the labours of the interrogator may lead to the discovery of discreditable facts which are of little interest to him.

Equally, the interrogator may encourage the suspect, by pointing out the absurdities in his story, to tell another one just as untrue, which has also gradually to be discredited; and when this has been done, the suspect may invent another tale and then another, while the ultimate truth recedes even further away. Or in other cases, a stupid person, or one who can pretend to be stupid (which is very difficult), will repeat the same story again and again in slightly varying forms, even when it has been clearly exposed as incredible; or else, after giving two or three quite different versions, he may obstinately return to his original story from afar, and deliver it up as if it were now a new one.

To break the deadlock, an experienced interrogator can make use of two sorts of technique: violence to the mind and violence to the body, or a combination in varying proportions of the two. His choice will depend on the personality and physique of the suspect, also on whether the particular interrogation concerns a matter of opinion, or one of fact. On whether, for example, a suspect is pro-German, or has sabotaged a bridge. Acts and ideas are involved in each other, but an interrogation will usually aim principally at detecting the one more than the other.

Interrogations on matters of opinion are by far the more complex, because the total personality of the suspect is in question, and also, if he is to discover anything, the total personality of the interrogator too. Mind must speak to mind if facts about the mind are to be known. In this case, the interrogator will not be so likely to use physical violence, though demoralizing doses of petty cruelty will be a help. Physical force might get an immediate, crude avowal; but as coherent statements may have to be secured from subtle men, and since it may be desirable for the suspect to repeat his admissions to the interrogator's superiors, and even to repeat them in public, the more intensive and durable technique of mental violence will be preferred. What the interrogator will aim at is to undermine the suspect's inner confidence in his own beliefs, whatever these may happen to be.

These psychological methods (as they are called) seem extraordinarily effective in the majority of cases if applied with relentless persistence. By these means it may be possible to make most men admit to any opinion in the long run; that is, not only to admit what they themselves believe, or think they do, but even to admit what the interrogator wants them to say they believe. One reason for this may be that few men have beliefs that are entirely their own, reached by personal endeavour and held not blindly, but with free conviction. And where a man has clung to his ideas fanatically, it may be this very fact that leads to his collapse in the total solitude of the interrogator's room. There he may find that it was the will to faith, not the faith itself, which he was living by; so that the interrogator's own rival faith may now seem equally desirable. Or if the ideas which the suspect has long held involved its denial of other truths once clear to him, the painful weight of suppressing these truths will fall from him when he is invited to confess. It may be so even when his confession is compounded of half-truths he believes in less.

This is the moment at which the interrogator makes use of his enormous tactical advantages. All interrogators, however temporarily, have power, all suspects are alone and weak, their names (so easily reversible) describe their relative position in a given context. It does not matter that the interrogator may be inwardly guilty of the same heresy as the suspect, nor that he be one who, potentially, is in a similar psychological condition. However spurious his claim may be, he must try to cow the suspect with the moral and physical force invested in him by circumstance. He must be deity, father, tyrant, and force the suspect to his knees as sinner, child and slave. He must abet the deep-seated urge to confession that seems to exist in many men, and which in some arises from fear, in others, from humility. For men often have a prescience of some ultimate interrogation, of which this is the fraudulent parody.

So it would be revealing to compare the interrogator's report on the suspect with all that has been said and thought (if one could know it) in the concrete room where they have been alone together. If they are both persons of a certain degree of psychological complexity, a peculiar relationship may sometimes establish itself between them in which their minds, locked battling together, seem to desert their personalities and achieve a promiscuous intimacy like that of two bodies which have come together in lust. The further they advance into this mental forest, the more the questions begin to contain other questions and the answers, other answers. Till sometimes the initial object of the inquiry may partly be forgotten; and since the interrogator must necessarily reveal much about himself (as any question is always, in a sense, a statement), the answers of the suspect may themselves become questions, which fly back into the interrogator's soul and challenge him on points of human conduct far removed from the ones which were at first to be established. For everyone in the world has secrets he does not wish to reveal, and almost everyone has unworthy secrets. So that the interrogation, though it begins as an attack and may often result in the suspect's confession, can also become a defence on the attacker's part, or possibly even end in a mutual unspoken confession of the kind with which priests and psychiatrists, as well as political inquisitors, must be familiar.

But in fact, however much the interrogator may himself have disclosed during the struggle, his report to his superiors will confine itself to the admissions of the suspect. An interrogator can never afford to be interested in the total truth — even as he sees it. For him, truth is a raw material, and the confession he extracts from it, his commodity. He does not see that it is impossible to tell truth to a man who is himself untruthful; or that only in the case of two entirely honest men would truth and the confession ever be the same. And yet, what is striking about political inquisitions is how haunted they are by the presence of truth, how vehemently those who conduct them affirm, from out of their distortions, that they have found it. As if they knew that darkness cannot exist of itself, but only because of the absence of light which must at all costs be hidden.

This preoccupation with discovering truth by means that must destroy it, with mechanisms for extracting confessions by pseudo-scientific psychological tricks, by truth-drugs, by lie-detectors, by inflicting mental and physical wounds — all points to an immense fatigue with the mask men's mouths draw over their minds. And hints at a sick longing for simplicity, and even at a hidden wish for the relief that would come from the awful clarity of direct, wordless communication of thought.

In the present instance, my interrogation of the two men Vroons had caught was getting nowhere; perhaps because in this "matter of fact" I was not using "violence to the body". But I had never dared do that, and therefore didn't know what physical force would make a man disclose. I guessed that in most cases, if you went far enough, you could get him to admit any particular act he'd done, or that you wanted to pin on him. But this was conjecture.

So I gave up for a while, and went in to tea. Dennis was there, and I told him about them. When he said he'd soon get at the facts, I let him go in there without me.

After a while, I heard him walking with them down the corridor to the garden, and suddenly ashamed, I ran out and found he'd put them face to a wall, and taken out his pistol.

"Put that away!" I shouted.

"Don't interfere!" he screamed.

"What the hell do you think you're doing? Put that bloody weapon away."

His eyes had a killer gleam, animal, not vicious. "Do you want to get results or don't you?" he cried out.

"Not that way."

"Not that way! Do be realistic. You ask for my help and then come piddling out here to stop me." The men moved away from the wall and stood looking curiously at us. "If all our troops had your mentality, they'd drop their rifles and apologize to the Germans."

"That's different, and you know it. Shooting at an armed soldier isn't shooting an unarmed prisoner."

"What do you take me for? I was only trying to scare them." The gleam was fading, and his eyes showed irritated exasperation only. "Do you suppose if the Gestapo got hold of you they'd share your point of view?"

"No, I don't. Do you want to model yourself on the Gestapo?"

"Well, do you imagine if our people caught Himmler they'd just take down what he said on a typewriter?"

"No, they'd probably hit him."

"Well, then."

"They'd know who they were dealing with. What do you know about these two?"

"That's just it. They won't talk, so I'm treating them rough."

We took the men indoors, bustled them through to the mess, and went on with the argument in the corridor.

"Look here," said Dennis. "I'm not brutal by nature, but what you mild-mannered people don't realize is that most men aren't as scared of getting hit as you are. There are certain cases where a good, straight bashing will get at the facts without damaging a man all you think. It all depends on the man, and it's all a matter of degree."

"Of degree. Where do you stop?"

"That's a question of using your sense of proportion."

"A sense of proportion changes."

"Let's get this straight. Are you against violence because you're against it, or because you're afraid of it?"

I had no answer....

"Prison Governor by Chance"

BBC Home Service, June 1953

For six months I'd been arresting people. That was what we in Field Security used to do. Nazi officials, SS, Gestapo — anyone in the "Automatic Categories" — we grabbed them and slung them inside. "You were an *Ortsgruppenleiter*?" you said to some trembling idiot. "Yes, yes, sir, but I never realized...." "Quiet! Come with me!" You filled in a form and, hey presto! in he went. Those people were odious, I had no sympathy for them, but this tearing away of frightened monsters from their screaming wives and children did begin to prey on my nerves. I mention this to explain my state of mind when I accidentally found myself in charge of a prison in the last weeks of the war.

One day about a dozen of us — an officer and NCOs — arrived in a town where for some days we were the only British troops. The German army had surrendered, but it was still milling about fully armed. Hundreds of deported allied workers were roaming the streets marauding, and crowds of German refugees were doing much the same. The city was governed precariously by a ridiculous old German general who kept issuing proclamations but did little else, and by an extremely shaky Nazi Burgomaster torn between a sense of duty to his citizens and a terror that the British would arrest him — which in due course they did. As soon as we got there, they laid their problems at our feet. Could we get the gasworks going? Should they requisition food from the farmers? Ought there to be a curfew? And so on. *We* had no authority to solve these problems — let alone any technical knowledge — but as chaos seemed the alternative, we found ourselves making snap decisions until the Military Government arrived.

The first day we got there, some freed allied workers told me about the prison. They said it was packed with allied political prisoners, people who'd worked on our side, many of them dying. Couldn't I get them out? These allied civilians stood around and looked at me fiercely. I must get them out, they said.

I went along to the prison and found that the German warders, armed and trigger-happy, were keeping order by the skin of their teeth over 1,500 men (the prison was built for 700, by the way) — Allied and German political and criminal prisoners who knew the war was over and quite naturally wanted to get out. I learned this from the Deputy Governor, a cadaverous distracted man — he had a nervous collapse a few days later — and I went back and told my officer. He said, "Prisons aren't our pigeon, Sergeant. They're a Mil. Gov. matter. Besides, our job's arresting people, not releasing them." I said I thought if we didn't do something soon, there'd be a riot. He pondered deeply, then told me he'd try and get authority. He got it, because Military Government, when they arrived, were so busy with more pressing problems that they hadn't time for prisons. "Carry on, old boy," they said, "carry on, please do." So with my officer's blessing I set off for the prison with another NCO.

We drove in and asked to see the Governor. He turned out to be an elderly Colonel with a sad brutal face and about as much imagination as a plank. He escorted me to his office, waved me respectfully to his chair and stood at attention like an ancient monument. His first question was, "Do you take full responsibility for the orders you will give me?" I said yes, I did, and from that moment I had his job.

The Colonel told me he knew who some of the men in his prison were — he had documents about them. But there were hundreds more who'd been evacuated there from other prisons that he hadn't a clue about — didn't know their names even, let alone what they were there for. He said it as if this administrative confusion — not his fault, of course — was most distressing.

I told him to bring what documents he had, collect details about the other prisoners cell by cell, and to send me within an hour a representative of each allied nationality, to be chosen by the prisoners themselves. He sighed — yes, he actually sighed; he was the only man I've ever met who did it — and out he went.

I must tell you about two more of the prison staff — the ones who turned out most useful. The Deputy Governor was a minute man with wide hips and tiny feet, fantastically efficient and utterly humourless. He wore a huge pass-key round his neck on a string, and he used to touch it from time to time perhaps to make sure it was still there, but also as if it were a holy object, just as a cleric might reverently touch his pectoral.

The other, the prison Secretary, was a cunning and capable ex-soldier who'd been posted to prison duties after he'd been badly wounded. He seemed to despise the prison, and he was the only German there who treated us as fallible fellow-creatures and didn't think we were some sort of high authority disguised as NCOs.

Meanwhile the allied delegates arrived in the Governor's office — or rather, in *my* office. A dozen men in tattered prison clothes — French, Belgian, Dutch, Polish, Yugo-Slavs — every nationality. (I looked up their convictions afterwards, and found they were heroes from our point of view, with sentences to death, life imprisonment, twenty years or more.) But just now they came in with a courteous decided air, masking their emotion and very conscious of representing their nation at this critical moment. We handed round cigarettes (the first they'd had for years) and all sat down.

I asked them to take charge of their national groups for a day or two until we could get them evacuated. I told them the Germans had orders to take no sanction against any allied prisoner without reference to me, and asked them to prevent their men provoking the Germans if they could.

At this point the pattern of post-war political divisions in Europe already emerged. The Western leaders — French, Belgian, Dutch and so forth — all agreed. But among the Slav delegates there was a lot of argument in languages I couldn't understand. It transpired there were two rival delegates for each nationality. One pro-East, the other pro-West, and both wanted to be boss. I said no, each was to be responsible for the men who accepted his leadership. All said this was inadmissible, but eventually agreed. The Western delegates looked on pityingly while this discussion was going on.

Then they all asked me if I'd arrest the *whole prison staff*. They had dozens of witnesses, they said, to prove these men were responsible for acts of violence, theft of prisoners' belongings, violations of the Geneva convention. I said no, not till we'd got *them* out.

Then they asked had I seen the prison hospital. Because if I hadn't, I'd better go *at once*.

I called the Secretary and we passed into the control block of the prison; storey upon storey of metal stairs and corridors lined with cells. Prisoners shouted at me through grilles in a dozen languages and armed warders dropped their eyes as we passed by.

The prison hospital, intended I suppose for about twenty men, had about fifty men in packed beds and on the floor. Many were dying — and soon did. Some grew hysterical when I came in, grabbed hold of my arms and wept. One man — a Dutchman — said, "Look at me." I looked at him. He said, "No, look at me," and started fingering his blanket. A German orderly drew it aside. The Dutchman looked as if he'd snap if you touched him. As we went out the orderly came up and said, "This is shameful. But what could we do?"

Later our officer paid us a visit. He said troops were starting to come in, and he'd try to get the Garrison Commander interested. He said he expected the Garrison Commander would be glad to get the prison cleared, because the cells would be needed for our own War Criminals.

That afternoon I went through the documents of the allied prisoners — some hundreds of them — with my NCO and the Secretary. Most were political, and even those the Germans called criminal weren't, of course, to us. Sabotage. Slaughtering of cattle. Desertion from forced labour — these were admirable crimes. There were the odd murderer and robber, but I decided we'd release them all and let the Allied Missions sort them out.

Then I looked at some of the documents of the German prisoners, and found many were in for doing things we'd been telling them to do over the radio for years. Deserting. Harbouring allied deportees. Even listening to the BBC. So I decided to let out most of the Germans too. My NCO said,

"No, no, Germans are outside our terms of reference." I said we had no terms of reference. I found an unexpected ally in the Secretary. Even some of the criminals, he told me, were excellent fellows, and perhaps we'd kindly let out some of them too? I said, well, perhaps some but not all — we must draw the line somewhere. So during the next few days the Secretary, the NCO and I went through all the cases like Appeal Judges and decided who to keep and who to let go. There were about 200 left out of 1,500 by the time we'd finished — but that's anticipating.

When the Colonel heard that Germans were also to be let out, he looked as if he was going to explode. "German *convicts* are also to be released?" he cried. "Yes!" I shouted. "They are. Go to the Burgomaster and requisition clothing for them. They can't go out of here in those prison clothes." "Of course they can't," he cried. "Such clothing is prison property and will be needed for others to be convicted in the future." He looked at me with contempt and hatred, sighed, and shuffled out. Later he came back and said all he could get from the Burgomaster was naval uniforms. Would it be suitable for such men to wear such garments? I said I didn't think they'd mind....

During the next days we got the sick moved to the German city hospital — some refused to go, incidentally, and said they'd rather stay in prison among their friends. The new Garrison Commander arrived and told us he'd have a camp ready for the allies in a few days. When we asked him for decisions of principle he smiled and said, "Oh, you seem to be doing quite nicely — carry on." So we started releasing the Germans at once. Some walked out in a matter-of-fact manner, others sobbed and tried to embrace us, and one embarrassed us by shouting pro-British slogans in defective English just outside the prison gates. Two we'd let out came back for the night because they couldn't find accommodation in the town, and were very indignant when I had them ejected. Then a head warder lost the pass-key that opened every door in the prison, but found it when the Deputy Deputy Governor threatened to have him executed. Meanwhile the British prisoners — War Criminals and so forth — started arriving and began to fill up the cells that we'd been emptying. Among them was Dr Rosenberg, who asked me to deliver a personal message to the British Commander-in-Chief.

When the camp was ready and the day of the evacuation of the allies dawned, the national leaders mustered their parties in the huge cobbled courtyard and saw them on to the lorries one by one. Each group had somehow made a national flag and as the first lorry-load of every nationality drove off, they struck up their national song as they passed through the prison gates. These national anthems, usually so formal and so solemn — I have never heard them sung with such fervour and such ecstasy. Even the German warders, peering discreetly out of windows and of doorways, seemed to be moved and impressed.

After this came anti-climax upon anti-climax. No longer buoyed up by nervous tension, many among the allies died — and good food wrought havoc on most of their digestions. The German Colonel himself was arrested — still not quite understanding what was going on. Other German warders, seeing which way the wind was blowing, very sensibly fled. Proper British officials of various kinds began to arrive, and my usurped authority rapidly waned. But by this time I was heartily sick of the prison and only too anxious to leave the Governor's office where I had sat in state. And when I did leave I'd only one regret: that I hadn't simply, in the first few hectic days, opened all the cells and let everybody out. I'm convinced to this day that nobody would have noticed or very much cared. And I was haunted by the thought that among the two hundred or so I finally left behind, amid all the confusion over nationalities and identities and convictions, there might still be some who were completely innocent.

from MacInnes's unpublished "Thoughts" book

1948-1954 (University of Rochester)

1948

A writer, when he meets a person, tries to stir up the mud in his soul.

Other people's "wisdom" is something received at second hand. One can only become wise by listening to those who are not — who are excessive. One must beware of one's own "wisdom" also, since it must be constantly changing.

It is impossible to be generous unless you have nothing.

1949

If I were writing myself a letter of good advice, I should say: Be patient, & learn by listening to everybody, even to idiots.

With one woman to love, and one friend to tell the truth to, you can travel through the jungle of society in the necessary second gear.

When I fall back on my instinct, as I often do, it serves me wonderfully, but the answers it gives are those of an observant child.

Writing weakens your character and resolution. You become part of a process & live from day to day.

The degree of evil you see in the world is the degree of evil in yourself.

What an impression of solitude it gives if your lover lies to you.

Grant me a perpetual thirst for absolutes.

What is dangerous about writing *anything* that does not correspond to an inner need is the at first unrealized corruption of your honesty & sensibility that results from it.

One should not write anything of this sort — anything at all. That is the only solution.

Let us be less illusioned about friendship and friends; it never goes deep. The only human bonds that lift us out of loneliness are those of the flesh — even when indifference or hatred are also present in them.

The consciously evil handle the consciously good as a drunk man handles a vase that might break.

I cannot bear, cannot support, the sight of the consciously good.

Do not ever explain anything to anybody; if they cannot see, they cannot see.

The past! the past! that is English culture. I cannot pretend to the future, but oh, let me tell the present.

Homosexuals sip half-pints.

The dangerous Puritan is the Puritan who boozes.

You have to keep your heart exercised like your muscles, or it daily shrinks.

Men turn to God when weaned from human comfort.

A saint can only seem good to others; never to himself.

The theme and tragedy of [Benjamin Britten's] *P. Grimes* is homosexuality &, as such, the treatment is quite moving, if a bit watery.
Grimes is the homosexual hero. The melancholy of the opera consists in the melancholy of homosexuality.

Another reason why they all confess so readily is that they are so tired of lying.

I sat up in the night writing letters. I worked on through the night because I wanted to catch up with my work, because I was behindhand and wanted a new start.
I went to bed after breakfast.

I slept all through the morning and was woken in the afternoon by the phone bell, with a call from the woman I had been writing to.

She said, "The chairs & sofa look idiotic without you." I said, "I shall come back soon." She said, "They look idiotic." I said, "Don't move them till I come back."

She said, "Do you love me always, always, always?"

I said, "Always, always, always. Always, always, always. Always, always; always, always, always."

1950

All great achievements are in spite of, not because of....

Telling the truth or not is largely a matter of habit.

"Nostalgia" is the longing for what never existed, and its painful pleasures are more acute than those pleasures it seeks to recapture.

Only trust strangers.

All hosts are bullies.

The wisdom that comes with age is useless; one must be wise when one is young.

Two unpleasant characteristics:
— To give third parties advice which is in fact addressed to oneself;
— To make a parade of virtue for acts which have been done by inclination or, worse still, by fear.

If chastity were not considered a virtue, it would be quite attractive.

The bottomless pit: the Devil can give you one look, & claim you for his own.

The fallacy of the idea of the "Welfare State" is that it is a purely static conception.

Anyone who has not done something remarkable, really remarkable, by the time he is 32, need no longer worry whether he is Jesus Christ reincarnated, or even Napoleon.

1951

The reason why societies have insisted on filial piety is that the old men who govern societies know, from their past recollections and present observations, that most sons and daughters wish for their parents' death.

I am the donkey who hesitated between two thistles, & died of starvation.

I have no real critical spirit: my "judgements" on the work of others are my judgements on my own.

Everyone in England is soaked in privilege.

The whole art of the novel depends on the fact that people can't read one another's thoughts.

The only way to avoid misery is to expect the worst of everyone & demand the best of yourself.

1952

Men's idealism arises from the fact that they must get a stand; women's realism from the fact that they lie on their backs.

Evidently age does bring some "automatic" wisdom, since A[ngela] T[hirkell], who has behaved with passion more than wisdom, now has a sly, hard sardonic look in her eye, which she darts out at you in a penetrating, disturbing way.

Her unspoken thought is, your achievements do not match your pretensions.

Should like to go away from here and live somewhere else: have lost too much spleen on these surroundings. Streets reflect your own frame of mind....

The habit of worming a way inside a personality and then dropping it....

This idiotic preoccupation with evil... fly & spider attitude to it....

Throwing away capital of friendship & money....

The weak are often alone & hate to be. The strong are rarely alone & like to be.

Unpublished Thoughts

Ambition: to be a sinner who doesn't sin....

Oh, intolerable sight of the Katherine Dunham dancers† —
such animal beauty makes the streets & the days unbearable!
What is there to compare with animal beauty, grace &
intelligence? Nothing.*   It is a terrible punishment to grow old
& die.

The pain of falling in love is like the pain of a loss....

When you think that you have suffered everything, you find
that your capacity for suffering is virgin, untouched.

When you're older you've got to appear dignified despite
yourself.

Only the rich can afford to be mean.

I hate moralists with the same passion as that with which
they hate themselves.

1954
Your soul is never sold to the devil until you die.

The devil can take no initiatives, only manoeuvre on others
(but God knows that's a lot).

† *Editor's note:* The Katherine Dunham Dance Company, whose exotic appeal was part-
aesthetic and part-ethnic — its dancers were black Americans, mostly from northern
cities, and its musicians (drummers) were Cuban — first toured London in 1948.
MacInnes encountered the dancers on their return visit in 1952 and modelled Isabel
Cornwallis and her company, in *City of Spades*, on them.

* animal courage.

MacInnes continued to jot down "thoughts" until the beginning of the Sixties, but increasingly, they took the form of scribbled injunctions to himself to behave better: drink less, smoke less, be nicer to people, avoid meaningless sexual encounters, and so on.

The following letter, to his friend from pre-war days, Robert Waller, then a BBC radio producer in Bristol, gives some idea of MacInnes's state of mind at the time he was about to embark on the writing of City of Spades. *The letter is the final one of a series prompted by Waller's complaints about MacInnes's high-handed behaviour towards the landlord's agents of the house in Regent's Park Terrace in which MacInnes had a flat (a house which was still in Waller's name despite the fact that he had left London).*

from a letter to Robert Waller,
dated 15 January 1954

Let me first refer to "all your old friends" whom I cut and snub and try to make use of. I don't know who they are, which, in your eyes, will, I expect, make it worse. But condemn me as you may, I don't care about them: not 2d, my dear chap, even if I frizzle for it. In the first place, I don't believe, as most Englishmen do, that "old friendships" have anything sacred about them whatsoever. Friendship is like love, if it ceases to exist it ceases to have meaning. There are people I consorted with ten years ago who now mean nothing to me, and if I see them again all they'll get is a cheery wave at best. There are others whom I'm still attached to, whom I'll cling on to like grim death. But the sentimental blackmail of the good old days leaves me indifferent. And anyone who is small enough to complain to a third party that old So-and-so has cut them, deserves, in my opinion, to be cut. Can you imagine explaining to me, for instance, that old XYZ had snubbed you? You wouldn't give a damn. Nor do I.

A letter to Robert Walker

Please don't tell them I'm "really" a "loyal friend" and so on. It's not true as far as they are concerned, and even if it were, they wouldn't believe it. Don't "stick up for me", my dear chap: it's not worth it; if they can't see for themselves they never will. As for being nice to acquaintances if I think they can be of use to me, I don't blush at this as you seem to expect. Certainly, I would be. Certainly, for instance, I'd be prepared to lick, say, [D G's] arse if I thought it meant a broadcast even though I dislike her intensely. I wouldn't lick it long, but wd. certainly lick it.... You try being a free-lance some day, dear boy. You live in a different world when there's no pay-packet — try to imagine it, some time.

Now, my dear Bob, my "sensual allegiances" that fascinate and horrify you (largely, I think, because you are not sensual — though intensely passionate). What, my dear fellow, do you *know* about them? Aren't you...having illicit sex by proxy when you dream of all this? In my sex life, I have always (no, almost always) done what I'm sure *bloody few* in this world have done, always taken the burden of sin off the other person, always preserved their humanity intact. (It is this, not vestiges of morality, that has preserved me from spiritual damnation.) When I think back over my Negro period, for instance, I am amazed at the load I have carried for them in every possible way. What do you know about all this?

At this point, now I've struck back at you at any point where I think you're vulnerable (fundamentally, I mean, not merely tactically), I lower my guard and say, for your information, that I think my life is in most respects catastrophic and a disaster. Why this should be, I don't quite know, since what you would call vice bores me so painfully, and what you take for spiritual pride is as much [...] an ingrained loneliness of spirit that goes back, I should say, to circa 1917, has shown few signs of altering, and probably never will. Yes, my dear chap, my life on the spiritual (and artistic) plane is crippled and thwarted. *But:* unregenerate to the last, I would not trade my angry solitude, my exasperated contempt, my anti-social arrogance, no, no, not at any price, for the *dreadful moment* at which a human being becomes a judge and tries to eat somebody else's soul.

from "National Health Lottery"
New Society, 5 May 1966

The variety of treatment that can be had under the NHS is enormous. It ranges from the best to the worst, and in choosing which branch of it he will patronize, the potential patient must himself first diagnose the whole Health Service. If this diagnosis is correct, he will be saved; if it isn't, he may not.

I was reminded of this by a visit recently for a check-up at the Hospital for Tropical Diseases. As I've discovered to my cost, everyone who visits the tropics should have a check-up on his return. Those three or four obligatory inoculations mean little. There are dozens of other diseases you can catch, and only an early examination will reveal if you've got one of them.

Some time ago I started running temperatures for weeks. I visited my NHS doctor: no solution! I went into a hospital where several doctors had a go. They pumped me full of penicillin and discharged me. The temperatures immediately returned.

The thought then struck me that the illness might have something to do with a visit to Africa two years before. But could a disease lie dormant all that long? Indeed it could, I discovered — and much longer: retired colonial servants in Tunbridge Wells can suddenly be taken ill years later because a dormant bug they caught way back in the tropics ceases to be dormant.

So I found out there was a Hospital for Tropical Diseases and rang it up. It gave me an appointment, the doctor examined me for an hour, then said, "I don't know what's wrong with you, but you're coming in here at once and we'll find out." I was immensely reassured by that "I don't know." None of the physicians who had hitherto failed had said that.

In coming, by that lucky inspiration, to the Hospital for Tropical Diseases, I was fortunate. Being a teaching hospital, it has the pick of the doctors and nurses of the London area. The wards hold six, an ideal size, without the loneliness of the private room, or the Dickensian conditions of a multiple ward.

Then the tests began. They took marrow out of my bones. They put tubes down my nose into my belly ("some prefer putting it down their mouths," said the nurse — "you just try whichever doesn't make you vomit"). They used an embarrassing instrument known to patients as the "shuftiscope". ("We're very interested in the reactions to this thing," said the doctor, as he inserted it. "Some show marked signs of resistance, which we consider psychologically significant.")

There was a lot of taking and giving of blood. After multiple transfusions, I can no longer speak of the purity of my gore. Who were the donors? Pakistanis, possibly? The removals were made by a gleaming African lab attendant. He used to heat the blood with a spirit lamp beside the bed. "You look like a demonic chef," I told him. "Oh, yes," he said glintingly, "and I am making a crepe suzette."

The first clue came from a female foreign doctor (I think Czech). While I was upended on the mobile X-ray machine, filled with revolting barium meal, she noticed the liver was inflated. However, the actual discovery was made when they were looking for something else. They were inserting a long hooked needle between my ribs to nip off a bit of flesh to see if I had lung cancer (as they cheerfully told me afterwards). In doing so they pierced the liver.

"Call all the nurses!" cried the doctor. "A perfect case — the fluid's the colour of anchovy sauce." He extracted a pint and a half of this to begin with. It was caused by an amoebic hepatitis, and was indeed the result of an African microbe and its millions of progeny.

Czechs, Africans, West Indians, Australians, Hong Kong

Chinese and the dozens of Irish girls — where would our hospitals be without our immigrants? Old timers in the ward used to watch with interest the reaction of colonial newcomers to their saviours. A chief of police, who rather threw his weight about, blanched visibly when an African house doctor bore down on him. Dark nurses were okay, but *doctors*...though even in America, I read, without alien surgeons the system would collapse.

But there was one stalwart Briton — Sister T, with a breast like Queen Mary's covered with medals. We took an instant dislike to each other, and battled for five months like a drill sergeant and a barrack-room lawyer. I am a strong believer in the absolute necessity, for reasons of morale, for refusing to be bullied even by nurses who are saving your life. Their tactic is to try to reduce grown men to cradle status ("Have you been a good boy? Come along now, beddy bies" — to middle-aged gents).

This must be resisted at all costs — even if you have tubes in your arms and stomach, can't walk, and feel like the death you're close to. "Why did your visitor stay half an hour after the bell went?" Sister T cried, flourishing the book of rules before my blanched unshaven face. "Because he enjoys the pleasure of my company," I shouted. She tried to bar me from bringing in food from outside, that in the local diet being inedible; pointing out that if tinned pâté poisoned me, I might sue the hospital. I asked what about those revolting sardines she'd given us on the official menu? She appealed to the doctor, I appealed to the matron. The matron, being by good fortune a Scot with a taste for Nicholas Monserrat, upheld me. Before her might, even the doctor quavered. Sister T glowered.

Fame came to me when I learned that slides of my "case" were being used by the doctors at their lectures to the nurses. Some months after I was discharged, there was an international congress of tropical doctors at the hospital, and my own asked me and others of his star patients if they'd mind coming back to the wards as exhibits. I thought this might take an hour or two, but not a bit of it! Sister T made us all get into bed, though cured, and took our temperatures and supplied bed pans.

Now supposing I hadn't thought of ringing up that hospital? Well, I'd probably be dead. This suggests to me that what is needed are doctors who, in grave cases, do nothing but try to route patients in the right direction. Unless your illness is fatal, there's probably someone somewhere who can cure you. The thing is, to find him....

"Bankruptcy"
New Society, October 1962 *(Out of the Way)*

I was dying in bed, with tubes stuck into my arms, at the Hospital for Tropical Diseases, when a small man in a bowler crept into the ward and placed a grubby piece of paper on my belly. With faltering hands I raised the document to my feverish eyes: it was an Order in Bankruptcy.

For some years prior to this nearly fatal illness, I had neglected to pay my Income Tax. Forms came, and the usual warning notices in black then red, next letter peremptory or pleading, then admonitions from legal departments at ominous south coast addresses (the greater the danger, the further away the menacing office), till at last I was waylaid, in Camden Town by a stranger who handed me a summons. I was to appear at the High Court to explain my neglect of civic duty. I failed to do so, and the Inland Revenue set the bankruptcy machinery in motion.

Everyone knows about Carey Street, but perhaps not so many have entered the Dickensian construction called, with somewhat sinister realism, Bankruptcy Buildings. It is a vast, dank pile of huge corridors, enormous cellars, bleak courts and then a profusion of little cubby-holes inhabited by the Examiners. From the moment you are made bankrupt, your Examiner takes over your existence and has powers over you greater than those of any man except a warder.

I was fortunate in mine: he was a sandy, ruthless, amiable

man who, from the outset, clearly regarded me (not altogether unjustly) as an imbecile. What surprised him most was that my only debt was to the fisc; for usually, it appears, a person heading for Bankruptcy Buildings runs up debts in all directions. He was also puzzled, since I was his first writer client, by the peculiarities of publishing: by the fact, for instance, that an advance on a book is a debt and yet no debt, since it is not recoverable from the author if the book, when put on sale, fails to recoup the amount of the advance.

My Examiner began by putting me through an inexorable third degree about my entire life since childhood, and then called on me to produce every relevant document I possessed. He was favourably impressed by the mountains of incoherent papers I shovelled on to his desk, and ferreted through them for several happy hours. Then he produced the most formidable schedule — of thirty or more printed pages — that I had ever yet seen. He gazed at me with quizzical despair and said, "You're supposed to fill in all these, but perhaps I'd better, hadn't I?" On these sheets he entered the most remarkable lists of assets, debts, and double-entry balances, which I thankfully signed blind on the dotted lines he indicated.

Meanwhile, the Examiner was fiercely pursuing all *my* debtors — one of which, surprisingly, turned out to be the Government. I hadn't had my war gratuity, said the Examiner, frowning. Well, he'd get it for me, even if it wasn't normally payable until I was sixty. Did any periodicals owe me fees? I rejoiced to hear that he was hot on their trails, recalling the weeks and even months that so many had made me wait before paying for a piece they'd already printed long ago. I was beginning, in fact, to warm to my Examiner. Here was this expertly competent man, vigorously conducting my affairs that I'd been so incompetent at handling myself. I would like to add that, however professional he was, at no time did my Examiner in any way bully or rebuke me. It was like being in the hands of an able, if rather impersonal, doctor.

Then came the day of my public Examination. Fortified by an adequate dose of pep pills, I faced the presiding judge and the cross-examination of the Official Receiver (or of one of his deputies, I believe). He took me remorselessly, yet courteously, from the time of my birth up till the present day, giving due weight to my achievements, and sparing none of my numerous follies. The total effect of this confessional was not, I must record, unpleasant — it had the effect of a psychological purgation, a sort of last judgement on a miniature scale.

But all the time the Receiver was heading me towards the inevitable Moment of Truth. My situation now laid bare, he slightly lowered — yet sharpened — his voice and asked how, if I was earning this much, and the tax was only that much, I hadn't paid it up as was my duty? At this point I realized that if I didn't come clean, he would turn ruthless. So I said, with truth (though perhaps also a part of duplicity) that I had been irresponsible and unwise. This admission once wrung from me, the Receiver turned off the heat and raised the question — with some sharp prompting from the judge — of how I proposed to rectify the situation.

As is generally known, the Receiver has, during your bankruptcy, complete control over your assets and earnings, and can decide what portion of these you may retain to keep yourself alive and enable you to pursue your vocation. By a curious convention, the sum allowed to the bankrupt person is related to his financial status before bankruptcy: the more you had, the more you can have. This may be partly an instance of the class bias that survives in English legal practice, but it is also, perhaps, based on the commonsensical theory that a businessman, say, needs more to get on his feet again (supposing he's going to try to) than does a manual worker. In my own case, it was soon apparent that I would be able to pay my debts in full, so that the Examiner didn't bother to check on my actual earnings.

As for the disadvantages of being a bankrupt, in the case of an artist they are slender. You cannot go into business or borrow more than £10 without disclosing you are undischarged, but as you don't want to do the first, and don't mind admitting the second, the constraint is negligible. On the positive side, being relieved of your creditors' pressure, you have a breathing space to turn around and get organized. (A theatrical agent even told me that artistically writers do their best work when bankrupt, because they think more of quality than of fees that must in any case be paid into the Receiver's hands.)

For a businessman — the more usual kind of bankrupt — there would also seem to be pros as well as cons. If, by ill fortune, he is genuinely unable to cope with creditors, then bankruptcy will afford him a respite. If he is — to be frank — a crook, and operating in areas of business whose standards of probity are not high, the disgrace will not worry him much, and he will probably continue to function through his wife, relatives or associates. It is only, I imagine, to a man of affairs in circles where personal honour is most prized — for example, a solicitor — that bankruptcy might prove fatal.

As soon as you have been examined, you are advised that you can apply for a discharge. The Court will give you this if it esteems you have made a genuine effort to pay a percentage of your debts, and if your creditors cannot advance valid reasons why you should be kept bankrupt till you pay in full or, at any rate, pay more. Before my own examination, I witnessed an appeal for discharge which was opposed by an enraged creditor who alleged he had seen the bankrupt at race meetings and in night clubs; nevertheless, he was discharged. So far as I could understand the ideology of bankruptcy, as one might call it, the principle is to discharge wherever reasonably possible — presumably because most bankrupts are, so to speak, sterilized commercially, and their talents useless to the community. This doctrine — if I am right in thinking it exists — is clearly open to abuse, but I expect the Court can distinguish the crafty goats from the rather more innocent sheep.

In my own case, I was not discharged, but annulled. This happens when you pay 20 shillings in the £, and the dossier is then, I believe, destroyed, as it is when you are acquitted on a criminal charge. The ceremony of annulment takes place not in the Court, but in a private room; and in my own instance, the official (whose exact status I could not determine) was a benevolent, rubicund person wearing a carnation, whose attitude was cordial, if mildly admonitory. This process of annulment took some time, however: months passed after the payment into Court of a sum well in excess of the total debt (thanks to the sale of a film right to Mr John Osborne, for whom the heavens be praised), and there are legal costs amounting to several hundred pounds (whose severity, it seemed to me, might actually have the effect of discouraging anyone from trying to pay their debt in full). Humanly, and even practically speaking in most respects, it is hard to fault Bankruptcy Buildings: but in the matter of expense and delay, the law hasn't altered much since the days of Dickens when this grim palace of disaster was erected.

"The Schweitzers — Who are they?"

Queen, February 1962

What IS a "Schweitzer"? You mean the Doctor personally?

He is the best example, but is far from being the only liberal saint.

"Liberal saint"?

A Schweitzer is saint of the anti-clerical liberal church, and is worshipped by progressive persons who despise superstition, and believe themselves above it.

How can one recognize a Schweitzer?

Major clues: **1** He will not be of your nationality. **2** He will operate in some distant land of which you know next to nothing. **3** He will be successful in some humanitarian endeavour of whose beneficial effects you know far more than do peoples on whom these benefits are bestowed. **4** His public attitudes will be peremptory, not to say bullying. Minor clues: **1** He will be artistic, literate, or eloquent in some striking manner. **2** He will never be criticized, not indeed objectively assessed, by the *Guardian* or the *New Statesman*. **3** His admirers will describe him as "compassionate" and his attitudes as "deeply moving". **4** To attack him — even criticize him — will be deemed blasphemous, and arouse liberal ire.

We may now see how the Doctor himself meets all these requirements to perfection, and is thus the symbolic Schweitzer. He is an Alsatian, lives in Equatorial Africa which few Englishmen visit, runs a hospital most Africans have never heard of (and when they have, disapprove of its antiquated paternalism), and his public declarations are *ex cathedra*. He is a writer and musician of note, much loved by the progressive press, he radiates (at least, on English admirers) benevolent compassion, and not to appreciate him is, in liberal eyes, a sign of original sin.

But all this is unjust to the Doctor, surely?

The question misses the point. Liberal saints are not self-elected; they are chosen for worship by their progressive congregations. A Schweitzer may be an admirable man, or one less so; he may not even wish to be a saint; but once the progressive have decided that he is, there is little he can do about it.

The phenomenon might more accurately be called Schweitzerism, since it derives from the needs of those who create the cult, rather than from the men (or, more rarely, women) selected for adoration.

But why do liberals need saintly Schweitzers?

All men seek heroes, especially those who scorn men who seek heroes. And to the progressive temperament, it is essential to feel:

a: that however dreadful things are in England, *in some land out there* (for which I am not responsible, and where I can take no direct action whatsoever) progressive things are being done.

b: that so long as my liberal hero is *in situ*, operating in a land beset with "problems", these problems will somehow cease, or at any rate be diminished — or at all events I needn't worry about them much.

c: that provided this hero is doing something miraculous far away (like running a primitive hospital for Africans, while playing J.S. Bach on a pedal organ), then *I* am absolved from doing anything there (still less at home), because I have appointed him my saint.

In short, the chief virtue of the liberal saint is that he must be as ineffective as possible while appearing to be effective, and as irrelevant to English life while deemed in some way to be relevant to it.

Is the Doctor, then, the original Schweitzer?

In the modern sense he is, yet looking back, we may detect some "Ur-Schweitzers" of the nineteenth century, and some Pre-Schweitzers of the recent past.

The two great Ur- (or "precursor") Schweitzers are Ludwig van Beethoven and Leo Tolstoy. They have in common a talent of genius, domineering and ill-tempered dispositions, and the faculty of evoking in their followers not just the admiration due to art, but a mystical regard amounting to a religious (though non-clerical) cult. Thus, while Mozart was esteemed a great composer only (which is surely more than enough), Beethoven aroused in his public — and still does — emotions of fearsome awe: his music is not excellent, it's holy. And while Pushkin is allowed to be a fine writer, Tolstoy is seen as a literary Moses, founder of a dogmatic faith.

	Rational reasons for admiration	Progressive reasons for admiration
Gandhi	Superb politician and empirical mystic	He slung us out of India, disliked factories, wore a dhoti, was English-educated, and his triumph frees us from imperialist guilt.
Einstein	Physicist of genius and noble man	His brilliant discoveries led to the invention of the atom bomb, but so long as he was around it was spiritually de-fused, and couldn't blow any of us up.
F.-M. Smuts	Able white African political soldier	Admired England, liked English-speaking South Africans, climbed mountains and devised Holist philosophy, and though he rigorously applied *apartheid*, did not say he liked those dreadful Nationalists.
B.B.	Highly paid expert for top international picture dealers, and eminent art historian in a limited field	Invented Italian renaissance painting, transformed his art-expertise fortune into cultivated one-man Florentine museum, and if he neither liked nor understood the art of his own century, that is excusable since our era is deplorable.

Prominent Pre-Schweitzers of more recent vintage are Gandhi, Einstein, Field Marshal Smuts, and Bernard Berenson. In considering their achievements, we may compare the reasons for which they may be rationally admired, with the mystical motives for their transformation, by the faithful, into Schweitzers.

And who are the contemporary Schweitzers?

The list is long, but we may select these names from it, and suggest reasons for their liberal sanctification.

Paul Robeson.

By his presence in the United States, the "colour problem" there is neutralized, and doomed to elimination. Through his performance, by generous English invitation, in the part of Othello at Stratford, a great blow against racialism was struck (despite the fact that, until he plays a "white" part like Lear, no "colour break-through" in the theatre has occurred, and that casting him as Othello is a polite way of continuing racial discrimination). His spirituals are to be admired (since these dismal songs perpetuate the slave concept of the Negro), and the infinitely greater achievement of American coloured jazz "greats" (like Armstrong, Ellington or Gillespie), in breaking down race barriers by advancing their own people, and educating white audiences, are of far less significance, since progressives do not care for jazz.

Charles Chaplin.

The decline of Chaplin's talent, and of his creative influence in the cinema, are in direct relation to the increased esteem in which progressive people hold him: so that now, at his lowest artistic point, his Schweitzer-rating stands higher than ever. It is a progressive dogma that Chaplin is the great clown of all time, whereas he is a fine mime and comedian (stemming from the English Music Hall where he learned his art), and in no sense a true clown like Leno, Grock or W.C. Fields. His message is mocking and pathetic, not tragic and authentically subversive as a real clown's is; but as progressives have no tragic sense, and (despite their image of themselves as rebels) are in fact conventional people, their error is understandable. In addition, Chaplin is a Jew, which enables the liberal-minded to indulge in their cherished philo-Semitic instinct — which is really an inverted form of anti-Semitism, thoroughly insulting to Jewish people, and which absolves them from the tougher necessity of making organic, acceptive, human contact with Jews in England, Israel or elsewhere.

Danilo Dolci.

The first reaction of any human creature to Dolci's work in Sicily should be — why is it necessary at all? Why has Sicily been left a rotting, corrupt slum amid European prosperity, and how can this be altered? Why have so few of the billion dollars poured into Europe found their way there (in return for which neglect, the Sicilians have now exported the Mafia to the United States)? But the progressive feeling about Sicilian poverty is that it enables Dolci to do his charitable work (splendid in itself), excuses anyone else from doing anything, and affords the vicarious spiritual thrill of "selling all and giving to the poor" — a thing even progressives do not want to do. That poverty is odious and remediable, rather than that "saintliness" is admirable, is a distinction liberal sanctifiers do not see.

Nehru.

He is perhaps the only liberal saint whose qualities are so great that he has somehow managed to evade canonization. Goa of course has helped, but even before that shattering of liberal illusions by the sensible step Nehru took, he did not quite measure down to Schweitzeresque requirements. Nehru is too tough, rational, effective to be a Schweitzer; and so far as India goes (a country much loved by progressives, to the total indifference of the Indian population), the recollection of Gandhi must suffice, unless his land-reforming disciples can be built up as acceptable substitutes.

And what of England? Have we no Schweitzers?

By definition (see above) this is not possible, since it behoves the perfect Schweitzer to be one who is adored from afar, and whose activities are international. It may nevertheless be possible to suggest some Native Schweitzers who, if not quite fit for local worship, could be candidates for sanctification by Schweitzer-seekers overseas:

Mr Victor Gollancz.

The combination of formidable commercial acumen, automatic and fervent espousal of all good causes, a built-in tendency to forgive every kind of enemy (without asking the enemy's permission), and the propagation of liberal-religious concepts on a supermarket scale, seem hopeful characteristics.

Lady Violet Bonham-Carter.

High-minded declarations on every topic, the *grande dame* air with which these are delivered *de haut en bas* to mortals, and the resolute creation of an atmosphere of "what I feel is right, and good for you whether you know it or not", are promising symptoms.

The Rev. Donald Soper.

It is the rare achievement of Dr Soper to be hero both of Nonconformists and agnostics. This is achieved (in the manner perfected by Dr Hewlett Johnson) by transferring the tones of clerical authority to the hustings, without forcing the irreligious to realize the distinction.

We have also some Junior Schweitzers on whom expectant eyes may be directed.

Mr John Berger.

The blend of a tough temperament and loving manner, of persuasive appeal to sweet reason backed by a menacing hysteria, and, above all, the deft art whereby this candidate contrives to suggest his personal speculations have the force of absolute moral sanction (that if you don't accept his love or threat, watch out) make his development worth watching.

Mr Philip Toynbee.

Once a most promising candidate, in the days when he was inviting us to march to the Hungarian border and, in a notable interview with Graham Greene, contrived to say more — and far finer things — than his illustrious interlocutor, his prospects have since been marred by the unfortunate injection of an element of common sense (inappropriate to a Schweitzer), which puts him out of the running for the moment.

"Vicky" (*of the Beaverbrook press*).

Those ill-drawn, mawkish, "humanitarian" drawings of famines, disasters, and atrocities, contrasting with the mild astringency of his critical productions, reveal him, in this aspect of his art, as an emotive, mindless suppliant for progressive sympathy. Unlike great caricaturists, whose theme is the follies of mankind, he also departs from satire when himself drawing international Schweitzer-figures, whom he invariably flatters. His self-portrait "signature" drawing, hinting at the harmless "little man", contrives, by its juxtaposition with the attack in the cartoon, to suggest he both loves power and rejects it (a characteristic Schweitzer attitude). He appeared most effectively as a potential minor Schweitzer in a *Frankly Speaking* broadcast, in which he obliged his three interrogators (themselves, it's true, Schweitzerettes) to treat his pronouncements with respectful awe, and with total lack of the critical sense a real satirist engenders in his admirers.

Any more? Miss Jacquetta Hawkes? Sir Charles Snow? Dr Bronowski? Mr Laurens van der Post...?

Enough is plenty. You may draw your own list by applying the tests hitherto suggested, and chiefly by employing this one: is the potential Schweitzer a man seeking to create a personal empire by morally blackmailing the gullible into supposing he is not, like the rest of us (and however good or gifted we may be), a fallible human being, but a person entitled, by the law of God or non-God, to authority over the minds and deeds of others?

Note: When Low and Vicky are praised for propounding ideas hostile to those of their employer, has it been noticed that in both their cartoons Lord Beaverbrook is invariably portrayed as a gay, sympathetic, imp-like creature, and that he appears in them far more often than his real political significance merits?

But such attitudes, surely, are neither liberal nor progressive?

No: a true liberal loves freedom, material and spiritual, for others and himself. A real progressive wants health, wealth and happiness to grow among us here and now. But persons who seek Schweitzers are mere mannerist liberal-progressives — professionals at it, one might say; and their use of these fine terms as aggressive, domineering war-cries is just as meaninglessly sterile as is that of "duty", "honour", "service" by reactionaries they despise. Each group is as hidebound, conventional, and negative as the other, and closer in spirit — or lack of it — than they imagine. In each, the absence of self-criticism is directly proportionate to their instinct to criticize the world. In each there is a decayed "religious" sense which seeks "faith" as a substitute for felt and reasoned action. Each, beneath the bare banner of "progress" or "tradition", is indifferent to the real life of our country, because wherever life is surging now in England, it cannot be moulded to these dead categories.

So it seems we should speak not of "liberal saints", but "saint-seekers"?

Yes. A saint has no need of followers, or he would not be a saint. The saint-seekers make of liberal heroes they select, the scapegoats for their unfulfilled, frustrated aspirations. They call them "saints" to avoid trying to be likewise, and, by setting them apart, to increase the difference between heroes and other men. Schweitzers cannot exist without Schweitzer-worshippers. And it is only when the liberal progressive becomes, by acts in his own life, the saint in whom he tried to exteriorize his weaknesses and limitations, that the need for Schweitzer-figures will depart.

"Chief Boy"

New Statesman May 1961

The prophetic book was *Kim*, and the new revelation *Scouting for Boys* — a startling example of the power of the Word: for when Baden-Powell issued his six fortnightly messages in 1908, there were no Scouts except for those he had camped with a year earlier on Brownsea Island. The Book came before the Movement and created it.

To propagate his idea, the hero of Mafeking possessed the skills of a maverick general and, less remembered, those of journalist, actor, artist, spy and copper — all of which talents were reflected in the Movement's burgeoning ideology. This swiftly grew into the weirdest blend of Old Tory militarism, Arthurian mysticism, masonic secrecy and ritual, non-sectarian religiosity, nature and beast worship, and a passion for peoples (Red Indian, Australian aborigine, African tribesmen) whom Christian imperialism had tried for centuries to destroy. To thousands of urban, industrialized lads in fat, crumbling Edwardian England, his call sounded like a sacred dinner bell. They donned shorts, seized staves, pledged dangerous vows, and rallied to their self-elected Chief.

Above boy level, B-P's support came from his monarchs (all four of them, consistently) and from those few in high places who shared Kipling's exacting, never-realized vision of their country's destiny. Orthodox (that is — then as now — empirical) Conservatives had no time for him, especially top military brass. In Africa, while they had blundered blindfold yearly on to the Transvaal, B-P had filched their laurels by his strategically irrelevant and brilliantly publicized exploit in Bechuanaland. (Perhaps they suspected, too, that he admired and understood Boer tactics — disloyally to brother generals using those of the Crimea.) Such stalwarts may have also sensed that if Scouting belongs unquestionably to the Right, a lot of its concepts were subversive — or seemed so fifty years ago; indeed some of them, though gripped within a framework of conformity, still are.

The most disquieting was B-P's notion of the soldier. It is closer to Wingate's or Montgomery's (who both surely learned from him — in public relations if not tactics) than to any beloved of British brass. Apologists for Scouting tie themselves in granny knots trying to prove their Movement is "non-military", though Baden-Powell's writings make it very clear for which activity his Scouts should chiefly be prepared. Yet para-military in the manner of the Boys' Brigade — twenty years older than the Scouts and never, despite formally swapped salutes, friendly to them — the Movement certainly was not. B-P believed in the discipline of consent, given freely by individuals to an acknowledged leader; and if anyone is his true military heir today, it is Dayan.

Then, his ambiguous attitudes to class and race. He was in both a paternalist; but he did believe that if you thought yourself the better man (boy scouts are "men"), you must prove it by drastic personal ordeals, unprotected by "background". Anyone with youthful memories of cosmopolitan Scout camps can vouch that — if only within that closed, artificial, momentary world — guile, brawn and personality alone forged the master race. Accent and colour lost their power — as they do in the army itself (among "other ranks"), or in the republic of a prison, whatever the structure of society outside may be. Within these three institutions there may be found a rough parody of communist existence, which capitalism has unconsciously created in its midst.

His feeling for "primitive" peoples was disturbing. It was "romantic", sure enough, but not condescending. He thought our skills finer, but respected and envied theirs and taught his Scouts to. His instinct for nature was the same. We English, great country-lovers, are its cruellest vandals; and animals, which we so much cherish, we slaughter, debase into pets, and devour in ravenous platefuls. The wonder of animal life, and our ancient kinship with it, we have lost; B-P tried to rediscover them, and bring the jungle into towns. He also restored the night to city boys who'd switched it out, and told Scouts how not to fear the dark.

But his most original and, in its day, unorthodox conception was of what young boys are and need. They like to be bossed — and trusted: not bullied, adulated, or neglected. B-P, born in 1857, was no Victorian in his attitude to kids. Right from the start, in *Scouting for Boys* Part I, he issued instructions, asked for reactions. He knew boys can teach men; and he didn't try to "teach" anything he couldn't himself do. In an era of bad food and pauper hospitals, he fussed sensibly over the lads' health: though best remembered for his sermons about knots, his Ambulance Badge was the one he told them to value most.

Those who mistrusted these qualities could find reassurance in the fatal limitations of his message. In *Scouting for Boys* and, even more, the later *Rovering to Success*, the pallid passages are on politics and sex. The earlier book — naturally, considering its period — is downright and brisk on empire and onanism: this good, that bad — take it or leave it, men. By 1922, in the Rover book, B-P had mellowed. On sex, there's still much on the pistil's reception of the stamen, and the corrective raptures of "a wet and scrubby towel"; but he does allow that "if we were living in a primitive state of nature, boys would behave about sex matters just like our friend the stag!" (his exclamation mark). In the chapter on politics, he admits that "Labour has gradually and steadily raised itself on its merits as a National institution, through the work of a succession of earnest, far-seeing men." Short of this, his thought halts at a cartoon wherein Employer and Worker throw off Profiteer and Communist, and join hands with John Bull to exchange Contracts for Tools.

This failure to confront adolescent maturity has kept the Movement permanently in short pants. In its *Official History* [*B-P's Scouts,* by Henry Collis, Fred Hurll and Rex Hazlewood] the three writers (all "Scouters") report on the leadership's recurrent and perplexed dismay that so few Cubs become Scouts, and even fewer Scouts want to be Rovers. The clue to this mystery may be that an adolescent boy starts to think of girls, and of what sort of world he's got to work in: and finding the Movement vague in these key matters, he hangs up his lanyard and departs. Thus, at its senior levels, Scouting attracts mostly the man-boy of Anglo-Saxon cultures — of which the Chief himself was a notable example. The *History* tells us, not surprisingly, that Senior and Rover Scouts are only a fraction of the whole, and that Wolf Cubs already outnumber Scouts themselves. Mowgli still howls compellingly from the wilds; young Kimball retired when the last troopship left Bombay.

The case of the Left against the Movement, in substance correct, has often been unjust in detail. The Scouts were never, as has been alleged, incipient fascists. As early as 1920, when John Hargrave, then Commissioner for Woodcraft and Camping, tried to transform the Movement into a neo-pagan cult, B-P smelt heresy and sacked him; whereupon he founded his own Kobbo Kift ("The Strong"), anointed himself "White Fox", and in 1929 became a Social Credit Green Shirt. When fascists on the Continent grabbed power, they promptly suppressed local Scouts — not merely as rival storm troopers, but because some measure of individualism and international goodwill were by then built into the Movement's ethos. (On the advent of Hitler the swastika "Thanks Badge" had promptly to be withdrawn — a confusion of emblems that may also have vexed Kipling's final years.)

The charge of clerical indoctrination (revived as recently as 1954 in the Lords by the first Viscount Stansgate) also needs qualifying. B-P's God, like Kipling's, was non-denominational; and the scope of the Movement proves that non-Christian peoples find it acceptable and — perhaps a harder feat of persuasion — Roman Catholic nations as well as Protestant. Primitive sectarian endeavours to make Scouting itself a "religion" were also roundly pronounced anathema. As for the notion that Gilwell Park, the Scouts' international shrine, is a sort of Caux for congresses of do-badders masked as gooders, the Movement's chronic poverty is the best disproof. Unlike divinely subsidized MRA, the Scouts are perpetually obliged to beg by public appeals or by the amiable blackmail of *Gang Show* and "Bob-a-Job".

B-P has also been accused of Caesarism. Certainly, in earliest days, the Chief himself loomed large on the Movement's widening horizon: perhaps because he knew that until he got Scouting moving, he really was it. Hints were heard too, in the 1920s, that the hereditary principle had much to recommend it; but this concept failed to impress the Scouts' increasing confidence in their own right to shape the Movement. As this broadened, so did B-P's ideas. So far as he could, in what had perforce become a complex organization, he decentralized authority on to counties and, later, nations. Five years before his death in 1941, he chose a Deputy (Lord Somers) who was in fact Chief Scout elect. Today the succession seems, if not democratic, papal; with B-P not over-sanctified, but remembered as the unique Founder.

There are now over six million World Scouts of all ages, about a third of them in the Commonwealth. As the figures rise annually, the force of the Founder's vision wanes, if only because so many of his novelties have faded or become familiar (shorts, for example, deemed "indecent" in 1908, are no longer thought to be so). Boys mature earlier, "spending money" offers other alternatives to the tyrannies of poverty — and of Mum and Dad. The "problem" of youth is no longer its constriction, but its freedom not to know what it wants to do. Boys, as they always have and will, like to move in mobs; but suspect adult organization, and aren't very satisfied with their own.

The Right, by tradition, steals the Left's ideas: this custom could be reversed. So far as it's possible to judge, the teenage and sub-teenage youth of England remain uncommitted — "non-political" but radical, even anarchic. A young educated élite is now increasingly involved in socialist thinking; but between them and the vast mass of youngsters (let alone between all youth and the titular leaders of the Left) an enormous chasm gapes, without a bridge. B-P was keen on bridges — no doubt he thought them a useful extension of his cherished knots. He saw his chance to build one between the young and the Old Right in 1907; and if anyone of the Left feels like mocking at what he did, the last laugh (or smile and whistle, as he might say) is still so far with Baden-Powell.

from "The Anarchists"

Queen, May 1962

The great inhibition to anarchist endeavour in our country hitherto has been that, until about the mid-1950s, everyone who thought at all had faith of some kind left in one of the orthodox parties, or in the communists. Then suddenly, from 1956 onwards, there came a crack in the social-political situation that released old allegiances and left the conventional parties frozen into postures that ignored these changes. There came Poland, Hungary, Suez, death of Stalin, rise of Africa, the New Left, the teenage phenomenon, the race riots, the teacher strikes, Osborne and the new-wave writers, and, for what it is worth, CND. In this atmosphere of instability (which is still, I believe, very relative in its depth and extent), anarchists could at least begin to breathe, look about, and act [. . .]

Despite the frenzied efforts of politicians of all hues to persuade, bully and frighten us into their parties — or at least acquiesce in their activities — I believe the vast majority of the human race detests, mistrusts and despises the purely political animal — where it is safe for them to do so. Yet I also believe, with the anarchists, that the instinct to unite with others — at any rate, at some point and for some objects — is equally widespread among mankind.

The anarchists are the only non-political — indeed, anti-political — party in existence. They're not even, in fact, a party — you can't join, take out a card, pay a subscription (though donations would be welcome), and anything you do or don't do is because you want to. The only way you can "become" an anarchist is to wake up one morning and find you are one.

From what I have read of anarchist lives, and observed of those I know, they have also the peculiarity among political groups of behaving, in their private lives, according to their philosophical doctrine. They don't love the masses from afar (which has always seemed to me a way of hating and fearing them) — in fact, they're not interested in "the masses", but in creating a mass movement based on self-persuaded, not converted, individuals; and if they do like particular persons, then they will work with them and for them. Temperamentally, they are informed, versatile and resourceful, indulgent of human weakness, but set high standards for themselves. Like all political groups they have sectarians and extremists, but fewer I think than other parties, because they nod kindly to these wayward brethren, and then get on with the business.

To the popular belief that anarchists are "destructive", the replies come pouring into any rational mind, it seems to me. Historically, the confusion is with nihilism, though even that desperate doctrine had, in the Russia of its day, some positive aspects — as gifted a man as Turgenev thought so, anyway; and if "anarchism" is misunderstood in that direction, then the arch anarch of our times was Hitler who, needless to say, finds no place in the anarchist pantheon. And anyway, if it comes to bombs — who has them? The Pentagon, the Kremlin — or men and women building Adventure Playgrounds?

In my own lifetime (b. 1914), we Europeans have murdered 25 millions of one another, and a fair number overseas: and done this ruled by governments of impeccable orthodoxy, and for the highest reasons of state and national interest. In the past twenty years we have seen authoritarian nationalisms growing and sprouting and shrieking and terrorizing like hysterical children (non-anarchist assisted), and in every industrial country we have witnessed the worship of *gigantism*: of the bigger city, the taller building, the more massive production of undrivable vehicles, the vaster (and less productive) state farm, the greater (and monopolistic) industrial combine, the wider and more powerful state control. We have seen laws busily enacted and old ones piously preserved (why not, I wonder, a second parliament concerned entirely with abolishing decrepit statutes which, though totally irrelevant to late twentieth-century life, can be whipped out of the musty legal bottom drawers at the drop of a wig in case of need), and enormous bureaucracies entwining us in idiotic and unenforceable regulations. But we must not trust the anarchists — the great destroyers of human order — even when they ask us what is the

244

true purpose of the good human life, and pertinently remind us that it is by decentralization, and the dismantling of these vast social edifices, that we may hope to inhabit a globe that is not a nightmare.

To the devastating stricture that anarchism "wouldn't work", if one neglects the evident reply that its various alternatives aren't working all that well, one may reflect that this negation betrays a total mistrust of human nature; for if one can't trust that, at least in some ways, what is the use of having a human nature? Yet even apart from the historical instances of anarchist societies that have indeed "worked" harmoniously, there can surely be few of us who cannot recall an instance in our lives of anarchist principles working to perfection. For example:

Short of the courts and prisons, the most authoritarian institution in our country is the Army (or Navy, or whatever), in which I had the honour to serve for six surrealist years. At one point in these I found myself senior sergeant in a unit comprising an officer plus batman-driver, a fellow sergeant, and fourteen junior NCOs. The duty the Army had assigned to us was to flit over liberated and occupied Europe hunting for spies, saboteurs, national socialists and suchlike.

We left base in orthodox formation but, thanks to our officer being a man of fantasy and brain, and the other ranks impenitent individualists, we soon reformed the structure of our unit on novel, non-military lines. The officer always messed with us (contrary to King's Regulations), and by the deft expedient of indenting for fourteen sergeant's stripes, I promoted, without benefit of military writ, all the junior NCOs to the same rank as my own. Duties were allotted on the principle of finding what each man was best at, telling him to do it, and the officer and myself, aided by a devoted if somewhat pedantic clerk, clearing up any resultant muddle. When revolts broke out against my slender surviving authority, I told the promoted sergeants anyone could take my job whenever he wanted to — no one volunteered. As well as all this it was noticeable how, in any emergency, the real "rank" of the man bore no necessary relation to that sewn on his arm or

245

shoulder. Sometimes the batman would take charge, sometimes the Scots sergeant controlling the stores, often the most "irresponsible" of them all (an ingenious near-delinquent now prospering in Canada), at times even the captain. The result of this anarchistic set-up was that we enjoyed ourselves, and acquired an embarrassing reputation for efficiency.

Yet I must come to what seems to me inadequate in anarchist philosophy. I think there is an unconscious deception or self-deception — about their belief in the innate goodness of man. When I read Prince Kropotkin, although I am charmed and awestruck by his formidably generous humanity, I feel he is leaving something out: that he is writing immaturely for so fine a thinker. Perpetually, he appeals to our better natures in the blind confidence they exist. But do they? In all of us? Or in any of us always? Do they even — and perhaps specially — exist in children, and even in adjusted children?

In short, it seems to me anarchism is a religion without a god. To say why this embarrasses me, I must briefly explain my own religious "position" (such as it is, and without wishing to give offence or to presume I am "right" about all this). That any man should be deemed divine, that such things as miracles ever existed, seem to me vulgar notions since natural creation is more miraculous than any virgin birth or juggling with jars of wine. Though organized churches have produced men and women of noble deeds and nature, their total effect on human life, both in the past and now, seems to me disastrous. Nor have Jehovah or Satan much reality for me as they are presented in holy writ, as I understand it. Nor also does the hope held out of personal immortality seem to me even desirable, let alone credible. But that there is a spirit of good, and as certainly one of evil, both in and outside each one of us, seems to me sure. So that if ever I do anything worthy, or anything I know not to be so, I cannot feel these to be only by the dubious light of my own nature, but in response to these two forces in myself and everything.

A tolerant anarchist, I am sure, would brush this courteously aside saying something like: "It's what you do, not what you think, that matters" (and would no doubt make the mental reservation I am a follower of Tolstoy — a genius for whom I have a particular horror). But to his kindly gesture my reply must be that while anarchist prophets of the past, and those anarchists I know today, seem to me good men and women, I regard such goodness as exceptional. There are also less good men, and men more bad than good despite every advantage of birth and nurture (yes, and children too, if I may commit this anarchist blasphemy), and societies are made of all men, not just the best.

So, the kind anarchist may reply, what then? Must we have churches to correct the evil? Dictatorships to coerce into proper conduct? To this I answer no, but also that the anarchist message seems to me incomplete as a total understanding of the human situation. To coerce men by politics or religion is to destroy them. But to appeal to their natural good is not enough.

To illustrate my faltering thesis I would choose as the perfect anarchist a man whose name I've not yet seen quoted in anarchist writing, and that is Anton Tchekhov. Writers are usually unpleasant people, and Tchekhov is exceptional not only in this but in his courage, practical social conscience, charm, generosity, austere self-control and radiant, forgiving kindness. He was not what is known as a "believer", yet his life and writing seem to me profoundly religious in his constant awareness alike of creative spirit, and of malevolent evil, in himself, all nature, and mankind.

The scanty success of anarchism hitherto presents it with one intangible advantage over all political systems yet invented — it is the only one we have not yet seen in general operation; and what we have seen of the others arouses, to say the least of it, serious doubts. Over a hundred years ago Karl Marx, from his tenement in Dean Street, let off an intellectual atom bomb that has altered the lives of every human creature on the earth. There can be no doubt that at some time, somewhere, in this century, an idea of human life and destiny as novel and disturbing as his own, and yet quite different from it, will change our ideas about ourselves and our societies once more. About this idea, one thing only can be certain: it will spring from a minority, and its triumph will seem, to reasonable men, impossible.

"Everything on Our Raft"
New Statesman, June 1963

To think, in casual recollection, of *The Adventures of Huckleberry Finn* is to see in the mind's eye the splendid Mississippi, an image of creation and eternity, and a feature of nature and history which so many writers and musicians (among them, elsewhere, Mark Twain himself) have made as vivid as any in the western world. Upon this wide, essentially benevolent river, safe on their raft (however perilous the shores), float Huck and Jim, a white boy and a Negro man, united by accidents of cause and temperament against the pressures of the world beyond — both sailing, though through dangers, to safety and fulfilment of some kind. Figures, some of them comic-tragic, like the Duke and King, some tragic-comic, like the young men slain in the feud, may be remembered; but once encountered, it seems as if our memory, like the broad waters, will pass them by. The reader then may recall villainies and horrors on the journey, yet the overall impression of the heroes' course will be serene: the river seeming a protective, if apparently indifferent mother, the story lyrical and joyful on the whole. That, more or less, is the total feeling that the book may leave — so long as one isn't reading it. As soon as one does, with a sharp jolt one sees that the tale is mostly terrible, often ghastly, and at all chief points a tragic one. Left unread again for even a short period of time, the horror evaporates, the kind stream mysteriously flows on again, and the sensation of bliss invades the reader's faithless memory once more.

Huckleberry Finn is one of those stories, rare even among masterpieces, on which grace has descended absolutely; and this is because the narrative, so charming and arresting in itself, is constantly and effortlessly sustained by underlying theme and symbol. In his own prefatory note, Mark Twain reminds us that he did not wish readers to probe its motive and its moral. But since to try to divine the secret of the tale's simple magnificence is irresistible, we may begin by reflecting on the nature of its themes and characters.

Huck: Huck is at the golden age, 14, when youth becomes a man. He is a superstitious realist, but in fact far more imaginative than his merely "inventive" buddy, Tom Sawyer. The most remarkable thing about him is that, although he is a tough little character, at no point in the story does he resort to violence, even when to do so would be normal, and even sensible. For example when, on the raft, the Duke and King behave abominably, Huck — let alone Jim — never thinks of simply hurling the two mountebanks into the Mississippi, which would not have been difficult since both rapscallions are often asleep, and the decrepit King is over 70.

Huck is the only character in the book who undergoes a human evolution. His spiritual crisis comes when he must make a moral choice about what is, in reality, the chief theme of the book: namely, the relations, in America, between white and coloured men. When Jim, the escaping Negro slave, is treacherously sold by the Duke and King, Huck first prays that he should do his white boy's "duty" of betraying Jim as well. He realizes that he cannot find the words to pray until he actually writes the fatal letter that will ensure Jim's return to slavery. "Religion" then descends upon him, and the "holy" words fall pat: until, revolted by the inhumanity of what he is about to do, he decides to be a "sinner" and help Jim to escape. From now on, he considers himself damned (Huck has a lively credence in the Devil), but has of course in fact encompassed his own salvation.

Jim: Twain's attitude to the Negro slave Jim remains — like Huck's — ambivalent. Jim is strong, brave, practical and devoted, though at times depicted as an astutely comic simpleton, and throughout with a certain literary sadism. For we must remember that whereas Huck, on the journey, has really little to fear — since he has committed no crime save to succour an escaping convict — Jim is threatened constantly by a return to slavery and even death. Yet Twain plunges Jim 1,100 miles downstream further from the North and freedom, and the final episode of his liberation is cruelly protracted by the antics of Tom Sawyer, which Twain seems to find amusing since he describes these at such length and with such relish.

All the same, his placing of Huck and Jim together bang in the centre of the story does show that, though he half despises Jim, he realizes that the white dream and Negro wisdom are the keys to the true American destiny, and that the love and trust that grow up perforce between the Southern Negro and the Southern white lad are the only possibly fruitful outcome for the South. For almost without exception (these being only some young girls and old ladies), the Southerners we meet when the raft is washed ashore are either idiots or picturesque monsters. Huck's Pap, a drunken Negro-baiter, or the silver-haired Colonel Grangerford with his ridiculously destructive feud, or the mobs, the religious fanatics, the multitudinous murderers — these are the South as Twain sees it, apart from Huck and Jim.

Tom Sawyer: However much one may love Tom of the earlier book, in *Huck Finn* it is impossible to do so. Mark Twain, in his dual role of Huck-Tom, clearly admires Tom's domineering bounce and resourcefulness, yet establishes him from the outset as cruel, insensitive, and petty-bourgeois in all his instincts. Even his help in the rescue of Jim is morally valueless because of the mean intricacy of the way he achieves this and, even more, because Tom secretly knows that the Widow Douglas has already freed Jim by her will. "He was always just that particular. Full of principle," says Huck of Tom, and one cannot but feel that in describing Tom Sawyer, Twain was prophetically evoking the modern American organization man. So that of his three chief characters one might say today that Tom Sawyer is in the White House, Jim still struggling off his raft...and that Huck himself seems to have momentarily vanished underground.

The Duke and King: Throughout Twain's writing there is a

love-hate (or envy-contempt) in his attitude to Europe. He despises — rightly — European pretensions to superior "civilization", yet realizes America has not yet found its own. His portrait of American culture is mostly atrocious (Huck is escaping from Hannibal-St Petersburg life as much as Jim is from slavery — the indecisive river is their wavering escape-route) and Mark Twain, by contrast, makes even Jim interested in royalty (which I simply do *not* believe), and erects these "European" puppets only to knock them down. Yet notice his obsession with all things European and ancient in time, of which he evidently felt the lack in the United States, and which impelled him, perhaps unconsciously, to try to create an American past and legend of his own. Notice also that he is "fair" to the ignoble Duke and King — giving them credit for nerve and ingenuity, and pitying them genuinely at their downfall. His — or Huck's — comment on their ultimate torture, "Human beings *can* be awful cruel to one another," is one of the most convincing sentences in the book.

The Opening Pages: The first two chapters of *Huck Finn* are a lesson to us all. Mark Twain is faced, at the outset, by two major technical tasks — how to establish Huck, in this sequel to *Tom Sawyer*, as an even finer character than Tom, and how, in this most tall of stories, to make his readers suspend large chunks of disbelief.

This he achieves, initially, by the throwaway device of referring to his earlier book and hero (and even to himself) and by creating, from the outset, the atmosphere of an *epic* story: so that one is bound to think of *Huck Finn* in terms of *Gulliver's Travels, Robinson Crusoe,* even of *The Pilgrim's Progress* — this last a volume, by the way, of which Huck later tells us that he "read considerable in it now and then". (Note that, as in all these masterpieces, Twain adopts frequently the device of supplying enormous *lists* of apparently irrelevant objects as "then I done the same with the side of bacon; then the whisky jug; I took all the coffee and sugar there was, and all the ammunition: I took the bucket and gourd, I took..." and so on.)

Notice also how, in two brief chapters, Mark Twain

announces all his essential themes and characters: there are already blood, premonitions, prophecies and the first essential introduction to the river — "a whole mile broad, and awful still and grand". Readers of Twain must have known by now that they were dealing with a "comic" writer; but in the first pages of *Huck Finn* he makes it clear as Mississippi fog that his fun is going to be frightening.

On the third page of the present edition there is one of those superb passages of terse description of nature that have rightly won for Twain the reputation of daddy of twentieth-century American writing. But rather than quote this, I prefer an extract that comes much later —and which demonstrates his extraordinary gift for verbal *syncopation*, which makes me believe he heard Negro music as well as coloured voices:

> I had the road to myself, and I fairly flew — leastways I had it all to myself except for the solid dark, and the now-and-then glares, and the buzzing of the rain, and the thrashing of the wind, and the splitting of the thunder; and sure as you are born I did clip it along!

The Raft: The raft is washed ashore for Jim and Huck after a hurricane, and the parallel with Noah's ark is evident, the more so as we have the impression, throughout the story, of all *real* life being concentrated upon it. "By that time everything we had in the world was on our raft," says Huck.

Did Jim and Huck love each other physically on the raft? It has often been suggested — sometimes mischievously (in a story, like the others I have mentioned, so bereft of female characters) — that they did, and though Twain is not specific about this, he plants all sorts of (possibly subconscious) clues. Jim and Huck were alone together on a journey of more than 1,000 miles, they love each other emotionally, Jim calls Huck "honey chile" and "would always pet me", "we was always naked, day and night", and it was Jim who had the idea of dressing Huck up as a girl when he went ashore, on his celebrated and disastrous errand to spy out the land.

But does all this really matter? For the raft is so much more than whatever happens on it: it is a birth-life symbol, and therein lies its fascination. Huck is entering adolescence (notice that he no longer fears his terrifying father), he respects Jim's wisdom, is ashamed when he betrays him, and finds his own moment of truth through their association. So long as the raft does not touch the treacherous shores (or be rammed by some wanton steamer, or come alongside a wreck which is sure to have a corpse or two aboard it), Mark Twain suspends us in a moment of history wherein America had lost its innocence, but was still filled with invincible hope and promise.

He also resolves, as an artist, all the human dilemmas he has posed. Jim is free, and ready to buy the freedom of his beloved wife and children. Tom, his last prank played, prepares for his life of delayed adolescence at a Northern business school. Even the feud is ended, because Harney-Romeo and Sophia-Juliet are united. And Huck, his ordeal completed, his moral stature won, can face his own future that one feels, with regret, should also have been America's.

"Second Test, fifth day"

New Society, July 1963 (*Out of the Way*)

"They won't be playing," said the taxi driver, gazing at the windswept skies, and with that joy-in-gloom so characteristic of our island race. But at Lord's they were, and I arrived just at tea-break to witness the most exciting hours of cricket I have seen in forty years.

Fearing the elements, only 6,000 of the faithful were now scattered round the wet cold darkening ground. To the west, cosseted in mackintoshes, sat the members, like senators at some Roman spectacle. To the east, the Caribbean contingent were massed enthusiastically as if preparing for some Birmingham or Little Rock. The displaced clergy wandered purposefully, very gentlemanly chaps mingled with gnarled provincials and hearties from the Tavern, and dotted here and there were rare members of the sorority of female fans. "If a woman was hard pressed for a man," one of them said to me, "this might not be a bad spot to look around in."

The West Indians now reappeared, loping, elegant, casual and dynamic, and placed themselves strategically at spots where the balls rarely failed, later on, to come. The embattled Close, looking stocky, reassuring and prodigiously *English*, stepped calmly onto the ground, accompanied by his junior partner Titmus. England were 171 for 5, and had to make 63 to win before stumps were drawn at 6, or the rain fell, or the light vanished — both of which latter seemed all too probable.

With the exception of a few vicious overs from Lance Gibbs (who "slow" bowls with a whiplash like a scorpion's tail), the bowling was by Hall and Griffith: each with a run of over 40 yards and a jet delivery so electric that one half expects the bowler to hurl himself, in person, like a long-jumper, at the distant wicket; and if Griffith seems deadly, what word can one use of Hall, who's like a hurricane force of nature? He had been bowling in all, from the pavilion end, for 3 hours and 20 minutes, and his last ball was as lethal as his first.

The four overs after the tea-break took 20 minutes to bowl, and the hearties in the Tavern manifested some impatience — beginning to barrack in that deliberately non-gentlemanly style which is the approved mode of audience participation at the super-gentlemanly game of cricket. For this they were rebuked by many a shocked "shush" and, more specifically, by a party of elderly and dignified Caribbeans who, braving the native wrath or envy, had ensconced themselves among the patriotic Taverners. "Fair is fair," one of these elder statesmen from the Islands reproachfully repeated. "Win, lose or draw, what matters is the *game*."

Close was now lashing out, hitting impossible fours off balls that must have been invisible to any naked eye but his, and sometimes carrying the war into the enemy camp by charging down the wicket before the ball had been delivered. This so disconcerted Hall that, on one occasion, he stopped, as if in acute physical and mental agony, before hurling his ball, and began his 80-yard safari all over again — this provoking more shouts of sabotage from the audience, and shriller remonstrations from the Caribbean representatives. Close made his 50 amid wild applause from the British sector, and decorous clapping from his courteous rivals on the field; then Titmus fell (caught McMorris at the chest off Hall), then Trueman, no longer Ferocious Freddie, on the next ball off Hall again in the same over. Only Allen and Shackleton remained, and Colin Cowdrey encased in a plaster cast.

When Close fell to Griffith at 70 the game belonged to anybody — and more, it seemed, to the fierce West Indians than to England's tail and one-armed casualty. The light was growing dimmer; rain occasionally swept in horizontal showers across the pitch; there was also the matter of whether Worrell would, or not, use the new ball (he eventually didn't, largely because in the poor light it would be more visible). All eyes were on the clocks; confusing instruments, since one registered six minutes advance upon the other. And time, which had seemed earlier to favour England, when Close was still on the attack, now seemed to favour the West Indies in their task of demolishing our weakest batsmen.

Could the tail hold on and win at least a draw? Could they almost incredibly hit a few fours, or even a six, and win? Nerves became so strained that a vulgarian holding a transistor radio blaring a superfluous commentary on the game was almost lynched.

When Shackleton joined Allen, 15 runs were needed in about as many minutes. Almost to the end, these bowler-batsmen bravely risked defeat to win victory, and restored their faith in cricket as a thrilling spectacle to every one of the 6,000 present. (It has always seemed to me hard, incidentally, that the poor bowlers must all bat, and not vice versa: something should be done about this, I feel, and batsmen be made to bowl and suffer an identical embarrassment.) When the last over began (Hall bowling), England were but six runs short.

Two singles were made off the first four balls, and on the fourth Shackleton was sensationally run out. Allen had started bounding down the crease, Murray threw the ball to Worrell at forward short leg, and the sagacious Captain, not trusting himself to throw, raced down the field, ball clutched in hand, and whipped the bails off at the bowler's end before Shackleton could make it.

Now one-armed Cowdrey appeared and if, in the two remaining balls of the over, England could score six, or the West Indies get a wicket, the game could still be won by either side. An even more fascinating possibility existed, which was that Allen might hit a single and leave Cowdrey to make the final stroke. If this had happened, would Cowdrey (against Hall) have hit a one-handed six — like Harry Wharton at one of those crucial matches at Greyfriars School?

But this did not occur: for Allen, preferring the fair chance of avoiding defeat to the near-impossibility of snatching victory, decided to stay put at all costs during Hall's two final whirlwind deliveries — and who can blame him? Tension at this point was, as they say, "unbearable". Twice Hall hurtled down the field, and two times Allen prudently stayed stuck. The Caribbean spectators immediately invaded the ground, their heroes raced for the safety of the pavilion, and soon a mass of dark and wildly gesticulating figures were confronting the equally excited members. For in this memorable contest, no one had won because both teams deserved to.

My last glimpse, as the emotional temperature subsided, was of an athletic policeman, helmet awry, snatching away a wicket from an enthusiastic West Indian souvenir hunter (what did the copper *do* with that wicket afterwards, I wonder? Hand it in to the Black Museum at Scotland Yard?). And as we tottered into St John's Wood Road, I reflected how silly I had been to write, earlier in *New Society*, on the tedium of cricket. What I had forgotten is that though it can be inexpressibly dull, it can sometimes be more nerve-racking than any other sport that I have seen — including bull-fighting, racing, motoring, and soccer with Pele on the field.

What is the explanation? I think it is that, when grace descends upon a game, cricket is *mathematically* exciting as well as physically: it's like a game played by champion athletes who are also Grand Masters at chess. Additionally, there is the battle against time and the correct use of it, which is an allegory of the part time plays in all our lives. For few other sports last, as this one does, for several days, during which teams, and specially captains, must calculate their time-and-effort strategy to a nicety.

A final appeal is that the game is both so polite and yet so ferocious. There is all that clapping of your opponents, all that tactful by-play between overs, all those flannels, those caps and sweaters, those oranges and cups of tea! But there is also the hazard, which is greater even than in boxing; so that if — which *heaven forbid* — I had ever to face Wesley Hall or Cassius Marcellus Clay, I would choose Cassius as the lesser peril. Cricketers are brave men and, at the same time, so casual, so apparently unexcited; and when they are locked, as in this match, in a really vital struggle, and yet behave so coolly, they restore one's faith in human dignity; for to be valiant and calm is a marvellous human combination.

"Life with Time"

New Statesman, December 1965

Last year, for six delightful months, I travelled all over Australia and New Zealand, garnering material for a book on those countries for Time Inc. This was for *Time*'s Book Division, and it is perhaps not generally known that the production of millions (literally) of copies of books annually is an important, if subsidiary, activity of this stupendous firm. These come in different series, and the one to which I contributed is called "Life World Library", which consists of descriptions, pictorial and verbal, of all the countries of the globe.

After sending a final draft from Australia to New York, I was asked to spend three weeks there at the *Time* office revising the text with the Book Division's editors. I had anticipated, I must confess, that these would try to maul my modest text, and was agreeably surprised to find that they regarded as sacred any flight of fancy, or opinion, or criticism of either country. What they turned out to be chiefly concerned with was getting the multitudinous facts as accurate as could be, and making sure the meaning of each sentence was entirely clear to their imaginary reader... who is thought to be a Ford car salesman in Wichita (though some believe he may be a Cadillac salesman). There were also certain house rules to be observed — as, for instance, the convention that the writer doesn't say "I", but uses some abstract formula like "the visitor" when describing his experiences. All this involved many hours with their researchers — bright and highly literate girls — who checked remorselessly on every date, statistic, factual detail, and on the clarity of meaning in the text. These exercises saved me from many minor errors and several clangers, but any judgement of mine (unless obscure, or based on an erroneous fact) they left religiously alone.

All the same, I became rather haunted by the relentless pursuit of meaning of these sharp girls. And this led me to imagine what might happen if a poet, and not a writer of prose, should have come under their inexorable care. In the following dialogue, therefore — a copy of which I presented to my hosts before my departure — it is supposed that the poet Shelley goes to work in the *Time-Life* building.

RESEARCHER: May I come in, Percy?

POET: Certainly. Take a chair. What's your worry?

R: No worry, Percy. It's just this line in your copy. I quote:

> I am the eye with which the universe
> Beholds itself, and knows it is divine.

Well, we feel that needs some little clarification.

P: Okay. Shoot. What?

R: The word "I". We don't use that, you see, shouldn't we just say "people in general"?

P: Sure. What else?

R: Besides which, "I am the eye" strikes us as awkward.

P: The point's conceded. So what next?

R: Well — "eye": which eye? I mean left or right or what?

P: Let's say left eye.

R: Good. What colour eye?

P: Let's say blue.

R: That's better. So to date we have

> People in general are the left blue eye.....

You okay that?

P: Sure.

R: I'm not harassing you?

P: Not a bit.

R: You want me to clear it with Grace? Oliver? Norm? Anyone else?

P: No, no. You're doing fine. What else?

R: "With which" — that strikes us as ill-phrased.

P: What do you suggest?

R: "*Through* which". Our research on the optical nerve establishes that you don't see *with* the eye, but *through* it.

P: You sure of that?

R: Sure we're sure. We've checked with a professor at the MIT.

P: Gee! All right. What now?

R: "Universe". That strikes us as a nebulous concept.

P: That was rather the idea.

R: Yes, yes, but we have to consider our readers. Now then. Couldn't we define it a little?

P: Sure. What about "solar system"?

R: No, no. If we say that, we lose *your* fine poetic concept — which is after all what we've hired you for (if I may put it that way).

P: Thanks. Well, what do you suggest?

R: Listen, Percy. I don't want to *dictate* to you. *You* just suggest something.

P: Okay. What about "solar system and its ancillary galaxies"?

R: Fine! That wraps up line one. Thanks for your cooperation.

P: Not at all. So what have we got so far?

R: I'll read it back to you:

> People in general are the left blue eye through which the solar system and its ancillary galaxies....

You okay that?

P: Sure I do. What next?

R: Well, now we come to line two.

P: So we do.

R: Which must of course be related to line one — I mean we don't want to lose *that* quality in your writing, now, do we?

P: I hope not. Go on.

R: Well — "beholds". That strikes us as a somewhat archaic word.

P: Well, yes, it is.

R: So what about just "sees"?

P: Okay for "sees".

R: Okay. But now, Perce, we come to the really awkward moment. I ask you: how *can* the universe see, or for that matter, behold, itself? You see our difficulty?

P: I do indeed. I guess it's the universe's difficulty too.

R: Sure, sure, but we don't want to get too metaphysical,

now, do we? We don't want to get bogged down in abstract concepts.

P: Sure we don't. Let's avoid that at all costs.

R: Well — I have a suggestion. Only a suggestion, mind you.

P: Which is?

R: Instead of "the solar system and its ancillary galaxies sees itself", what about "the solar system and its ancillary galaxies becomes aware of the existence of similarly related heavenly bodies"?

P: That strikes me as just perfect.

R: Sure?

P: Sure. Right. Let's go on.

R: You're not getting impatient with me?

P: No, no. What next?

R: Well — "*knows* it is divine". That strikes us as overstated. What about "guesses"?

P: Or "suspects"?

R: All right-y — "suspects". Now, "it is" — that's okay — but we're still left with "divine".

P: What's wrong with "divine"?

R: We'd prefer "religiously inclined". The universe, you see, just can't *be* divine. That's theologically inaccurate.

P: How do you know?

R: We've checked with Bishop Sheen, Cardinal Cushing, the Pope, the Chief Rabbi of Jerusalem, the Dalai Lama and Dr Graham.

P: Oh. Why didn't you ask the Almighty Himself?

R: We may have to get round to that if you start turning argumentative.

P: Sorry. So what have we got now?

R: I'll read it back to you:

> People in general are the left blue eye through which the solar system and its ancillary galaxies become aware of the existence of similarly related heavenly bodies and suspects it is religiously inclined.

How's that?

P: Marvellous! I wish I could have written it myself.

R: You mean that? You're not ribbing me?

P: Of course not. Anything else?

R: No. You got anything else?

P: Yes. Please give me my $100,000,000,000 and let me get out of here.

"A Peculiar Neighbourhood"
New Society, November 1964

In New York, only a Negro can wander where he will — provided, that is, he has a white shirt, a tie and ten bucks in his tight hip pocket. Thirty years ago, when I first visited the city, the situation was exactly the reverse: the white could go slumming up in Harlem, and the Negro came down town off duty at his peril. But today, despite the accumulation of white magnificence, and even despite the ghetto conditions of Harlem and Bedford Stuyvesant, New York has become a Negro city.

I did not believe that whitey was so unpopular in Harlem as the papers said — but soon found out their case was understated. I arrived at John F. Kennedy airport at 7 on a Sunday morning after a direct flight from Hawaii, tired, drunk, dirty, and only wanting from New York City a bath and six hours of sleep. But on reaching the hotel where I was booked in, I found I wasn't expected till the evening, and no room was available. Desperate calls to alternative hotels were unavailing, since all were full because of the World's Fair. So faced with a homeless Sunday in the city, I dug out my address book and looked up names.

I hit on that of Minnie W, a coloured dancer I had known in London, with whom I had kept more or less in touch. I called her and was immediately asked to drop right by. So leaving my heavy luggage at the hotel, I took only an air bag containing passport, money and other precious possessions, thinking it would be safer to have these with me. I hailed a cab, and was a bit nonplussed when the driver asked me if I really wanted to go to *that* address. I said I did, and we set off to Harlem through the empty streets.

New York, as I discovered afterwards, is zoned. The varied areas do not melt into one another as they do in London, for everywhere there are invisible frontiers: of immense wealth and squalid poverty a block apart, of racial groups divided by a single street. This thoroughfare is safe, or relatively so: travel a short block, and you're in hostile territory.

Such territory we now entered (unbeknown to me) and the driver decanted me, collected his fare, and moved off again at speed. I found myself in a crowded street with no white faces in it, and hundreds of black ones that did not look at me though I was aware that they were watching. Grasping my precious bag, and trying to suppress a rising palpitation, I set off to look for the right number.

But in that mysterious way of unfamiliar streets, the numbers seemed to run direct from 1468 to 1474, without any figures in between. I walked back and forth, peering for 1470, and at last decided I'd have to ask someone where the hell it was.

But these were not the affable, if menacing, dark faces of Africa, nor even the crafty ironic features of Smethwick or Ladbroke Grove. These faces were shut, locked and hostile. Nor had these bodies the lissom confidence of Lagos or Kampala, but a taut tense desperate animosity. I suppose it sounds as if I'm exaggerating to make a story, or it may be that my own conscience, or my cowardice, invented all of this. But I do not think so. The Negro peoples of America are at war: and you, if you're white, whatever your intentions, are the enemy.

Feeling (and I'm quite sure rightly) that one false move would have landed me in hospital (if not the mortuary), I approached an elderly woman sitting on some steps, and in the hopeful belief that one of an older generation — and a woman at that — might prove more indulgent, I asked her for 1470. She pointed vaguely and said nothing. Figures around her noiselessly moved slightly closer. I caught the eyes of children, and their looks were just as cold.

At last I found it, entered a lobby, and pressed the elevator button. It came down with three large men inside. I stood aside for them to exit, but they didn't: they stayed in the elevator saying not a word. Breathing a prayer, I got in and pressed the floor. Up we went shakily, I waiting for the blow that didn't fall.

Now I was in a corridor of doors with spyholes and no names on them. I pressed several bells, brown eyes appeared, gazed and vanished. Apart from just not liking me at all, I believe they thought that, with that absurd white bag, I was the rent collector. At last Minnie's eye appeared and she admitted me. "Hullo, hon," she said. "How you been keeping?" "Minnie," I answered in severely trembling tones, "you live in a peculiar neighbourhood." She gave me that Negro "will they never learn?" look, sighed slightly, offered me a triple gin, and said, "Well, Collins, you had to find out for yourself."

I stayed there all day, afraid to leave. At last Minnie said she had to go down town: I was delighted to have a (female) bodyguard to the taxi rank.

This totally minor incident is, of course, in reverse, what millions of Negroes have known for centuries in circumstances that were not minor at all: those of blood and horror and humiliation: not just once on a casual Sunday, but daily throughout whole lifetimes. And if the treatment is now reversed, we may not like it, nor in any human sense approve of it, but we cannot be surprised.

Yet America is a land of contrasts and extremes, and what is so astonishing about New York is that once you're outside these danger zones there's infinitely more inter-racial exchange than there is in London. If we here see a coloured boy with a white girl, or vice versa, we're still apt to stare. In downtown New York you see these pairs in hundreds. At Washington Square on Sundays, these mixed groups are out there in their thousands, strolling and listening to the music of a dozen *al fresco* combos.

Also, not all Negroes live in Harlem or Bedford Stuyvesant, though the vast majority do. But with those that don't, there seems no "problem". I went to parties and apartments where you couldn't imagine exclusive ghettoes existed only a few miles away.

I do not believe that a "solution" of America's racial situation (or anyone else's, for that matter) is possible in terms of any kind of "racial adjustment". Races are *not* going to love one another — or even put up with one another — for any of the sensible reasons that they ought to. But races may tolerate one another when there is some sort of political and, above all, economic equality.

America has spent billions on overseas aid in the past twenty years. Until it decides to spend billions on an internal "crash" programme of aid to its own Negro population, the "Negro problem" will remain. The fact that the cost of this, in the long run, would possibly be far less than the cost in misery and horror which the present situation will produce, does not, of course, mean that any such programme will be undertaken.

Coming from Honolulu direct to New York City, it is hard to believe they are cities in states of the same nation. For Hawaii is one of the few areas in the world where, on the whole, racial harmony has been created. This is partly because when the Hawaiians were poor and stateless no one cared, and now that they're prospering, there's little or no racial bar to rising in the world. It's also because they've not been afraid of miscegenation — in fact, hardly notice it exists.

And is all this to conclude that the American Negro people, burdened with wrongs, are without fatal defects? Must Mr Whitey always be the villain? I think the answer is, in both cases, no, but the great white failure has been one of imagination. People will accept almost anything except humiliation. The whites, operating from a position of strength, humiliated the Negroes, and this will never be forgiven. Also, although I know it's tactless to say this, a people can't be slaves for three hundred years, then economic serfs for a hundred more, without their gifts and virtues being twisted into cynicism and violence.

America is passing, it seems to me, through its third civil war. The first was against the English who in those days were, after all, fellow countrymen. The second we all know about. The third is now — and it really is a war: not just because, in the richest city in the world, you can't walk up hundreds of streets without getting mugged, but because, even though the violence, relatively speaking, has as yet been slight, psychological postures of total denial have been taken up by most on either side.

And in my vulgar Scottish way I do believe that the breakthrough to any kind of sanity will only come when Mr Whitey forgets about those dazzling office blocks, and Lincoln Centres for the Performing Arts, and World Fairs, and lethal freeways, and starts to unbutton and pay back for four hundred years of toil in terms of schools, houses, jobs and all those basic essential banalities that make life supportable and enable you, if not to love, at any rate to put up with your neighbour.

"The Green Art"
New Society, May 1966

George Orwell once remarked that if you want to provoke an embarrassed silence in a public house, the most effective way is to talk about poetry — or any other art, for that matter. Yet there is one art to speak of which evokes a sympathetic response in almost any surroundings: the art of gardening.

For though gardening has its utilitarian aspects (not that other arts — for instance, architecture — don't also), its practice is essentially an aesthetic one. No one who lays out and cultivates a garden, even of the simplest kind, can avoid making choices that reveal an aesthetic feeling of some kind. All gardeners, though they may be unconscious of it, are artists.

This becomes most apparent when one listens to gardeners — amateurs as much as professionals — talking. People who might be horrified by a discussion about music, or painting, or literature, will embark on the most recondite analyses of gardens. And what is additionally attractive about this obsession is that it seems absolutely classless: I mean that a passion for gardens can be found in every social group.

Of course, a love of gardens is far from exclusive to England — or indeed to Europe — yet with us it does seem to be a major, and widely diffused, affection. As to why this should be, I offer some theories culled from gardeners I have consulted, and a few from my own imagination.

1. **Climate.** However much we may complain about English weather, it is almost perfect for variety and subtlety in gardens throughout ten months of the year. Tropical gardens, by contrast, however beautiful, have far greater monotony and even harshness.

2. **Nostalgia.** Being essentially an urban people, gardening satisfies an instinct for a lost rural heritage. Also, perhaps, the pride of being, even if in only a minuscule way, a landowner.

3. **Grandeur.** Though English people consider ostentation ill-mannered, it is possible, in a garden — and even quite a small one — to indulge an instinct for display that is socially acceptable.

4. **Exercise.** This comes with gardening, in the most pleasurable form, since honest toil is blessed by a visible result. When you've banged a golf ball round eighteen holes, there's not much to show for it. When you've dug and raked and weeded, you get the double reward of agile muscles and a herbaceous border.

5. **Nature.** Most of the great English painters were landscape artists, and this instinct to interpret, or improve on, nature, also reveals itself in gardeners. Gardening is a direct and intimate means of communing with nature, learning from it, and adapting it to a sympathetic human will.

6. **Meditation.** Gardeners don't hunt in packs: the image of the gardener is that of a solitary, silent figure, lost in a flower bed. This corresponds to the ruminative, reflective aspects of

the English temperament.

7. **Expense.** Except when the garden is on a grand scale, gardening remains one of the least expensive recreations imaginable.

8. **Growth.** This is perhaps the strongest motive of all, and not, of course, confined to English gardeners. To take an empty plot, and a year later make it blossom, satisfies a profound instinct for creation.

As soon as one examines, even in the most superficial way, the activities of English gardeners, one finds oneself on the threshold of a vast new world, seething with unsuspected activity. On the organizational level, there is a huge gardening industry for growing and selling plants, shrubs, trees, bulbs, seeds and gardening tools, with a turnover of millions, and a considerable export content. There is an enormous gardening press, ranging from learned periodicals like that of the Royal Horticultural Society, to specialist journals on roses, allotments, orchids, fertilizers and cacti. Books on gardening surpass in numbers those on cookery, and one is not surprised to find that one of last year's best sellers (among books of all kinds) was about English wild flowers. There are countless gardening societies and exhibitions, of which the finest and most famous is that of the RHS at Chelsea (though professionals, I understand, prefer the society's specialized shows at Vincent Square).

Trying to discover the motivation of a fragment of this colourful spectrum, I visited different gardens recently. I should perhaps explain that, though abysmally ignorant about gardening (even if I once had tea, as a lad, with Miss Gertrude Jekyll), I love visiting gardens, and listen respectfully to what I am told — in so far, that is, as I can understand it, for I must repeat that gardening talk can be highly sophisticated and indeed mysterious.

Stately Home. I wanted to see a garden still kept up like those of before World War II, and visited one in Scotland. As is well known, Scottish gardens are usually far more formal than those in England where, since the eighteenth century, the landscape style replaced the earlier patterned gardens of Tudor and Jacobean days. This is thought to be due to the closer relations Scotland maintained with France, where the *jardin anglais* is still exceptional, and the more regimented or chess-board garden the rule.

The stately home in question is quite small, with a central medieval tower and later accretions fortunately ceasing before the nineteenth century. It stands beside a burn, and on two other sides the fields come right up, casually, to the house. But on the fourth side there is a large walled garden which is one of the loveliest I have ever seen. This is because, although it is laid out with geometrical paths, there is a great variety of smaller trees, and the shrubs and flowers are planted, in contrast to the general pattern, quite informally, so that the whole effect is of a place at once classical in spirit, and yet romantic.

I asked the owner (or rather, his wife) how she managed about gardeners. Apparently there are only two (who also look after the kitchen garden and do other work on the estate) and the secret, as one might expect, is that she and her family do a lot of the work themselves. According to this lady, once a garden is mature, it does to a great extent look after itself (though other gardeners to whom I repeated this laughed sardonically). All the same, this lady admitted that a formal garden is hard to keep up properly unless professionals are employed: which explains why such gardens are disappearing, since only the rare rich, or aristocrats charging 2s. 6d, or national bodies, can afford them.

Although the castle is not "open to the public", anyone can see the garden who asks, and many do. I asked my hostess if she detected any resentment, by her visitors, of the relative grandeur of her garden. She said not at all — the more so as they often find her hard at work in it. I think it is striking about garden-lovers that they seem to have little jealousy about gardens bigger than their own.

I next asked whether a walled garden was for beauty or for protection. For both, she said. In England and Scotland, the most favoured areas for gardens are, it seems, to the west (north or south, except for the seasons coming later, is more or less irrelevant), and since her own lay in east Scotland, the climate was more rigorous. But walls, she thought, were right, in any case for a formal garden.

Did she think, I asked, there were other European peoples who had finer gardens than we? "Oh, yes," she said at once. "The French — possibly the Italians: but only the grand gardens. I don't think there is such a variety of fine gardens as we have." And what did she think of the Capability Brown "landscape" style of great English gardens. Here she grew very scornful. "All you have to do," she said, "is root up everything except for a few trees and let cows wander up to the drawing-room window. I don't call *that* a garden."

Rural Bliss. This one was on the Thames in Oxfordshire, quite large, yet entirely looked after by two gents who live, as they say, together. These gents, one of whom has modest personal means, do absolutely nothing except garden, and though I suppose one could be censorious about such a life, it seems to me harmless and estimable.

They have let the reeds and rushes of the Thames bank come right up wild half way to the house (sound instinct this, I feel — laundered swards beside a river look somehow horrible). Then comes a large lawn, severely mown, but the land left with all its natural bumps, and declivities, and a large pine in the middle (which I, hating conifers, would chop down). Beds all round with bushes and flowers. A small lawn at the back with nothing but fruit trees growing in it and a rock garden in one corner. By the side of the house (where the main entrance is) a plain lawn, with fields beyond, separated by a closely clipped hedge. Peacocks strutting, doves fluttering. Inside, a conservatory with tropical plants, chiefly creepers, originally brought back as cuttings from a trip to the West Indies.

I fell rather foul of my host by making, unintentionally, non-G remarks (gardeners are very touchy about these, I found). "*Not* 'rockery' — rock garden, please," he said. "Rather out of fashion just now, but believe me, it's a complicated and *scientific* matter acclimatizing these Alpines." I asked, nervously, if the hens sitting on nests, clipped out of the hedge on the side lawn, were "for fun". "Not at *all*," he said. "The topiary garden is one of the finest English contributions." A crack about "herbaceous borders" went down worse. "You say you knew

Miss Jekyll," my host said severely. "Well, if you *did*, you'd know she did away with artificial Victorian bedding out, and by growing herbaceous borders found a practical natural way of planting, staking, and then thinning out which gave the garden shape and beauty and found room for everything."

To show me another of Miss Jekyll's innovations, he took me back to the riverside garden again, and pointed out a number of shrubs whose appeal was in their leaves rather than their flowers. "That's *it*," he said. "A lavender bush looks lovely even when it isn't flowering. Miss Jekyll did her own gardening, and if you can't afford gardeners it's sensible to have as many shrubs as possible that are attractive in themselves and need little attention."

I admired the roses — not yet in flower, of course — and asked if he was trying to cultivate a blue rose. "*That*," he said, "would be very vulgar." But weren't others trying to do this? He sighed. The rose, he explained, is regarded by everyone — somewhat as the lion is the King of Beasts — as top flower. But there was a ridiculous cult of "fashionable" roses — for instance, the Elizabeth Glamis at present. Of course, the variety of roses was one of their splendours. But a sad innovation of Miss Jekyll's day (not *her* fault, of course) was that hybridization of plants became a fetish, hundreds now being created every year. Particularly in the case of roses, this became big business, since there are fashions in plants just as there are in dogs.

Was there such a thing as an *un*fashionable garden, then? He mused. "Some might say so: but I think *any* garden can be beautiful, if the gardener has taste." He frowned. "Of course," he added, dropping his voice, "there *is* such a thing as a *vulgar* flower." Which? Well, a lobelia, for example. But could anything in nature really be vulgar? Certainly: what about a monkey-puzzle? I saw his point. But wasn't it, I suggested, how gardeners juxtaposed flowers, rather than the flowers themselves? Yes, principally that, he agreed. "Of course, there are some flowers that are *always* right — both aristocratic and modest, like a geranium. But others... well, hollyhocks, for instance, are rather proletarian. A garden, you know," he

271

added, "does reveal *class*." (This rather shook my notion of gardeners being classless people.)

After tea (it was one of those freak March days, and we had it under the fruit trees which were already budding), he lamented the disappearance of cottage gardens. "The French," he said with asperity, "*never* had them: far too mean; they grew only vegetables. But when I was young, there were dozens in the village here that were little jewels. Rather over-ornate and crowded, and perhaps too many wall-flowers and marigolds, but a *profusion* of delight." He took me to see a surviving specimen, but it was too early in the year for one uninstructed like myself to judge its potentialities. "Come back in the summer," he cried. "It's like an embroidered tea-cosy!" Why had they stopped growing them, I asked? "Cars and TV," he said bitterly, "but you can't blame the poor dears. Thirty years ago they had absolutely nothing to do, so they gardened. Now, they watch Malcolm Muggeridge and drive into Oxford."

London Pride. Although London's parks are the loveliest in the world (the subtlest, I think, is Green Park with only trees — no flowers), one doesn't have the impression of there being hundreds of private gardens tucked away behind the dour façades. But in fact there are thousands, some I visited of amazing variety — and size — in the most unexpected streets.

The finest I saw lies south of Hyde Park, and the gardener is a female dramatist. She does most of the work herself, except for the lawn which her husband — retired, and not an enthusiast — mows as his weekly chore. The garden is surprisingly large because, thanks to a land agent's freak, her neighbours on either side have only little paved-over plots, and her own garden branches out behind theirs, taking in land that must once have belonged to the adjacent houses. The smaller part near her house is fairly conventional, but in the larger strips annexed from either side she has created a kind of maze of paths, hedges, pools and beds, like a miniature Versailles.

"Contrary to what most people think," she said, "there is more gardening in London than there used to be. Before the war, everyone went to the country on Friday, but now there is a real Saturday-to-Monday life in London. Besides which, gardening has become *fashionable*, rather like exotic cooking. Why! even girls in offices have plants on their window sills, which they never used to do — or so my husband tells me. Many people have found — I'm one — that in the days when you could afford a gardener (and there *were* any gardeners) you really missed three-quarters of the fun. Both my daughters, who live in London, are gardeners (when they're not having babies), and they've even converted their husbands — which *I've* never managed to do."

I asked her what she thought the secret of being a good gardener was. "Oh, you want me to be pompous," she said. "All right. Well, in the country, you have to know about soil, aspect, climate, drainage, and principally, the general *effect* you want to get. Here in London, where you can't pick and choose where you'll put the garden in the first place, only the effect matters, really. To be *really* pompous, I'd say you need study, science, and some taste." "Green fingers?" "*That*," she said firmly, "is just nonsense. Everybody's got them.

"You know," she went on, "there are added satisfactions, apart from just growing things. Flower names fascinate me: so pretty if they're English, and I don't mind the Latin ones, they're quite fun too. Then if you learn about plant migrations, natural as well as artificial, you have practical history as well as geography. You can look at a flower bed and feel it's a kind of United Nations — though not so dull as *that*, naturally.

"Of course," she continued, "there are garden snobs, I'm afraid, just as there are wine snobs: I mean people who have peculiar fads and fancies, about which they're so dogmatic. For instance, have you met any rhododendron people?" I said no. "Well, that's a cult, rather like being a Zen Buddhist." Then she frowned. "Another cult," she said, "is that of the garden-haters." What? I asked. Are there any of *those* in England? "Architects!" she said darkly. "They *hate* anything that grows. Urban *planners*, you know. This terrace is coming down before long, and if they don't build on this garden, do you know what they'll do with it?" I asked what. "*Pave it in*," she said. "like those poor little people have done next door."

Allotments. Feeling I had been moving in rather too grand a gardening world, I sought out an allotment holder in Fulham. He lived in a semi-detached, whose small garden seemed neat but unremarkable. But after a cup of tea, he took me round several blocks to one of the most unexpected sights I have seen in London.

This was an oblong strip of perhaps half an acre which ran between the back yards of two rows of houses on either side. What had happened, my host explained, was that the original speculative builder of the estate had put up for himself the much larger house I could see at the far end, linking the terraces, and simply hacked away his tenants' garden so as to have an enormous one for himself in between them all. In fact, he hadn't used it as a garden, but as a stable and grazing ground for his horses. Some years ago, my friend had heard the land was not now used for anything, and had persuaded the estate of the long deceased builder to rent it to him.

There it was, in the middle of a thoroughly built-up area, almost like a country kitchen garden. Though the plants were only beginning to sprout, the whole strip was arranged with meticulous care, stakes for the beans and peas, nets for the fruit bushes, neat rows of furrows where the lettuces and broccoli and cabbages would shortly burgeon. There were also pears, apples, cherries and a fig tree on the end wall — planted, apparently, by the builder, or perhaps even a survival of the days when Fulham was semi-rural, for they seemed to me quite old.

"But what on earth," I asked him, "do you do with all this produce? Surely, there's enough here to feed a regiment." Here he looked rather embarrassed, and I suspected he probably sold them (why not?) and didn't want to say so for some reason. But no: after assuring his own family's supplies, he distributed the surplus veg to neighbours and, occasionally, hospitals. "But why don't you sell the rest?" I asked. He looked distant. "Well, this isn't my *profession*," he explained. "I work for the Gas Board, and that's quite enough for me." He asked me to come back later, when I could see the garden in full spate. "And bring a basket," he added slyly, "and we'll see what we can do."

I asked why, if he wasn't growing for profit, he didn't give some part of the allotment over to flowers. "Oh, I grow some of them at the house," he said, rather remotely. "The wife likes them." "And you don't?" He stopped and said rather solemnly. "I've nothing whatever against flowers...but after all, once you've grown them, what can you *do* with them?"

I am bound to say this minute, and perhaps untypical, exploration of the gardening world has impressed me greatly. To quote Orwell again, he once suggested that each time we do an evil deed, we should plant an acorn somewhere as a gesture of penance. And certainly, there is something highly attractive about those whose preoccupation is to *grow*. Although the allotment keeper in a way impressed me most, there is perhaps something even more delightful about people who take endless pains to produce "only" flowers — I mean an activity (unless, of course, professional) which seems entirely disinterested: the creation of beauty just for the satisfaction of creating.

It also seems to me that gardening must foster, in the gardener, a number of admirable virtues: patience, skill, imagination. And when one thinks of the wasteful, harmful ways in which so many of us spend our leisure time, it is salutary to imagine, all over England (and Scotland — sorry), thousands of forms bent solicitously over rock gardens and herbaceous borders and clumps of rhododendrons and even blue roses, restoring to our in so many ways blighted land some of the simple glory of which so many of us have deprived it.

"Another Story"
New Statesman, April 1971

Even the dedication was startling: "To the Wittiest Woman in India". For at Simla in 1888, it must have seemed strange a woman was so honoured in a man's world; while in London two years later, the notion there were *any* wits, let alone female ones, among the exiles of the far sub-continent, may have appeared bizarre. Most breathtaking of all was the splendid effrontery with which the millions of Indian women were ignored; for "the wittiest woman in India" was white.

The very first story accentuated the shock. In the verse with which, following Emerson, [Rudyard] Kipling introduced his tales [*Plain Tales from the Hills*] , this author of twenty-three announces:

> To my own gods I go.
> It may be they shall give me greater ease
> Than your cold Christ and tangled Trinities

and then goes on to tell how Lispeth, daughter of a Himalayan hill-man, falls in love with a young Englishman, brought wounded to her Mission station and, when he abandons her, abandons Christianity. Reeling from this racial-religious paradox, rapt readers of both continents were plunged into forty further episodes so vivid, novel, macabre, and even scandalous, that sales soared, *The Times* erupted in a leader (though "we believe he is not yet twenty-five"), and Henry James wrote to Stevenson in Samoa, "Kipling is far the most promising young man who has appeared since — ahem — I appeared."

What is amazing is that, though Kipling was later greatly to extend his range and depth of theme and feeling, everything is to be found potentially in *Plain Tales from the Hills*: all that makes his writing so memorable, so haunting, all the crudities at which even his admirers blush. His youthful attitude to race was, as it remained, a complex one. He did not deny love between the races, nor that this can be true love; "Beyond the Pale" is specific about this. What he did declare was that "a man should, whatever happens, keep to his own caste, race and breed": the social consequences of rejecting this dictate were disastrous. Nor, though he portrayed the white male as the pursuer as often as the pursued, would he allow that the white woman is ever attracted by the dark male. As for Eurasian unions and their fruits, these are described with sympathy but condescension: love, yes, but marriage — even concubinage — is a catastrophe. The man, if not already a cad, becomes a wreck; or, if he escapes, is symbolically "knifed into one of the muscles of the groin"; while the woman ends up as Lispeth did, a "bleared, wrinkled creature, exactly like a wisp of charred rag".

The Indian cast list, in *Plain Tales*, is quite as large as the Anglo-Indian, and they steal most of the scenes where they appear. Kipling was, of course, a paternalist; and this attitude has been attacked as much by those of whatever ideology who had no personal feeling for Indians at all, as by critics who, on political grounds, deemed paternalism even more repugnant than outright hostility. But given Kipling's terms of human reference, which were well in advance, so far as intimate knowledge goes, of those of most Englishmen whether in India or at home, his Indians are the heroes and heroines of the stories. "He did not know," says Kipling, satirizing a white official, "that no man can tell what natives think unless he mixes with them with the varnish off. "

Did he himself do this? Those who deny that Kipling really "knew" Indians are right if they think this was quite impossible from the posture of the late Victorian sahib. But allowing that Kipling, even in his youth, was always this, he penetrated the Indian world to the uttermost point of a sahib's social limitations. As a child in Bombay, his mother-tongue was Urdu, and he had to be re-taught English. As an apprentice, from the age of just seventeen, on the *Civil and Military Gazette,* Lahore, he was often in charge, during his editor's absences and fevers, of 170 Indians of diverse faiths and races. He was an obsessive noctambule, a deft interrogator and, rarer still, a patiently questing listener. With a prodigious natural talent on top of this, it is quite possible no Anglo-Indian — not even Strickland of the Police — knew as much about Lahore as he did.

One cannot help speculating on what might have happened if Lockwood Kipling, his father, had been posted to Madras, say, and not Lahore; for the warrior Punjab was the perfect nursery for a paternalist, while the quarrelsome, rebellious "East side" would have posed different questions to which this youth of genius might have found different answers. As it was, Bengal is "full of Babus who edited newspapers", and Madras the sort of place where "Grubby" Pack, a nasty officer, "can do no great harm even if he lives to be a colonel". What excites Kipling is "the real native — not the hybrid, university-trained mule". And so his chosen Indians are those who challenge the Raj only by the sword and spirit: warriors, fakirs, women, children, even criminals... though not, be it noted, only servants, who were all most Anglo-Indians knew at all.

The white heroes are the administrators: soldiers, engineers, doctors, anyone seriously engaged on a practical job who doesn't boast about it — "they trusted Strickland as men trust quiet men". Legislators — and not only liberals — are lambasted:

> As if any Englishman legislating for natives knows enough to know which are the minor and which are the major points, from the native point of view, of any measure!

Except for an occasional banker, working out on a station, not in a big city, traders are given short shrift: when "Young" Gayerson makes a fool of himself, this "proves that he had been living in Bengal where nobody knows anything except the rate of Exchange".

To liberal critics — let alone Indian nationalists — "Kipling's India" was quite unreal since they saw politics and money, whose importance Kipling denied, as precisely what the Raj was all about. Yet Orwell, in his nagging, righteous way, has pointed out that if the Raj offered anything real to

Indians, it was Kipling's administrators who gave it; and that if liberals don't like Kipling, it is because they won't assume the responsibilities administrators must undertake. In *The New Machiavelli*, Wells had already said as much:

> The prevailing force in my undergraduate days was not Socialism but Kiplingism.... He helped to broaden my geographical sense immensely, and provided phrases for just that desire for discipline and devotion and organized effort the Socialism of our times failed to express, that the current socialist movement still fails, I think, to express.

And what of Kipling's women? What of the dreaded Mrs Hauksbee, *dea ex machina* of Simla, or of such goddesses of this Himalayan Versailles as Tillie Vernon, "a frivolous, golden-haired girl who used to tear about Simla Mall on a high, rough waler, with blue velvet jockey-cap crammed over her eyes"? All Kipling's personages — even the men, and even the Indians — seem less real "characters" than persons with distinctive attributes, or who reveal, by their antics, certain marked — and often morbid — psychological states. Mrs Hauksbee, who pops up in several stories, and "who could forgive everything but stupidity", seems something of a vivacious puppet, manipulated by her creator; who is, indeed, "possessed of many devils of malice and mischievousness" about her, as she was with her victims. "She could be nice, though, even to her own sex," said Rudyard. (I have an irreverent suspicion Mrs Hauksbee was based, at any rate in part, on "the Mother", Alice Macdonald, the formidable matriarch of the Kipling family. For when a character "vowed that Mrs Hauksbee was the greatest woman on earth" the young author adds, "Which I believe was true, or nearly so.")

But if Kipling seems rather boyish, however knowing, about women, we must remember he *was* almost a boy when he wrote the stories, though extraordinarily intuitive and observant. He is well aware of the memsahibs' powers behind the thrones, and writes "in India where ... you can watch men being driven, by the women who govern them, out of the rank-and-file and sent to take up points alone". Prefacing "The Bronckhorst Divorce-Case", there is a verse of remarkable cynicism — or profundity, according to choice — which echoes the mature Meredith's *Married Love*:

> In the daytime, when she moved about me,
>   In the night, when she was sleeping at my side —
> I was wearied, I was wearied of her presence,
> Day by day and night by night I grew to hate her —
>   Would God that she or I had died!

But the real heroes and heroines are the bit players who, as in Shakespeare's plays, steal our sympathies when the monarchs and noblewomen begin to make us yawn. *The Three Musketeers,* Mulvaney, Ortheris and Learoyd, make their debut in several tales, and if one may find their dialects a bit much, and their adventures highly improbable, one must admire Kipling's virtuosity in juggling with Irish, Cockney and Yorkshire, and his penetration, if from the outside, of other-rank mores. He delights in amazing names — Aurelian McGoggin, indeed, or Mrs Cusack-Bremmil! Slang, in languages and "the vernacular" pepper the pages — perhaps he shows off a bit, but their use always heightens the reality of odd or lurid scenes. His most fascinating character is Me: "but I am only the chorus that comes in at the end to explain things. So I do not count." No, Ruddy? "But that is another story" (as he himself says no fewer than seven times).

One realizes, at last, how absurd it is to call Kipling "a journalist", unless in the sense that Balzac and Dickens were as well. "The Gate of the Hundred Sorrows" (written when he was 18!) is, by any standards, a masterpiece. An "opium den", and what goes on there, are just the kind of theme that "journalism" would get quite wrong. But here young Kipling is not only entirely convincing, but actually tells the tale in junkie jargon, with all its meaningful ramblings and precisions amid hallucination. His staccato style is so telling it is hard to believe Hemingway did not read this story. Nor, according to Charles Carrington, his official biographer, was Kipling guessing: for while still in his teens, a bearer cured him of fever with doses of opium.

Between the bliss of Bombay and Lahore, Kipling had an atrocious childhood in his English exile, and this kind of experience tends to make a man excessively rebellious, or conforming. Kipling, I believe, remained both all his life: the inward poet with the protective covering of a philistine. Thus, speaking overtly, he says:

> Never forget that unless the outward and visible signs of Our Authority are always before a native he is as incapable as a child of understanding what authority means, or where is the danger of disobeying it.

Thus there is approved bullying, though much less violence than is often alleged against him — only Mulvaney's beating of a dacoit with a "clanin-rod", and the wronged Biel "cutting Bronckhorst into ribbons" with "a gut trainer's whip": in the one case to get vital information, in the second to avenge gross injustice, and in neither mere sadism for the sake of it.

"Trial of a Trial"
New Society, August 1971

All criminal trials are about a society, not just a case. Even at the most insignificant of trials, wherein the culprit's guilt is manifest to all, the proceedings just, and the sentence plainly reasonable, the trial can never be about these things alone, but is also, each time this drama is enacted in a court, about the social assumptions of a nation; about the legislative process which enacts our laws, the administrative bodies which enforce them, and the judicial forms by which their effect on erring citizens is assessed.

It is not only philosophers who have pointed out the dual nature of criminal trials — it is lawyers and judges who recognize it most of all. For while judges invariably insist that the trial is about the particular charge, and that all else is irrelevant, they are equally conscious of the ancient majesty and power of their profession. And how could this power exist were it merely that of some arbitrator deciding on facts and penalties in particular cases? Manifestly, no judge thinks that he and his court are only this. And by his frequent interjections during the proceedings, and his hours of summing-up at their conclusion, though he may remind the jury that the facts, and the facts only, must be weighed, his own orations make it clear that he deems himself and his court the ultimate arbitrators in our society.

Lawyers, and connoisseurs of courts, know well that this is so; but the public, usually, regards a trial as just an isolated event, affecting chiefly the accused and other participants, but not themselves or society as a whole. Yet, occasionally, a trial takes place which arouses unusual interest: a preoccupation at once made manifest not by mere declarations of any minority of "informed opinion", but by massive coverage of all news media. Of course, this popular interest may be morbid, as in sensational murder or corruption trials; and, of course, it by no means necessarily implies any sympathy for the accused. But what it does show is that the public, for once, feels itself somehow involved in the outcome of the trial.

The *Oz* trial being of this nature, we may try to determine why it hit and held the headlines.*A trial apparently about "youth, sex and drugs" has, of course, promising elements for arousing wide public interest, and yet there have been dozens of such cases that failed to excite it on anything like this scale.

The decor of the Old Bailey, the length and cost of the proceedings, the procession of unusual witnesses, and the battery of advocates both amateur and professional, were further unusual factors that caught the popular imagination. But perhaps the public preoccupation had a deeper reason. Perhaps it steadily became apparent to them that the importance everyone directly involved was attaching to the trial — prosecution, judiciary, defence and information media — was one they found reflected outside the court in the larger world around them. Perhaps they grew to feel this mammoth contest couldn't be just about a dirty magazine, but must be about some major principle, and reveal some major social

---

Editor's note: Oz, an Australian import founded by Richard Neville, was, like its "underground" rival *International Times,* very much a product of the later Sixties, the heyday of the hippies and "counter culture" in general.

confrontation.

Had they seen inside Court No. 2, this impression would have been confirmed. In the dock, the three defendants, in style, garb and tone almost perfect exponents of the "alternative society" and, when they spoke (which all of them did for hours, and one of them for days, on end), so pointed and eloquent, that whatever anyone might think of them, no one could possibly mistake them for cynical purveyors of smut. The galaxy of advocates and solicitors with, among the former, a celebrated dramatist and, seated among the latter, as assistant to the defendants, the startling delegate of Gay Lib, attired in appropriate gear. The stars of the press box, intent on creating instant stories, books and films, usurping the monopoly of the habitual "crime reporter" hacks. In the seats for the privileged public, a constant to and fro of celebrity spectators, social and legal, as if at the dress rehearsal of a smash-hit of the year. Poised in their balcony above, the schoolkid counterparts of the juvenile *Oz* editors, as if both a second jury and a fresh batch of the accused. And surmounting these, a judge in the weirdest fancy-dress of all, who was to tell the court, among so many other things, that the trial which invoked this spectacle was not political.

Lying around in piles, and fingered nervously, disdainfully or with familiarity, were copies of the offending publication. It is a curiosity of literary obscenity trials, that "a case" is usually made over the less successful specimens; thus Lawrence was judged (in spirit) on *Lady Chatterley,* and the *Oz* editors on No. 28, one of their less brilliant productions. The chief objection, really, to the number, is that it is rather silly: its kid editors playing 10-12-year-olds rather than the 15-18 that they were, and the adult editors over-indulgent, purely as regards quality, to their productions.

In trials where, beside fact, opinion may be advanced by witnesses — opinions which, whether hostile or favourable to the defence, must be judged by a jury of middle-aged ratepayers — there was inevitably a great deal of oversimplification and confusion. Thus "obscene", "pornographic" and "erotic" were used as if they were interchangeable. In reality, though all denote attitudes to sex, their intentions are entirely different. Obscenity is the gross safety-valve of sex, that exists in all societies (and fails to at their peril), alike in their citizens' daily lives, as in passages of their popular and "high" literature and art. Pornography is the portrayal, verbal or visual, of perverted sex, and since it aims directly at the masturbatory fantasies of the frustrated, is of no social value. Erotic art, rarer west of Suez than east of it, is mankind's hymn to sensual beauty, and the glory of sexual communion. It is the only one of the three that has consistently produced great works of art, beside which those of pornography seem idiotic, and those of obscenity, merely crude. For most major artists have used obscenity as a minor device and not, as a great artist can erotic forms, exclusively.

In *Oz* 28, there is, alas, little that is erotic, some near-pornography (including the unfortunate cover), and chiefly, frank obscenity. The real question was, therefore, whether these texts and images corrupted and depraved. On this key question, in the court, we heard two utterly different languages, as if of Japanese speaking to Peruvians: for all the defence witnesses, as well as the teenager technically speaking for the prosecution, affirmed that they would not, and all the prosecution witnesses, as Inspector Luff, Leary QC and, one must objectively record, the judge (whose total wordage of interjection hostile to the defence, even prior to his summing-up, must have run into thousands), were positive that it would; an opinion, in the end, that was shared by all but one of the members of the jury.

This decision runs contrary to centuries of folk wisdom. Our folk songs, our very nursery rhymes are, in their unexpurgated versions, resolutely obscene. For the songs were a means of harmonizing, by art, society's spiritual and social imperatives with the realities of our animal natures; while the rhymes were a means whereby adults wittily instructed their young in sexual matters, revealing mature secrets in a way that would not scare or alienate their children. Yet adults today, who have disastrously lost this ancient art of naturally imparting sexual wisdom, have condemned the obscenity which was, in happier days, our ancestors' chief means of doing so. So how are the young supposed to know? By finding out for themselves, as the kid editors made the mistake of doing — or rather, of saying so in print.

Our writers must shudder in their hallowed graves. Shakespeare, Swift and Burns, to name but these, used obscenity as a means of revealing the complexities of our human condition; and these, precisely, are writers deemed by authority to be "classics", whose example should instruct the young. Joyce and Lawrence — whose works now sell in millions, are translated into every civilized tongue, and are textbooks in schools and universities — were also accused by courts, in life and even after, of corrupting and depraving youth.

It almost seems that if a book, or a magazine, is singled out for prosecution among the multitudes that could be, this very choice is, by implication, proof that it *has* some literary or social merit. For while prosecutions of "pure" pornography do occasionally occur, the favourite target is precisely some publication that takes sex seriously, and thinks it matters. Thus, in its way, our Directorate of Public Prosecutions is an able literary and social critic: and the cases it brings to court are a tribute by conventional morality to the alarm aroused by artists trying to rediscover what social and moral precepts are really relevant to our present lives.

As for the general public, which of them are unaware of cheerful obscenities, and how many think these harmful? In this holiday season, our resorts are garlanded with festoons of "comic cards" whose obscenity is removed only in degree from that of *Oz* 28. Millions must have heard, and enjoyed, obscene variety performances. Whose ears are deaf to saloon bar stories, or barrack-room tales and songs? And who, that hears and sees all these things, would consider himself depraved thereby? It is surprising (by which I of course mean it is not) that no prosecution witness and, in particular, no juvenile, was called to declare himself corrupted by *Oz* 28.

It happens often in political trials that the defendant, though convicted, wins the moral victory; and this not only after, and outside the court, but during the trial, and in it. Thus, Richard Neville successfully upstaged all other performers; and viewed simply as a sustained intellectual feat, his hour-long speeches, testimony in rebuttal, and cross-examinations, were masterly, as were his rejoinders, always courteous and measured, to Leary QC and Judge Argyll. To defend oneself without counsel may seem superficially attractive, but to do so effectively demands tremendous energy and concentration.

Yet it can also afford the opportunity, which Neville quickly grasped, of seizing the initiative from the prosecution, lifting the trial out of the narrow limits they sought to impose upon it, and appealing to the jury, and to the public outside the court on far more general terms than those dear to Mr Leary, who sought constantly to bring the proceedings back from Neville's considerations about society and morality, to a precise examination of some dubious word on page something, line something else, of *Oz*. I would guess it was Neville's performance, ably abetted by Mortimer QC, that led the jury to reject the gravest charge, that of conspiracy.

Another curious victory of the convicted defendants was that whereas the legal element sought, somewhat naturally, to impose their conventions on the accused, the *Oz* group contrived to infiltrate their own ethos into the Old Bailey. Never before can so many "unprintable" words have rocketed about those hallowed walls. For not only was the defence bandying them cheerfully about, but surely few prosecutors, and certainly fewer judges, can ever have used so many, and so often. True, each contrived to impart to these terms bizarre pronunciations which made them sound doubly obscene, and in this the palm went to Mr Leary, who managed to make even an innocent word like "art" seem absolutely revolting.

As for the defence witnesses, their chief difficulty was that observations that would sound perfectly natural in the House of Commons, in the mouth of a member supporting a reforming bill, were made to seem almost blasphemous in the context of Court No. 2.

For one of the many peculiarities of a parliamentary democracy is that ideas that may, during the legislative process, be hotly and eloquently disputed, assume, once they are formulated into law, a hallowed and rarely questioned sanctity. Thus, one real, yet unspoken, question of Court No. 2, was not "Is *Oz* obscene?" but "How do laws about obscenity ever come to be passed by intelligent and balanced men?" But laws, whatever they may declare, and whatever individuals or party enacted them, become sacred texts to judges; which is why they instinctively detest those rare cases wherein the law permits testimony as to opinion, and seek to contradict and denigrate the witnesses that provide it.

What may the consequences of the trial be — apart from those to the defendants? In the short term, an encouragement to harassing of minority expression, to sterile public busybodies, and even to additional prudence among "respectable" publishers in all media. For the prosecution is one manifestation among many of the new morality of the "silent majority" — whose chief characteristic, both here and in the United States, is its vociferous clamour to deny.

In the longer term, I would guess the result will be the opposite to that intended. By younger generations the trial will be seen as yet another proof of their elders' mistrust and dislike of them, which they will increasingly reciprocate. Nor do I believe many schoolkids will alter their life-styles because of this trial — rather the contrary. Nor yet do I think that these legal fingers stuck in a shaky dyke to withhold the flood of what the old call "permissiveness", and the young call living, will hold back the rising waters.

For it may be we are emerging from the puritan period that began in the mid-1600s. In its purer forms, puritanism created many fine things, and it is hard to think of modern England without its lingering presence. Yet it also became increasingly a motive-force of a commercial, industrial and imperial expansion which, from the last century onward, grew increasingly destructive to ourselves and other peoples. Now that the empire and supremacy are gone, the puritan urge may seem less justified, less attractive. The young, at any rate, born into a post-imperial age, see little use, let alone virtue, in it.

Yet though an official puritan ethos survives on the

defensive, it has also permitted, because vast sums of money are involved, an acceptable commercial sexuality. Our cities abound with its images in millions: corrupt and depraved because titillating and not frank, yet surely encouraging to "lewd thoughts" whose physical expression authority nevertheless discourages. The young, bored with these adult pin-ups, want the real thing: but seek it at their peril.

None of the middle-aged should worship the young mindlessly, by fear of their force, or regret for a vanished youth. Yet surely they should have the imagination to see why the world seems so different to young men and women of the age of the *Oz* defendants. Those of my generation, and Mr Leary's, and Judge Argyll's, were born into a world of a certain stability. There could be, and were, wars, revolutions, sudden changes. Yet the present seemed to hold hands with the past, and the promise of some continuity in the future.

But to those born after 1945, the world is different. Because the future can be annihilated, the past means little, and the present everything. This fact, seemingly so hard for anyone over 40 or so to grasp (not just intellectually, but to feel it), explains so many youthful attitudes. It accounts for their mistrust of an older generation that created, and still holds, the boasts that it may use these instruments of terror. It explains the youthful compulsion to explore life intensely while there is time; not in three score years and ten, but maybe in half as much, or less, or none.

This thought hung over Court No. 2: at times, in the exchanges between those who had lived most of their lives, and those who knew the beginning of theirs could be aborted, you could feel it almost palpably. And what, to me, was most painful about the trial is that so few of my generation seemed to understand their absolute duty to keep contact with the young: not in a doddering spirit of "anything goes", but when in authority, to show some understanding of their hopes and fears. For a war of generations, in any society, is a disaster; and of either group, it is the older that should show forbearance. Well, the judge, the advocate and myself will soon be asking the young to pay our pensions, and maybe even defend us; let's hope they do so.

And what of the convicted defendants? I regret they lost, because I think our society will too, but I hope they can take it and go on. *Oz* 28 was certainly a provocation; and if you advance a new life-style, yet know the ancient rules, you should expect to be clobbered for meaning what you say. So many of the "revolutionary" young are political cock-teasers: with no idea that a serious radical attitude involves sacrifice without glamour, and perpetual self-discipline.

Though the prosecution pored, like scholars studying a codex, over every line and image of *Oz* 28, there's one picture I didn't hear referred to. It is, as it happens, the largest in the magazine, covering two pages just inside the cover. It's a photograph of the schoolkids editorial team, surrounding headmaster Neville in a garden. Mr Leary taught us, in the trial, that you can read much into images, and so let's try with this one. These twenty young men and women look to me bright, healthy, handsome and irreverent; and if that's what corruption and depravity do to them, I hope a lot more get hooked.

"Hustlers"

New Society, August 1971

As soon as men built villages, hustlers appeared in the plausible guise of Mr or Mrs Fix: those dubious personages who could arrange, at a price, for anything, provided it was illegitimate. As cities waxed, so did he and she; and with tourism annually displacing millions, male and female hustlers in big cities must now number tens of thousands.

Their favourite hustle is on the sexual scene — chiefly, because that's all they've got to offer. And here tourism is a godsend (if that's the word), for tourists, unless self-disciplined or regimented into protected groups, are all obsessed by dreams of "adventure" far from home, and have the means to buy their artificial paradise. As such, they are perfect fall-guys-and-dolls for hustlers.

Here are two cruel rules about sex outside the nuptial bed:
1. Anyone over 23, or thereabouts, has to pay for it, one way or another.
2. Whatever your age, and however glamorous you are, you can't get it for free if you're in a hurry.

So if you're over 23 and eager, you have only three alternatives: to take a sleeping pill and forget about it, to chase yourself, or to go out looking for a hustler. (In fact, you don't have to "look for" him or her: he/she soon finds you.)

Beware, however, of these invariable characteristics of the hustler. He/she is:
1. Totally incompetent at the job, and of unbelievable sexual vanity, based on next to nothing.
2. Amazingly impractical about the details of the hustle: wrong hotel, lost keys, endless waits, pointless taxi rides to nowhere....
3. Totally and unselfconsciously venal: of whatever noble nationality, the agreed bargain means nothing.
4. Almost always a minor criminal to boot, or dependent on others in such ways as the victim will all too soon discover.
5. Frequently, on top of all this, a police informer.

6. Of insatiable appetite: not for drinks — let alone for sex — but for piles of grub, *de luxe* if possible.

Yet notice that hustlers can also be:

1. Incredibly optimistic: convinced you're delighted to see them again, however disastrous the previous encounter.

2. Sentimental, even devout, and almost always compulsive chatterboxes.

3. Very occasionally, irresistible: children of nature, Lucifer's angels before the Fall.

I am myself a born and perpetual sucker for the hustler: they can spot me coming, anywhere, from a mile off. This is not only due to lust or solitude, but because, however bad or silly they may be, I find their company frequently delightful. Truth to tell, I rather admire them, despite every disillusionment; for their lives have a sort of desperate courage, and isn't their fragile independence, in our structured societies, rather admirable? As for "guilt", I have always believed, and ever shall, that if anyone is "guilty" in a client-hustler relationship, it is — whatever the law may say — the one who seeks to buy the ultimate unbuyable, which is love, or even affection.

I have also a theory (which may be a rationalization of more questionable motives) that sex is the quickest and surest way to find out what any people you don't know are really like. Put me in any city of any nation, and I'll learn more about it after a week with hustlers than I would in months of conventional inquiry. The same, I believe, is true of individuals: what man knows any woman until the day when...and then, how fast he learns!

And what becomes of hustlers? Well, some go on for ever: it becomes a way of life, and doesn't seem an activity confined to any age-group — save, perhaps, that it excludes the aged and infirm, and even then....Some cut out, marry, and get jobs: but often continue as part-time hustlers, since it's habit forming. Some take to crime, or take more seriously to crime; some few, on the contrary, make the big time: I know an ex-hustler, for example, who is an eminent film-director, another, a semi-star.

And curiously, there often is a certain lack of greed and guile in their performance: the born hustler is, however crafty, a kind of innocent. It's the situation that fascinates him, more than the expected revenue. Thus, a rich hustler is a contradiction in terms. First, because most people don't need him anyway: and then, if he expended all that energy and ingenuity on legitimate business of some kind, he'd certainly make more money.

What he or she is really left with is a way of life: best comparable, in "respectable" society, to those of an agent, advertiser, telly personality or society hostess. For the existence of such persons depends not so much on what they are themselves, as on how useful they can be to others — or seem so.

Let's consider, as a perfect specimen, whom I've known for nearly twenty years, Emmanuel Deedes (alas, a pseudonym). He lives in that paradise of hustlers — where once a weekly was published, actually called *The Hustler* — The Grove, London, W11. He is in his forties, occasionally does odd jobs (usually of a nocturnal catering-trade nature), and lives in a reconditioned municipal flat which he secured by squatting in a condemned building, and then persuading the authorities, after two years of continually harassing them, that he should be officially "re-housed".

On the credit side, he has virtues most of us sadly lack.

He is, to start with, unfailingly pleased to see you, at whatever hour, in whatever company and whatever, momentarily, your state of fortune. If he has anything to offer, his hospitality is without stint. He never seems ill-humoured or, though a terrible gossip, argumentative. His chief defect, hustle-wise, is that he is totally unreliable: not through ill-will, or fraudulence, but because he believes his promises, yet has never learned the mechanics of how to keep them.

During your visit to him, there will be a stream of callers, bent on mysterious errands. Sometimes, with his eyes alight with professional zeal, he will make off with one of these upon some errand: from which, as often as not, he will fail altogether to return — leaving you, apparently without a qualm on his part, in full possession of his flat. Occasionally he throws parties at which, after the first free drink, you buy those following — the food, however, being on the house.

No proposition astounds him in the least, and on only two kinds does he impose an instant veto: on anything that is flagrantly illegal, or deplorably conventional. Thus, he would not entertain a project to rob a bank, nor one to show some tourists round the Tower of London. But if you asked him to organize for you an orgy of one-legged shoe-fetishists, he would give this serious consideration.

Remarking that he should have lived in imperial Rome, I asked him once what he got out of it all. He sighed, smiled, and said, "Well, you see, this life, it is a *style*."

Did he expect ever to get rich on it? Of course not — yet he is equally certain he would never starve. Nor will he, probably, his greatest qualities being resilience, buoyancy, and a profound faith in human gullibility. Moralists will condemn him for the parasite he undoubtedly is — yet it seems to me that the real menaces to us all are eager-beavers, bent on dominating and improving us. For if it is certain Mr Deedes has never done anything worthy, it is equally so he has never done anyone much harm.

And, after all, how like so many of us he is — save that he is more candid. For hustling, looked at one way, is so like what we all do — if not directly and immediately (whatever our long-term hopes), for money. Everyone is, to some extent, a hustler in human terms: that is, offering services in return for favours. Professional hustlers are more bleak and stark about it, that's all. Thus, as so often, one finds that an "underworld", or part of it, is but a reflection, a bit bent, a bit distorted, of the society it underlies.

Though patriotic to a fault, I'm bound to record my travels reveal the world's best hustlers are not Britons. In Europe, the palm goes to the Italians, since they throw in dollops of utterly spurious charm, with the Greeks as runners-up, because splendidly unscrupulous: not for nothing was Odysseus the legendary hustler of all time. Native hustlers lack grace and plausibility: that is, they announce too openly, by their behaviour, that they *are* hustlers, whereas the true artist will convince you he is simply himself.

On the other hand, north Europe produces finer female hustlers, chiefly because, while southern social convention permits the prostitute, its restrictions on women's social mobility make it difficult for the she-hustler to operate freely. For while the whore offers one thing only, the woman hustler offers anything she thinks will match the fantasies of the client.

The best, and nicest, girl hustler I know in England has two children (different non-husbands), a cosy flat in a municipal block, and a job in (not inventing this) a morgue. Her speciality is introducing seekers of either sex who've not yet found each other; and each is expected (not just the man) to make her a "present". If anyone thinks this is the same as pimping — well, technically no doubt it is; but not in social terms: for the contacts are received like guests and, once approved, can always use her decorous pad for subsequent encounters.

On reflection, I have come to think the reason why so many seek out hustlers is not so much that they couldn't make it on their own, as that they like the idea of an intermediary, with whom they can discuss the other prospect both before and after they have met. And the fact that such retrospective chats are so often stories of disaster, doesn't seem to prevent the victims coming, ever hopeful, back for more.

from *Loving Them Both: a Study of Bisexuality and Bisexuals*
(Martin Brian & O'Keeffe, 1973)

Since all nations have the deviates they deserve, let us glance [...] at some other peoples. Of course, notes of this kind will be partial and subjective — but are they not bound to be, on a subject about which there is such secrecy? And how else can one find out anything about this topic other than from within it? For instance, how does anyone know in which places a man finds it easiest to pick up, or get picked up by, men, unless he, or his friends, have done some field-work in these areas?

I am unimpressed by views held by doctors, lawyers, sociologists, coppers or whatever upon sexual matters of which they have learned at second hand. Such people, however intelligent, open-minded and so forth, are *voyeurs*.

Greece: This noble nation is the Shangri-La of educated English homosexuals, who dream of holding hands with lissom athletes, while they hearken, in the Agora, to Socrates's honeyed words. Unfortunately, this is a masturbatory fantasy dreamed up by studious dons, for what people were madder about women than the ancient Greeks? Who else named their capital city and chief temple after a goddess, and conducted their legendary epic war to redeem a woman? Bisexual they were certainly, but homosexual? The *Greeks?* And now? Well, the scholarly don, if he's got a drachma or two to spare, will certainly find a kindly mariner in a Piraeus bar, but he'll have to hunt hard for queers among this virile people. (His best bet would be to go to Hydra, and scan the Nordic tourist scene.)

Arabs: Another people about whom educated Englishmen have extraordinary fantasies. Because, in a Muslim culture (when it's strict), girls, unless expensive harlots, are almost impossible to get at, Arab lads may have it off with one another, and can be remarkably kind, tender and long-suffering to frustrated visitors. But when it comes to women,

Arabs are one of the most eager and expert peoples in the world. Once again, Arab queers (in the sense of "female" homosexuals) are far from typical.

Africans: Though black Africans, whichever part of the huge continent they come from, may have much in common, they differ as much as, in Europe, Norwegians do from Portuguese. This variety is reflected sexually, since in one place you may be picked up at the airport, and in another, deploy your charms for weeks in vain. Thus, when a hustler from one tribe says, "I think you would like to meet my sister" (who is not, of course, but a whore from whom he hopes to collect a cut), and you answer, "I'd rather meet your brother," he says, "Oh — ho! I think we must find you a ———— fellow" (naming a more appropriate tribe). The general rule is, in East Africa far more bisexual (doubtless due to the Arab influence), in the West, very much less so.

Caribbeans: Unusually bisexual. I hope Barbadians, in particular, will not mind my mentioning the Caribbean legend that the virtue of anyone who, in Barbados, bends to retrieve a coin, is in dire danger. If any Caribbean is going to have it off with you at all, the conditions are that he must really like you (indispensable), that you are discreet, and that the time and place are very right. The general situation may be best defined by a father of three from St Kitts who once said to me reflectively, "Me, me like the pussy, see; but from time to time me like a piece of arse."

All, or most, blacks, incidentally, blame white influence for the habit. This may be true for all I know (though I certainly doubt it), but since blacks now blame whites for all their defects, while attributing all virtues to their own unsullied primal natures, one can but say, "Of course, of course".

An incidental word here on the white obsession with black sexuality. At the root of all racial clichés and stereotypes, there is usually a grain of truth, and in this case, the characteristics of black sex are not chiefly skill or potency, which whites tend to fear, envy or admire, but a generosity and absence of hypocrisy; for blacks regard a bed as a place of joy, and not as a confessional.

Loving Them Both: a Study of Bisexuality and Bisexuals

Americans (white): All sex in the US has been blasted by the ravages of WASP puritanism in decay, and sexual hatred of the blacks. Nowhere else does the act, in all classes, seem so obsessively discussed, and yet so unharmoniously performed; and the current pornographic wave is less a liberation than a proof of the old preoccupations in a modern guise.

The impression is that the nation produces more vicious "male" homosexuals, and more frantic "female" ones, than anywhere else in the Western world; even bisexuals seem unrelaxed and afflicted about their "problem". On the other hand, "gay" militants in the US are far more brave and outspoken than in Europe.

The least gay sight in the world, however, is the American "gay" bar: a voluntary slave-market, in which anxiety, duplicity, and a rather desperate respectability are all horribly apparent. Not surprisingly, the conventional attitude to homosexuality is more frenziedly censorious than elsewhere. "Queer" and even "poof" are mild terms compared with "faggot" or "closet-queen".

Communist countries: All Marxist countries and, indeed, all revolutionary ones, are resolutely puritanical. All persecute deviants from the accepted sexual norms while asserting, in the same breath, that no such deviants exist in Marxist lands. English homosexuals may consider themselves "martyrs", which they rarely are; but in Cuba, for example, they rate high in the revolutionary demonology.

There seems a contradiction, in "revolutionary" views among many of the young (whether "normal" or in any way deviant), between their attitudes to sexual emancipation, and to political liberation in general; for often they fail to grasp that the two, after a short revolutionary dawn, turn out to be incompatible.

Japan: Information here is entirely at second hand, from travellers' tales and current Japanese writing. If these are to be believed, bisexuality is not unusual. The Japanese, incidentally, in their heterosexual aspect, are a splendid denial of the philistine puritan notion that sexual abstinence denotes virility. For not only are the Japanese as sensual as they are virile, but their toughest men love to adorn themselves in clothes of the utmost elegance and refinement.

European Latins: In the Latin countries of Europe, homosexuals tend to be a race apart — specialists, as it were, a recognized part of the scene, but not merging into the mainstream, as in the North. The Spaniards, even more extreme Catholic puritans than the Irish, are the most disapproving. Italians more acceptive, as they are of everything, and more overtly bisexual. (Italian rennaissance painting is the most bisexual ever devised, men and women being depicted with an equally admiring sensuality.) French homosexuals are rather segregated (following the French law that anything is admissible provided it can be placed in, and does not stray from, some recognizable and hence acceptable category), while bisexuals, such is the national cult of woman (or the Frenchman's idea of woman), tend to keep quiet about it. *Germans:* Very bisexual, though highly indignant if this is suggested. However, the Nazis evidently thought so, since their laws on homosexual *Untermenschen* were exceedingly brutal. In the much-maligned Weimar republic, sexual quirks blatantly emerged, and though everyone seems to remember chiefly transvestite Berlin bars, the libertarian youth movements were sexually emancipated in a healthier way, and very bisexual in their social customs. These *Wandervogel* are now seen by some as crypto-fascist, just as modern youth movements are said to be; but is this not, rather, a case of the old corrupting and transforming naïve youthful energies? *Celtic Fringe:* The Irish are the most passionate, and least sensual, people in Europe. Late marriages, militancy and love of liquor can all be explained by political-religious factors, but also by a release of sexual energy into these other channels. Legend among homosexuals about Irishmen is that they will often come home with you, but afterwards beat you up before going to confession.

The Scots are the reverse of the Irish: sloppily sensual and lacking in passion, for which they substitute sentimentality and wanton violence. When caught in the right mood, however (e.g., at the point between the sixth and seventh drams), they can be delightful lovers. Understand bisexuality, but don't like to discuss it, since they don't think it's reputable.

"Fallen Angel: The Life and Writings of Arthur Rimbaud"
Gay News, No. 95, 1976 *(Out of the Way)*

Heterosexual critics, when speaking of homosexual artists, are apt to imply that although it is well known that homosexuals are "artistic", they do not produce, as do heterosexual creators, really major figures in any of the arts. Ballet dancers, yes; interior decorators, of course; even minor poets, painters and musicians. But the great figures of genius who have transformed their own art and public sensibility in a lifetime? Oh, no! That is beyond the limited talents of the homosexual.

Like so many heterosexual ideas, this condescending notion is as arrogant as it is ignorant. For whatever may be that mysterious proportion of the world's men and women who are homosexual, so will a similar number of homosexual artists of the first magnitude be found. And among these, few are more extraordinary than Arthur Rimbaud who, in the five brief years of his creation in poetry and prose, completely altered not only the literature of France, but of almost every country, oriental as well as in the west. And more: his prophetic vision of life itself — of the very nature of mankind and human destiny — has created a whole climate of behaviour and opinion, so that countless thousands who came after him, and who may not have read him or even heard his name, have adopted as their own his revolutionary concepts of what man is in the modern world.

Rimbaud was born in Charleville, in nothern France near the Belgian border, in 1854. His father, a soldier commissioned from the ranks, was, despite his excellent military reputation, too easy-going a man for his tough, cold possessive wife Vitalie, whom he abandoned when Arthur was a child of six. Thenceforth Vitalie reared and educated Arthur and his brother and sisters with little money, great devotion and no love, until Arthur entered a conventional local school, redeemed by the presence of one teacher, George Izambard, himself only twenty-one in 1870, who fired something of Arthur's amazing talent: an achievement doubly remarkable, since Rimbaud — in utter contrast with his later hooligan and even manic behaviour — at this time appeared to be a model pupil; his seething revolt against his family, ultra-bourgeois Charleville, and French society of Napoleon III's tottering empire, as yet masked by the bland appearance of the virtuous scholar.

Already, the reader should realize that in Rimbaud's unique case, a severe readjustment of normal ideas about the time-span of a creative life has to be made. Certainly, in the past, there have been poets, painters and musicians who have created masterpieces in their teens: Shelley, Raphael and Mozart come to mind. But with Rimbaud, his entire creation in poetry and prose was between the ages of fifteen and nineteen, after which, though he lived to be thirty-seven, he stopped writing completely; and what is more extraordinary is that these are not just good adolescent works quickly maturing, but a total spiritual, intellectual and technical development, as if of a whole lifetime, crammed into five frenetic youthful years.

And indeed, right from the very start, he wrote as if already a minor master. His first poem was published with Izambard's help when he was fifteen which, in itself, is not remarkable: poets, like mathematicians and musicians, perhaps because their "knowledge" derives from intuition rather than experience, are freqently precocious. But what *is* remarkable in Rimbaud's case, is that his poetry, even at this age, never seems that of a beginner: he is, at fifteen, already writing "classics" comparable in quality with those of his "Parnassian" masters, who were the vogue poets of the time. Of course, it is not this kind of poem on which his later reputation rests, and within a short while, he looked on his own early creations with horror. Nevertheless, a poem like *Sensation* — a summer elegy

of boyhood known to every French schoolboy since his day —
already shows a poignant perfection.

Par les soirs bleus d'été j'irai dans les sentiers,
Picoté par les blés, fouler l'herbe menue;
Rêveur, j'en sentirai la fraicheur à mes pieds,
Je laisserai le vent baigner ma tête nue!

(By the blue evenings of summer, I'll go along the footpaths,
pricked by the corn, to trample the slender grass; dreamer,
I'll smell its freshness at my feet, I'll let the wind bathe my
naked head!)

Now came, in 1870, the Franco-Prussian war, with its
disastrous consequences for France, and much of it fought in the
vicinity of Charleville. This, and the interior development of
his bursting talent, seem to have released the "real" Arthur
within the "model pupil", and overnight he became a violent
rebel: hating the Germans yet also the "patriotic" imperial
war, openly loathing the Charleville bourgeoisie, violently
critical of his family, although attached to them. "One is an
exile in one's own country," he wrote to Izambard, on his
school holidays. Now also began the first of many flights to
Paris, where he invariably arrived penniless, lived on his wits,
was frequently arrested, and returned home in disgrace with
more and finer poems written. On one such safari, he lived
through revolutionary moments of the Commune — the
working-class revolt against the bourgeois capitulation to the
Germans. He also probably lost his virginity in squalid
circumstances, for he now developed a morbid dislike of
women.

Back at Charleville, he was the despair of his family, and
especially of his domineering mother who demanded so much
of him. He ran wild, refused to wash, cut his hair or return to
school, and gave vent to blasphemous obscenities in such
squalid cafés as the respectable town possessed. As best he could
at the local library, he studied satanism and magic; but his real
and richer reading was in the private collection of a rare good
friend, Charles Bretagne, an older man and the only kindred

spirit he found in his detested native city.

So as not to interrupt the story, I shall defer till later a description of Rimbaud's chief mature works, *Le Bateau Ivre* (The Drunken Boat), *Les Illuminations* (The Illuminations) and *Une Saison en Enfer* (A Season in Hell); saying only now that the "descent into hell", of which he was so often to write later, was already beginning. "The poet makes himself a *seer* by a long, immense and reasoned disorder of all the senses," wrote this adolescent of sixteen; and in 1871, he took the fatal step that was to be critical to his whole life and poetry — he wrote to Paul Verlaine, sending some of his verses, and asking to see this master poet who, though still young, was ten years older than was Rimbaud. "Come, dear great soul," wrote Verlaine, "one calls for you, one awaits you!"; and more practically, sent money for the rail fare, and an invitation to stay with himself and his pregnant wife in Paris.

All love affairs between older and younger human beings are perilous, and those of homosexuals especially so. The older man offers experience, encouragement, admiration, and often material help; the younger, really, offers nothing but his love — yet what a "nothing" that can be! Most usually, and sadly, the younger takes all the older can give and teach him, and then moves on; and unless the older man is wise enough freely to turn the younger loose in time, what could have become a lasting affection, is apt to end in bitterness and regret. This will be all the more so, if the younger man's potential talent is infinitely greater than the older's known one; and especially so, if the young man is beautiful, and the elder not.

About Rimbaud's beauty, contemporary opinions were sharply divided. Those who later saw him in Paris as an overgrown, uncouth hobbledehoy, always ill-clad and frequently drunk and dirty, thought him abominable. Others found him, however wild and unruly, startlingly handsome. Photographs, which are few and bad, unfortunately tell little; in the only painting of him, an insipid work by Fantin Latour, he looks quite improbably pretty, like a French Shelley. Victor Hugo, France's greatest living poet, saw him only once, and instantly called him *"Shakespeare enfant"* (child Shakespeare).

To Verlaine, himself an attractively ugly man, Arthur seemed a sort of fallen angel — a startlingly handsome infant prodigy. For great minor poet though Verlaine unquestionably was, he sensed at once that this divine layabout had the seeds of genius; and from their first meeting, he was captivated. This occurred in the inappropriate setting of Verlaine's in-laws' extremely bourgeois establishment at Montmartre, where Verlaine and his wife had moved because he had lost his civil service job as the result of "intemperance", and of past association with revolutionaries in the Commune. This wife, Mathilde, though devoted to her Paul, was quite unsympathetic to his "bohemian" past, and she and her mother were trying to set up the wayward poet, whose work they genuinely admired, as a respectable man of letters; and it was the mother-in-law, hoping to subject young Arthur to the same remedial treatment, who rashly suggested he should move into this decorous household.

As well introduce the serpent into Eden, for the experiment in bourgeois-bohemian co-existence was a disaster from the start. Rimbaud, who deeply resented his kind hosts' condescension, and what seemed to him their grotesque literary pretensions, set out to shock them by behaving as if in the bar parlour of one of the shadier joints of Charleville; puffing a smelly pipe with his elbows on the table while they ate being one of his many maddening gambits.

The birth of Verlaine's son George, which his family hoped would wean him from his dreadful incubus Arthur, seems to have had the opposite effect. They so often returned, soaked with absinthe after all-night sessions, that at last Verlaine's lawyer father-in-law threw Arthur out and the family found his room infested with lice. "He keeps them in his hair to throw at priests," said Verlaine — loyally, if not so convincingly.

About this time, in a studio Verlaine had taken for Arthur off the Boulevard Montparnasse, the poets became lovers: an experience infinitely productive for the younger man, and almost as disastrous for the elder. In his love for Verlaine, Rimbaud found his sexual identity and, until his greater talents outgrew those of the older man, a wise and helpful critic who taught him to control his verbal eccentricity; while more profoundly, the debauch that surrounded their affair was, to Rimbaud, an essential means to full self-understanding. For Verlaine, the affair brought ruin to his marriage, his career, in the long run to his talent, and even the fate of being considered, historically, as the lesser associate of the greater, younger man; and yet one cannot but feel that, in human terms, he judged rightly to live so dangerously.

Rimbaud, who had a strong streak of sadism, soon established an ascendance over his older lover, with whom he quarrelled increasingly, and often violently. Verlaine, in turn, tried to strangle his wife, and even assaulted his infant son; the family separated. Until September 1872, the two men played a kind of hysterical hide-and-seek in France and Belgium — parting violently, reconciled rapturously, then quarrelling again, with members of both their families, though mutually hostile, trying to intervene to "put things right"; till at last, following the footsteps of so many forced and voluntary exiles of the period, they ended up in London.

They lived first in Howland Street at a house (No. 35) pulled down in the late 1930s for a new telephone exchange (the one that now has the Tower), and when I lived in Fitzroy Street nearby at the time, I used to pause each time I passed and think of them. "A flat black bug", was Verlaine's description of London, and they found even the Soho pubs dreary and unsociable. They may have met English literary figures — Swinburne, probably — but this isn't certain; for mostly, they stayed among the foreign colony, giving French lessons to live, on whose proceeds Rimbaud most improbably bought a silk topper.

They discovered the East End and the docks, and it is possible that in Rimbaud's chatting up sailors there, lies the origin of his longing for the Orient. By now Arthur was sure he wanted to leave Verlaine of whom at this period, he later wrote brutally, *"Ainsi j'ai aimé un porc"* (Thus I loved a pig). In April 1873 they left London, Rimbaud for his family's farm at Roche, near Charleville, to write *Une Saison en Enfer* (see below); and Verlaine, to try to reconcile himself with his deeply wounded wife.

But next month they were together again in London: it seemed only a fatality would ever sunder them, and this, indeed, would soon occur. Now they lived in Camden Town (8 Great College Street), in poverty and mounting venom. It was Verlaine who at last walked out in July, and sailed to Belgium: a manic correspondence ensued; Rimbaud summoning him back, Verlaine buying a gun and threatening suicide — and in Brussels, his mother turning up once again to "help". Rimbaud came over: and Verlaine shot him three times from three yards, one bullet only hitting Rimbaud's wrist, and Verlaine then handing his friend the gun and begging to be shot too. Rimbaud said he would leave for Roche, and when Verlaine tried to shoot him again outside the station Rimbaud called the law, and Verlaine was charged with attempted murder.

After a week in hospital, Rimbaud tried to get the charge withdrawn — unsuccessfully, though it was reduced to one of criminal assault. Mathilde's lawyer arrived, trying to use the occasion to get a legal separation for Verlaine's wife. Though Rimbaud pleaded in his friend's favour in court, when their sexual lives "came out", all leniency was refused, and Verlaine was sentenced to two years' hard labour. (One is reminded of the Casement trial, for though he would certainly have been convicted, he would probably not have been hanged had not his sexual habits been "made known". Verlaine served his full two years (writing some poignant prison poetry), and Mathilde got her separation on grounds of cruelty and immorality. On his release, Verlaine became a devout Catholic convert, yet not even clerical critics pretend that his later "religious" poetry has the quality of his earlier pagan verse.

After finishing, at Roche, his master-work *Une Saison en Enfer* (A Season in Hell), Rimbaud saw it through the press — it was the only one of his works he himself published — and burned all his remaining manuscripts. And since, if the word means anything, *Une Saison* is a work of genius, it may be the moment to ask why this man of nineteen, at the height of his powers, never wrote — save for letters and a few geographical articles — another line. This question, naturally enough, has puzzled scores of poetic and scholarly minds ever since, and these have come up with several theories. These, roughly, are: that he was discouraged by the total incomprehension and indifference with which his work was received; that like Shakespeare in his final silent years, he had said all he had to say; that his "season in Hell" had so endangered his soul, that he paused on the brink of total lunacy; that like many writers, he longed for the life of a man of action, and now embarked on one. Yet none of these theories seems to explain the mystery — which, significantly, he did not discuss publicly himself; so perhaps we had better admit we just don't know.

During the next six years, from 1873 - 79, Rimbaud lived a vagabond life all over Europe — *l'homme aux semelles de vent* (the man with heels of wind), as Verlaine called him. He was in London again in 1874 with the homosexual writer Germain Nouveau, where there are traces of him as a reader at the British Museum, and in Scotland, as a schoolmaster in Glasgow. (This seems to me the oddest episode of Rimbaud in our country. What *on earth* did the young Glaswegians of a century ago make of their French dominie?) In Germany, Verlaine sought him out again — "with a rosary in his paw," said Rimbaud — and tried to convert him; but Rimbaud, despising his lachrymose repentance, made Verlaine drunk and beat him up, and Verlaine departed for England to become a schoolmaster at Bournemouth. Rimbaud crossed the Alps on foot into Italy, visited Vienna, enlisted for service in the east with the Dutch army (he had by now learned Arabic and Hindustani), but deserted at Liverpool, and made his way to the Middle East and Cyprus, where he was foreman of the men building Government House at Troodos. By now, though only twenty-five, he was bony, weather-worn, his hair prematurely greying.

In 1880, he came to the region where he was to spend the last twelve years of his extraordinary life: this was in Aden and, across the Red Sea, Ethiopia, where he became at first a trader, and then gun-runner and even dealer in slaves. His headquarters were in Harar, six thousand feet up in the Ethiopian mountains, and then almost totally isolated, with few other European inhabitants.

Rimbaud embarked on enterprises so hazardous, that it was

almost as if he sought disaster. He caught syphilis, and was possibly never properly cured by an Egyptian doctor. He lost more money than he made. His belated recognition as a qualified explorer by the *Société de Géographie*, who invited him to write for learned periodicals (though they had no idea he was their nation's greatest poet), was some small consolation; more so, was the devotion to him of his servant Djami, whose name he was to call in delirium on his death-bed. Back at Harar, his right leg became infected, swelled to twice its size, and with no medical help, he was carried in agony in a litter to the coast. The doctors there were afraid to operate, and shipped him back to France, where his leg was amputated at Marseilles.

At Roche, after twelve years' absence, he found his grim mother and devoted sister Isabelle working the farm almost alone. He took opium for pain, and found his right arm growing paralysed. Determined to regain the Orient again, and Djami, he set off, against all counsel and accompanied by his pious sister, for Marseilles; but there he fell ill, was taken to the same hospital, and died in November 1891, aged thirty-seven. The devout Isabelle had engineered a "death-bed conversion"; by which the orthodox may claim Rimbaud as their own although, however deep his feeling for God, there is nothing in his life or writing to suggest he was one of the conventionally faithful.

His mother came down to fetch the body, gave him a funeral *de première classe* in Charleville, attended by absolutely nobody; and yet, by now, Rimbaud's name was already legendary in Paris, though most thought him long dead, for he had done nothing whatever to revive his reputation. In 1901, the citizens of his native place, which he loathed, gave him a monument in the *Square de la Gare* — perhaps appropriately, since it was from the railway station there that he often fled the city. Immediately after his death, a colossal scholarly exegesis of his entire work began; and France and the literate world set about assimilating his extraordinary genius.

And what is the nature of his genius? It is, in brief, to have seen man in the modern world in a fresh way, and to have found a new language to express this vision. *Le Bateau Ivre* (The Drunken Boat), written at sixteen before he had even seen the sea (though he loved sailing on the river Meuse at Charleville), is possibly influenced by Baudelaire's *Le Voyage*. The boat is allegorical, and its voyage symbolic of experience, both spiritual and mundane. Horrors are seen, as well as beauties; and the voyage — and the poem — end at the very moment when the boat is sailing into infinity . . . and also end with some of his most celebrated lines:

Mais, vrai, j'ai trop pleuré. Les aubes sont navrantes,
Toute lune est atroce et tout soleil amer.
L'acre amour m'a gonflé de torpeurs enivrantes.
Oh! que ma quille éclate! Oh! que j'aille â la mer.

(But true, I've wept too much. The dawns are harrowing, every moon atrocious and each sun bitter. Sour love has swelled me with intoxicating torpors. Oh, let my keel explode! Oh, let me go to the sea!)

Une Saison en Enfer (A Season in Hell), his ultimate and most considered work, written in 1873 when he was nineteen, came at the crisis of his whole life between his youthful writing and great love affair, and the beginning of his years of exile and of silence. It is clearly written from despair — yet not surrender, or we would not have had it at all. He recognized its importance: "My fate depends on this book!" he wrote — and we may take it he means his psychological fate, his very sanity and spiritual equilibrium, as much as its merely literary fortune. In brief, the varied sections of the work express his disillusionment with love, art and philosophy, and his search for the nature of good and evil, and for the meaning of life itself, and God. It is as if Rimbaud realizes that earlier, he had tried to take heaven by storm, almost to become God; and that now he knows in anguish that however far a mystic, by suffering, may penetrate, all he can see of the unknown is a momentary vision.

The most difficult assimilation of Rimbaud by posterity has been, curiously enough, in France: for France is the great nation of measured, classic art and, if "romantic", decorously so. And is not Rimbaud closer in spirit to an English, or even a Slav, imagination? To Shakespeare or Dostoievsky rather than to the passionate lucidites of Racine or Moliere? In fact, this "assimilation" has been effected not so much by the French adapting Rimbaud to their national genius, as by their adapting themselves to him by altering, over the decades, the very nature of their national sensibility.

And indeed, have we not all, in a sense adapted ourselves to him? For was not Rimbaud, a century before his time, the precursor of millions of young rebels in the western world — with his arrogance, his scorn, his challenge to conventional values, his restless search for a finer, truer reality than that of the faked forms he saw around him? And above all in his compulsion to experience life of the body, mind and spirit to the ultimate, and at whatever peril to his immortal soul? Let us then bid him farewell on a note of youthful defiance:

Et toute vengeance? — Rien! — Mais si, toute encore,
Nous la voulons! Industriels, princes, sénats:
Périssez! Puissance, justice, histoire: à bas!
Ça nous est du. Le sang! Le sang! La flamme d'or!

(And all vengeance? Nothing! But yes, everything else, we want it! Industrialists, princes, senates: perish! Powers, justice, history: down! That is our due. Blood! Blood! The flame of gold!)

"Cancer ward"

New Society April 1976 *(Out of the Way)*

To join the cancer club is to fear this disgusting affliction more or less. More, because you feel what it can do to you, less because the alarm at a perpetual threat has gone. To say you "have cancer" is, except in a general way, meaningless, since everything depends on which of the nasty scores of fungi attacks what part of the human body. Cancers can thus range from those curable by an injection, to terminal cases from whose agonies death is a deliverance. My version was a growth at the junction of the stomach and the oesophagus, which involves a familiar operation, and small danger. Nor, except for forty-eight hours after surgery, does it involve unbearable pain.

Doctors now know almost everything that cancer does but despite a vast international research effort, nothing about what it is. This humiliates them, and leads many to propound ludicrous theories as to its origins — whence the campaign against smoking which, while certainly an unhealthy addiction (shared by many doctors, one discovers), is probably blamed by medical puritans because it is so delightful.

My own theories as to what cancer is are so eccentric that I offer them with diffidence — but here goes. I don't think doctors are the right people to seek its causes. I would guess that mathematicians, psychologists, chemists, or even mystics are more likely to discover its real substances. I think it also likely that as nature has ordained a seventy-year span, if your strength and fortune (in escaping lethal disease and accidents) enable you to surpass this, nature uses cancer to dispose of you.

Rationalists please skip this paragraph, but I also think cancer is an invention of the devil. In both the religious and scientific-atheist views, there is a belief in the logic of cause and effect — God being the prime mover for the first, and casual chance (as in Jacques Monod's version) for the second. In short, whatever cause (or "non-cause") is propounded, in both systems rules, divine or natural, can be discovered. But Satan's object, usually thought to be simply to encourage evil, is really to supplant laws of any kind by chaos.

My reaction, on discovering what was wrong, was one of resentment even more than terror. For though I have had many body blows, and spent about a year, off and on, in hospitals, I was convinced cancer was one I wouldn't get, both because it's in neither of my families, and I didn't think I was the psychological type. The medical snob in me (we're all this about diseases, I believe) was outraged too. "In his early sixties, he contracted cancer...." What a drearily conventional addition to my *curriculum vitae*! And what a foul infliction like leprosy — so different from the classy tropical disease that nearly killed me twenty years ago, but which was such a lovely one to name-drop.

For more than a year I'd known something was wrong, since I had increasing difficulty in swallowing: but by switching to less solid foods, though I lost weight, I could lead a perfectly normal life until quite recently. The reason I didn't go at once to see the doctors was twofold. First, I believe you can rid yourself of many ailments if you trust nature, both consciously and sub-consciously — and indeed, many ominous aches I've had at various times have gone as mysteriously as they came by following this method. On the other hand, I must admit that on two prior occasions, and now this one, my "system" has failed and I went to the doctors in the nick of time.

In view of this, it may seem rank ingratitude to declare that, save in the rarest cases of one physician or surgeon in a thousand, I profoundly mistrust the medical profession. This is not due to being "chicken", for I am reasonably stoical about medical ordeals, nor is it because of blind prejudice. It is through learning the history of the profession, plus several disastrous encounters with it at its most pretentious and incompetent.

Until 150 years ago, and save for rare pioneering spirits, the ignorance of the medical profession was almost total, though it was none the less confident and arrogant for all that. In more recent decades, especially the past few, its knowledge has increased enormously, yet not to the extent of justifying any pretensions to omniscience; nor will most doctors admit that sloth and lack of time prevent them from catching up with many essential innovations. The next doctors' defect is that they are mostly — and surgeons in particular — "activists". "When in doubt, do it" seems to be their attitude to treating the patient's ailment, when "let's give nature a chance, and wait and see" might be the better answer. Another characteristic is a mastery of the cover-up that makes Nixon look like an amateur; for when their "solution" fails, as it often does (even to the point of death), they never admit error, and can absolutely rely on their colleagues to disguise any incompetence. Concurrently with this, and most unfortunately, the growing public lack of faith in anything has left doctors as the only trusted gurus they believe in; a factor of which the profession doesn't hesitate to take advantage, often with disastrous consequences to the credulous patient.

What finally decided me that the "nature cure" method wasn't going to work, was the abrupt development of unpleasant side-effects: dropsically swollen feet, so that I could hardly walk; a constipation like the great wall of China; and a sharp increase of pain which, hitherto quite mild and yielding to an Aspro, now began to feel, if not unbearable, like a severe toothache.

So I took myself and my troubles to the only doctor I have ever known whom I trust completely, and whom I had the good fortune to meet, again "by accident", when I lived in Stepney in the Fifties, where he had practised for more than half a century. My pretext for seeing him was the swollen feet; but spotting at once that these were a mere symptom, he invited me to come clean, and I gave him the whole story. To which he replied that he, with the modest facilities of a GP's surgery, could make no reliable prognosis, so would I be willing to go to a hospital consultant for serious tests? Only for *tests*, I said, with no action until I'd heard the results and — if the proposed cure involved surgery — had the opportunity of refusing. Well, said the sage, since I'd be seeing only physicians for the tests, and they don't operate anyway, my options would still be open. So in I went to a London teaching hospital for ten days' tests.

They came up with the conclusion aforesaid, and seemed rather surprised I didn't want to meet the surgeon at once and get carved open. Was it all *that* urgent, I asked them? No, possibly not, but the more anaemic I became, the more difficult I would make it for the surgeon, let alone myself; so I said I would give them a firm answer in a week.

Even now, I was not sure I wanted the operation; and I truly believe this wasn't due to cowardice, or a subconscious suicidal urge, but rather to a combination of quite rational factors. First, I wasn't sure I trusted their prognosis — they'd been so certain about it, whereas the tropical doctor who'd saved me had made no prediction at all until he'd defined the malady. Then, if I mistrust physicians, I mistrust surgeons even more, as I've said.

Since the operation would be a "major" one, of some hours' duration, the shock to the metabolism is equivalent to being hit by a truck; and whereas this didn't worry me twenty years ago, I wondered if my older body could take it. And if there's one place I didn't want to die, it was in a hospital and, in particular, on an operating-table. So why not soldier on as before, and see if I could lick the cancer (if it *was* cancer), and the side-effects as well? And if they won, I'd had quite a long and certainly fortunate life, so that instead of risking sudden death on that table, I could at least go out in my own time and in my own way.

I put all this to my Stepney doctor, who then gave me a masterly analysis of the pros and cons of accepting the operation. He conceded all the strictures about his own profession, and said if I decided to go it alone, he'd see to it I didn't suffer unnecessary pain. On the other hand, if the cancer *was* one, and didn't go away, death was certain, through starvation if nothing else; while if it was true the operation could be lethal, it was a conventional one by now, with a fair recovery rate that often extended life for years. So which should I do, I asked him? Oh, no, I must decide, though now he advanced the clincher which was, suppose I decided to soldier on solo, then changed my mind, I might find I'd become too weak for surgery.

313

So I told the physician yes, and while awaiting the summons to the theatre (appropriately named, in view of *Wozzeck*, as the word "patient" is inapt), I set about the psychological therapy indispensable, I believe, to facing any ordeal; which chiefly is, by patient yet ruthlessly truthful self-examination, to make sure the whole psyche, including the subconscious, is going to work as one. When the summons came, I had some other strokes of luck. My chief surgeon "had some beds" at a smaller annexe to the giant teaching hospital, where the tone, though just as efficient, was far more relaxed and helpful. The sisters were the nicest I'd yet met and even the nurses (a tribe about which I am far from starry-eyed, having found most to be bossy, opinionated and insensitive, however able) were supportable.

As for the surgical team of three, I again had a stroke of fortune. The chief, a taciturn Scot, looked the sort of fellow who on a farm could turn his hand successfully to anything; his colleagues, both FRCS and FRCP, were a benign yet tough Hindu, who radiated confidence and helpful courtesy; while the houseman, Dr and not yet exalted to Mr, was dynamic, able and delightful. They were all utterly frank about exactly what the operation would involve and, perhaps because I asked them no hypothetical questions, answered all my queries with reassuring candour. They also decided on a further week's build-up, both physical and psychological, before the operation, so that when the day came, we were working as a team.

From the surgeons themselves, plus blow-by-blow accounts from friendly students, I learned exactly what happened. As to the location of the growth, the physicians' diagnosis was entirely accurate; but not as to the nature of the particular fungus. They had guessed it to be one that grows in a single clump, so that once this was cut out, and the stomach itself possibly reduced a bit in size, I could then be fed intravenously while recovering. But when they opened me up, what they did find was a nasty variety of fungus that spreads itself everywhere in tiny patches. They consequently decided to remove the oesophagus altogether and replace it by a plastic one (thereby making it impossible, henceforward, for me to speak ill of this unpleasant substance), and to clean up the stomach as best they could — for to remove all the growth from it would have left me with no serviceable stomach at all.

My instant reaction, however, when emerging from anaesthesia, was one of rapture. According to the students, who found it comical, my first question was if I was alive, and on hearing that I was, I began telling everyone about it; and I certainly remember the first hour back in the ward was one of bliss at being in the world again.

A chief task in the ten days before discharge was to learn how to eat all over again. For though the natural oesophagus has not all that many valves and muscles, being a living tissue, it can control the passage of food to (and, in case of vomiting, from) the stomach; whereas the plastic substitute, being inanimate, serves merely to get the grub down by gravity. Dangers are that, since you feel nothing between gullet and stomach, you may suppose the plastic conduit fuller or emptier than it is; and that until the food is thoroughly digested, if you lie too flat on your back, it may flow in the wrong direction.

Despite real gratitude for all the surgical-nursing team did for me, I cannot conclude without beefing about three current hospital practices, the more so as I believe them avoidable, and one positively pernicious.

Diet. At the tropical hospital aforesaid, I was amazed that such a concentration of brains and skills trying to cure you was frustrated by meals unfit for human consumption. I had heard that, in the past two decades, the quality of hospital diet had vastly improved, with succulent choice of menu, and so on. Well, if so, not that I could discover. No doubt the diet embodied every dietetic refinement, yet its taste and appearance was unsavoury in the extreme. The patients seemed not to mind this, for Englishmen and women, apart from being poltroons about complaining to those set in authority, have a curious double standard about food. At home, they can be quite choosey; but when it comes to institutional food, they'll put up with almost anything.

Medicine and pills. Connoisseurs of hospitals will know the bizarre regulations for the issue of medicine. That pills must be swallowed at once in the nurses' presence is doubtless to assure you don't hoard, or pop them in the trash can. Yet often, these pills are useless to you at the moment of distribution — the more so in view of strict regulation No. 2, which is no medicine after midnight — possibly to ensure you're drug-free by the time the doctors make their morning rounds. Take sleeping pills, for instance. Since these ensure only one to two 2 hours' fitful slumber, the best moment to swallow them is in the cruel early hours. But no; you must have them at 10 p.m. when you least need them, and can't get them when you do.

Pain. I come now to the grave defect in English public hospital treatment, which to my mind is a cruel and callous disgrace. This is the nonchalant attitude of the medical profession towards unnecessary suffering — so much so that the one place in the country where you can get least relief is a hospital itself.

All hospitals insist that no medicaments, even if prescibed by their own doctors, may be brought in by patients. One can see the sense of this since, once the hospital accepts responsibility for your life, they must also have control of the means of preserving it. But the tacit implication of this rule is that they inflict on you no pain other than what might be necessary (by revealing the source of the complaint, or the effects of treatment) to ensure an accurate prognosis and swift cure.

But while they are adamant about the first part of this rule — no imported pills — they are quite unscrupulous about accepting the corollary of preserving you from fruitless pain. Thus, during my first visit of ten days for tests, they offered as pain-killers two products that were totally ineffective, and when I complained of this, assured me something stronger would be prescribed. Perhaps it was at doctor level, but at sister and nurse level — especially at night — they still offered nothing but the routine placebos.

Now, knowing hospitals, I had smuggled in a product prescribed by my own doctor which I knew was strong enough to stop the intermittent yet acute pains caused by the cancerous growth. I also took care to ascertain from the physicians that pain, at this stage, was not necessary to assist them in any test. Yet so as to preserve my "cover", and in support of my claim that something stronger was needed, I took the useless hospital pills as well. Unfortunately, through over-confidence and poor security on my part, they detected my use of pills other than their own, and that night I was subjected to a third degree by a house doctor and sister, demanding that I hand them over. This I absolutely refused to do, and they let the matter drop for the moment, though labelling me a trouble-maker; whereas my chief aim in any institutional situation is to preserve as low a profile as possible.

When I was released from the test hospital, to await my recall to the surgical one, and they prescribed pills and medicines for me to take meanwhile at home, the " pain-killer" they supplied was the identical one I had smuggled in, and which they had refused me.

Planning my return visit for surgery, I realized that this product, clandestinely brought in again, would serve me during the ten days prior to the operation; but once this was done, I'd be entirely at their mercy, since if the growth was removed pills appropriate to its pains would now be useless, while this product I had would certainly be inadequate for post-operational pangs; besides which, I at that time imagined I'd be fed intravenously anyway, and thus be incapable of swallowing. So when I got to know the surgeons well, I asked them if they'd any objections to sparing me any pain not strictly relevant to the cure. They assured me that they hadn't and would see to it I didn't suffer; though the strongest they had to offer was "substitute morphia".

Well, I'm sorry to say they didn't keep their promise — or perhaps couldn't do so through administrative muddle. Thus, during the forty-eight really hairy hours, the best I got (administered by a nurse, not doctor, or at least sister — always a sign of a minor medical manoeuvre) was an injection which made me dozy, and didn't affect the pain at all. When I reproached them for refusing me the substitute morphia, they told me a tale of my blood pressure having fallen slightly — which I regret to say I don't believe, or believe to be relevant.

In hospitals abroad, I have had morphia injections, and though their effect is of short duration, the boost to morale is prodigious; for pain, if persistent and believed to be avoidable, can be demoralizing, and surely unhelpful in the total cure. The English medical establishment has always taken the hardest line at international gatherings, and tried to get addictive drugs banned in hospitals altogether. Paradoxically, English curative policy towards addicts is remarkably liberal, so that at the junkies' clinic downstairs they get soothing fixes, while in the main body of the building, orthodox patients toss in superfluous pain.

Is this policy based on strictly medical considerations? I don't believe so for a moment. England is, after all, the land where children are beaten, wives and babies bashed, football hooligans crunch, and Miss Whip and Miss Lash ply their trade as nowhere else in the western world. Despite our belief we are a "gentle" people we have, in reality, a cruel and callous streak in our sweet natures, reinforced by a decadent puritan strain which makes some of us believe that suffering, whether useful or not, is a fit scourge to the wanton soul.

How come, then, that the stalwart Briton, so independent, so insistent on his rights, puts up with this? Either, I'd guess, because in his heart of hearts he shares this masochistic view; or through superstitious respect for authority — "Doctor knows best," as the nurses love to tell you; or, as is so often the case, just doesn't know the facts, nor have the intellectual vigour to ascertain them; and because those whom hospitals are there to serve don't yet realize the potentialities of patient power. For though there has been a NHS for a generation, the spirit of the charity ward still lingers, and the people who pay for it haven't yet learned that it's *theirs*.